GLASS HOUSE 51

Also by John Hampel

Wherever You Go, There You Are

A NOVEL

GLASS HOUSE 51

JOHN HAMPEL

BZFF BOOKS
MILWAUKEE

BZFF *Books*
P.O. Box 270243
Milwaukee, WI 53227

bzffbooks.com

First Edition
2013-9991

Library of Congress Catalog Card Number
2011933028

ISBN
978-0-9627992-2-8

Published in the United States of America

For Linda

It's nobody's business but ours.

— Bill Clinton

A tragic sigh. "Information. What's wrong with dope and women? Is it any wonder the world's gone insane, with information come to be the only real medium of exchange?"
"I thought it was cigarettes."
"You dream."

— Thomas Pynchon, *Gravity's Rainbow*

My storehouse having been burnt down,
Nothing obstructs the view of the bright moon.

— Masahide

GLASS
HOUSE
51

PROLOGUE

IT IS THE back door to the brave new world. A tremendous gateway. Leonard Huxley's eyes reflect the glow of his heated computer screen as he prowls the soft silicon bowels of AlphaBanc, the largest financial services company in the world, jumping from file to amazing file. This last one is really fabulous, one of a collection of video clips obtained from God knows where, labeled NSXMD71109, depicting an attractive scantily-clad young woman in red high heels holding a glass of wine and traipsing around what appears to be her living room, obviously enjoying herself.

"F-fantastic stuff," Huxley softly stutters, licking his lips and banging the top of his ancient battered monitor to try to jump these jangling chartreuse and violet images back into a semblance of real colors. Regretfully, he closes the clip and yawns, glances at the time: two a.m. He's been at it for four hours straight, but he can't stop now, he's finding almost too much to comprehend: electronic acres of bank records, credit reports, medical archives, criminal records, phone call listings, video and audio files, all elegantly sorted by social security number, DMV code, surname, maiden name, credit card numbers . . . dozens of primary keys, relentless unending columns of people's frantic lives—incredible, amazing, and strangely evil. Geoff was absolutely right.

It is even more than Huxley had imagined. Ever since Geoff had hinted to him what was behind the silicon curtain, Huxley had begged him for a way in, an ID and a password. And finally, in the last encrypted email Geoff Robeson had sent, he had attached them. It was the gift of gifts, but the decoded letter, which Huxley feels compelled to open again this late hour, is unsettling:

Leonard: I fear I'm in trouble. I confronted Bergstrom this morning and he was, as I predicted,
extremely upset with me. I finally told him that our
current activities at AlphaBanc are clearly beyond
the pale and that we must reconsider our plans. He
was so violently angry that I walked into the door
jamb on my way out, something I have never done
before. So, I must confess, aware as I am of the
magnitude of the dangerous game they are
playing, I now fear for my life. Until later, my anarchistic friend.
— Geoff.

Huxley closes the message again, wonders exactly how much
trouble his friend might be in. He has never known him to exag-
gerate, one of the reasons he loves to correspond with him; the
man is a straight shooter. So many others out there are frauds
and liars but Geoff Robeson is just who he appears to be, a fifty-
four-year-old economist at AlphaBanc in Chicago, a caring, intelligent, blind black man, and most importantly, a great friend. And
he, Huxley, is pleased to be actually himself online, a poor
twenty-year-old computer science dropout who takes great
pleasure in trying to refute Robeson's thoughtful observations of
a world that both of them have really never yet seen.

It is only one week later that Huxley wanders by a newspaper
vendor on Lincoln Avenue, idly scans the front page of a Chicago
Sun-Times and finds: SIGHTLESS MAN PLUNGES 64 FLOORS.
The story that follows describes the windows removed for maintenance at One AlphaBanc Center and the firm's chief economist
(described by AlphaBanc employees as seeming to be depressed
lately) who must have wandered past the barriers to take the
fateful, weightless step.

J-just like that Tarot card, The Fool. Huxley fights back tears,
trying not to believe what he reads. He should have tried to do
something; he knew that Geoff might be in great danger. He

knew of the ruthlessness with which AlphaBanc pursued its
objectives, fuel for many encrypted tirades to his blind mentor
which just might have persuaded him to take the dangerous steps
he had into Karl Bergstrom's office and thence to an evil free fall
. . . the fool.

He begins sobbing softly on the street corner. His great good
friend . . . gone. In the end, nothing more than one of Alpha-
Banc's pathetic doomed fools. . . .

CHAPTER ONE

RICHARD CLAYBORNE CAN'T seem to breathe.

Who could do something like this?

The photograph embedded within the email he has opened is vivid and disturbing, centered mutely, outrageously, on his computer screen.

Oh God . . . there must be some mistake, Clayborne thinks as he forces himself to examine more closely the message and the repugnant image. But it is specifically addressed to him alone at alphabanc.us.west and worse yet, contains what seems to be a warning, just for him.

He can't believe it. Just when everything was beginning to go so well for him again—actually, spectacularly well.

"Richard, don't you have a meeting right now?"

"What?" Clayborne jumps, exhales hugely, looks up from his monitor.

Mary Petrovic, one of the members of his marketing team, is standing in his office. "Don't you have a teleconference now with Chicago?"

"Oh! Omigod!" He checks his watch. "You're right!"

"Are-are you okay, Richard? You look kind of sick—"

"I'm fine, I'm fine . . ." he mutters, quickly clearing the picture before she can see it. He takes a deep breath, momentarily closes his eyes, wishes he could dismiss the image from his mind as easily as it disappeared from the screen.

"Are you sure? You don't look very—"

"I'm *okay!*" he nearly shouts, immediately regretting his anger. It's not her fault he's upset. He pushes away from his desk and grabs his suit coat. This is definitely not a good omen. The most important meeting of his career—maybe his entire life—and he almost missed it.

Breathing hard, Clayborne blinks in the daylight that assaults him as he hurries down the windowed corridor on the thirty-fifth

floor of AlphaBanc West, the San Francisco branch of Alpha-
Banc Financial Services, the largest banking, consumer credit,
and marketing services firm in the world. It's still hazy this time
of the morning, but considerably brighter than the dim staircase
he has run up from two floors below, rather than wait for the
elevators.

Now I really don't feel good about this, he thinks as he lopes down
the hallway, the disturbing email adding a quantum jolt to the
nagging bad feeling he's had ever since he was offered this
special assignment.

"A tiny bit of subterfuge," was how it had been described to
him by Alan Sturgis, AlphaBanc's senior vice-president of corporate marketing who had flown in from Chicago to personally
pitch him on the project. Which immediately impressed Clayborne with just how big a deal this really is to them.

All to catch a Gnome.

"Er, did you say, Gnome?" he had asked Sturgis, sitting across
from him in his small office hugging one of the interior walls in
AlphaBanc West's prestigious marketing department.

The chair squeaked as Sturgis leaned back before answering
him. He was a big thickset man with a florid face and a balding
head surrounded by a reddish scruff of hair on the sides. He
panted slightly as he talked, his voluminous dark blue pinstripe
suit quaking as he shifted repeatedly in the small chair, trying to
get comfortable. "Well, that's what he calls himself—on the Web.
The Gnome. His real name is Norman Dunne. But he takes great
pride in being 'the Gnome,' believe me. He's a computer genius,
and we know that for a fact because he used to work for us. Not
all that long ago, actually."

"No kidding? Why did he leave?"

Sturgis sighed. "It's a long story, not worth getting into now,
but it certainly hasn't hurt his efforts to break into our computer
systems. He knows every weakness, every flaw. I'm embarrassed
to say that he's recently—hacked, is the appropriate term I've
been told, into our corporate databases and stolen quite a bit of
valuable client information."

"What did he take?"

"Sorry," Sturgis smiled at him, "can't tell you that. It's clas-
sified. But I think you can understand, Richard, how important it

is that news of this crime is never made public. AlphaBanc is recognized as an ultra-secure institution, particularly our McCarthy operation, and if word of this got out it could cause us tremendous damage. It would take years and cost us a fortune in PR to regain our customers' trust."

Clayborne nodded. He understood. AlphaBanc's reputation for security is unparalleled in the financial world.

"So, you can see why it's so important that we track him down before he gets a chance to peddle this information—and stop him before he can do it again. And you can also see why we're not immediately involving the police in this matter. At least not until we've positively located him, when we can be assured of a swift, hopefully, very low-key arrest."

"I understand. I assume then that he's . . . hard to find?"

"Oh, yes, exactly," Sturgis snorted. "That's the whole point. He's gone completely underground. Goes by any number of fake identities when he does happen to surface. Even with modern electronic means and our surveillance, er, what we call sentinel, databases, he's impossible to locate. He knows all the tricks. You see, Richard," Sturgis leaned heavily over the desktop and lowered his voice, "that's exactly why we need your help. Instead of us trying to find him, we're going to get him to come to us. . . ."

As Clayborne rushes onward to his teleconference he reconsiders the assignment: could he possibly back out? It seems unthinkable now; he's already accepted and this high-visibility meeting with AlphaBanc's top executives is partially his reward for signing on. How would it look if he just quit? Besides, it's the opportunity of a lifetime, one he's been waiting for since he first came here six years ago. He can't give it all up just because of one errant email.

"Whoa! Richard, watch out, man!" says someone jumping out of his way, a blur in his peripheral vision.

Clayborne stops short, realizes he has almost run into a coworker carrying a stack of printed reports. "Sorry, Stevie, I guess I wasn't watching—"

"You looked like you were in another world, man."

"Yeah, got a lot on my mind, I guess. And a teleconference in the library—right now. Gotta run!" he says, still startled by the glimpse he had caught of himself in the corridor windows as they almost collided. Beyond the basic good looks he had inherited from his dynamic father, the supersalesman Bruce Clayborne— square jaw, keen blue eyes and the unruly skein of chestnut hair on top—he looked frazzled. Certainly not the image he wants to project at this meeting.

He shrugs it off, tries to smooth his hair as he sprints into the empty library, buttons his coat and fidgets with the tie he has chosen to wear for the meeting, the two hundred dollar *Stefano Ricci*, his best, and runs over to the big monitor on the wall. He powers it on and flops down in the red leather chair facing the small camera perched above the unit. He leans forward, picks up a thin keyboard from a side table and logs onto the system. A series of numbers immediately scroll across the screen. He wipes sweat from his forehead and waits for the response from Chicago, world headquarters of AlphaBanc Financial Services, or AFS, as proclaimed by the ubiquitous golden insignia centered on the startup screen of every computer in the enormous AlphaBanc network.

He slowly shakes his head as he glances around the small sumptuous library, its walnut paneling softly illuminated by green glowing banker's lamps on each table. *Here at last.* He still can't believe his luck. At thirty-one he is a senior marketing manager and one of the project leaders of AlphaBanc's wildly successful "Biggest Best Friend" campaign. Obviously a very good place to be in the organization for in only a few minutes he's about to meet the big man himself, the one at the top of the gigantic AlphaBanc pyramid of 350,000 employees, Karl Bergstrom.

Hurry up and wait, he thinks as he sees his name added to a long queue on the screen. He pushes his fingers through his hair, wonders if he's worrying for nothing. Maybe the message was just a hoax, or some kind of sick joke. His part in the scheme is quite simple, anyway, a little harmless online chit-chat with some woman in Chicago, nothing more. Piece of cake.

Of course, he's got to assume a fake Web identity and make contact through NEXSX, the dubiously popular Internet adult conferencing service—but in terms of the greater good of the

mission, really not a big deal. AlphaBanc, he's sure, has everything worked out.

Or have they?

He wonders again if he should just tell them to get someone
else. Or tell them about the ominous email? His stomach tightens; it's an excruciating decision. He's worked so long and hard
to get to this moment. Of all the possible candidates available to
them, they've asked *him* to help them out. No one else.

Maybe it was all the blood. He's always been squeamish about
blood and that photograph of what seemed to be a police crime
scene had been virtually drenched in it. Who was that poor young
woman? Who could have sent it? The From address, which had
seemed real enough, he was sure now was undoubtedly bogus,
untraceable, but the brief message that accompanied it seems to
have found its mark, him:

> This is what they are hiding, Richard. This is what
> has happened to the others. It might happen again.
> Think about it.

CHAPTER TWO

IN A SMALL northside Chicago apartment, a grimy, smoke-blackened window separates the outside world from the Gnome's lair, a darkened room crammed to the ceiling with humming computers and networked electronic gear. The window is always closed and shaded, but this particular fall morning it has been propped open in an attempt to refresh the heated atmosphere of the electrified space behind it.

The outside air is quite cool, however, and it is not long before Norman Dunne, a slight, balding man sitting before an array of computer monitors, pulls his worn sweater closer and squints in the unaccustomed brightness. He gets up from his swivel chair and shuts the window, draws the shade. The room darkens once again, lit only by glowing monitors and a multitude of red, green, and gold indicator lights—just the way he likes it.

He turns his attention back to the screens, stops to scrutinize one containing a series of online accounts he has been monitoring. He moves his mouse, clicks, and enters the private realm of a young woman logged onto the NEXSX site. A few moments later he smiles and enlarges a particular window.

She's wearing red today, and not very much of that.

Dunne licks his lips and taps on the keyboard to more precisely calibrate the screen color.

A study in scarlet. How very lovely.

He grins. He's touched. She's choreographed this sweet and minimalist video ballet just for him. The unbelievably beautiful and absolutely unattainable—in the real world—Katrina Radnovsky, has done it for him. Or, actually, for the glib, gorgeous, blue-eyed muscular hunk she thinks he is.

Dunne sighs. *Anyway, I've got her now.*

An amazing catch, and right here in Chicago. *Perfect . . . absolutely perfect,* muses Dunne as he idly browses the massive amount of data he has gathered on her: email and phone logs, credit card numbers and pins, summaries of her financial transactions, cross-referenced listings of all known family and friends, business associates, suspected lovers, past and present . . . and recently, the lab test results of her latest physical exam. He knows who she talks to, what she says, where she shops, what she buys . . . who she is. But in the end it was she, herself, as it always was, who let him all the way in.

Dunne smiles as he scrolls through her file, thinks that this is a very good specimen indeed. One of the finest in his collection. The only bothersome thing is that she now wants to meet him, in real life.

Damn . . . not again.

He gazes at her incredible image and smiles bitterly. He's simply too good at being who he is not. Too suave, too convincing. Just too damned good. It's a thrilling and satisfying game, but it always comes down to this, a looming real-world encounter that the diminutive computer genius simply cannot pull off.

As always, he frets, mutters to himself, wrings his hands. Time's run out with her. She's forcing his hand and he's out of excuses. He'll have to be cruel, present a challenge. Truth or dare. There's nothing else he can do.

He sighs again. It's time now to be someone else, someone much, much better than himself, and she's expecting him. He reaches toward the keyboard and is suddenly startled by a beeping sound and a message flashing red on his screen—one, actually, that he has been waiting for.

He quickly opens a window on another monitor. *Aha.*

It seems that some jokers have been repeatedly hacking into the new AVAVISNET air traffic control system at O'Hare airport, one of the world's busiest, just down the road. He's been remotely monitoring it since he first suspected intruders, and it appears that they're in there again.

He chuckles softly. These clowns don't realize that they're playing with fire; in a very short time thousands of innocent lives will be in jeopardy. There's a lesson here that they will have to learn. From the master himself.

CHAPTER THREE

"SO THE GIRL will be in danger?"

"Considerably," says Tobor "Toby" O'Brian, nervously kneading his long pale fingers. "I'm afraid there's no way to avoid it. But, of course, it's a relatively small price to pay."

"And Clayborne, too?"

"Yes, yes . . . him, too. What can I say? It's such a dangerous game."

O'Brian, director of information systems at AlphaBanc's enormous McCarthy complex, is speaking to the senior vice president of finance, Edward Van Arp. They are sitting on very soft, very expensive leather chairs in the offices of Karl Bergstrom, president and CEO of AlphaBanc Financial Services. The long walnut table before them is aligned with floor-to-ceiling windows that enclose three walls of the huge office. From the sixty-fourth floor of One AlphaBanc Center, the view is usually stupendous, with the Hancock building, Water Tower Place, and the broad blue expanse of Lake Michigan to the east, and to the west, the complicated gridworks of metro Chicago, sprawling into the great rolling plains of the Midwest.

Today, however, an unusually cool morning in early September, the upper floors of the building are enclosed in fog, and O'Brian and Van Arp float in a vast Olympian whiteness that seems to insulate them from the rest of the gritty business world that grinds below them, far away.

"Toby, Edward, I'm sorry I kept you waiting." Bergstrom strides through the open double doors that separate his office from the anteroom of his secretaries. He is a tall athletic man with perfectly trimmed silver hair and icy gray eyes that immediately lock on his fellow executives. "Al Sturgis won't be able to join us; he had something to take care of in New York. But the others should be here in a few minutes."

"Okay, Karl," says O'Brian. "We're ready."

"Good. Let me refuel on java here and we'll get started," he says, absently fiddling with his heavy gold cufflinks engraved with the AFS logo. "Darryl's going to give us some sort of super systems demo, I gather."

"Oh, what's that about?" asks Van Arp.

"I'm not really sure. Something that only another propeller-head could love," says Bergstrom, casting a wicked grin toward O'Brian. "You know anything more about this, Toby?"

"Well, actually I do—"

"All he told me was that it was an alternative solution to our problem with Dunne—and that it would knock my socks off!" Bergstrom continues. "Well, I damn well hope so, because we could use a solution about now," he adds with a sudden frown as he walks out.

"So what's going on?" Van Arp asks O'Brian. Van Arp, a shorter, less perfected version of Bergstrom, has thinning gray hair and watery blue eyes, upon which he wears contact lenses enhanced with a slight tint which he thinks no one notices. But everyone does, especially O'Brian, a pale lanky man with a dense thatch of wavy dark brown hair, who is used to keeping a keen eye on his computer systems, alert for the slightest blip, blink, or other incongruity in the cyber-status quo.

"Well," O'Brian sighs deeply, "Gates thinks that we might be able to get along now *without* Norman Dunne."

"You're kidding. So the plan with the girl, Darrow, and with Clayborne in San Francisco is a no-go?"

"No, not at all. But suppose our little trap doesn't work? Gates is going to give us a demonstration of some super system penetration—supposedly as good as Dunne's."

Van Arp sniffs. "Well, all I've heard is that Norman Dunne is a genius, absolutely irreplaceable."

"Well, yes, that's my opinion, too."

"What's Gates think he's going to do?"

"I don't want to spoil the surprise. All I can tell you is that I'm not too thrilled with it; I just hope he can pull it off."

Van Arp looks intently at O'Brian. "Do you think we could actually go it alone? Without Dunne?"

O'Brian shrugs, intertwines his fingers. "With the extremely critical nature and magnitude of this, er, project, and the time constraints we've got, I don't see how it would be possible. No one has ever been as good as he was at compromising supposedly secure systems. And with his, ah, indiscretions, of late—"

"The killings."

"Yes. Have you seen the pictures of the crime scenes?"

"No, I always seem to be out of town when—"

"Well, here then," says O'Brian, reaching down to open a briefcase he has under the table. He brings up a thin folder, pulls out several color photographs, pushes them over to Van Arp. The photo on top depicts a horrific scene, the blood-smeared head and upper torso of what had once been an attractive young woman, her throat viciously slashed open.

"Oh my God . . . oh God . . . so this is what he is doing?"

"Yes. That one is frightful. Incredibly bloody . . . but the ones of the garroting are almost worse, I think . . ."

"Oh Jesus. These are disgusting." He shoves the photos back at O'Brian. "We've got to stop him. Now."

"Yes, you see, that's why we've got to find him and bring him in as soon as possible."

"I agree completely. The man's out of control."

"And yet," O'Brian smiles ruefully, "we need him now like we've never needed him before."

CHAPTER FOUR

THE EXECUTIVES HAVE been joined by Darryl Gates, senior vice president and CIO of AlphaBanc's formidable information technologies area, and Maury Rhodden, a rumpled little fellow who works for Gates as a senior systems engineer. They are all seated around the end of the long table in Bergstrom's office watching the CEO fitfully pace around the room before he takes his seat at its head. "Okay, let's go," he says. "We might as well get started."

"Say, Karl, wasn't Pierre going to be here today?" asks Van Arp.

"Well, he said he was going to try to make it—"

"I'm here, I'm here . . ." calls a voice from across the room.

They all turn to see a tall, thin, somewhat stooped elderly man in a black suit fastidiously close the office doors behind him. He looks up and smiles. "Sorry I'm late."

"Well, Pierre," Bergstrom smiles, "you know we couldn't start without you."

"Bah!" says Dr. Lefebre, adjusting the steel-rimmed glasses perched upon his long Gallic nose. "Sure, sure you couldn't . . ." he mumbles as he shuffles over to the table.

Bergstrom stands and pulls a chair out for the old man, helps him get seated. "Okay, *now* we're ready," he says, looking over at his CIO.

"All right, Karl," says Gates, nervously fingering his new electronic wand, a sleek pencil-size remote unit that controls practically everything in the room. "Before we proceed with our little demonstration I want to report to everyone how things are shaping up with our communications grid."

Gates points the remote toward the back wall and a large dark panel suddenly illuminates and a color animation sequence commences, of the earth surrounded by a spheroidal grid of silvery satellites.

"Uh, is that the latest model, Darryl?" O'Brian asks.

"Hmm? Oh, yes, this is the 5000 series," he shrugs, flicking the unit, which sends a red laser pointer to the screen. "So . . . now that Datacomsats 28 and 29 are in orbit, the North American communications network is ninety-two percent complete, with the addition of the northern and southern states of Mexico, including, of course, all of Mexico City. But the infrastructure down there is still pretty feeble, and we mostly consider this a future opportunity. Anyway, this will enable us to bring data into the network nearly instantaneously, without having the two to three day wait we had previously."

"Was it really that long?" asks Van Arp.

"Sure, sometimes even longer. But with the new mainframe we've installed here, we're able to get almost as much processing power as we had previously, when we relied solely on McCarthy."

"Oh? I didn't think there was any comparison," says Van Arp.

"Well there's really not," O'Brian chimes in. "For our statistical modeling routines, there's nothing, actually, that comes close. For sheer horsepower," O'Brian smiles, finding it difficult to hide the thrill he gets talking about the gigantic supercomputer installed at his McCarthy complex, "there's nothing on the planet that can compare to the processing power of—the Source."

Gates winces at the latest name O'Brian has chosen to call the big machine. But maybe that's an improvement; it used to be the Magic Mountain.

Karl Bergstrom tilts slowly back in his chair, smiles, says softly, "And we're actually getting there, Grand Unification," apparently to himself, although everyone at the table hears him and becomes attentive, as they always do whenever the president speaks.

They all understand that he—and each of them—has a right to be proud. Nearly ten years of concentrated effort finally coming to an end. As if basking in their shared thoughts, Bergstrom relaxes somewhat. At sixty-one, he is showing his age, the long days and nights taking their toll around his eyes, but he is still handsome, tall, deeply tanned; he exudes pure CEO—the only thing, with these looks, at his age, he could possibly be in the world. And this upcoming project with Norman Dunne, he and everyone in the room knows, is going to be the capstone of his career. And yet—as they also all know—if all goes well, no one, other than themselves and a small cadre of expendables, will ever know of it.

"Grand Unification . . . bah!" sputters Pierre Lefebre. "Our petty bastardization of Albert Einstein's name for his noble concept, his great dream. And we are doing *this*!"

Everyone turns toward Dr. Lefebre and at the same time stifles a smile. Lefebre is nearly eighty, easily the eldest of their group, and is also indisputably the most intellectual among them.

"Well, Pierre, you were in the meeting when we decided upon this project name. In fact," Bergstrom smiles cagily, "as I recall, you might have come up with it."

"Me? I—well, perhaps. But now I see all too clearly the dark side of this thing. And it troubles me, Karl. More so than ever before. Einstein—you know I met him once, many years ago at Princeton, of course you do—searched for universal truth, and we are searching for, for what? Wretched, miserable, little beastly details about people's lives—trivia! And that is not any sort of truth or enlightenment, no beauty to it, none at all—just the opposite, in fact: ugly, sad minutiae, very sad indeed!"

The room falls silent.

Bergstrom grimaces, shakes his head. "Now, Pierre, you know as well as the rest of us what the fruits of our labors will be. Don't forget that all those, what you call details, in the aggregations that we will be able to produce for the first time in the history of the world, I might add, are extremely valuable, for marketing, for political polling, for crime prevention and the very honorable fight against terrorism—"

"And for governmental domestic spying, corporate espionage, the tracking of humans like they were just so many inventory items . . . the potential abuses are mind-boggling!" Lefebre snaps back.

Bergstrom sighs. "Pierre, you certainly know how to put everything in perspective." Bergstrom is really the only one who can lock horns with Lefebre. They are very old friends—Lefebre had been his chief mentor in the firm—and Bergstrom knows that whenever the old man goes on like this it is best to simply change the subject. "Well, I happen to think that it's quite a noble—and extremely profitable—goal. And of course some parts of the project will be more, ah, enjoyable, than others. Now, has everyone seen the dossier on Christin Darrow? She's a senior financial analyst in mergers, originally from the Seattle branch. There's a cutie, hey?"

Everyone perks up immediately, including Dr. Lefebre.

"Oh God, yes. That looker in M&A, good choice."

"She's the one, all right."

"Ed always gets the best ones, anyway."

Van Arp grins. "Well, I understand she's essential to the, er, plan . . . unfortunately."

With the addition of this last word, everyone's smile dissolves, including Van Arp's.

Bergstrom picks it up again. "Well, it's nearly eleven. Are we ready to proceed with this demonstration? Darryl?"

"Karl," says Gates, "we've got Richard Clayborne on the line right now. AlphaBanc West. Maybe we should first—"

"Yes," sighs Bergstrom. "Let's get him out of the way. Oh, by the way, Zara is going to be out there with him, with Clayborne. She's heading up this phase of the project."

"Oh boy," someone groans.

Bergstrom grins, "Well, we all know she's damn good, er, at this sort of thing."

"Amen," grunts Van Arp.

Everyone chuckles. Gates points the wand across the room and the second panel illuminates, turning deep blue with the golden AFS logo displayed in its center. After a few seconds the logo vanishes, replaced in the upper left hand corner with the legend: SF ACCESS . . . PLEASE WAIT.

"Hmm," O'Brian mutters, "the satellite link appears to be a little slow this morning . . ."

Just then, the legend appears: SF INTERLINK - ACTIVE, a quick sequence of numbers, the date and military time, then another blink and a menu of approximately twenty names is displayed. The name: Clayborne, R.W., is blinking in green.

Gates flicks his wand again. The screen goes completely black, then reappears, presenting a smiling well-dressed young man sitting attentively before a large bookcase in what everyone in the room recognizes as the library and conference room of Alpha-Banc's San Francisco branch.

Bergstrom clears his throat and speaks, "Clayborne, how are you today?"

"Fine, sir. Thank you."

"Good. How's the weather out there?"

"Oh, cool. Foggy today."

"Here, too. Now, Richard, I guess you know everyone in this room, except perhaps Dr. Lefebre and—"

"Actually, sir, your side of the video link isn't up."

"It isn't? What—?"

Gates and O'Brian immediately lean over to Bergstrom, Gates tapping the mute button on the wand. "Forgot to mention it, Karl. We thought it might be best that he not see us all together on this end. It's not exactly a normal piece of business he's about to undertake. This NEXSX thing."

"Oh, yes. Well, good idea, then."

Gates taps the mute button again and nods.

"Clayborne," says Bergstrom, "can you still hear me?"

"Yes sir."

"The link is temporarily down here, son. Some technical difficulties."

"Yes sir, I understand."

"Now, I am told that, aside from your MBA, you hold an undergraduate degree in psychology from the University of Wisconsin. Is that correct?"

"Yes sir. I developed an interest in marketing, the psychology of it, during my time at Wisconsin and went on to pursue it at Northwestern."

"So, besides your help in setting up this . . . little scheme to locate Dunne, you also understand, on a psychological level, what we want you to do, communications-wise, with Darrow?"

"Yes sir. I do."

"And you understand that the young woman might be in some danger. And possibly even yourself?"

"Yes sir, although I was assured that you would be constantly monitoring—"

"Oh yes, yes." Bergstrom glances over at O'Brian and Gates. "Of course, we'll be on top of everything, but the man we're after is a genius, a-a demented genius—and that's why we have to be so careful."

"I've been briefed, Mr. Bergstrom."

"Good, good. Well, then I guess that's all we have here. You are to initiate contact fairly soon now, I am told."

"Yes sir, I'm ready."

"Good. Well, we'll sign off here. Good luck, Clayborne."

"Thank you, sir. Good-bye."

The red light below the camera lens in San Francisco blinks out and Clayborne loosens his tie, shakes his head. "Damn this old system!" he mutters. "I didn't even get to see them . . . but at least they could see me." Which he considers much more important, but still frustrating. He gently whacks the side of the monitor as he gets up. A piece of junk. There always seems to be some kind of problem with it. He's about to power it off when he hears Karl Bergstrom's voice coming through the speakers: "Do you think Clayborne's in any real danger?"

"Not really. The Gnome only goes after women, you know, lovely young women," says a voice he thinks might be O'Brian's. Clayborne looks up at the unit's camera; the little red light is still out. It appears they can't see him, and most likely have no idea he is still on the line.

"Like our Miss Darrow." Bergstrom's voice is quieter now.

"Yes, our little Miss Christin."

"Bait. Gnome-bait. Jesus, it's ugly."

"Does Clayborne know about the murders?"

"No. They've been in the news, of course. Locally, here. Unsolved. No one knows that Dunne is involved but us."

Oho. Murders, thinks Clayborne. Now the evil message he had received made some sense. That bloody photo of a young woman was the victim of a slasher. Who now apparently seems to be Norman Dunne, the Gnome. A gruesome serial killer? This is what they are hiding from him? He continues to listen.

"So Clayborne knows nothing about them? The murders?"

"That's right. We only told him that Dunne has stolen some of our data and that he might be dangerous. Not how dangerous. Clayborne's PERSPROF indicates he might be a person of some integrity. We think he's presently quite loyal, but we don't want him to get weird on us. Go outside or something."

Clayborne's ears burn. *Might* be a person of integrity? Well, maybe they'd better take another look at their idiot PERSPROF, which is of course AlphaBanc's infamous statistically correct personality profile whom every AlphaBanc employee has lurking within their online personnel file. And why would he go "outside?" Where exactly is that?

It's extremely risky, but in the most daring decision he has made thus far in his carefully cultivated career, he decides to continue eavesdropping. He's just got to know what's going on.

CHAPTER FIVE

THE FOG IS beginning to burn off around the sixty-fourth floor of One AlphaBanc Center in Chicago and Bergstrom, looking out over the ghostly Chicago skyline, suddenly seems jumpy. "Okay, enough about Clayborne," he grumbles. "He's got a job to do and he knows how important it is to us. Enough said. Darryl, can we get on with this demonstration?"

"Yes sir, Karl. Are we ready, Maury?"

"As we'll ever be."

"Okay," says Gates and nods to Rhodden, who taps some keys on the console before him and both panels on the wall suddenly light up again, each becoming a field of black containing the same message:

TARGET: O'Hare

"So what the hell is that about?" snaps Bergstrom.

"Uh, you'll see, Karl," says Gates a bit nervously. "You wanted us to prove we could get into secure systems, right? Well, we've tackled one of the most secure we could think of, the new air traffic control system at O'Hare. Maury here worked on them before he came to AlphaBanc."

"I can't believe that you actually came up with a graphic for this—"

"Well, maybe we went a little overboard there, Karl." With a nervous flourish, Gates signals the systems engineer to begin.

Rhodden hits some keys and after several seconds a network of bright white lines against a deep blue background appears on the left screen. At various points in the web are small clusters of letters and numbers.

"This . . . is O'Hare's new AVAVISNET air traffic display, the system which replaces the old suite sector display," says Rhodden with an air of pomposity. "It depicts the airspace the controller is responsible for. These labels represent aircraft info generated by the transponder on each plane."

"Don't we have audio to go with this, Maury?" asks Gates.

"Oh, yes. I almost forgot," smiles Rhodden and hits several keys on the console.

Immediately the voices of air traffic controllers and pilots fill the room:

"United eight forty-eight, turn right heading one five zero join victor ninety-seven, cleared for takeoff runway one zero."

"United eight forty-eight. Roger."

"American three thirteen heavy cleared to the Chicago O'Hare Airport via last routing cleared, maintain flight level one eight zero."

"American three thirteen. Roger."

"See, there's United 848," says Rhodden excitedly, walking over to point out a small label in the list of planes queued for departure: UAL848. "And here's AAL313 coming in. That's the American flight we just heard."

"So, what exactly do we have here, then?"

"To put it crudely," says Gates, "we've 'hacked' into the new AVAVISNET system at O'Hare."

"And what is this AVA-what net, again?"

"It's the latest in air traffic control. Runs on a mainframe host. It's supposed to be virtually impenetrable, as well it should be. But, of course, we're right here inside of it."

"You mean we're seeing—and hearing—the very same thing that they're seeing in the control tower at O'Hare?" asks Pierre Lefebre, staring intently at the slowly-changing, softly blinking display on the wall.

"Precisely," Gates purses his thin lips and smiles, obviously relieved that the demonstration is proceeding so well. "We're also monitoring the air traffic VHF frequency, one-twenty-something megahertz. For realism."

"Amazing. And could we, ah, *do something*, to what is going on here?"

"We certainly could. Once we've gotten this far inside we could do just about anything."

"We could wreak unbelievable havoc," Lefebre grunts.

"Well . . . yes. We considered altering their display just slightly to demonstrate our capabilities. But being inside is quite enough. Besides, those poor controllers have a tough enough job as it is."

"And this is a difficult—hack?" asks Bergstrom.

"Extremely." Maury Rhodden turns from the screen to face them and smiles proudly, almost sneers. "We've gone through the back door of back doors in this system. It was closed tighter than a drum, but of course we found a way in. The funny thing is that the tighter they close their systems up, once we do find a way in, it's nearly impossible for them to figure out how to shut us down. I truly doubt that the Gnome himself would be able to get in here as easily as—"

"Wait! What's that?" Van Arp jumps up and points at the screen.

"What?" Gates and Rhodden both turn quickly around to the display. To their horror, the screen has suddenly gone completely black and in its center is a particularly evil-looking gray and white skull.

"God*damn* it!" shrieks Gates.

"I-I don't believe it," Rhodden looks up at the screen wild-eyed. "How could he have . . ."

"It's him," says O'Brian resignedly.

The voices in the control tower are crackling:

"Good God! What's this? Jack, you see what I see?"

"I do. I do. What in hell is it?"

"Damned if I know. Maybe it's a-a joke, or something, or—"

"It's who, O'Brian?" screams Bergstrom. *"Who? Who?"*

"The Gnome," says Gates, O'Brian, and Rhodden, nearly simultaneously.

"The—him? Norman Dunne? But, how—?"

"I-I-I don't know," Gates stutters, not taking his eyes off the screen, running over to the console on the table.

Maury Rhodden, quite pale, beats him to it, begins typing at the keyboard. The other screen suddenly blinks, displays a list of job names headed with AVAVISNET SYSTEM / ACTIVE JOBS.

"What do we do? What do we do?" pleads a frantic controller.

"Jesus, I don't know. Call systems, pronto!" answers the other.

"So they're obviously seeing this same—insanity, on their monitors in the control tower at O'Hare?" asks Van Arp.

They all look over at Gates and Rhodden, who both nod solemnly, looking intently up at the screens.

"American three thirteen to O'Hare tower, request landing clearance. American three thirteen to O'Hare tower . . ."

"Oh no . . ." O'Brian whispers.

Everyone looks in horror as the central skull is suddenly displaced by the previous web of lines, but with an ugly added feature: a small skull in one corner moving rapidly across the screen, flashing black and white, its little jaws seeming to chomp up a swath of screen, white grid lines, transponder tags, everything—leaving nothing but terrifying blank display in its wake. After the row is gone, the skull instantly turns around and begins consuming another. In a few seconds United Airlines 848 and American 313 have disappeared as well.

"My God, this is horrible!" Bergstrom gasps. "They must be panicking at O'Hare, and—" he stops in mid-sentence as though remembering something. Then he speaks, surprisingly softly, "Brittany is coming in this morning on American."

An unspoken thought fills the room, one that everyone immediately shares: Bergstrom and his third wife are not getting along, are in fact rumored to be estranged, and she is at this time perhaps little more than alimony liability to his burgeoning estate.

"Well, we've got to fix this," Bergstrom continues. "There are a lot of lives at stake here."

"God yes, what a lousy, rotten joke," moans Van Arp. "There are thousands of lives in danger! O'Hare is the busiest airport in the world!"

"Actually, I think it's Atlanta, now—"

"I don't care! Goddamn it, Gates, how did Dunne get in here?"

"I-I don't know. He must have been watching us somehow. Online. There must be a leak somewhere. I thought we were secure. I-I don't know how he could've known—"

"Are we sure that it's really Dunne, the Gnome?" asks Van Arp.

O'Brian, grim, answers him, "Yes, Ed. You see, that skull is the Gnome's signature graphic. He used to pop that evil little thing on the monitors of unsuspecting programmers when he worked for us. Used to eat up all the graphics on their screens. Was a brilliant joke at the time. No one else could ever come close."

"Well," says Gates grimly, "the crazy fool has got it running here now . . . just to do this to us!"

"To *us*?" screams Bergstrom. "What about all of those planes in the air? And will somebody please turn off that goddamned speaker?"

In the background, anxious communications have been crackling between the pilots and the control tower. Maury Rhodden clicks a button and it ceases. The large office suddenly is filled with silence and the thoughts of a group of very worried men.

"Maury, can't you find that program and kill it, for God's sakes?" Gates pleads.

"I-I've been trying to! I can't even get to it! The Gnome's revoked our authority."

"God*damn* him!" curses Gates, his face beet-red. "That crazy son of a bitch! He's got to be *stopped*!"

"Such a shame, such a foolish, dangerous game," says Lefebre, shaking his head. "What can we do? What can we do? Surely, there must be—"

"I-I don't know," Gates stammers, begins to gnaw at his fingernails. "He's locked us out."

"My God, my God . . ." mutters Bergstrom as the room becomes quiet again, the only sound, Rhodden's frantic useless tapping on his keyboard. "What have we unleashed?"

CHAPTER SIX

BACK IN SAN Francisco, Clayborne sits riveted before the speaker. He can't believe what he's hearing. This is AlphaBanc's elite inner circle, the highest of the higher-ups, headed by Bergstrom himself. What in hell have they gotten themselves into? For that matter, what has he gotten *himself* into? This Norman Dunne is a bona fide *serial killer*. What kind of craziness is that?

His heart sinks. Was he chosen because of his ambition, loyalty, and overall stellar rise in the organization . . . or because he's nothing more than a patsy? Though he now fears it might well be the latter, it's something he mercifully isn't able to focus upon right now—there's a disturbing but ultimately fascinating high-tech train wreck going on at the moment and he's got to stay and hear more.

Like a cornered animal, Bergstrom circles his office repeatedly, as though looking for an escape route. "Is there any chance that this, this—*crime* might be traced back to us?" he snarls.

Maury Rhodden answers, his smirk all but evaporated. "Well, we were pretty sure our hack was invisible. We thought that the closest anyone could trace us would be to a phone booth in Peoria. No one should ever have known we were here. Uh, except the Gnome, of course . . . I guess there's no fooling him."

"Well, we've got to do something! We just can't let O'Hare come to its *knees*!" Bergstrom pounds the table.

"I hear you, Karl. But I-I just don't know what to do." Gates appears to be on the verge of weeping.

Up on the wall panels, the skull, triumphant after consuming all of the flight data, slowly blinks in the center of the now frighteningly empty screen.

"Oh God . . ." murmurs Van Arp. "What have we done?"

"Well, it's what the *Gnome* has done!" yells Gates. "Don't forget who's really to blame here—"

"As long as it's not traced back to us!" screams Bergstrom.

"Look! Look!" Rhodden points up at the screen.

Just below the blinking skull the words: BYE-BYE have appeared, flashing mutely underneath it. After several seconds they disappear and the entire screen is replaced by the previous AVAVISNET display.

"Thank God!" someone says.

"He-he's gone, I think," Gates gratefully whispers. "Turn on that speaker, Maury."

"Oh, lookee here, we're back again, I think," crackles a voice that sounds clearly relieved.

"Hope so. United eight forty-eight, how do you read?"

"Loud and clear. Go ahead."

"We've got to check things out here, eight forty-eight. But, ah, for now it looks like we're back . . ."

"Well, can you believe that?" asks Gates of no one in particular, wiping his brow with the back of his shaking hand.

"I don't want to believe it. But I saw it with my own eyes!" snaps Bergstrom.

"He's just playing with us . . ." sighs O'Brian.

"Gates, I'll tell you this," Bergstrom growls, face deep red, voice shaking. "We had better be damned careful in the future. Damned careful! There's got to be no more—stunts, like this. No more. Otherwise, there'll be no more future . . . for us. For any of us."

Gates looks sheepish and very worried—but not about losing his job. He knows that he, they, all of them, are in far too deep for that. If anyone is going to lose anything, it will be his life.

They're saved, apparently by Norman Dunne himself. Sitting before the dark video screen, Clayborne is overwhelmed, nearly in a state of shock himself. His ears are ringing, mouth is dry, finds himself reaching in his pocket for a Deludamil, but remembers that he's trying to quit. He winces . . . really a smart move, quitting the ubiquitous antidepressant now that his therapy is over with, his sessions run out. Real smart. But something he wants to do. Something, a last thing, for Natalie. She had wanted to quit, too. He'll do it for her.

Numbly, he walks over and powers off the unit. If there is any more to hear, he doesn't want to know, can't take the chance they might find out he was listening. He rubs his eyes, slumps back down into the chair. So this is the kind of game they are playing. And now, like it or not, it appears that he also is one of the players. The worst part is that his opponent, the weird fellow they know as the Gnome, appears to be the best player of all.

CHAPTER SEVEN

AFTER ALL THE turmoil, the sudden silence in the library is unnerving; Clayborne instinctively looks over his shoulder. The heavy oak library door is still closed, thank goodness, which means to everyone on the floor that a conference is probably still in progress and he won't be disturbed. Good. His head is reeling. He needs to be alone right now. He takes a deep breath and meditatively touches the arm of the rich leather chair he sits in, attempts to consider his position, which up until an hour ago, he considered to be very good. Very good indeed.

AlphaBanc, after all, is the pinnacle of the business world for him, for anyone. Known for decades as AlphaQuerian Credit Services, a giant in the consumer credit verification business, the corporation has redefined itself over the last two decades under Bergstrom's shrewd leadership. Beginning with the acquisition of several large regional banking groups, primarily in the West and Midwest, and taking the bright new name: AlphaBanc Financial Services, it became a key player in the growing diversified consumer banking industry. Its next big move was into the nascent marketing demographics business, and then, as it acquired the computerized infrastructure required to manage its growing collection of databases (including the fastest supercomputer in the world), it added, almost as an afterthought, an Internet and satellite telecommunications division and a highly profitable data storage venture. The multi-layered firm headquartered in Chicago now has branches in over one hundred countries with revenues exceeding two hundred billion dollars a year.

It is certainly a very good place to be, Clayborne thinks, with nearly unlimited career growth potential, generous compensation and benefits . . . and office politics that might rival those of the court of Louis XIV. He groans, shakes his head, realizes that this strange unforgettable morning has given him a glimpse into the

future, one that, if he continued his upward rise in the huge
organization, would not normally be visible to him for years to
come. If at all.

He gets up, rubbing the back of his suddenly stiff neck, opens
the door and walks unsteadily into the hallway. He stops at his
favorite bank of windows and looks out. Most of the haze has
lifted and he happens to spy a small plane glinting in the misty
sunlight over the bay. His mind blanks as he follows its flight for
a few moments, feels a sudden hollow sadness in his heart.
Natalie. He finds himself wishing that he might somehow turn
this apparition into the little silver plane that had flown away
with her.

Or at least, he wishes he could stop the dreams.

Too many times at night he sees Natalie again, landing that
silver plane on the dream street in front of their apartment, she
emerging in unreal golden light, pulling off goggles like Amelia
Earhart, tossing her hair in the prop wash, turning to smile at
him . . . brings midnight-hard tears every time.

But so does a real memory he nurtures beyond that twilit land,
of that pure perfect moment that occurs only once in a relationship, when dating ends and real love begins. It was back in
Chicago, several months after they had met, sitting behind two
pilsners in Pippin's on Rush.

He was first with a strange perception he tried to convey,
about the first time he saw her, bubbling and vivacious, on
Michigan Avenue in the afternoon sun of early spring in her dark
navy suit, auburn hair pulled back, Ms. Business, somehow seeming to be as out of place in her corporate pinstripe suit as the
gleaming glass and steel skyscrapers that sprouted so unnaturally
from those wind-blown Chicago prairies . . . and at the same time
he suffered a brief intense vision in the back of his mind, seeing
her as she might have been one hundred fifty years ago, an eager
pioneer maiden wearing gingham and an apron, willing to turn
the prairie, birth the babies, shoot the wolves . . . whatever it
took to survive, to prosper, to prevail. All this he told her as best
he could.

She listened, with her nose and upper lip screwed up in that wonderfully cute way she had when she was intent on understanding something, and then—now well into her second brew—she burst out laughing and told him that *her* impression of *him* was that he looked like a snobbish fop!

Ooh. "Aw c'mon . . ."

But she cackled wildly and told him how, in his Burberry coat and Brooks Brothers suit and Gucci shoes and Oscar de la Renta sunglasses, she wasn't sure if he was really *real,* as through Lyle, their mutual friend who had introduced them, was playing a joke on her. She thought maybe he was a model for a magazine photo shoot or something whom playful rich Lyle had paid a quick fifty to come over and put the make on her.

Well, Clayborne had to admit that maybe he did get a teensy bit pretentious at times. . . . They howled together over that little remembrance of things pompous, over that, yes, and the shared realization that something else, something really good, had settled in around them.

But life always wants to balance. After their wedding and the reception at her parents' big home in Wilmette, and after the move to San Francisco so he could start his new job at Alpha-Banc, she decided to take some time off to pursue a childhood dream: to learn to fly. That same pioneer enthusiasm that had attracted him to her in the beginning seemed to lead her heavenward, to begin the lessons of which Clayborne, cowardly confirmed earthling, nervously resigned himself to hear the tales. He could tolerate being one of two hundred semi-anxious passengers in a sleek, pressurized, humming air-behemoth, but flying in a small noisy plane with all that wide open *air* out there so close he could reach out and *touch it,* terrified him.

But he knew he couldn't put off forever the day that he would have to see his jaunty aviatrix do her thing, and on a bright Friday morning she had called him at work to say that she would be taking her first solo flight later that day, so would he please, please, please, come out to watch. . . .

How could he refuse such buoyant enthusiasm? So he sneaked out of work early to see—witness—as it turned out, the tragedy.

The little trainer was a too-brilliant gleam in the bright sun on a strangely too-warm day in early March, a fragile temperature for that time of year in northern California . . . yes, as he remembered it now everything seemed so fragile, her happy excitement, his foolish anxious pride, the clear blue sky somehow unnaturally able to support noisy oiled machinery, a shining brightness that suddenly tumbled in midair and began a sickening spiral down to the tarmac and a waiting explosion—a soft terrible noise and thick clouds of rolling black smoke. The impossible, the unthinkable, had happened. She was gone.

Clayborne's cell phone suddenly buzzes, jarring him from his thoughts. He pulls it from his jacket pocket, still staring out into the sky as the little plane floats farther away from him. "Clayborne."

A strange male voice, obviously mechanically altered, whispers into his ear, "So now you see what they're up to . . . and it's not very pretty is it?"

"Hey, who is this?" says Clayborne, but the voice doesn't stop.

"But you'll just have to play along . . ."

"Hey, hey, hey! Who *is* this?" Clayborne finds himself whispering too for some reason, but the monologue continues.

". . . through the danger. Stay alert, keep your eyes open and your mouth shut, and maybe . . . you'll learn the truth about your wife." The line suddenly goes dead.

"Hello, hello . . . ?" he says feebly, with the metallically-intoned word: "wife," lodged harshly in his ear. *The truth? About Natalie?* Clayborne braces himself, as though encountering a sudden stiff wind. He closes his eyes. Now what in God's name is *that* about?

CHAPTER EIGHT

"E. P., TAKE A look at this," says Sapphire Atkinson, sitting behind a computer screen in the strategically dim environs of AlphaBanc West's computer room. "The G50-112 server group in Red Rock is spiking like crazy."

"You're kidding," replies Elmo P. Quentin, a short rotund fellow with a beaky nose who lately goes almost exclusively by his Web name: Epenguin. "My God . . . you're right," he says as he pops up a new administration window on his screen.

They are seated together at the main console in a subbasement of AlphaBanc's San Francisco tower, deep within a warren of steel gray cubicles surrounded by miles of wiring and racks of humming servers, disk arrays, routers, and switches that comprise a sizable measure of AlphaBanc's computing power west of the Rockies. Though huge by commercial standards, it is a negligible eight and a half percent (according to the latest internal systems audit) of the colossal collection of high-speed computers they are monitoring thousands of miles away in the McCarthy complex, AlphaBanc's subterranean data fortress in southern Wisconsin.

"Wow," says Sapphire, clicking on her keyboard, "it looks like the whole server group is engaged."

"Yeah," the Epenguin mutters, clicking through screen after screen. "That array is only supposed to be used for maintenance and utility routines. It almost looks like . . . we've got a hacker."

The Epenguin and Sapphire exchange glances and smile. They are both hackers, or as AlphaBanc information technology management would like to think, *reformed* hackers. Sapphire, who is also known on the Web as Sapphirika, is pale and thin, with short jet black hair, dressed in a black leotard and tights and a huge black shawl containing silver bangles fashioned in the various phases of the moon. The Epenguin wears a rumpled white shirt, a red bow tie, and a vintage baggy brown pinstripe suit coat with pants to match. Incongruous as they might appear in the buttoned-down hallways of AlphaBanc, they are the truly the cyber-elite, the best of the best in computer systems administration.

With its enormous investment in information technology the huge financial services firm can afford to have nothing but. And the single thought that their exquisitely calibrated brains both currently share is that the Epenguin has just posited an impossibility, there could never be a hacker in the AlphaBanc files. At least not in those accessed by what is presently the largest and fastest supercomputer in the world, currently referred to as the Source (and lately, perversely, among those systems personnel who work most closely with it, the Beast). Nothing or no one could ever get behind the formidable firewalls, and yet . . .

"Well I'll be damned," whispers the Epenguin, his bulging eyes intent on the monitor, reviewing a long listing of active jobs. "The user ID on this job here, the one that's sucking up all the CPU, is a real old one, old format . . ."

Typing so quickly Sapphire can't follow his fingers, he accesses a history file of IDs and is amazed at what he finds. He pushes his chair back, slaps his soft white hand on the desktop and smiles wryly. "I can hardly believe it . . ."

Jewelry clinking, Sapphire leans over to look at his monitor. "So who is that? Dunne, Norman . . . ?"

"A little before your time," says the Epenguin. "This happens to be the only person on the planet who could possibly get inside here. Used to work for us, actually. Maybe you know him better as the Gnome."

Sapphire's jaw drops. The Gnome is a legend in the underground hacker community, as well as in the topside world of information technology. It's like a neophyte theoretical physicist meeting, albeit virtually, Albert Einstein. "Wow! The, the Gnome. He's like . . . a freakin' *genius*. Here. Inside of us," she says breathlessly. "God it's . . . almost kind of arousing. What is he doing?" The Epenguin blushes and gives her a sidelong look. "Let's find out."

Clicking his way through several layers of screens with ever-restrictive security authorizations, the Epenguin finally is able to see the source of all the intense processing. It's a dizzying series of file joins and excludes, numerous temporary files that are built, discarded, and rebuilt, with many data sorts along the way.

"Jeeze, look at all the file groups he's accessing," says Sapphire, leaning farther, her head almost touching his.

"Yeah, a lot of psychological profiles and, it's weird . . . some military service files we've got. But mostly . . . a lot of the financial files. He's even pulling in some of the credit check programs as subroutines!"

"Wow. This guy is . . . really, really good," Sapphire murmurs, entranced.

"The best," sighs the Epenguin. "Oh look, the job just finished. A bunch of temp files are deleting and . . . it's down to just this one file."

"A small one, too. Tiny. Only one KB."

"Well, it's obviously reductive. It's a distillation down to . . . whatever he's looking for."

"Open the file, E.P., let's take a look."

"Okay. Let's see . . ."

They find themselves looking at a simple address-format file, like any of thousands that might exist across the myriad databases of AlphaBanc: name, address, city, state, zip, phone, email address, along with some cryptic numeric codes. And it contains less than a dozen records.

"Huh, no telling what he wants with these." The Epenguin squints at the data. "Let's just look at it from another perspective—"

"No, don't close the file E.P., don't—"

"Oh damn. I just did. Do you think that he'd . . . damn!"

"It's gone." Sapphire jumps back to her monitor and begins typing frantically on her keyboard while the Epenguin does the same on his.

"We've lost it," the Epenguin says ruefully. "He's set everything to delete—all the history, everything!"

"Yep," Sapphire nods after a couple of long minutes, "it's amazing. Every trace of himself. Even the system logs are cleaned. It's like he's never been here."

The Epenguin sighs. "That's the way he operates. Like a thief running into a store while nobody's watching, stealing something, and running out again. If you hadn't seen that spike, we never would have known. Damn! I never should have let go of that file. Did you remember any of what you saw there?"

"Well, I only remember the name we saw at the top: McClelland, Theodore. I once had a computer science professor with almost the same name."

"Huh. It wasn't sorted alphabetically, so it must be prioritized. That was his number one result: Theodore McClelland."

CHAPTER NINE

GEORGE BLAIR DOESN'T like what he sees, a very pretty young woman lying rigid and pale and cold on a slab in the Grosse County morgue, toe tag reading: Katrina Radnovsky. The slit that runs from ear to ear below her delicate chin is thin and exceedingly ugly. Even now with the transition to pure angel complete, she seems merely a sleeping beauty, not really gone, only waiting to awake.

But Blair, an ex-Chicago cop with twenty-one years on the force, the last sixteen in homicide, finds it unfortunately not hard to imagine the shock and confusion of her final moments, the brief sensation of someone very close behind her, the sudden swift sting at her throat and then the sight of all that brilliant red blood, so much blood, the odd wonderment of where it had all come from and then . . . the awful realization of what horrible thing had happened . . . walking back to her apartment in Lincoln Park with a bag of groceries on a warm autumn night, the whole world ahead of her.

"I hate these," says Murphy.

"Never get used to it," mutters Blair, reaching inside his coat for a cigarette. "Let's get out of here."

"Wait a minute, Georgie, as long as you're down here, take a look at this, tell me what you think."

Murphy leads him over to another drawer and pulls it open. It is a white male, about forty, fifty, hard to tell, the guy obviously a derelict, a drunk, with matted graying hair. Blair has seen hundreds of them before, living corpses, in doorways and alleys all around the city, but there's something strange with this one, all right. Blair finds himself looking at something he's never seen before in all his years as a cop, something unbelievable.

"What the *hell* is this?" Blair breathes aloud.

"Don't know, we just got him in. Never seen anything like it."

Blair takes a closer look. The man has a great number of odd thin purplish lines etching his face, chest, arms, shoulders, and legs.

"You should see his back."

"Same?"

"Uh-huh. Even more. Want to see?"

"That's okay."

"But, this is what really weirds me out," says Murphy. He points to the man's wrists and ankles. They are scarred, discolored in ugly shades of purple.

Blair walks around, looks intently at the man's ankles for a few seconds, then up at Murphy. "Shackled. Prisoner. For some length of time, too."

"Can you believe it?"

"I don't want to. Where'd they find him?"

"Northside somewhere."

"What do you make of these marks?"

"Well . . . that's what I was going to ask you, Georgie. Some kind of weird . . . torture?"

"Hmph. Looks more like . . . tattoos."

"Like some kind of weird cult or something."

"Poor bastard. Jesus, just when I think the world is so screwed-up that it can't get any worse, I see something like this."

"Takes the cake."

"What do you think killed him?"

"Don't see anything obvious . . . lethal injection, maybe."

"Potassium chloride or something. This is sick. Let's get out of here. I need a smoke."

"This way—"

"I *know* the way."

"Yeah, okay," sighs Murphy as they walk down the old checkerboard-tiled corridor past NO SMOKING signs on the cracked and stained walls. He motions to Blair for a cigarette, takes a Pall Mall and a light from Blair's battle-scarred Zippo.

Blair, of medium height with graying hair and intense blue eyes, exhales and shakes his head. He is nearing sixty and knows that this is the last round for him, thinks that if AlphaBanc wasn't counting on him, wasn't paying him a lot to handle this depraved shit, he'd walk right out of here. Never look back.

"Haedler was supposed to meet us down here," he grumbles. "I don't know where he is."

"Who's Haedler?"

"Complete horse's ass. Head of AlphaBanc's ISD, internal security. My boss, supposedly. A real cracker. Good old boy. Gives me the creeps."

"He must be something else then. So how come they want you to come down here, Georgie? See this shit? That girl. I don't mind bending the rules a little here for you—or your boss, but I thought you were out of the trenches now."

"Deeper trenches at A-Banc—believe me," Blair smiles for an instant, then coughs. "She was an AlphaBanc employee. They want me to check this out."

"Any suspects?"

"Not that I know of. I'm not sure why they're so hot on this. She's—she was damn pretty."

"Friend of the boss?"

"I don't think so. But I'll find out."

"I'm sure you will, Georgie."

"Thanks for letting me in here, Murph. I don't know what happened to Haedler."

"Suppose he shows?"

"Show him. Let the son of a bitch see what we're dealing with here."

CHAPTER TEN

IN A SMALL, richly appointed office in the northwest suburbs of Chicago, financial planner Ted McClelland stares at the monitor sitting on his cherry wood desk and analyzes the extent of his troubles. The market's miserably down, he's been losing steadily, and one of his largest pigeons has been talking about moving his funds elsewhere. He is rather seriously debating the possibility of pulling a bank job somewhere, maybe up in Wisconsin: ski mask, fatigues, his 9 mm Glock, in and out in under two minutes, easy, and then back onto I-94 southbound before they'd have a friggin' clue.

He'd be able to do it, too. Without a doubt. He starts to breathe faster, reaches into a desk drawer and pulls out the gold medal, the Navy Seal's Trident, an eagle perched on an anchor looking over a flintlock pistol and Poseidon's three-pronged pitchfork, a true medal of honor for those who've earned it. But not, according to the Navy, for him. He'd endured the grueling BUD/S training and was about to go on to specialized sniper training when he pointed a loaded Heckler-Koch at his commander's head. What the hell, he hadn't pulled the trigger had he? Well, the idiot never should have crossed him, although, funny thing, now he couldn't quite remember exactly what it was that had pissed him off. But that did it, he was out of the Seals and the Navy, too, within a week, dishonorably discharged for "clear and consistent malign psychopathic tendencies inconsistent with the desired psychological makeup of this special warfare unit."

He fingers the medal that he had purchased in a pawn shop, revolted that anyone could relinquish for money an honor so dearly won, and at the same time disgusted at himself for having to buy it. Sometimes he wears it under a jacket; one time, while very drunk, he pinned it to his bare chest, nowadays sometimes running a finger over the scar when he feels sorry for himself. But each time he touches the medal, nicknamed the "Budweiser," due to its resemblance to the famous beer can logo, he knows that he earned it. He deserves it; it's too much of an honor to give up because some jerk needed to be put in his place. At any rate, the rigorous training has served him well, taught him how to be bold, to be fearless, to be ruthless, skills that, up until now, have paid off very well in the investment world—which he sometimes thinks is really hilarious, because one of the primary things he's been trained to do is to be a professional assassin.

The buzzing of his office phone abruptly interrupts his reveries. He picks it up and it's some guy whispering on the other end, "You're in big trouble, my friend. You've lost a lot today. Now you're in much deeper . . ."

McClelland is amazed. Who could possibly know this? Sounds like someone foreign, possibly disguising his voice though some kind of mechanism. "Hey, who is this?"

"Ted, listen to me. You have been stealing from your clients. You have been gambling with money that is not yours. You have been losing and are down exactly eight hundred and thirty-three thousand one hundred twelve dollars and seventy-nine cents as of today, by my calculations."

"Hey, who *is* this? How do you know . . . ?" McClelland is shocked. The man seems to be right. Probably to the penny. But, no one could have this kind of information. He himself isn't sure of the exact amount.

"As a show of my good faith, Ted," the clipped voice whispers on, "I am going to help you out by depositing one hundred thousand dollars into a bank account of which I have given you access—"

"Y-you are?"

"—but I need you to do something for me."

"Okay . . . what?"

Chapter Eleven

MIDNIGHT IN CHICAGO. Christin Darrow gazes into the cool silicon glow of a near-infinite spreadsheet that stretches across metropolitan cyberspace, from her home computer here in an upscale apartment on the 41st floor of Lambert Towers to AlphaBanc headquarters downtown via high-speed Internet, the ubiquitous electronic umbilical. She sighs. Talk about taking your job home with you. Now her job is at home. In fact, with her laptop, iPad, cell phone, and her new home workstation from AlphaBanc, her job is *everywhere*.

As she enters month after month of projected sales into slot after virtual slot, she idly shakes her soft brown hair and broods: *I made a deal with the devil . . .* angrily breathing the thought aloud, remembering how she had actually been excited when AFS had announced that all the senior financial analysts in Mergers and Acquisitions were going to be given state-of-the-art workstations with large ultrathin spreadsheet-wide monitors so they could work at home. If they cared to. Or in an emergency, when some hot-hot deal required a tremendous amount of analysis, or made it necessary to be in constant communication with any of AlphaBanc's far-flung branches, the device to be set up on a separate high-bandwidth carrier so that it wouldn't interfere with any other, personal, online business they might transact.

But who were they kidding? *Every* day at AlphaBanc is an emergency. *Every* deal is hot-hot. There seems to be no end to the string of businesses preyed upon by AlphaBanc and its rapacious clientele, no end to the speculation and the ghostly configuration of deals, each of which carries its own invisible mycelium of cataloged electronic data.

As if I might actually have time to ping someone, or . . . have someone ping me, Christin grumbles, checking the clock, now half past midnight on this lonely Friday night, er, Saturday morning, the home-alone scene replaying itself again, and now not even her pal

Marcia around to do anything with. Really, the way it is. Once someone hooks up with a guy, you see less and less of her until either they break up or move in together. Marcia's boyfriend, Vern, lived in Georgia and it had been pretty much a long-distance affair. But now Marcia's transfer to the Atlanta branch had come through and today had been her last in Chicago. Christin had helped her pack up her assortment of coffee mugs, plants, pictures of the venerable Vern-o and other cubicle junk, had taken her out with the girls for lunch and impromptu shower, had bestowed the group gift, the requisite burgundy teddy. She knew the routine well, had done it more times than she cared to remember, and of course, one time it had all been for her.

It was still difficult to think about, but not even six months ago she had been engaged also, to one Michael Burnie for a blissful year and a half during which time they shared an apartment, a life, and, ultimately, she learned, her best friend.

It was a crushing blow; they had known each other for nearly three years and had planned to marry in the fall. He had been smart and very funny, with an endearing zany streak. But Michael's craziness jumped, perhaps inevitably, outside the box. She still remembers that late spring afternoon when looking deep in the hall closet of their apartment for a spare set of keys she knew he had tucked away somewhere, happened to look through his workout bag and inside a zippered pocket that she never knew existed and found a completely out-of-place set of photographs of Katelyn (best friend!) in various states of dishabille and indolent repose—along with a couple of Michael himself, naked and rampant. At that moment the closet light suddenly exploded, the floor under her feet gave way, and her world, now forever abominated with ugly gleaming squares of just too much glowing cream and pink flesh, collapsed.

He had been her life. No one in Chicago had even come close. In the long empty months since, she has been pondering, recapitulating. What had she missed? What hadn't she seen? She racked her brain, trying to remember all of them together, at tennis, at parties, sailing Lake Michigan on a mutual friend's yacht . . . maybe he had spent an inordinate amount of time with Katelyn, whose bikini *had* perhaps seemed too skimpy, and-and maybe there was a reason for that now, and, God . . . *why anything?*

During the accusation and the ugly heated exchange between them, Michael, furious, trying to wound Christin even further, sputtered that she was just too prim, too quiet, too spineless, to try anything new. But Katelyn wasn't. No way. "Jesus, compared to you, Katie is wild, totally hot, in or *out* of bed!" he screamed, and just to show her exactly, cruelly, what he meant, ran out to his car and stomped back in with yet another evil sheaf of prints that he spread on the table like a winning hand at poker. They depicted the fair Katelyn in about a dozen exhibitionistic outdoor poses in various locations around Chicago, in the wintertime, no less.

Wasn't she cold? was all a thoroughly numb Christin could wonder at the time, but in the end, it was indeed an unbeatable hand. She couldn't begin to compete with such craziness. She was out of her league. Absolutely crushed, she jammed what she could into her BMW and left the ruins that same day.

Starting over in a world free from incorrigible Michael and the treacherous Katelyn was lonely, yet surprisingly exhilarating. Her new apartment in Lambert Towers was pricey but gorgeous and life might have been fairly tolerable until she rediscovered that her beauty, always a strange undeniable entity of its own, was as much a liability as an asset.

After the knowledge became widespread that Christin Darrow in M&A was available, she found herself fending off numerous entreaties. It was just too soon; she needed some time to think and heal, and besides, there seemed to be a total lack of depth to these AFS finance-jocks, no subtlety whatsoever, especially after she had overheard a couple of accountants briefing a new hire: the first thing he needed to do was learn where the cafeteria and the men's rooms were, the second was to know which VP's to suck up to and which to avoid, and the third, to get a date with the ice queen, Christin Darrow. And if he hit a home run with her to report back immediately, for there was a $1,000 pot in the office pool to the first guy who did.

That did it. She wasn't about to become a notch on the side of anyone's desk—or bed. She certainly wasn't going out with anyone from AFS. Which meant, in effect, that she didn't really see anyone at all.

That was nearly six months ago and she sometimes stops in the midst of her killing workload to ponder: what is happening with her life? Whatever became of the simple dream she had had (since childhood, for God's sake) of being an artist? What has her life become?

She looks guiltily over at the unfinished oil still clamped in the big expensive easel she had bought when she first got the job at AlphaBanc, her brushes and paints neatly laid alongside. It's a sort of cityscape, but with many sun-washed children playing in Chicago's Oz park, and she still remembers how happy she was at the time, under the blank benign eyes of the Tin Man sculpture, sketching away on a truly gorgeous and warm spring day in early May.

How long ago was that? At least two years ago—or was it three? Even when she thinks she might have the time, she just can't seem to get herself to pull the easel out of the corner to complete the painting. It's as though the magic has left forever; AlphaBanc absolutely seems to suck all the life out of her.

One thing is sure, it certainly takes a lot of energy to make it through a week, even a day, at work. Her new manager, Bernice McKrell, aka Bernice the Bitch, or more casually, "Cruella," seems to have it in for the attractive Christin, certainly never misses an opportunity to pile more work on her. A hopeless situation. She can't allow herself to kiss up to Cruella but she can't bring herself to confront her either. She just doesn't have the guts. And Marcia (only slightly less cowardly than Christin), after listening to her striking friend's lamentations during a zinfandel-fueled Bernice-bitch session, teasingly called her the "Queen of No Self-Esteem."

Christin considers this now, blinking back tears as she walks to the window, realizes that Marcia was probably right, seeing exactly the same thing that Michael saw her as, a miserable little mouse who'd sooner die than speak up for herself, and she hates herself for it. She sobs softly and wipes her eyes with the back of her hand, gazing out over the blurry lights of Chicago, thinking wretchedly that there once was a time when she could have stood up to her, when she feared nothing, it seemed, certainly not a miserable little twit like Bernice—but that was long ago, at an entirely different time in her life, and in a much different place.

CHAPTER TWELVE

FEELING SORRY FOR herself and staring absently out at the random lights of the apartments that surround her, Christin is momentarily startled when her computer chimes softly. Incoming. At this time of night probably another AlphaBanc-important memo, she thinks, mousing over to her mail icon and clicking, but no, it's from Marcia Deaver—

> Hi Chris. Finally finished packing up everything. Tomorrow I leave for Marietta. Thank goodness I started weeks ago. You know me. Miss Efficiency. Not too smart though, I dropped my cell phone into the bubble bath while I was talking to Vern! Hope it starts working again after it dries out. So now I've got my laptop on top of some boxes and thought I'd drop you a note before I shut this thing down. Mainly want to thank you for the lunch—and the teddy. Sorry I didn't get more time to talk to you today, but this transfer came so quickly it seems that all I've been doing is work, pack, and sleep! Well, you know what kind of workload we've got. Anyway, we should be able to move into our house on Monday as long as the movers don't screw up, so wish me luck. Chris, I hope your ear problem doesn't turn out to be like mine. Would that be a coincidence? At least we know that AlphaBanc is sympathetic ever since Bergstrom's own daughter came down with the very same thing. They sure took care of everything for me. Let me know how it goes for you, Okay? Let's keep in touch.
> —Marcia.

> P.S. Wonder if you've gotten on to NEXSX yet?
> You've got to give it a try, that is if you're up to it.
> Some of it is pretty hot stuff!

Up to it! Hot stuff? *Yes, let's keep in touch,* Christin mentally mocks Marcia's closing, then thinks better of herself. *I'm not being nice at all.*

Well, she's really tired, plus she and Marcia hadn't really been *that* close as friends. They had both worked in the same department for the evil Bernice, were both single, and, with Marcia's boyfriend in Atlanta most of the time, were relatively free to hang around together. But that was about it for things in common, until, of course, Christin started getting sick too—with apparently the very same thing that Marcia had had. Very strange.

Marcia had described her symptoms to Christin many times, so often, in fact, that Christin couldn't believe that she was experiencing apparently the same ailment, thinking that perhaps it was psychosomatic—but there was no denying the strange and sudden attacks: ears ringing, the full feeling in her head, and then, the worst part, the room would begin to spin so badly she would have to white-knuckle the arm of her chair, nearly dropping to the floor, *exactly like Marcia.*

The last time was about two weeks ago; the attack had lasted more than ten terrible minutes and she had vomited her breakfast in the ladies' room at work. Then she knew it was real. She had to tell Marcia, find out the name of her doctor. There was no longer any doubt, she needed help.

And just like Marcia had said, AlphaBanc was there for her. She had gotten in right away, the same day, in fact, to see her primary care physician, Dr. Albanese, a thin, pale, unhealthy-looking man who smelled faintly of the cigarettes and menthol lozenges he sucked between patients. He actually spent substantially more time with her than the nine minutes that the AlphaBanc HMO had deemed necessary for each patient visit, nearly a quarter of an hour. But he had scheduled another appointment with her for a more complete assessment, one he cautioned her, raising his eyebrows, that might require nearly a full hour. She understood then, how serious this must be.

I don't have any life at all anymore! Christin returns to the stupid spreadsheet, realizes that she's just plain miserable, tired and lonely and frustrated that she doesn't seem to be able to get any, any *anything*—any romance, any friendship, even any simple good conversation. She isn't one to hang out in bars, hasn't run into anyone at the health club, and had been thinking seriously about taking out an ad in one of the online singles dating sites. But now she thinks that maybe there's another way . . . with this NEXSX thing.

Before they had said their final good-byes, Marcia had written down the enigmatic name for her, and then almost insisted that she try it out. She had explained that NEXSX is like a crazy-fun albeit oversexed version of Facebook with zillions of different user forums and chat rooms. It also supposedly had a very slick postings area with listings of eligible people—two of whom, at one time, had been Vern and Marcia. *Hot stuff?* Well, Christin had met Vern a couple of times and though he seemed okay, he didn't in any way resemble: hot stuff. Whatever, exactly, that was.

She pushes away from the computer, goes to get her purse and the card on which Marcia had written the URL. She passes by the full length mirror in her bedroom and catches sight of her reflection: cute, slender, dressed in beltless faded jeans and a faded plaid blouse with its near-topmost button primly fastened. *Jeeze, am I losing it all so soon? At twenty-fucking-six years old?*

She unbuttons that button and one below it. She looks again at herself and then unbuttons the next button. She isn't wearing a bra and is pleased with the racy look. She sighs. At this miserable point in her life, it is, she has to admit, pretty daring for her. Maybe Marcia knows her better than she thinks. Maybe Michael did too. But what does it matter anyway? Who cares? Who can see her now? No one, no one at all. She takes a deep breath. Maybe that is the whole problem.

After she logs off her account at the bank, she brings up her browser again, enters the URL, and watches as a black screen rapidly appears, emblazoned simply with the silvery letters:

NEXSX. She clicks on the logo and encounters a page featuring the legend: *Welcome to NEXSX, the Largest Adult Conferencing Community on the Planet!* This is accompanied with a blur of information and links to pages about joining the community, membership costs and benefits, interest groups, privacy guarantees, and blah and blah. Well, what the heck was Marcia talking about? So far this sure isn't anything like the Facebook *she* knew.

Christin sucks in a deep breath and, what the hell, clicks on an inviting chartreuse label: "Take a Free Tour!" and up pops a sign-in screen that asks for a username, a personal "handle," and a password. Marcia had told her about using a handle at the site, a NEXSX specialty—Marcia's is "Chica"—so Christin enters "Kitten," a term of endearment that Michael had once had for her, and for her unique username: "newh0tgal." Perfect.

I can't fucking believe I'm doing this, she thinks as she presses the enter key and is immediately presented with a screen of instructions describing how to become a member—privacy guaranteed—by entering her real name and her credit card number. The subscription fees are actually quite steep, $39.95 a month, but Marcia had raved about NEXSX, had met her fiancée here, and had hinted that it might be, well, a bit *too hot* for Christin. This immediately angers her, what the hell, what's she got to lose? Screw the free tour, if the site wasn't too hot for Marcia, it's certainly not too hot for her. She pulls her AlphaBanc Promethium Card from her wallet and signs up. For six months, anyway. What the hell.

She proceeds straight to the heart of NEXSX and finds a huge array of menu options, ranging the gamut of social and sexual interest, with a bewildering number of forums and chat rooms available for each. Not really knowing what she should do, Christin clicks around until she finds pages of more prosaic links, stops at: *Women Looking for Men.* It seems almost too blatant, but it's really what she's doing, isn't it? She is presented with several lines of instructions and then a list of women's names or, for the most part, it appears, their handles, along with their small, nearly indiscernible images, that fill the screen. She's surprised that the initial images are so miniscule for such an expensive site, but at the same time, she's suddenly excited. This must be the personals listing area that Marcia had told her about. Clicking on any of these links will apparently bring more personal information and better images, although Christin quickly realizes that this isn't actually what she wants, and she thinks now that she really should access another link further down, *Men Looking for Women*, where she presumably would find listings of interested men. But while she is in this area, she figures she might as well see what other women post about themselves. She might soon be doing the same.

The instructions she read when she registered had stated that most persons elected to use a handle, but if someone wanted to list their full name it was up to them. Also, she could list her phone number directly, or require that anyone wishing to contact her do so only through NEXSX messaging. Christin can't imagine anyone, any woman, anyway, actually listing their full name and real phone number on NEXSX. God knows who's out there. Besides, it would spoil the fun of being anonymous on the web. It's the incognito factor that intrigues her; all she has to do is post a personal message and an image of herself. She smiles wickedly.

Her first thought is of sending a completely scandalous (well, Katelyn-esque, she winces) snapshot that a salivating Michael had taken of her in disgracefully skimpy black bikini underwear last year. It was after a wild party and she was heavily made up—and not a little drunk and stoned, and had slipped on a cute blonde wig she had bought just for the fun of it. She smiles broadly, still remembers the crazy lovemaking that had followed that little adventure in costumery.

Despite his pleas for a repeat performance, she had only done it that one time—a serious mistake, she realizes now. And anyway she knows that she could never put that picture on NEXSX. No way. No one besides her and Michael has ever seen it. She sighs, thinking that it's really kind of a shame, though, because it just happens to be her best picture ever, the one where everything looks just right, even if it is totally outré. Even if it isn't exactly her.

Or is it?

But no . . . no way, that's getting way too wild, she'd be stooping right down to the level of that disgusting tramp Katelyn. She has another picture that she can send, a dignified but very nice head and shoulders portrait of herself in a gray business suit that AlphaBanc had commissioned for their files.

But now she's curious to see what other women have posted. She selects one on the first page: Aimee. She once knew an Aimee in high school back in Seattle. And she would be about twenty-six now, the same age as Christin. She clicks on the link. Suddenly she's presented with a fairly sharp hi-res image of, presumably, Aimee. She gasps.

It's Aimee Effinger! It has to be her, never quite a friend, but an acquaintance from high school who had been, and obviously still is, quite pretty. She's someone with whom she had always felt a vague rivalry even though they had never really competed for the same boyfriends. But wow! Christin can scarcely believe her eyes—what a picture! Here is Aimee holding a cigarette and defiantly eyeing the camera in a drop-dead red leather miniskirt and sexy white satin blouse that is open nearly to her waist, with one sandaled foot perched jauntily on a wicker chair, long legs open quite provocatively in a full frontal assault on whatever anxious fellows happened to browse the listings of NEXSX. Poised to kill.

Aimee Effinger! Who had always been so quiet and soft-spoken, who used to work the ticket booth at all the varsity basketball games. Christin puts her hand to her throat, has to catch her breath. Wow. *Aimee!*

Well, Marcia was right. This certainly is no place for dilettantes; this is the real thing. But if this is what the women's postings are like, what will she see in the men's ads? She can't wait to check them out. But one thing she's sure of now, the photograph she'll post will be the one of her in the wig and the hot underwear. Absolutely. She's going completely incognito; it'll be crazy fun. Forget the stupid business suit.

CHAPTER THIRTEEN

IT'S THE SLOW time at Lambert Towers in Chicago, early Monday afternoon, everyone at work. Louis, the doorman, yawns as he checks the ID card of the serviceman from ABV Elevator although it hardly seems necessary, the man is dressed in gray coveralls with an ABV patch and the stitching: "Chuck," and a worn gray ABV cap. Besides, he's seen him at least once before, he remembers, the last time only about a month ago. Same time of day. Friendly guy. Talked to him about fishing downstate. But someone else is at the entrance so he doesn't have time to chat; he sends Chuck over to the security desk to register.

A bored-looking woman sitting behind a row of security monitors recessed below the marble counter checks the serviceman's ID again and enters it into the computer. The name tag on her uniform reads: Angela.

"Crazy computers," says Chuck appreciatively, smiling and slowly shaking his head. "These crazy computers are everywhere nowadays. They run everything. Elevators, too. But I don't know much about it. I just pull out the circuit boards and plug 'em in—whatever the manual says."

The woman stops chewing her gum, "Oh, yeah. We log in all repair services now. Used to have 'em sign a sheet, then cross 'em off after they left. Now we do it all 'online.'"

"Modern times," the serviceman smiles at her.

"Yeah. But if you ask me," she says, cracking her gum, "I liked the old way just fine. These things ain't all they're cracked up to be."

"Oh no?"

"No *way*. Sometimes this stupid system is down for an hour or more at a time. Sometimes half the day. Then what do I do? They took my old log sheets away."

"Sounds like a problem, Angela."

"Their problem. Not mine," she smirks, handing him back his card. "I just wave 'em by."

"Gotcha. Well, you have a nice day, okay?"

"Sure. You too, Chuck."

He smiles, swings his battered leather tool case from one hand to the other, walks to the first elevator and touches the UP button. Immediately the doors slide open and a feminine voice intones: "Going up." The serviceman enters and touches the button for the 41st floor. He smiles and waves back at the doorman just as the doors slide shut. Once inside, he takes a key from his pocket, unlocks a maintenance panel below the rows of buttons and sets several switches; the voice purrs "Express mode," and the elevator begins its ascent, though somewhat more slowly than normal express mode.

Immediately, down in the lobby one of the views on the security monitors blinks out. Elevator One. Angela shakes her head and tries thumping it with the palm of her hand: nothing. Stupid computers.

Inside the car, however, "Chuck" is quickly pulling off his coveralls. Underneath he is wearing a gray herringbone sport coat and dark gray slacks. He bends down and opens his tool case, snaps open a plastic container inside, removes an already knotted necktie and pulls it over his head. He fastens his collar button and straightens the tie. Then he quickly folds the jumpsuit into a tight parcel, stuffs it into the container and snaps the lid shut. He removes the container completely and sets it on the elevator floor. With swift practiced movements he trips a tiny lever on each of the toolbox's hinges and the top and the bottom of the case comes apart. He picks up the bottom, pushes a tab on each corner, the seams part, and he turns the panels inside out. He flips over the top, replaces the hinges, and snaps the handle onto the other side of the panel. He now has an elegant red cowhide briefcase. He quickly places the plastic container inside the case and closes it. He reaches inside the maintenance well and resets the switches, pushes the door shut and locks it. The voice announces the forty-first floor. He stands up, smooths his hair and drops the key into his pocket just as the doors slide open.

He nods and smiles at an elderly couple waiting for the elevator as he gets off and walks casually down the hall. At the door of 4131 he glances briefly up and down the corridor, inserts his key in the lock, turns it, and steps inside.

He wastes no time, pulling on a pair of latex gloves while he quickly walks through the spacious apartment, straight to the bathroom. He opens the medicine cabinet and finds the pills: Ovultodt's, one tablet already punched through the foil backing. Today she won't be sick. He sets the briefcase on the toilet stool and opens it. He opens another container. It contains an assortment of birth control pills, many different brands. He selects a plastic strip of Ovultodt's and punches out a pill. He drops it into the sink, turns on the faucet and washes it away. Then he puts the strip of pills he has taken from the cabinet into his briefcase and places his strip in its place. He finds two other unopened strips of Ovultodt's in the cabinet, replaces them with others from his case. He carefully closes the medicine cabinet, takes off the gloves, places them in the briefcase and snaps it shut. Then he walks back to the door, opens it slightly, peers down the hallway. It's deserted. Everyone at work. He pulls the door shut and walks quietly toward the elevator.

No one is on the sidewalk outside and the lobby of Lambert Towers is momentarily empty. Louis ambles over to the uniformed woman behind the marble counter, "Say, Angie, would you look up the name of that nice fella from th' elevator repair. Here about fifteen minutes ago?"

"I'm trying to get this stupid thing to work." She bangs the monitor again with her hand and, miraculously, the image reappears, of elevator One, presently empty. Angela chuckles, "All it needs is a little friendly *per*-suasion. Now, what did you want, Louis?"

"Thought you might see when that elevator fella would be comin' back down here. I know I talked with him just a month before. About fishin' around Carbondale. Wanted to ask him just where he went down there."

"Well, he didn't say how long he was going to be and he didn't check out yet," she says, typing at her keyboard, "but we'll just look right here . . . huh!"

"What'sa matter, Angie?"

"Well, damn. I know he didn't check out, I haven't left here for a minute. But this doesn't even have him on the log for today!"

"It don't?"

"Did you see him go out?"

"No ma'am. Not hide nor hair."

"Well, it looks like he was never even here!"

"Don't that beat all."

"Stupid computers."

CHAPTER FOURTEEN

THE MESSAGE HAUNTS him. Of all the things Clayborne has to contemplate lately, the one he can't get out of his mind is the mysterious phone call that he received after the Chicago teleconference. *". . . maybe you'll learn the truth about your wife."* Even now, a week later, sitting in his office at AlphaBanc West, he still can't imagine who it might be from, let alone divine what it means.

Did it mean she was . . . unfaithful? Natalie? Running around? A possibility perhaps, but a wildly remote one. It just couldn't be. Not Natalie. Is it about her death? He saw the FAA accident investigation report, saw the wreckage itself, though he was spared, mercifully, her sad remains *in situ.* The official cause of the accident was unspecified engine failure, but since that was also the crash impact point, one of the investigators told him confidentially that they would probably never know for sure.

What the hell is going on? He idly glances over at an empty space on his desk between his computer monitor and a plastic figurine of the amiable AlphaBanc mascot, Darby O'Banknote. It was where Natalie's picture used to be, and he immediately feels the lump rise in his throat. He hated to remove it, but his therapist had insisted, at least temporarily; it was time to start putting his loss behind him, to get on with his life. He shakes his head, knows logically that this is the right thing, but his heart can't seem to accept it. The only thing that gets him through the day and, very often, the night, is his work. Twelve to eighteen hour days have become the norm, with all-nighters not an unknown. He knows that it's probably not the healthiest of options, but at the least it can only help his career—all, at this miserable juncture, he has left in his life.

The only way is the way up, one of the very few things he learned from his father, the big Bruce, the apotheosis of drive and ambition. It could be that he's followed that proverb a bit too single-mindedly, especially since Natalie has been gone. She had once been a moderating factor, but now there is nothing to slow him on his journey to get to the top—any damn way he can.

Even now he can't help but bask in the sweet satisfaction he gets as he looks out his office door at the long rows of gray cubicles that sprawl across the thirty-third floor of AlphaBanc West; he's quite proud just to be here, even more so to be *succeeding* here. And although he'd be the first to admit he hasn't "made it" yet, he's fairly pleased with himself; it is certainly nice to have the private office that sets him apart from most of the other marketing minds that diabolically buzz together out there. On the other hand, he has to think that at thirty-one some guys are already vice-presidents, or at least department heads, and he's only a senior manager. But one, he keeps reminding himself, at a very, very large place. To make it to any upper level in this gigantic organization has got to be going somewhere. And to be actually working on a special project for the man at the apex of this colossal pyramid (with whom he personally discussed this mission) is a fantastic opportunity.

He still can't believe his luck at being selected for this gig. He likes to think that it's because of some of the traits that might have surfaced in his PERSPROF: intelligence, dedication, perseverance, loyalty. But in his darker moments he can also come up with: deceit, deception, and blind ruthless ambition . . . qualities which he sometimes thinks that AlphaBanc prizes more highly. Especially on a mission such as this. But he knows he's only fooling himself, the real reason he got this is assignment is probably due to one person: Zara LaCoste. Other than his hard work, she's his only other route to the top here, a depressing thought indeed.

"Richard?"

Uh-oh, rapidly approaching at 3 o'clock is Mary Petrovic, the young and pretty math whiz who is, or was, on his team, and who usually exudes entirely too much enthusiasm.

"Richard?" She's all too quickly in his office and in front of him. "Did you talk to Mattie? About dropping me? Or did you talk to Roger?"

"Um . . ."

"C'mon Richard, Mattie just told me I'm off the team. And Grayson is moved in as project statistician."

"Well, I guess we just decided it was time for a change."

"Look, I'm sorry that I screwed up that presentation, I really am, but like I told you, I've been having these weird dizzy spells and every month they seem to get a little worse, and—"

"Then you'd better see a doctor," Clayborne snaps.

"I *have* seen a doctor, one I've gone to for years, not even in the A-Banc system, and she can't find anything wrong, I told you. It just comes and goes . . . I'm really, really sorry I messed up that meeting, Richard."

"Oh, yeah," says Clayborne as coolly as possible, "*that* meeting, the Darby O'Banknote quarterly review, with Roger, my boss, and Alan Sturgis in from Chicago, just to get a look at—"

He pauses, realizes that his next word would have been: *me.*

"—all of us, and then we look like idiots. Didn't you think to check over the deck before we showed them?" Clayborne briefly closes his eyes, the memory of the debacle replaying in the back of his mind, the slides out of sequence, the graphs unfinished, percentages calculated incorrectly . . . which Sturgis, another math maven, detected immediately.

"I-I'm terribly sorry, but we were rushed and I didn't really get a chance. I was in the bathroom a lot, being sick . . ."

Clayborne reflects. As project leader he's responsible for the presentation and she really had made him, all of them, look bad. In truth, he always reviewed the slides of a major presentation himself beforehand, but they were rushed and he had let her handle it. Ultimately it was his responsibility, but he also understood the next order of business at AlphaBanc for a shrewd manager caught in such a situation: *find a scapegoat.* So he simply had to throw her off the team. It was expected of him. A lesson to others that Richard Clayborne has some clout. Anyway, it was all too easy: just a word to Roger and she was dropped. He felt bad for her, but it all came down to power, and at AlphaBanc, power is what it's all about.

"Richard, listen, I'm really sorry I screwed up, I apologize again, okay? I really was sick. Listen, I-I can go to another doctor, one in the AlphaBanc network, okay? Get a second opinion. This is my career here and it doesn't look good at all for me to get bumped like this, so could you . . ."

Clayborne considers, one word from him and she's back in, but how would he look? He had made sure that Sturgis knew that he had gotten rid of her, blatantly to cover his own ass, but it was something that Sturgis understood. He has to cut her short: "Mary, there's nothing I can do now, it's entirely out of my hands—"

"Bullshit!" she leans in, eyes flaming. "You know you could get me back on in a heartbeat. But you won't because you think it'll make you look weak or-or maybe even human! You know something, you really are a son-of-a-bitch! Have a nice fucking life!" she yells as she strides out.

CHAPTER FIFTEEN

CLAYBORNE WATCHES MARY run out and shakes his head, really wishes he had a Deludamil. After all, it wasn't as though he had gotten her fired. Which, unfortunately, is something he's going to have to do now. It's really too bad; she's a good kid. Could she really be that sick? He begins to ponder the implications of this, then notices somebody else standing in his doorway. Oh God, it's Lance Girardeau.

"So, Richie," he croons, "I hear that you're gonna get onto NEXSX and do some prowling around for Gates."

Clayborne blinks, glances quickly around, nearly whispers even though he's inside his office, "Huh? How'd you hear about that? Nobody's supposed to know about this—project."

Girardeau, tall, lanky, with a thin, mean smile, smirks, "Relax. The Epenguin told me. He and you are supposed to work on this together. You and Rascher, Mr. Psycho-dork himself."

"Yeah, I guess that's the team."

"And, uh, Richie-boy, I hear that Zara's heading it up."

"Uh, yeah, so what?" Clayborne hiding the instant anger he feels about this jerk knowing so much.

"So what? Oh boy!" Girardeau laughs hideously. "Zara! I love it. Watch out for her, man. She's gonna try to cut out a piece of your miserable bod. And we know which piece."

Clayborne slowly shakes his head, smiles weakly. Zara. Damn. It's happening, he can't stop it . . . she's come back to haunt him, just as he had always feared since he came to work here, all the way from the summer of his junior year in high school.

It was so long ago, so far away, maybe the scientists are right, the universe, all time and space are circular, tending ever to curve back on themselves . . . all the way to dreary here from a fiercely hot bright August afternoon in Chicago, far from any future San Francisco.

His father, Bruce Clayborne, who had been the top IBM salesman in Chicago back then for mainframe computers, big iron, had sent him on an errand, for fifty bucks, to deliver a package for the AlphaBanc account to downtown Chicago. The actual destination turned out to be a cool dark suite at the Drake, where Zara LaCoste, thirty-something then, already an AlphaBanc senior manager and incredibly hot in garter belt and purple stockings and a satin robe that wouldn't stay shut handled the rest.

A wonderful setup. And as much as he was grateful for this tremendous, thoughtful gift (which endured, sporadically, over a steamy short month, until stupid school started again), it was the fact that the old man—Mr. Never-around, whose family legacy up until this point consisted of late nights at the office, continual travel, and missed birthdays—had cared enough about him to bestow it that touched Clayborne deeply. It was one of the rare times when bodacious Bruce had actually shut down his sizzling sales machine and paid attention to his only son, leading to a great, albeit short father-and-son season, winks in the hallway and snifters of Maker's Mark in the den during that blissful chummy month—though they never at any time actually spoke of the *gift*.

And unfortunately, they never were as close again, that is, until years later when Bruce understood that his son needed a better job and then acted so amazingly effortlessly to get him in at gigantic AlphaBanc at substantial coin, which was one of the reasons, come to think of it, that he took the AlphaBanc West position so quickly—*because the old man had done it for him.*

It certainly seemed like the right move at the right time; Clayborne had been at the same little marketing firm in Chicago he had started with after college, desperately unhappy, overworked, underpaid, no real time to spend with his then new wife, Natalie—and Zara, the *possibility* of Zara, was only a dim afterthought. But then he never would have thought that she would still be working for AlphaBanc so many years later.

"Yeah, I can't wait to get started," Clayborne says to Girardeau. "What are you doing in here anyway?"

"Just slumming, pal. I got a few prints to drop off. Secret stuff. But I kid you not, buddy. You had better watch out for that old babe. She's hot stuff."

"Shut up. Get outta here. I've got work to do."

"Whoa! Wait a minute Richie, don't get so riled. I was just kidding. You're not her type. Not at all, I'm sure. Now, c'mon, do me a big favor and give this envelope to Dutch for me, will ya?"

"No way. Do it yourself." Clayborne isn't kidding. He can't stand Erich "Dutch" Dienstbach, a little overbearing blowhard who had somehow made it to director in telemarketing systems. He is not well-liked, and no one, including Clayborne, wants to have any more to do with him than is absolutely necessary.

"I can't, I gotta run. He's not in his office and I can't just leave it on his desk, if you know what I mean." He winks knowingly, infuriatingly, at Clayborne. "C'mon buddy, give me a break, he might be in meetings all day—"

"Okay, okay! Hand it over," says Clayborne, just to get rid of Girardeau, who, he knows, will pester him forever until he agrees.

"Hey, there's the A-Banc team spirit! Thanks buddy." He tosses him the manila envelope and turns toward the door.

Watching Girardeau wink again and smirk before walking out, Clayborne understands all the reasons he can't stand this guy either. And Girardeau doesn't even work for AFS; he owns a small prepress service on Van Ness and makes himself invaluable to them through his work with Photoshop and other sophisticated imaging software that enables him to retouch, restore, and recombine the elements of a photograph any way he, or AlphaBanc, wishes. Clayborne has to begrudge that Girardeau is actually quite a skilled artist who, prior to the AFS work, had thoroughly mastered the art of airbrushing nudes for skin magazines when the new technology replaced airbrushes and camera film. Now his results are flawless and a picture isn't worth a thousand words anymore. If fact, it isn't worth anything.

Maybe that is it, the fact that Girardeau does an increasing amount of dirty work for AFS that makes Clayborne so uncomfortable in his presence, except that he suddenly remembers that's exactly what he is going to do—dirty work for AlphaBanc. On NEXSX. And now this Dunne guy is a vicious murderer? He feels a pain in his stomach. What the hell *is* going on?

"Hey Richard, time to punch out."

"Huh?" A shadow looms in the doorway of his office. He looks up at the hulking figure of Stevie Denton, a marketing analyst in his department. Big Friday grin.

"It's five o'clock, man. Time to put the toys away. Want to catch some brews with us? Down at Sailer's?"

"Uh, I don't know. Got to finish this report."

"Aw, c'mon. The report can wait. A nice Friday afternoon like this can't."

"Well, maybe I'll be down," Clayborne says, just to get rid of him. He watches Stevie walk out, happy, whistling a tune. Once he was happy, wasn't he?

He looks over at the envelope Girardeau had dropped on his desk, picks it up, sees that the flap has popped open—stupid moron. God knows what dirty business—the only business that Girardeau seems to do nowadays for AlphaBanc—is contained herein, and he is too lazy to even properly seal it. But . . . hmm. Clayborne reckons that he will take a little peek here; he can't see why Girardeau would be dealing with geeky Dutch anyway.

He shakes out a set of black and white 8x10 glossies and, oh God, he should have let well enough alone, it's a bunch of pictures of, unmistakably, Dutch's wife, Lauren—or Laurie—he thinks, in flagrante delicto with, well, several fellows, it seems. Clayborne is instantly incensed; he's positive these are some of Girardeau's fakes because he knows that she is divorcing Dutch—everyone in the office cheered that she was finally dumping the little creep—and Dutch is of course fighting back, with a vengeance.

Well, he's not going to be a part of it, even as an innocent courier. He takes the pictures over to the office shredder—a satisfying, but purely token gesture, Girardeau will have the originals anyway—and proceeds to destroy all the bogus "evidence." In a few seconds it's done. Now he's finally given himself a reason to be proud today.

But the rest of his work at AlphaBanc remains. He truly hates to stay late on Fridays, but with Natalie gone it doesn't really matter anyway and the work of a senior marketing manager is never done. Due Monday are the latest numbers on the consumer acceptance and recognizability of AlphaBanc's venerable mascot: Darby O'Banknote.

No greater amount of test marketing, consumer surveys, and focus group studies had been conducted in AlphaBanc history before emerging with the apparition of the now ubiquitous Darby smiling kindly down over his broad white moustache, his bemused eyes making him look a lot like the cartoon character Gepetto in Disney's *Pinocchio*, with the reassuring tag line: "YOUR BIGGEST BEST FRIEND! ALWAYS WATCHING OUT FOR YOU!"

Although only one of several leaders of the multifaceted project, the Darby character itself had been solely Clayborne's baby, he having pushed and promoted the family-friendly computer animation ever since he saw the artist's original rendering so many months ago. At that moment he *knew* that was it; he somehow just knew it would all work, and after more creative decisions and conference calls and late-night team meetings than he could remember, he's been proved right, Darby O'Banknote is a gigantic success.

Now Clayborne's team is involved in the more mundane, but unusually rewarding task of gathering the numbers, and luckily for him the stats are not at all bad. In fact, they're terrific. Thanks to the hundreds of millions of dollars spent on a colossal marketing effort over the past five years, the latest data shows that Darby O'Banknote is now known to a phenomenal 94.2% of adults 18 to 54 years old in the United States. Within a 95% confidence level. The numbers for those who actually *trust* the grandfatherly banker-buddy is 74.3% within the same level of confidence. No, it is not bad at all to be associated with the Darby campaign. It was probably this notoriety—along with Zara's influence, and whatever god-awful information existed in his PERSPROF—that helped get him assigned to this dubious Gnome project.

The one set of stats that keeps appearing, though, the one that bothers him every time he generates it, is the summary of children's recognition of the old fart, the 5 to 12 year old group. It is an amazing 84.7%. They certainly aren't a major part of the target market. It is all business, of course, and it is certainly positive that these kids, America's next purchasing generation, will grow up to know and love the great Darby—and thus friendly Alpha-Banc. But for some reason these damn lies truly disturb him, 84-plus points seems like way too much recognition for their boy. Ronald McDonald is first, of course, at 88%. Santa Claus comes in third.

CHAPTER SIXTEEN

THE EXAMINATION SEEMS thorough enough. Christin has carefully answered a battery of questions on the nature of her dizzy spells. How often did they come? How long did they last? How severe were they? Had she noticed any hearing loss? Have they ever caused her to faint? Fall down? And on, and on. Dr. Albanese checks off her answers on a clipboard, grunting quietly as she answers, telling him that the spells usually begin about midday, when she is at work, but also, sometimes on weekends. Some days she's just fine, but on the whole, the spells seem to be increasing in frequency and intensity, and it's beginning to scare her.

"Well, this is something we can't ignore," says the doctor reaching absently toward his breast pocket as though there might be a pack of cigarettes there. "I'm going to set you up for a hearing test with an audiologist, an electrocochleography, or ECOG, an electronystagmography, or ENG, and a CAT scan at a clinic downtown I'm associated with, a part of AlphaBanc's Wellness Network."

"An electrocogli—what? Do you really think all that's necessary? And a-a CAT scan?"

"Yes, I do," the doctor purses his thin lips and looks at her with tired eyes. "It certainly appears to be Ménière's to me, but we have to be certain. It is associated with so many different maladies: allergies, physical trauma to the head, hypertension, estrogen levels . . . and yet responds so poorly to most treatments. We won't have the results of your blood tests in for a couple of days, and I can get you in for a scan almost immediately. Tomorrow, in fact. It's a state-of-the-art facility and—"

"Tomorrow? Oh, no. I've got to be at work."

Dr. Albanese lowers his eyes. "Ms. Darrow, believe me, your health is more important to your employer than whatever work you have to do at the present time. AlphaBanc is extremely concerned about its employees and—"

"So you think it is Ménière's syndrome?"

"That is a distinct possibility. I'll give you some literature to take home with you," the doctor sighs, as though he has discussed this diagnosis with patients many times before.

"But, that's just what Marcia Deaver had! I can't believe it. You treated her didn't you?" Christin asks, although she knows the answers, that Marcia was in fact Dr. Albanese's patient, and had discussed Ménière's syndrome with her many times. She had even read the literature he had given Marcia, a couple of pamphlets and a much-reproduced copy of an article in *The New England Journal of Medicine* on the disease and the pioneering treatment of Dr. Bokanovsky.

"Yes, your friend is also my patient. Although Dr. Bokanovsky performed the surgery—"

"Do you really think I'll need surgery, too? And-and an implant?" Even though she sees it coming, Christin is still appalled at the idea of surgery for this stupid thing that has come from essentially nowhere.

"It's simply the best treatment to date. There is no drug therapy that we've found to be successful, and past treatments have provided limited success, such as the surgical insertion of a tiny shunt in the inner ear to drain excess fluid, and the vestibular neurectomy, in which we sever the vestibular nerve, which is more successful in returning your balance, but the nerve is very close to the hearing and facial nerves and sometimes—"

"Okay, okay," Christin sighs, defeated. "So there's this implant surgery. And the pulser thing."

"Phaser. Yes, I can see you've probably been talking to your friend. By the way, how is she doing?"

"Oh just fine," Christin gloomily admits, "since the operation."

"Well, there you have it. The Bokanovsky implantation is actually a simple inpatient procedure, the insertion of a minuscule electronic device below the ear which emits a tiny phased electrical current into the nerves that service the inner ear. We're not even precisely sure why it works, but it does, and quite dramatically. It's really quite a tiny device, essentially a single microchip. It even augments its own battery with a bio-nano cell that generates power through a chemical reaction with glucose in the bloodstream. You'll never even know it's there."

"But-but we're not sure that I even *have* this, Ménière's syndrome, yet," protests Christin.

"We'll have to wait for the results of the tests," the doctor sighs again. "But if you *would* require it, the procedure is really quite simple. Very minor. Only one night in the hospital."

"But how could she, Marcia and I, have exactly the same problem? If it is the Ménière's? It seems uncanny. Like a crazy coincidence."

"I can understand your concern. But the fact is, this malady is not all that uncommon. We, Dr. Bokanovsky and I, that is, have treated more than two dozen people with this disease in the past year. With this very same surgical procedure. With the implant we get a one hundred percent cure rate, drug free. I'm sure your friend has told you how much better she feels now. I leave it to you to decide."

Appalled by the very limited options available to her—essentially down to this invasive procedure—Christin fends off a wave of dizziness as she walks from the examining room to the reception desk. She schedules a time the next day for further tests and is about to turn to leave when she notices a newspaper clipping lying in an open folder on the desk. Although the text is facing the other way she can easily read the headline: ANONYMOUS TIP SAVES ABDUCTED WOMAN. Christin tilts her head to view the label on the folder, Deaver, Marcia, M., discovers the receptionist looking up at her inquisitively while reaching over to close it.

"I-I know her," blurts Christin. "She's a friend. I worked with her."

"Yes, Marcia was one of our patients. We heard about the incident. Very lucky gal."

"I'll say . . ." says Christin, thinking back on the fateful episode about three months ago, only a few weeks after Marcia had had the same operation that may figure in Christin's immediate future. She had heard the story many times now from Marcia herself, of how she had gotten lost in a bad part of town while looking for a reception at a newly-opened art gallery, and how, horrified to find herself being followed by a car full of young thugs, she had panicked and driven into a blind alley. The car quickly pulled in behind her, blocking her exit.

Christin momentarily closes her eyes, remembering Marcia's description of the absolute terror she had felt as she frantically fumbled for her cell phone when the driver's window imploded in a shower of glass, the door pulled open, the thugs' hands reaching in and dragging her out into the alley and then shoving her, screaming, into the back seat of their car.

Holding her down while they drove, they wrapped duct tape around her wrists and ankles and her eyes and mouth, leaving only her nose free to breathe. After what seemed an excruciatingly long time, the car stopped and they lifted her out, threw her onto what seemed to be a mattress on the floor. As though trying to cause her the most pain, they quickly ripped the tape from her eyes, and Marcia saw that it was indeed a very filthy mattress upon which she lay, on the concrete floor of a dimly-lit garage. They held a pistol to her head, and even if they had removed the tape from her mouth she was so terrified she could barely utter a sound as they cut the tape from her ankles and began to methodically tear off her clothing.

She lost all hope, she knew that no one would know where she was; by the time they found the car and started to track her down it would be too late; she knew this was the end for her.

But it wasn't. Amazingly, at that moment a side door burst open and a heavily armed squad of Chicago's finest rushed in and rescued her. No one was more surprised than the desperadoes themselves. They had driven her more than a mile from the kidnapping, taken her to a shuttered garage well outside of their normal turf, and yet, not even twenty minutes after the attack they were in handcuffs and Marcia was on her way to the hospital.

The detectives on the scene had told her that they had received at least two anonymous calls telling them where her car was and then the exact location of the garage in which she was being held. They were confounded at how good the tips were, and of course, how timely. They had managed to trace back one of the calls, and strangely, it turned out to be from a phone booth in Peoria.

Outside now on the windy street, Christin tries to clear her head, wonders if she had asked the doctor everything she wanted to. When she was in the examination room she was so rattled, she realizes, she was lucky she was able to ask him anything at all. Then she remembers what she wanted to tell him that seemed so important. As if it was a clue to what might be her problem. She meant to tell him that the dizziness always disappeared completely once a month, during her period.

CHAPTER SEVENTEEN

SAILER'S IS CROWDED as usual on a Friday afternoon but Clayborne finds a seat right next to Stevie, feels vaguely uncomfortable as the big bear of a guy is a relatively new member of his team, coming to concept marketing only a year ago from telemarketing systems, and he realizes he doesn't really know him all that well. But he seems to be a hard worker with a great sense of humor, somehow able to keep a good perspective on the crazy, cutthroat business they are in—that is, he seems to be relatively sane. And, at this moment, fairly drunk.

"Hey, here's Richard! What're ya drinking? I'm buying a round for all of us dedicated AlphaBanc-ians. Tell this pretty waitress what you want."

"A draft please, Anchor Steam. So, what's the occasion?"

"The occasion is . . ." Stevie giggles, taking a swallow of beer and looking at Clayborne with squinted eyes and his famous big grin, "I'm getting out! I'm leaving A-Banc!"

"You're kidding."

"Nope. I'm gettin' out! Yee-haw!" he whoops, circling his mug of beer wildly above the table.

"You're kidding. Where are you going?"

"Up north. My girlfriend and I bought us a little farm in Washington state, outside of Burlington. We're going to grow veggies. Organic. We'll truck them to restaurants around there. Good business nowadays."

"I'll be damned. Well, that's good news then."

"You know it. I'll make it official to you and Roger on Monday. But to tell the truth, I just couldn't take it anymore. The pressure, the grind, the crazy way our computers tie everyone and everything together anymore. The goddamned things really are taking over, just like everyone said they would. I've just gotta get

away from all that. To someplace where I don't have to wear this
suit and suck up to all the—"

"Yeah?"

"Well, let's face it, Rich, much as I hate to say it, you're one
of those guys. You just love it when people kiss up to you. Even
worse, now, I think, you expect it."

"Huh . . ." Shocked by Stevie's candor, Clayborne tries to
keep smiling but feels the realization of what, quite possibly is
the truth, sink in.

Stevie leans toward him, guileless, eyebrows raised, whispers
beery-confidentially, "Rich, I know I'm only tellin' you this
because I'm leaving, but I think you oughta know: a lotta people
around here think you're really pretty much of a jerk. Big-time."

"A-a . . . that . . . they do?" Clayborne finds it nearly impossible to maintain the smile, feels his face flush, mind racing the
floors and labyrinthine corridors of AlphaBanc West, searching
out the ghostly faces of his coworkers, thinking, *is he right? have I
been too driven, too rigid, too—*

"You're just too tight-assed, is the whole thing, Rich," continues smiling Stevie, looking at him closely, seriously, surprisingly drunken-kindly. "Maybe you're just trying too hard to make
it to the top, and you think that's the way everyone up there
acts—like mean sons of bitches. And maybe that's so at A-Banc,
and you're just trying to be like them. But ya know, Rich, I think
that you're not really like that. Not at all."

"R-really?" Clayborne now truly smiles, embarrassed to be so
greatly relieved by this observation.

"Nah!" laughs Stevie.

"Huh. Ha-ha."

"Just kidding, pal. No, seriously, I think you gotta lighten-up.
I know it's been really hard since Natalie—is gone, but I don't
think acting like a real creep at work is the way to deal with that
scene, ya know?"

"Huh. Well I-I never thought . . ." Clayborne, wounded, tries
to lick his lips, mouth gone incredibly dry, reaches for his beer,
which he hasn't yet touched, so intently is he listening to Stevie.
"I-I guess I never thought about it that way." He takes several
big swallows, almost downing the glass.

"Yeah, it's kind of funny isn't it. Me, just a nobody at A-Banc compared to you, and I'm telling you all this stuff, and the bitch of it is," he pauses dramatically, "it's all true. I'll bet you don't even see what you've become. Well, you're awfully damn lucky that I'm here to tell you, my friend. As I said, I think you're actually an okay guy, somewhere inside there . . ." Stevie chuckles and reaches up his big hand, playfully pokes him in the chest a couple of times.

Clayborne begins chuckling too in spite of this wholly miserable revelation; it isn't really possible to dislike Stevie, and even though he barely ever talked with him, except to demand reports and, well, maybe snap at him when they were slightly late, just like . . . it begins to dawn on him . . . just like Dutch Dienstbach! Oh, Jesus, Stevie's right; he's becoming one of them! A tight-assed AlphaBanc son of a bitch! Stevie's right!

This strikes him as actually kind of funny, with the truth smacking him across the face, the beer loosening him, Stevie poking him, and he suddenly finds himself laughing, and then laughing madly, so hard that tears run down his cheeks. Stevie laughs drunkenly along too, both of them whooping and howling at what only the two of them know to be the salvation of Clayborne's battered soul.

Clayborne calms down after a while, snuffling and gasping for breath. "Oh God, I needed that, man, I did."

"Yes," replies Stevie, radiant of kindness itself, "you did, pal. That you did."

"Yeah," sighs Clayborne, wiping his eyes, feeling quite wonderful, relieved, as though he might have seen a way to avoid a very unpleasant something in the future. "So, uh, you said you got a farm . . ."

"That's right. Gonna get away from it all. All this. I can't deal with it anymore. What I really need to do is to get my hands in the dirt and feel the sun and rain and all that real stuff again, you know what I mean?"

"Well, I guess maybe I do." Clayborne loosens his tie, unbuttons his shirt collar and takes another big swallow of beer.

"Can you make any money at that?"

"Money's not everything. You know I was raised up there, on my parents' farm. And, back then, I couldn't wait to get off of the farm, go to college, get to the big city. And now I did just that and I'm here and I hate it and I can't wait to get back. I *hate* it!"

This last is spoken so vehemently he has to smile sheepishly at Clayborne, who says softly, "It's okay, Stevie. I understand." And he knows that he does.

"Well, what I really find I hate," Stevie on a roll here, "what's really, really—diabolical, is the best way to say it, I guess, are the goddamned marketing databases. The unbelievable information we have on people. You know when I worked in telemarketing we set up an 800 number that anyone could call for info on AlphaBanc services?"

Clayborne nods, takes another swallow of beer.

"You know the computer screens we gave the operators to record the information they'd get from the callers? Well, we started loading them with data that we could pull together from their phone number as a primary key, okay? Well, we got it so tight that as soon as a call came in, we automatically pulled up on the screen all sorts of family data, you know, married, divorced, ages, kids, automobile registrations, and of course whether or not they were a current AlphaBanc customer. Then, with a few key-strokes, our folks could bring up other information, like credit history, estimated income, unemployment claims, and as much purchasing history as we could find.

"It amazed me. It amazed all of us. We couldn't believe how much stuff we actually had on people. All legal, more or less. We knew everything. Everything! In fact, if we pulled up someone with no info, that number was flagged for further identification. Sheesh!"

"So, how's the system working now?"

"Well, the industry has been changing, to email and chatbots and such, completely computerized. We took the people out of the loop about two years ago. Laid off or relocated nearly fifty operators, mostly disenfranchised-type women, undereducated, unskilled, you know. By going to complete automation we cut our costs—and our problems—by ninety percent. With savings like that, who can justify having people around?

"Anyway it was probably the best thing for them, actually. You know we had all their WORKPROFs, AlphaBanc Work Profiles, online, each one updated electronically, instantly: the calls they took, the information they obtained, the number of new customers they enrolled, what time they came to work, what time they left, how many times they went to the bathroom, how long they were there, you name it. Plus, we had video cameras constantly monitoring the work area, as well as routine monitoring of exactly what they said to customers.

"We also could interface the WORKPROFs with their PERSPROFs, which as you know keeps a hell of a lot of information on every AlphaBanc employee, so we had a lot of info about their personal life, too, their finances, medical problems, marital situation, almost everything. It got so we could spot employee problems before they would occur, just by watching graphs of their keystrokes, and they knew it. Say what you will about the benefits of the information age, these poor folks were working in a modern-day sweatshop! They were under tremendous pressure."

"As are we all . . ." muses Clayborne, wincing, knowing that Stevie is quite right, AlphaBanc knows a great deal—a very great deal—about everyone in their employ, and whenever they deem it necessary, they aren't afraid to use it.

"You, maybe," Stevie looks seriously at him. "Not me anymore. You know, I was actually glad when we let all of them go. It was like releasing them from prison."

"That how you feel now, Stevie? Like getting out of prison?"

"Sure. Wouldn't you?"

"Hmm," Clayborne can't think of anything to say to that, wants to just tell the truth: maybe Stevie's right; the rest of the world, this world, AlphaBanc's world, seems somehow wrong . . . and suddenly wonders if he might be somehow, ah, monitored, here in the tavern, but thinks that's paranoid, crazy, no way . . . and then he feels Stevie's elbow nudging him.

"Uh-oh. Look, he's up there, he's watching us!" Stevie laughs as he points up at the TV over the bar. "Good ol' Darby. Be careful what you say, Rich. He's everywhere!"

Clayborne looks up to see an AlphaBanc commercial and the fatherly face of Darby O'Banknote smiling benevolently down on him, on all of them. He has to look away.

CHAPTER EIGHTEEN

IT ALWAYS TAKES a minute or two for his eyes to adjust to the muted undersea glow of rows and rows of computer monitors, but after that Toby O'Brian knows he likes no other kind of lighting better. He is in the nerve center: AFS Data Command Central, the global hub of NATALNET, the North American Telecommunications Alliance Network, and its resemblance to Mission Control in Houston is no accident. After government cutbacks in the space program in the 1980s, AlphaBanc had hired its pick of exiled NASA electronics engineers eager for challenging work, along with the most brilliant systems designers and programmers they could find. O'Brian feels no small measure of pride as he shows his guest, Richard Clayborne, through Alpha-Banc's huge Joseph McCarthy complex, which sprawls ten stories below the farmland of central Wisconsin.

Above ground, the two hundred acres surrounded by chain link fence contain an assortment of trim modern buildings which appear no more imposing than the campus of a medium size high-tech concern of some sort, but because it includes dual banks of four huge satellite dishes that aim at various angles into the sky, an imposing microwave tower, and an assortment of variously-shaped antennae bristling from the tops of several structures, it appeared to locals that it might have something to do with communications. Definitely communications.

It was only later that new silhouettes appeared on the cluttered horizon, a pair of sleek cylindrical structures that looked for all the world like cooling towers. And then, as if function truly followed form, they began issuing steady clouds of steam, summer and winter, day and night. The locals feared at first that a nuclear reactor had been installed at the secretive site and it was only after an escorted tour through the underground facility that the concerned mayor and councilmen of the town of Red

Rock learned that their bucolic central Wisconsin community, once famous for its quarries of magnificent rose and mahogany granite, was now home to thousands of networked disk storage arrays and the largest supercomputer in the world: the Magic Mountain (O'Brian's whimsical appellation at the time, picked-up on immediately by the local press). They had been installed in the lowest levels of the complex, and the heat generated by the many thousands of processors and drives was so tremendous that it had to be vented into the atmosphere. This amazing technology was a little unnerving to the farmers plowing on its periphery, but welcomed for the high-paying jobs it brought to the area— even if it did exist far underground, and belched never-ending steam as though from the fires of Hades.

"So, Richard, what do you think now of our little operation?" O'Brian asks as they stand in "command central," as everyone calls it, dimly-lit and nearly three stories high with huge panels on the walls currently glowing deep dark blue with, variously, outlines of the United States, all of North America, a close-up of northern California, a greater close-up of the San Francisco Bay area, and an outline of Mexico and Central America. Thousands of colored points of light dot the maps overhead, with clusters around major metropolitan areas, interconnected by glowing lines that occasionally blink out to be replaced by another of a different color or intensity or suddenly diverging to connect with a cluster on the other side of an electronic continent. Beneath the screens dozens of technicians sit before smaller monitors, typing at their keyboards, murmuring to each other, glancing occasionally up at the illuminated landmasses above them.

"Well, sir, it's quite impressive. I have to admit I never expected that all *this* was way down here." Though he tries to maintain that air of mildly bored professionalism that pervades the upper ranks of AlphaBanc, Clayborne can't keep from breaking into a stupid smile at the sheer scale of the place. It is pure NASA. Mission control.

"Well, I'm glad we were able to get you down here, Richard. We're ten stories underground at this point, you know," O'Brian smiles and sizes up the eager young man that stands before him. O'Brian is the director of the operation and, despite a busy schedule, always is ready to show a visitor around the facility, especially on orders from Bergstrom himself, which are to impress upon Clayborne the huge resources that AlphaBanc Financial Services has available to it, and, by extension, the importance of his upcoming mission for them.

"You're standing right now in the nerve center, you might say, of the giant network I've been telling you about, Richard." O'Brian smiles again, speaks mincingly, with a slight lisp, which Clayborne recognizes immediately as a voice on the other end of the blacked-out teleconference call a week earlier. But he hadn't been able to see him then and is fairly surprised at how pale he actually is.

"Yes, well, it certainly looks—busy."

"Oh it is, it is indeed. AFS provides central switching and primary satellite relay management for NATALNET, an ultrahigh speed business information exchange segment of the Internet. It is, of course, a private venture, a consortium of many different firms headed by AlphaBanc Telecommunications. The backbone consists of a vast network of fiber optics and satellites that now span most of North America, Europe, Japan, India, and Australia, and soon much of Central and South America, and eventually, we hope, all of the African continent—in short, the entire globe, linked with cable and satellites."

"A seamless network."

"That's the master plan, Richard," says O'Brian excitedly. "You know that our geosynchronous and medium earth orbit satellite network, the central control center of which is located right here in underground Wisconsin, happens to now include a positive *wealth* of various interesting remote site earth stations, generally small sub-meter antennas that are, ah, extremely flexible in terms of location."

"Which means you can put them wherever you want?"

"Exactly, Richard. We can put them almost anywhere! We're constantly trying to miniaturize our addressable units to provide instant worldwide communications to—practically anything: retail stores, trucking fleets, highway patrol cars, mobile military command posts or the troopers themselves, even individual citizens carrying on their daily lives . . . ."

"Individual citizens?"

"Oh yes," O'Brian chuckles, rubs his hands together, "and with or without their permission."

"With or without . . . I don't get it."

"Perhaps you will later," O'Brian snaps and turns away, as though he has said more than he wished.

"Uh, Mr. O'Brian," says Clayborne after a respectful pause, "I still don't think that I understand what you meant about the individual—"

"Simply understand this, Richard," O'Brian's face a dark void below the animated constellations twinkling above him, "information, refined precise information, is very much a commodity now, like petroleum or orange juice or pork bellies, and has never been more important to industries and nations than it is now. And we at AlphaBanc realized very early on that whoever controlled this information, that is to say, whoever could access great quantities of it and then manage its flow most efficiently would gain, ah, the upper hand in this business."

Clayborne wonders exactly what part of AlphaBanc's business that is, but decides not to look stupid by asking about it.

"Let me now show you our main repository, Richard," says O'Brian, turning abruptly and beginning to walk towards the doorway.

O'Brian leads him down a series of broad brightly lit corridors past technicians in lab coats pushing carts loaded with magnetic tape cartridges, stacks of printouts, and various pieces of computer hardware. They come to a large central lobby-like area which features a huge stainless steel door resembling that of a bank vault.

"This door isn't really as strong as it looks," O'Brian manages a smile and winks. "Pretty much for show, actually. Now and then we'll even have a guard stationed here when we take clients on a tour. All you really need is the proper ID." He takes a card from his coat pocket and swipes it through a slot in a unit affixed to the wall. "During busy times the door often stays open. Anyone makes it this deep into the facility, they've got to be secure."

A buzzer sounds, there is a whoosh of hydraulics and the steel panels part, sliding into the wall. They step inside and Clayborne can't help letting out a low whistle. The place is really huge, like the inside of an aircraft hangar. "So this is where you keep all of the, uh—"

"Data, is probably the most appropriate word. On the levels below this one are our arrays of online storage drives for our massive SANs, storage area networks, but this is where all the hard-copy material is stored, real stuff, which I think is somewhat more interesting than—"

"Real stuff?"

"Yes, real things" chuckles O'Brian, "as opposed to the magnetic bits and bytes on the floors below us. Here we store tapes, disks, microfilm, *real* film, such as x-rays, both human and industrial, and around a hundred thousand reels of cinematic film in our climate-controlled area. We also store many original sound recordings and tapes, from wax and vinyl to reel-to-reel. Anything that hasn't been digitized yet, and that is considerable, as you can see. And we also get many bales of printouts, along with stacks and stacks of binders, and pallet loads of sealed file containers. Whatever our clients need to keep safe.

"It's like a huge library," O'Brian continues, leading him farther inside, past a long counter lined with computer monitors, clerks busy behind each one. They walk into the main storage facility, peer down a long row of storage racks. "Two and a half stories, all the way back. Everything in the repository is checked in and out."

"So, how often do they save their, uh, stuff?"

"Well, it depends on what it is. The online data is updated continually, but this stuff," O'Brian looks up at the racking, "it can come in here at any time. And come in it does."

"And they think it's safe here?"

"Of course," O'Brian sniffs and turns to look at him. "Here it's unbelievably secure. You know, the tunnels we're in extend for nearly half a mile, carved during the late fifties and early sixties as an alternative to NORAD, out in Colorado Springs. It was actually begun several years before the Cheyenne mountain excavation through funding provided by Senator McCarthy in 1955. Say what you will about the man, you can't deny that he was absolutely pro-America."

"With all due respect, Mr. O'Brian, from what I remember about him from history class, I'd say he was absolutely pro-McCarthy."

"Well, yes, that's one interpretation. But the junior senator from Wisconsin saw back then—or thought he saw, anyway—that the red menace was threatening our country from within—and without. To handle the latter—and also send some tax dollars Wisconsin's way, I'll grant you—he pushed through a bill to fund the excavation of this huge granitic mound, properly called a batholith in geologic terms, which used to extend slightly above the countryside. We have old photographs of people, families, picnicking on it. It took nearly eight years at a cost of nine hundred million dollars back then; you can imagine what it would cost today. The granite was sold for building materials, cemetery monuments, and such, which reduced the expense somewhat. Afterwards, the site was cleaned up and landscaped and after a few years no one would ever think that there was such a huge artificial cavern directly beneath them. By the time it was completed, the senator was in disrepute, deceased, probably from alcoholism, and they, the idiots in congress felt, or so they went on record as saying, that it wasn't quite as impervious to nuclear attack as the NORAD facility, and politics got in the way and Colorado got all of it. Wisconsin was left with this, a series of huge empty chambers carved into solid granite."

O'Brian clasps his hands behind his back and looks proudly up toward the lights on the girders crisscrossing the ceiling. "Hah, I'm positive it's more solid than Cheyenne mountain. You know the rock out there is cracked pretty badly and they've had to pump in thousands of gallons of epoxy? There's not a crack in this place. Solid granite. Anyway, they were storing cheese down here before we bought it, tons of it; it's like a natural refrigerator. Of course, what we're storing now is somewhat more important—"

"More important than cheese?" Clayborne jokes. "This is Wisconsin, isn't it?"

"Oh-ho. Much more important. The nation's data. All here. Or most of it. About seventy-two percent of it, by our current estimates. We'd like to get it all, of course. It's a very good business. As it is, we're the largest repository in the United States for the vital records of quite a few of the country's Fortune 1000 companies: IBM, Coca-Cola, AT&T, Microsoft, Citibank . . . you get the picture. And many, many foreign concerns send their data here as well. From eighty-three different countries, I believe it was at last count."

"Why would they want it all the way out here?"

O'Brian chuckles. "Well, it's the perfect place for it. In the vast heartland of the United States. Here we're secure from everything, I would think, short of a direct nuclear hit. We're naturally cool, dry, and actually, we're quite cheap. We have a great deal of capacity here, so we can provide the largest, most inexpensive vault for storage of, actually, any sort of information. Even the Library of Congress is sending some of its volumes here now.

"Most people don't know this, but safe long-term data storage is a huge concern for companies, from AlphaBanc itself to Joe Schmo's Tool and Die keeping the ledger and inventory with a personal computer, they all need to keep information in secure storage. Preferably here."

"Er, for disaster recovery."

"Exactly, Richard. If something bad hits their facility: tornado, fire, flood, lightning, computer virus, you name it, they've got to get the most recent copies of their data back into their system as soon as they can. Online data is available instantaneously. For hard copies, we're only a half-mile from an airstrip and I can tell you that several times a month we've got a company jet out there waiting to pick up something that they've cached here."

"Are government records stored here?"

"Oh, yes. Certainly. We keep data for all fifty state governments. Also our federal government, and more than thirty foreign governments: nearly all of Latin America, and many in the third world. We're the world's largest safety deposit box, Richard. And we keep getting more and more business. Just recently we've completed negotiations with a sizeable United States federal agency for all their records. Care to guess which one?"

"I give up."

"Oh, just the IRS."

"The IRS . . . the Internal Revenue Service? Here?"

"The very same," O'Brian smiles proudly.

"The federal government's tax records? All of them?"

"Every last one."

"My God, that's a big haul."

"You're certainly right, Richard. The biggest," says O'Brian, so pleased he clamps a moist pale hand on Clayborne's shoulder. "Actually we calculate it to be about twelve petabytes, give or take several terabytes. But it's all in the current spirit of farming out more government business to private industry. Of course we've had to quote them a ridiculously low price, and because most of their data is on tape they insist that we partition our storage area off so their section is completely separate from the rest of our communal repository. But it's all been worth it, starting next month they're going to be shipping us their files. Literally tons of tapes. Many of them old twelve inch reels, too. I anticipate quite a few semitrailers coming down our road."

"I can imagine."

"Yes, so very much going on for us . . . and that's not even the end of it. You know that the other big, big news down here, Richard, is the elections coming up in just a month or two."

"Oh my God, that's right. I had almost forgotten!" exclaims Clayborne. "The national elections are going to be held right here!"

CHAPTER NINETEEN

CLAYBORNE'S HEAD IS spinning. Standing ten stories underground in the midst of much of the nation's archived intelligence, it seems ironic that he should be thick-headed, but this place is so overwhelming that he had forgotten all about the elections. It was in fact one of things he had wanted to ask O'Brian about.

Aided by a multi-billion dollar federal grant to once and for all modernize and streamline the elections process, the nation has been retrofitting many of its precincts to use new electronic voting machines, digital equipment supplied by any number of qualified manufacturers, each of which, in accordance with federal specifications, is to be connected to the Internet. The vote counts will then be gathered regionally and tabulated at a safe central location, which turns out to be right here, the most secure site in North America, perhaps the world, AlphaBanc's underground McCarthy complex.

"Yes, Richard," O'Brian smiles serenely, "although I wouldn't quite say *held*, here. Aggregated and tallied is perhaps how I would term it. But I have to tell you that it is an extremely heady event for us usually sedentary troglodytes."

"Oh, sure," Clayborne chuckles along with O'Brian. "Should keep you pretty darn busy."

"Well, yes, and no," O'Brian scratches his pale chin. "Workwise, the IRS data will require a great deal more effort; the elections much less so, as the feds will be bringing in their own systems engineers to install and run the tabulation software. We are voluntarily putting some of our IBM mainframes at their disposal for the effort, as a patriotic gesture and, er, we will of course pick up a tiny bit of publicity for that."

"A tiny bit? It's the first totally electronic presidential election. The press coverage will be tremendous."

"Well, yes," O'Brian grins, "I've begrudged several interviews to the press already. But I must correct you, Richard. It is only about seventy to eighty percent of the total vote that will be coming through here. Only the ballots garnered from the new electronic voting machines, most of which will be directly online to the fed's ElecTal vote tabulation system here. Of course, that's still a rather large piece of the pie. But it all makes us feel rather patriotic to play such a role in modernizing the elections."

"There's been a lot of buzz about it out at A-Banc West."

"I'm sure there is. Well, I suppose it was only a matter of time before the outdated voting equipment—particularly in the disenfranchised districts—caused some problems. Now most of the, ah, noise, that might have skewed the results in one direction or the other is out of the process. Pity."

"Er, did you say: 'pity,' Mr. O'Brian?"

"Well, let's see . . ." O'Brian ignores him again, scratches his temple. "Where should we go next? There's so much I could show you, but—"

Clayborne decides not to pursue the election issue any further, says, "Mr. O'Brian, one thing I've always wanted to see is the big computer area here, what I believe you call the Magic Mountain?"

"Oh yes! The Magic Mountain!" O'Brian seems delighted. "Excellent idea. Er, we've also been calling it 'the Source,' of late. It's on very nearly the lowest level, the safest place in the case of a nuclear attack—or anything else. Follow me."

O'Brian quickly leads Clayborne out of the repository. Neither of them happen to look over at the clerks as they pass through the busy registration area again, nor does it seem that any of the workers give more than a passing glance to the director of the facility and his visitor, except perhaps for one fellow who stops working long enough to take a fairly long look and then very inconspicuously jot something on the margin of his note pad.

"Hey, Lenny!" yells someone from behind.

"Wh-what?" Leonard Huxley, aka Mario Pfalser at Alpha-Banc's McCarthy complex, jumps and stabs his pencil into the pad, breaking its point.

"No, Mario. I was talking to Lenny over there, man."

"Oh," Leonard, aka Mario, thinks fast, "sorry, I, uh, a good friend of mine's name is Lenny. And I guess I just—"

"But your name's not Lenny, right, buddy?"

"No. Of course not. Guess I was just daydreaming." He winces and admonishes himself to immerse himself in his character more deeply, always, *always* remember his nom de guerre: Mario Pfalser.

"Well, since Lenny didn't hear me anyway, let me ask you, Mario. Could you sub for me in the softball game in Red Rock this Saturday?"

"Oh. No, sorry, I'm gonna work this weekend. Help them get ready for the IRS tapes and the elections."

"Oh, me too. That's why I needed the sub. I can use the overtime."

"Me too."

"Well, maybe I can get Lenny, or someone else."

"Good luck," Huxley, as Mario Pfalser, smiles weakly, puts his log pad away and turns back to his computer screen.

Clayborne has to hurry to keep up with O'Brian, who leads him down several stairwells and through anonymous long corridors until they come to another steel door which O'Brian opens with his security card.

"Yes, follow along, Richard, before we get to the Source, I want to show you our systems engineers, our programmers. It's directly on our way."

"Yeah, er, I've heard they're quite a strange crew." Looney Toons is actually what Clayborne has heard, but he isn't sure if he should mention that to O'Brian.

"Well, they are quite a bunch. But only strange in appearance. We-el, perhaps *some*what in their actions, but it really doesn't matter to us because they're the best in the country, probably in the world. Their average IQ is currently above 140, and you know, each time we test them it seems to go up! Of course, we think they might be memorizing the tests, but—"

Suddenly a gentle chiming issues from the phone affixed to O'Brian's belt. He pulls it off, reads the message on its screen. "Drat! Meetings, meetings, always something," he laments. "Well, let's hurry on over there."

Clayborne follows O'Brian into an area darker than the rest of the brightly lit interiors, with an obviously hand-painted banner overhead proclaiming: WELCOME TO THE MORLOCK ZONE.

O'Brian chuckles paternally, "They like to think of themselves as the subterranean creatures in the H.G. Wells' novel—you're familiar with the book?"

"Oh yeah. *The Time Machine.* Read it in high school."

"Me too. Actually, it was junior high for me. Well, come along now . . ." And O'Brian leads Clayborne through a series of dormitory-type rooms with Star Wars and Star Trek posters on the walls, laptops and computer monitors on cluttered desks, unmade beds, and piles of clothing strewn everywhere.

"Jeeze, it looks like my college fraternity."

"Yes, I'm not surprised. They're quite a bit like children, actually. Big children, but children just the same. We recruit them right out of college. Our recruiters jokingly call it 'anti-recruiting,' because we look for the ones who aren't in the scrubbed, clean-shaven group of suited-up overachievers that, I daresay, you might have come from, Richard."

"Oh, well, yeah, I guess . . ."

"No, we look for those with the straight A's in computer science and mathematics and the F's in English and History and Basic Hygiene 101," O'Brian laughs. "But seriously, it is the ones who fail to show up for the interviews, those who favor long hair down to their shoulders—or are shaved completely bald—and wear the same wretched plaid lumberjack shirt for weeks on end because they are positively glued to their workstations, those are the ones we seek out."

They pass one room where everything is absolutely tidy and austere, a dark green wool blanket drawn so tightly over the bed that a handful of quarters no doubt would bounce right off. There is a solitary framed picture of Captain Kirk (the William Shatner version) centered on the wall above a table holding an antique pitcher and washing bowl. O'Brian notices Clayborne peering inside. "Quite a contrast, eh?"

"Yeah, I'll say."

"Well, this is the room, or as he would have it, the *cell* of Jacob, probably our most brilliant programmer."

"Jacob?"

"Yes, just: Jacob, is how he prefers to be called. Ah, here he comes now."

Walking slowly towards them down the hallway is a tall gaunt man about forty, bald with a tonsure. He is dressed in a dark wool robe and sandals.

"I do believe he had aspirations for the seminary before coming here," O'Brian whispers out of the side of his mouth. "Jacob, how are you today?"

"Just fine, Mr. O'Brian. And how are you?"

"Oh just fine, also. This is my friend, Richard."

Jacob nods and bows slightly.

Clayborne does the same, withdraws his extended hand.

"So, how's the DDD system coming along?" asks O'Brian.

"Very well, sir. You will have to look at it presently."

"D-D-D?" asks Clayborne.

"Derived Dwelling Definitions. It's something quite wonderful we're working on here. I might tell you about it later on."

Just then the phone on O'Brian's belt begins chiming again. He snaps it up, checks the screen and sighs, "Now I'm into another appointment. I'm terribly sorry, but I absolutely must cut this short. Let's get back to my office. I've got a folder of information for you on Norman Dunne. Good-bye for now, Jacob."

"Fare-thee-well."

"Uh, so long," says Clayborne, then hurries to keep up with O'Brian as he strides quickly down the hallway.

CHAPTER TWENTY

"SO THAT'S OUR boy?"

"That's him," says Toby O'Brian, looking up at one of the monitors on the granite wall of his cave-like office in the McCarthy depths, watching Richard Clayborne walking down a corridor toward a bank of elevators. He is carrying a large brown envelope given to him by O'Brian. A moment later the picture on the big screen changes to show Richard inside the elevator, rising upward, to the sunny Wisconsin countryside.

"Well, I hope the kid is up to whatever mean-ass thing you've got cooking, Toby," says George Blair, squinting as he lights a Pall Mall with his Zippo. Backed by a rough-hewn wall of deep mahogany granite, tiny crystals sparkling in the track lighting, O'Brian's office is incongruously modern. Along with the wall panels, two ultrathin computer monitors are perched upon a long gray laminate desk, before which are two uncomfortable stainless steel and leather chairs. Blair sits in one, watches the monitor above and feels vaguely resentful that Clayborne gets to resurface, to return to the light, and that he has to remain subterranean, at least for another couple of hours, with O'Brian. He wonders how these guys can stand to work down here all day in this granite tomb. Though not a true claustrophobe, Blair still doesn't like being so far underground; it's as though all the thousands of tons of rock above are somehow squeezing him, compressing his heart, his mind, his soul. . . .

"George, just be assured that his PERSPROF indicates that Richard Clayborne is definitely our man, a perfect candidate."

"Well, you know that I don't put a hell of a lot of faith in your computer profiles. I just hope that you're right, Toby."

Blair sighs, wonders again why exactly he is here. He would have just retired from the force had not a connection at Alpha-Banc offered him a job as a consultant in the internal security division at such a ridiculously large salary that, in the end, he simply could not refuse. That was four years ago, and the consensus at A-Banc is that they have certainly gotten their money's worth. His years as a cop have taught him much about the myriad situations that people can get themselves into and the sometimes bizarre reasons that they do. As a detective he had a reputation for doing whatever it took to bring a perp to justice and then some. He had been relentlessly aggressive at times, brilliant in retreat at others, and had always carried cheap untraceable heat which he had had to toss away not a couple of times to a poor dead bastard who had definitely been in the wrong place at the wrong time. AlphaBanc had wanted a smart, tough Chicago cop, someone who knew the town and had connections, someone who could front for the outsider, Haedler, when it became necessary. And right now, in AlphaBanc's opinion, Blair's help has become quite necessary.

"We have refined our PERSPROF's to be statistically accurate within a ninety-five percent confidence level," replies O'Brian, sounding a trifle miffed.

Blair frowns. "You were going to tell me what was in the packet you gave him—which I gather is also why I'm here."

"Actually, what I gave Clayborne is a much-sanitized version of the information I'm going to give you."

"On who? On what?"

"It's almost more of a what, I'm afraid." O'Brian turns to look at Blair. "Have you ever heard of the Gnome?"

"The Gnome? Like, as in elf? Troll?" He almost says fairy, but thinks of O'Brian's pronounced lisp and checks himself. "Can't say that I have. Sounds like one of your wacky programmers."

"Well, you're right again, George. Actually, he is one of my ex-programmers. Probably, no—assuredly—the best we've ever had. The best ever."

"So, what have you got on this . . . Gnome?"

O'Brian leans across his desk, hands Blair a manila folder. He looks up, pushes a button on his wand and the panel above them with Richard Clayborne walking out of the facility goes dark.

Blair leafs through the folder, stops at copies of several newspaper clippings stapled together.

"He's really become quite a problem. As you can see."

"That girl in Lincoln Park. The AlphaBanc girl. I saw that. Very clean, almost professional."

"Now that's an interesting thing to say. Almost professional. Why . . . almost?"

"No pro would have slit her throat. Too messy. And it might miss. This was done by a very precise person. One, I would think, with a grudge against her. Wanted to be dramatic, mean, hurt her bad. With her looks I'd guess he might be a spurned lover."

"Very interesting, George. I'd say you're on exactly the right track. What else do you get from those clippings?"

"Hmph, it looks like two, no, three murders. Are you thinking they're all him? This guy, who you call the Gnome?"

Blair is eyeing a newspaper headline: WOMAN STRANGLED / NO SUSPECTS. "I kind of remember reading about this one. Says the guy—had to be a guy—attacked her from behind, only three blocks from her apartment. Evanston. Jesus, that sounds like a garrote. Ninja stuff. Ugly."

"Again, George, you're absolutely right. Piano wire on sawed sections of broomstick. From the tiny paint chips they found on the victim they even know the brand of the broom. That little piece of information could win someone an all-expenses-paid, decidedly one-way trip to—"

"But how do you know all this, Toby? If the cops are withholding this info . . . plus, why do you think this is the, er, Gnome? Here you've got a garroting, a stabbing, and now a slashing. I can tell you now these aren't the work of the same person."

"Ah, but they are, George."

"No way."

O'Brian smiles, leans toward Blair, wagging his bony finger, "I know you've been in this business a good long time George, but I can assure you that these crimes have all been perpetrated by our suspect. He's simply—creative. Your friends on the force don't know anything about him. Only we do. We've been kind of keeping it to ourselves, but now we feel we've got to turn it over to A-Banc ISD."

"Yeah, Haedler was real pleased you guys sat on this so long."

O'Brian's smile thins somewhat. "I know. I understand. But we wanted to run our data first. We wanted to be absolutely sure before we turned it over. Plus, we kept thinking we might be able to locate him ourselves. We knew that once you folks got involved, we'd lose control of it."

"Always happens."

"You're right. Anyway, I know that the police, and you, don't think the killer of the young women is the same person. In fact, all they have that might link this thing together is that the victims were all young, in their twenties, single career women, and—they were all quite beautiful."

"So what makes you think you're right?"

"We know something else about these women that the police don't," O'Brian purses his lips and pauses, looking expectantly across his desk at the detective.

Blair sighs. "Okay, Toby, so what is it you know that the police don't?"

"Well," O'Brian grins, "just the fact that each of these women owned personal computers and each happened to be subscribers to the virtual Internet community: NEXSX."

"Next-cess what?"

"NEXSX. They're letters, N-E-X-S-X, meaning exactly, God knows what. You can imagine. But it's the largest online adult conferencing service in the United States and the world, actually, with more than two million subscribers."

"This virtual computer stuff is still a little new to me, Toby. What do they subscribe to?"

"Actually, the chance to meet someone. It's pretty much an on-line connection service where you can hook up with anyone anywhere in the county, or even worldwide—they have quite a number of international subscribers—to get together with. Some of it's quite racy, but mostly it's just a huge lonely hearts club chat line. There are quite a few smaller, local services like this, but NEXSX is the largest. It also happens to be the one, or perhaps one of numerous ones, that the Gnome surreptitiously monitors."

"He monitors? Secretly? What do you mean?"

"Well, he hacks into the system. He listens in, or looks in, I should say, on the many thousands of online conversations that

occur over NEXSX's chat lines. And sometimes, he monitors certain individuals, such as these fair young victims, a bit more
closely."

"This is something I'm not really familiar with Toby. Maybe
you've got the wrong guy here—"

"Nonsense, George. You're our man. It's actually a very
simple concept." O'Brian briefly explains the way Web conferencing services work and how AlphaBanc plans to use Richard
Clayborne and Christin Darrow to lure the Gnome into their
trap.

"So the girl is bait?"

"Precisely."

"Sounds pretty weird to me. Sick, actually."

"I agree, George, it is weird. But it's a strange new world
we're in, and we're after a very sick character, believe me."

"So why do you want him so badly? Why aren't you working
with the police?"

O'Brian lowers his eyes toward his desktop and smiles again.
"Well George, you know as well as anyone that we hesitate to use
the police—in matters such as these. And the reason we want
him is because we want to stop these horrendous crimes."

"Sure. Sure you do."

"Okay. Well, we do want to stop the carnage, of course, but
the truth is, we badly need him. He's simply the best at what he
does." O'Brian leans over his elbows on the desktop to face
Blair, eyes shining. "We've got something very big planned,
Georgie," he practically whispers.

Blair, though presenting his usual aspect of bored gumshoe
nonchalance, is suddenly very attentive. O'Brian is dangling some
seriously interesting information in front of him. Repulsed as he
is by O'Brian's childish delight with whatever he's got going, he
manages to smirk, "Now that I believe, Toby. What?"

CHAPTER TWENTY-ONE

O'BRIAN, ABSOLUTELY DELIGHTED with Blair's interest in the "something big" they have planned, sinks back into his chair, smiling broadly, slowly shaking his head back and forth. "Can't say, can't say. Don't know if you'll ever know, in fact. But that's the beauty of it. You won't know, no one will know. But it . . . will . . . happen." He trails off into a whisper again.

"The perfect crime."

"Now, now, this is great big respectable AlphaBanc, you know, George."

"Yeah?"

O'Brian's huge quivering smile explodes into a laugh. "Well, then yes! Just between you and me, I do believe you've defined it precisely! Yes! The perfect crime."

"Well, I guess it's none of my business so I won't ask you again exactly why you need him."

"No. Couldn't tell you," says O'Brian with an unmistakable look of disappointment.

"Suit yourself." Blair shrugs and looks again through the file on their suspect, a man who actually appears to have the name of: Norman Dunne. Besides the gruesome news clippings, it contains a yellowed green bar computer printout of his past AlphaBanc employment record and a single faded photograph of, presumably, Dunne. It's a Polaroid that was apparently taken at a long-ago Christmas office party. In the background are old reel tape drives along with some tangles of red and green crepe paper hanging from the ceiling. The man is scowling at the camera in, Blair supposes, mock disgust, and is wearing a party hat that in the photograph has dissolved to a sickly pink color. He looks a little like Edward G. Robinson with thinning hair and sideburns. Blair dates the photo as late 1980s.

"This the only picture you have of him?" Blair asks incredulously. "At know-everything-about-everyone AlphaBanc?"

O'Brian smiles sheepishly and nods. "Before he, er, left us, he cleaned out our files on him. Deleted everything on himself in all of our employee databases," O'Brian winces. "He had access to everything. We were damn lucky to scrape up that printout and that picture."

"He looks like a gnome."

"Yes. He does. He's definitely on the shorter side, stocky build—"

"And his real name, I take it, is . . . Norman Dunne."

"Yes, Norman 'the Gnome' Dunne."

"These programmers always come up with these catchy nicknames?"

"Yes, they're endlessly creative. By the way, you'll be working with a fellow from our San Francisco branch who's called the Epenguin. And I might add, he looks very much the part."

"The *Eee*-penguin? Oh no . . . Toby."

"Now George, I actually think you'll like him. Apart from his, er, attire, he's a very levelheaded young man."

"Oh God, I can't wait."

"Really George, these people are a bit strange, but—"

"Okay, okay. Let's keep going here. Now, did you say that Dunne is a shorter guy?"

"Yes, maybe around five foot four, or—"

"Well, again, he didn't do it, Toby. The slashing, for sure. That girl was at least five foot ten, like a model, maybe six foot. He couldn't have reached her. Not enough to have done it so smoothly. He couldn't have."

"And I'm telling you he had to, George. We've monitored the messages between them."

"Between who? What messages?"

"Well, I suppose I should tell you what we know so far. Save you some reading in the file I've given you."

O'Brian settles back in his chair and begins to tell Blair what he knows about Norman Dunne.

"He was a California boy, a rather troubled child, actually. His parents had separated when he was five years old and he went to live with his mother in Pasadena. She ended up a barmaid and had a series of boyfriends who Norman might have liked to think would be a father to him, but they always ended up leaving his mother, and him. He was ignored by his real father, and since his mother was never around, he buried himself in understanding how his computer worked. He had one of the first Apple's and learned to practically take it apart and put it back together again. He was really a brilliant kid. Damn shame in a way. He was lonely and technology beckoned. He was also an early phone phreak when he was just a teenager."

"Phone freak?"

"That's right, George. And you know they spell 'phreak' with a p-h instead of an eff. Get it? Phone phreak?"

"I get it, but I don't. What is it?"

"It's a sort of a phenomenon that swept through the country in the 1970s, along with the whole rebellious youth movement. You might say it was a funny technological ripple in the cross-currents of a communications network that was growing rapidly from ancient electromagnetic relays to transistors and integrated circuits. It centered around what was called a 'blue box,' a little plastic box with a circuit board inside and a battery. When you pushed a button, it emitted a high-pitched beep in the twenty-six hundred-hertz range. You could hold the blue box against the speaker of a telephone, push the button, and make free calls anywhere in the country, or around the world, for that matter. It seems that Bell Telephone had configured their entire long-distance switching system to be controlled by those tones and then foolishly published that information along with the exact frequencies in a technical journal. Of course, it didn't take long for electronics hackers to come up with the little boxes. The color of the original box was blue. Ever hear of them, George?"

"Actually, I have. I think there was a fraud alert out for them in Chicago, at the time."

"I'm sure there was," says O'Brian. "Those blue boxes spread across the country. Many, many folks used them to avoid the long distance charges of Ma Bell, everyone from mob chieftains to small businessmen trying to save costs. In fact, it's said that Steve Wozniak and Steve Jobs, who created Apple Computer, used to have them. I even had one myself. It was a funny thing. At the time Bell Telephone and its parent, AT&T, was a monopoly, and no one thought much about defrauding the company. It was like striking a blow against the empire, or, you know, the 'establishment.'" O'Brian raises two fingers of each hand to supply quotes to his statement.

Blair winces. He hates when people do that.

"There was one relatively famous phone phreak, a so-called 'Captain Crunch,'" continues O'Brian, "who discovered that the little whistle they packaged in Cap'n Crunch cereal blew a perfect twenty-six hundred hertz tone. It was all you needed to switch long distance calls. Crazy. But what we were seeing, in essence, was the very beginnings of hackers—or phreakers, I should say—on Ma Bell's huge communications network. And then it just grew from there, as hackers moved from the phone system to the large VAX and UNIX computer networks that were beginning to be linked world-wide. Computer security in the early eighties was relatively lax, and hackers with a lot of patience and some key passwords could access the systems of some amazingly large corporations, and, of course, even more easily, government institutions, such as the Pentagon and the CIA. Piece of cake."

"Where'd they get the passwords?"

"Ah, good question, George. I can see that you aren't quite as computer-illiterate as you proclaim."

"Give me a break. I've got to get into my email."

"Quite right. Well, a perfect example of that is our quarry, Norman Dunne, bona fide alpha geek recluse. But as it turns out, he is surprisingly able to sweet-talk people out of their passwords. He is actually very clever with the spoken word—over anonymous phone lines, of course. He calls it social engineering, the ability to call a computer installation and sound like an irate user who has forgotten his password and needs it right away. Or calling an administrative assistant and kindly asking her to walk over to so-and-so's workstation and to read the password that's written there on a sticky note because they have to get into the system to get a report for so-and-so, who needs it right away—the joke being that Norman probably knows no one in the office, has never seen the office, and is probably halfway across the country, but of course, he knows that so often that damn note with a forgetful user's password is there!" O'Brian chuckles.

"But what did he, Dunne, do once he got inside the systems?" Blair flips his Zippo, lights a cigarette, exhales a cloud of smoke that rises above the monitors on O'Brian's desk.

"Well, essentially, Norman just looked around," says O'Brian, frowning and waving away the smoke. "He tried to get to any- where and everywhere he could in a system. He also tried to get himself as high a level of security as he could. Sometimes he'd leapfrog from one system to another, become sort of a hitchhiker on the Internet's highways. Quite a feat in the era before today's fiber-optic backbone, which is a two hundred fifty-six lane data superhighway compared to what would be two-lane country back roads in Dunne's early hacking days."

"So he really didn't take anything, any valuable information?"

"No, nothing that he tried to market, if that's what you mean, like company secrets, as in industrial espionage, or, ah, business research, as we like to call it nowadays. He didn't do anything like that. He, like most true hackers, has a curiously high set of ethics. He wouldn't have thought of attempting to profit from his explorations, or doing actual harm to a system. Until, of course, he came to work for us."

"You set him on the right track."

"Well, the poor boy was in need of guidance. Pity to let such vast talent go to waste on mere hacking!" O'Brian smiles. "He had lists of user ID's, stolen passwords, and voluminous notes on system peculiarities he had discovered: security gaps, 'back doors' into supposedly very secure systems, and the like. All of which proved extremely valuable when he came to work for us, I might add. But he himself never thought of using any of it for any sort of monetary gain!"

"But you changed all that."

"Of course. We offered him a very generous salary, free hous- ing, the ultimate in equipment, telecommunications, satellite links, the works, along with highly skilled teams of programmers and system engineers at his beck and call. Plus, he was in a bit of trouble—quite a bit of trouble with the authorities for hacking into places where he shouldn't be—and was facing a fairly stiff prison sentence, which we were able get dismissed. How could he resist?"

"So why did he end up leaving you?"

"Ahhh," O'Brian slowly stands up behind his desk, stretches, and looks reflectively towards the ceiling. "Like many of our computer geniuses, he was a touchy sort, and one day I made the mistake of prodding him to action on this new project—the new one I told you about—ever so gently, I thought—"

"The top secret one?"

"Yes, please don't ask me to describe it to you."

"Oh, I wouldn't think of it."

"Good. Yes. Well, anyway, the next thing I knew, he had left without a trace, erasing from the system all the information we had on him, even calling up the backup storage and erasing that, too. It was possible, because unfortunately all of our backups are here at Red Rock, too, you see, quite accessible to him."

"And that's the last you heard of him?"

"The last. Except for the murders, of course."

"Okay, so what makes you think that it's him?"

"Yes, that's where we're heading. Well, you see, when he left, we put together as good a profile as we could of him—a copy is in your dossier there, embarrassingly incomplete as it is. But one of the things in it is a penchant he seems to have developed, early on, for hacking the personals areas of the small bulletin board services that sprang up around the net's access nodes, like small towns at railroad crossings of long ago. Eventually, as the cyberworld grew, so did his horizons; he began regularly hacking all sorts of online forums, including NEXSX, the biggest meeting place of all. As I explained, it's a place for adults to meet in cyberspace, especially ones seeking partners, and, as you might expect, it runs the gamut of human sexual possibility. I think it quite intrigued him."

"Uh, define 'cyberspace,' Toby."

"Well, technically, it's the network. But it's actually sort of nowhere. It's the 'place' or 'space' where people who are online meet. Someone simply defined the common ground. It's not really all that new. It's the same place where phone conversations seem to occur. Somewhere between the two receivers, somewhere 'out there'—in cyberspace." O'Brian gestures widely with his arms, as though to enclose the vast ethereal terrain he speaks of.

"I think I follow you. Go on."

"Well, Dunne would quite regularly monitor the users of NEXSX, particularly the women, the beautiful ones."

"You say he hacked his way in."

"Yes, he, as usual, found a "back door" into NEXSX and proceeded to look around wherever he wanted. This allowed him to immediately learn the real name, address, and phone number of any subscriber on the system, and also their credit card number, because that's how they pay for their subscription. Most, if not all, of the women on the system, you see, use a nickname, a 'handle,' in order to remain anonymous. That way, of course, they're protected from any weirdos that might also lurk on NEXSX."

"Like Dunne."

"Yes. No protection from him though. He's absolutely diabolical." O'Brian chuckles and sits back in his chair. "His favorite trick, you see, is to monitor online conversations between two subscribers who happen to be widely geographically separated, a fellow on one side of the country texting one of the beauties he's been monitoring in the Chicago area, say."

"Where the girls who were murdered lived."

"You're a step ahead of me, George. But that's right, at some point in their conversation he breaks in and sends the fellow a message, pretending to be the *girl*, telling him that she is signing off. And then, he continues the conversation with the girl, as though the same fellow is still talking to her."

"Pretty damn weird."

"Quite right. But that's, of course, how we're going to get him. Our chief psychologist at AlphaBanc West, Dr. Roland Rascher, says that he's pretty much a control freak. He's got to dominate the situation through his superior intellect. Out in the real world, FTF, face-to-face, he's an absolute zero with women, no social skills at all.

"*But*," O'Brian smiles at Blair and raises his finger to emphasize the psychological insight, "when he's on a network, telephony or NEXSX chat room, *then*, he's this incredible social engineer, a real charmer."

"Does Clayborne know about the way Dunne breaks in and impersonates the guy who—"

"Oh, no, no, no," says O'Brian, chopping the desk top with the edge of his pale hand. "We don't want him to know. The conversation between them must appear as entirely natural."

"Hmm. That makes sense."

"Yes, it's an integral part of our plan. As it is, Dunne, as the Gnome, is terribly difficult to deceive." O'Brian shakes his head in grudging admiration. "If anyone was ever at home in a particular medium, it's got to be the Gnome in a network. Otherwise, he's a fish out of water. He's a man made for the digital world."

"So," says Blair, "why do you think he kills them? Rascher, I suppose, has a reason for that?"

O'Brian sighs, "Well, it all supposedly goes back to the Gnome's rejection by his parents, many years ago. He can't take rejection, and in his conversations with women as . . . whomever, he keeps urging them to reveal more and more of themselves to him, which beyond a certain point, of course, they won't do, and this seems to drive the Gnome crazy. He often makes some rather personal and exotic demands, you know. He is, presently, a very sick and dangerous man."

"What exactly does he ask them to reveal of themselves?"

"Well, it varies—" O'Brian's phone chimes. He picks it up, listens, then murmurs, "Okay . . . I'll be there right away."

"I've got to run, George. Someone from the IRS is here for yet another check on our facilities. You should have enough to go on. Everything's in the dossier. You can find your way out, right?"

Blair sighs, picks up the folder and starts for the elevators.

After a short upwards ride on a very fast machine, Blair steadies himself and walks across the polished red granite floor toward the main entrance. Off to his left, against a wall is a security desk with three bored uniformed officers who nod to him as he walks by. Blair reaches for a cigarette, grateful to see the light of the outdoors through the glass doors ahead, grateful to be out of the darkness of geeks and freaks and infernal machinery and into the bright and beautiful world of hackers and slashers and everyone else.

CHAPTER TWENTY-TWO

"I-I'VE NEVER HAD this done before. Even though I've always wanted to," says Mario Pfalser, nervously drumming his fingers on the barroom table. "I've read a little about it, the symbolism. It fascinates me."

"That so, sonny? Why have you waited so long? Why now?" asks Madame Salina, lovingly taking a deck of Tarot cards from a leather case.

"Before, maybe I was afraid. But now, it-it's because . . . I guess because I now find myself in the unique position of . . . perhaps causing something sort of big, to happen."

"Is that so?" Madame Salina's narrowly plucked eyebrows raise, scrutinizing the dark, slight young man before her in the light of the candle on their table. She sighs, wonders, *what have I got here?*

"Well, we've got a beautiful night for it," she says enthusiastically, as if to temper the somber mood she senses across the table. It's near closing time on a Saturday night and all of the regulars have gone home. In fact, she had been thinking of closing for the night, standing outside the doorway of the country tavern, looking over the fields and distant hills shimmering under the light of a harvest moon when this fellow had pulled into the lot, walked up and asked her for a reading.

A reading. He hadn't come for a drink, he made it clear, he wanted her to spread the cards. She was tired and wanted to tell him to come back tomorrow, but he kept talking, telling her that he had just gotten off the late shift at the McCarthy complex up the road and that he just had to get a glimpse into the future. Right now. Stone sober and absolutely earnest, he told her that he just had *to know*. And any other night she might have turned him away, but she was good with the cards, and with people; she understood them both. When someone knows that they need this

particular kind of help, whenever that might be, it is only she
that can provide it.

"It's so beautiful out tonight that it seems a shame to sit in
here and look into . . . the dark side, hey, sonny?" she continues
cheerfully.

"I guess," Pfalser answers seriously. "I didn't want to impose,
at this time of night. But I've been in here before and I saw the
sign—"

"Relax. I was just putting you on, son." Madame Salina smiles
kindly at him, asks him his name.

"Mario."

"Mario. There's a good honest name. No, I was just fooling
you a little—"

"It *is* nice out there. Maybe we could sit outside."

"No, the moonlight's perfect, but there's a bit of wind. We've
got to have calm and quiet, son."

She doesn't do the readings very often anymore; they seem to
come in spurts, usually a younger person, a girl from the countryside around Red Rock discovering her and wanting a reading,
and then telling all her friends . . . and then she won't do another
for a year. Those, the kids, she does over in her house. Others,
like this one, she'll do right here in the tavern, at a back table, if
there aren't too many people inside. And even though it's late,
there's no one else but them here, pretty unusual for a tavern in
Wisconsin after the Badgers have won. She takes it as a sign.
Then she asks, "Is Mario your real name?"

"Huh?"

"Your name's not Mario, is it?"

"I, uh, of course it is. Why would you . . . ?"

"Hmm," she looks at him with piercing green eyes. "Just a
strange notion I got. Don't even know why I said that."

"Well, look, maybe we shouldn't do this at all." He starts to
get up from the table.

"Son, I know you've got an important question to ask, and if
you get up and walk away you're never going to get an answer to
it. Now you sit back down here."

Pfalser looks sheepish, sits down again.

"That's a good fella. Didn't want to spook you again, sonny!"
Madame Salina laughs, and then quickly turns serious.

"Now, this . . . something big, that you're talking about, Mario. I hope it isn't something . . . real bad."

Pfalser smiles weakly. "I guess it all depends on your point of view. If, let's say, someone, or something, is destroying your home, your life, your country, and you put a stop to it. Is that something bad? Not for those you saved."

"Hmm. I guess I can see what you mean . . . maybe," replies Madame Salina warily. "And what would be the nature of your 'something big?'"

"Look, could we just do the reading?"

"Okay, son. Sure. Well, now you just take these cards and shuffle them up good, okay? Since you don't want to share what this big deal is all about, we'll just do a general reading. Just try to empty your mind as best you can. Got it?"

She passes the deck to him, a tried-and-true Rider-Waite set over twenty-five years old now. Although she has several decks, including a Royal Fez Moroccan (her favorite), a Visconti-Sforza Tarocchi reproduction, and an Aleister Crowley "Thoth" Tarot in which, among other modifications, the Major Arcana card: Justice, is replaced by a new card "Adjustment," and Strength replaced with "Lust," leading to interpretations which seem to deviate from the precise balance she finds in the traditional sets and thus doesn't use, the gorgeous and bold imagery of Rider-Waite deck, painted in London in the early 1900s by the inspired Pamela Colman Smith, an American artist and member of the Order of the Golden Dawn, always seems to work well with new inquirers.

Pfalser shuffles the deck and passes it back to Madame Salina. She closes her eyes, takes a deep breath and overturns Pfalser's covering card—the Magician, very interesting, in this embryonic Celtic Cross spread at this particular moment in time at this particular place in the universe. The next five cards fall as follows:

Crossed: The Emperor;

Crowning: The World;

Behind: 10 of Wands;

Beneath: 5 of Pentacles;

Before: Judgment

"We have determined the present situation," says Madame Salina, slowly shaking her head back and forth as she views the spread. "Well, none reversed, but . . . let's take a look at what we've got here. I will say this, son, if you've got something 'big' going on, you are certainly the person to do it," pointing to the lemniscate-crowned figure of the Magician. "This signifies yourself, and it tells me that you are imaginative, creative, and pretty much in control of yourself. I would think that you are a very meticulous planner, and that you may lead a group of followers, as you can be quite persuasive."

Pfalser smiles thinly and slowly shakes his head, "Okay, what else?"

"You're covered by the Emperor, which represents power, order, authority, great wealth. In my day we would have called it 'the establishment.' It's very much what's keepin' you *down*, boy," she chuckles.

"Now, son, I really hope that your 'big deal' is going to be something good. At least for most folks. Because your goal here is represented by the World, and that's just one darned big thing! It's like you're looking to make a real big change, somewhere, somehow. And . . . that would appear to be a kind of shift for you, as what's beneath you is poverty or deprivation of some sort, maybe abandonment, maybe sickness, but my impression is that it's a combination, maybe more material than not.

"For the past, it looks like you have been doing quite a lot of work . . . a lot of work on . . . whatever. You can see for yourself that fellow on the card bent over under all those staffs. He's overburdened, and according to this, so are you. You're working very hard at something, that's sure. But . . . see the future is Judgment, so a day of reckoning is coming. From the looks of this I'd say it's for you, son, and because of the World as your goal, well, the judgment is in regards to your 'big' thing.

"Anything you'd want to tell me, son, that might enable me to create a better picture here for you?"

"No, no, actually I think you're right on the money. Please, let's go on."

Madame Salina's eyebrows arch again as she turns over the next four cards:

Self: Page of Swords;
House: The Moon;
Hopes and Fears: The Hanged Man;

What Will Come: The Tower.

Madame Salina looks over the spread for several minutes saying nothing, at times nodding to herself, at others shaking her head solemnly from side to side. Finally, she speaks, a slight edge to voice, her earlier good cheer now all but gone. "All right, Mario, or whoever you are, the Page of Swords here represents yourself and it tells me that you are currently something like a small cog in a big machine, and are confronted with problems, but I think that you're quick-witted enough to solve them from the Magician representing you over here . . . but you're also secretive, like a detective, or a spy."

"Oh, really?" Pfalser laughs nervously.

"Really. And I get that because of The Moon above you here. This is the environment you live—or operate—within. It's a shadowy world, full of danger, deceit, dishonesty—an ugly fearful world. I don't mind telling you I get a real bad feeling about it. It's clear that you're enmeshed in this dark world and that you're operating, I would say, quite well within it, but I think, actually, against it." Madame Salina raises again her finely calibrated eyebrows and stops to listen. The wind has come up and whistles around the tavern windowpanes. It seems darker now outside, the moon having retreated behind a cloudbank. She says nothing, bites her lip and returns to the reading.

"The Hanged Man, which symbolizes your hopes and fears, is always an interesting card, and here it occupies an interesting position. It symbolizes sacrifice, abandonment of efforts—efforts which I would say you seem to be making toward your goal, your big something. Considering all that seems to be going on here, I would consider it a warning. It is quite possible that your goal may be accomplished, but only directly through your sacrifice."

"Really? And-and how would that be?" Pfalser seems to choke.

"I'm not sure. It's puzzling . . . and I have to say downright unsettling, because the final card is The Tower, a powerful symbol of sudden change, upheaval, destruction, chaos, ruin. And the strange thing, son, is that I think it means success—for you, for your big deal. But certainly not for whomever, or whatever, you're plotting against. And at what price? What sacrifice?" She falls silent, staring blankly at the cards. Outside, the wind seems to be gusting more strongly against the tavern.

"S-sounds like a storm coming up," says Pfalser uneasily.

"Do you think so, son?" Madame Salina's gaze is penetrating, but somehow kindly, truly concerned.

"I-I think I'm going to leave, now." Pfalser gets up from the table. "How much do I owe you?"

"For this truly interesting, ah, excursion . . . nothing, son. Just go on your way. And Godspeed. . . ."

Pfalser throws a twenty on the table, runs to the door and lets a gust of wind into the tavern as he leaves. The bill blows to the floor. Madame Salina ignores it, walks to the door the young man has left open. She stands in the doorway, hair blowing, skirt fluttering in the wind, watching the dark clouds rush before the moon, thinking: *and it was such a beautiful evening. . . .*

CHAPTER TWENTY-THREE

CLAYBORNE IS A haunted man. He keeps looking over his shoulder as he walks along Sutter on the way home from AlphaBanc West. A definite change in behavior, no more Mr. Happy-Go-Lucky here, but then that never really was him, was it? Certainly not according to Natalie, who, during squabbles would sometimes address him caustically as "Mr. Intensity," or at times of greater exasperation with her fiery marketing maverick, as "Mr. Ambition." And why not, what else has he known, son of the biggest IBM rep in northern Illinois, hard-driver Bruce Clayborne, who, in the sixties and seventies sold more big iron in Chicago than Central Steel and Wire, ha-ha, or so the old man liked to say. . . .

But maybe, Clayborne thinks, that wasn't all such a bad thing. It was undoubtedly some of that inbred intensity that helped him keep it together as well as he did after Natalie died—on the surface, anyway. No one ever saw the heartsick tears he shed every morning and every night for months after her death. Hopefully it will help pull him through this, this . . . strange paranoia, that has descended upon him—keeps him looking in the rear view mirror when he drives now—ever since he got back from the McCarthy complex in Red Rock.

That little tour truly made an impression on him; if that's what they wanted to do, *They* certainly succeeded. The information that they can get on someone, anyone, and then share with others, nationwide, worldwide, in a matter, quite literally, of seconds, is frightening. And now with this dubious assignment and the sickening-strange email and phone call, he feels truly haunted. And it doesn't seem to end.

Just the other day AlphaBanc West's premier systems' geek, the Epenguin, showed Clayborne what he had found out about a girl whom he happened to be secretly crazy about—and the poor fellow she was actually seeing—by accessing information available to him through AlphaBanc's colossal data network.

Clayborne has to smile in spite of himself as he thinks now of the short, chubby, beak-nosed reformed hacker whose real name is Elmo P. Quentin, which evolved over time, through E.P. Quentin, to, perhaps inevitably, Epenguin. The name and the plucky image certainly suited him. Prone to overheating to begin with, he decorated his climate-controlled office with Antarctic posters of windswept ice floes, chill-blue crevasses, bleak glacial snowfields . . . that fitfully rattled in the air conditioning he kept blowing constantly . . . and then there was the tux.

One day he showed up in an old tuxedo he had picked up in a secondhand shop, complete with a faded ruffled shirt, droopy bow tie, the works. He wore it every now and then, as a gag. But then he found another used tux, along with a dented top hat to boot, and it wasn't long before he started passionately prowling thrift stores and secondhand shops for superannuated formal wear, never anything new: ancient morning coats, retro chalk-stripe business suits, battered homburgs, spats—anything to add to his new look: shabby genteel geek. Soon, it was all he wore.

Clayborne had thought that Elmo was going deep-end eccentric, but the systems management folks at AlphaBanc West weren't concerned in the least—in fact, they seemed rather pleased that the Epenguin was strutting his stuff.

It was Clayborne's introduction to the exotic world of *uber*-programmers and he soon learned that they are the only breed AlphaBanc hires: the best of the best. And the more incredibly brilliant the coders are, the more fragile and way-out, and also perhaps the more disconcertingly diabolical they could be. What the Epenguin showed to an already shivering Clayborne in his icebox office made Clayborne's blood run truly frigid: both the girl's and her boyfriend's checking, credit card, and savings account balances, and, with a few keystrokes, an amazingly detailed profile of their lifestyles.

That was eye-opening. The program—one of many AlphaBanc standard systems, FINIRG in this case—had actually searched through the history of all their transactions: direct deposit payroll, checking, savings, and plastic card accounts . . . and had analyzed the patterns of their spending, the goods purchased, the times of purchase, the amounts spent, and from that had generated some chillingly accurate profiles of the two of them. Even the cool little bird confided to Clayborne that he was impressed with the latest iteration of the software. The girl's profile, he believed, was right on the mark, and he could only assume her boyfriend's was too, he told Clayborne with a satisfied smirk.

The Epenguin was also very pleased to find that the program had detected a distinct imbalance in income-to-spending ratios which indicated that her boyfriend was possibly embezzling from the construction firm he worked at as an accountant. He thought that it would only take a few more computer searches, and maybe an outside hack into the books of the construction company itself, to be fairly sure. The little bird also casually mentioned that he would be adding this guy as a "specimen," just like his dream girl was now. . . .

"Wh-wh-whoa, P-pengy," asked Clayborne through chattering teeth, "what the heck is a 'specimen?'"

Clayborne's blood temperature dropped another several points when the Epenguin explained to him that he happens to be a bona fide "collector," which is sort of the *ne plus ultra* of hacking, or actually, z-hacking, the current term for those who have been dismissed as renegades by the true hacking community.

Z-hackers, the Epenguin told him, are those who have ventured beyond the activity of exploring complex systems and pulling the occasional prank, to the dark side itself: the actual destruction of system software and hardware and other highly unethical practices (such as specimen collecting). Their singular name actually began life as *a*-hackers, or anarchist-hackers, a neologism coined by a techno-savvy New York city reporter writing about malicious hacking. The article was of course immediately repudiated by the recreant hackers themselves who spitefully proceeded to call themselves z-hackers. Of course.

The hacked appellation stuck and served to differentiate the true hackers, who, the Epenguin explained, would never think of trashing the systems they love to traverse, from the malign z-hackers, the most notorious of whom have banded together as the "Neanderthals," and have anarchy as their stated goal.

The Neanderthals . . . the name seemed to ring a bell. Clayborne had heard the unusual appellation in the press or somewhere but knew really nothing about them. The Epenguin filled him in: The Neanderthals are a group of electronic anarchists, or "neo-electronic-luddites," as they like to think of themselves, whose leader calls himself "General Ned Ludd" in honor of the vaporous leader of the much misaligned Luddites, the radical mechanized-weaving machine abolitionists of nearly two centuries before. On the surface they appeared to be just another hacker clan, although suspected to be larger than most (meaningful metrics being nearly impossible to obtain on the secretive group), with virtual chapters in all major cities in the United States and much of the rest of the world. But the tightly-knit and secretive clan also had an edge described best by a disgruntled compatriot as "organized evil," and they began to attract similarly annihilative souls to their dark cause.

Their infamy spread quickly throughout the hacker underground: no other club was first to place a portrait of Norman "the Gnome" Dunne on its cyberspace wall (no one else could obtain a true picture of the errant elf), and certainly no other club had (it was rumored), safely isolated on a computer called the "Clean Room," the ultimate killer computer virus: the Plague.

The Epenguin shuddered and said that it was only Net-speculation, but the Plague was supposed to be extremely deadly, an intelligent rapidly spreading stealth virus that reduces all of a computer's data to incomprehensible garbage before detection can occur. By then it's too late. And to complement this diabolical Neanderthalian infrastructure, no other group of z-hackers had (as far as anyone knew) a tremendously ambitious plan, as General Ned had stated in his recent e-epistles, "to bring the computer-industrial complex to its androidal knees!" It is their belief that massive modern corporate and government databases keep entirely too much information on individuals—the downtrodden masses in this brave new eworld—and that the only real means of cleansing these electronic infrastructures is to level them and begin anew.

Clayborne felt vaguely embarrassed as the Epenguin explained all this to him. He couldn't help sensing a certain ring of truth to their propositions. But what was this about "collectors," and "specimens?"

"Ah, yes . . ." the Epenguin replied somewhat guiltily, told him that the practice of "collecting" was started by the Neanderthals, under the leadership of General Ned, who began the accumulation of what they called "specimens," (as a lepidopterist calls the members of his fritillary collection) to exemplify the evils inherent in the multiple indexing of databased personal information. People, of course, were the specimens, who became such by the assiduous gathering of all the information available about them on the Net and elsewhere: phone, bank, medical, legal, educational, occupational records, and on and on, until a remarkably complete profile of the individual emerges, resulting in, as one angry sociologist has termed it, "the appalling total and complete annihilation of an individual's privacy."

Though it was only supposed to be a demonstration of the awesome power of the would-be cyber-sleuth, the challenge intrigued so many z-hackers that General Ned rapidly lost control of the scheme and it became a favorite Neanderthal pastime, one that, though never actually denounced by the General, was never encouraged again. The only supposed proviso was that the specimen not be personally known to the collector.

"Oh, sure," sputtered a shocked Clayborne, "I'm sure everyone's going to play by the rules. Especially an anarchistic Neanderthal."

"Well, *I* play by the rules," said the Epenguin, closing his big bug eyes momentarily. "At least for this particular specimen. But then I'm not technically a z-hacker, either. In fact, I'm not any kind of hacker anymore, I guess. I'm an insider now. But I'm inside at AlphaBanc with its libraries of data collection and analysis software, and that makes me the best collector ever. I've got maybe twenty-five to thirty specimens right now. The very best z-hackers only have a dozen or so—and I'm talking good specimens—because of the tremendous amount of work it takes to play detective and gather all the necessary information and piece it together. Premium specimens are wonderful things, you know.

You put such effort into it, you get to know them; you practically fall in love with them. It's hard to describe . . . you get involved in a kind of intimate relationship."

"Uh, kind of one-sided, I would think," said Clayborne.

"Oh yeah," the Epenguin admitted. "By its very nature. It's the ultimate in cyber-stalking."

"I would guess so."

"True specimens are always up-to-date," the Epenguin continued, "where you know so much about someone that you can make really accurate predictions about them. I mean, it's an incredible trip to be able to know such minutiae about them that you can predict where they're going to be at what time, who they're going to be with, what they're going buy at what store, what they'll eat, what they'll drink, what they'll read, practically, what they'll *think*. I'm even working on integrating security cameras on street corners into my collections. I found a way to get my hands on the data, through AlphaBanc, natch. Now I'm watching for any of my specimens walking by. Since most folks have their mugs databased through driver's license and credit card photos, it's fairly easy to locate specimens out and about in public—and, of course, within camera range. It's fun when you get a hit on someone in your collection.

"The recognition software we've got now can pull facial characteristics from people in crowds and match it with individuals in the database with ninety-nine percent accuracy. The FBI and CIA are using it—with the help of AlphaBanc and yours truly—to locate folks they're interested in: terrorists, of course, but also fugitives, known criminals who might show up at a crime scene, participants in political rallies, suspected narcotics traffickers, and so on. But I will grant you that the barriers have certainly been relaxed since September 11th and the Patriot Act. It's a hell of a lot easier to get ahold of this information now.

"And the next big thing is RFID tag tracking, that is, radio frequency identification tags, where the RFID chip embedded in driver's licenses and passports, or even the tagged T-shirt some poor clueless specimen bought at K-Mart will allow us to track them every time they pass a collection point. And these babies are tiny! Not only can they be made as small as a grain of rice, the circuitry is now *printable* on clothing! On say, the inner lining of a coat, so now you'll never suspect how you're being tracked! And they're readable at 60 feet or more! It's so crazy! Governments are already tracking people at political rallies and protests by collecting their ID codes through RF readers hidden in innocuous-looking poles and lampposts at the rallying site and then loading those codes into databases. Then all it takes is one click and the person's data comes up instantly on the screen, with a picture and all the info it has on the poor bastard."

"Yeah I've heard about these—tags, but there's supposedly no personal data stored in them. So it's not really that bad ... is it?"

The Epenguin laughed out loud. "Awk! That is the most colossal piece of disinformation that the RFID-er's are feeding us! To soothe the masses, I guess. The evil fact is that each RFID code is unique in the universe, and thus can uniquely identify a person once we link that code to anything *else* about them, like an SSN or a credit card number. Then we own them! They're dead meat. Like the person wearing that T-shirt that has an RFID tag embedded in it; that tag is unique, and it's not too hard—at least here at AlphaBanc—to find out when and where it was sold, and via credit card, to whom, and then we've made the link—we call it the "golden kiss," and once they've been kissed, they're ours. Wherever they go, there we are."

"Very dramatic," murmured Clayborne, but he was troubled by this frightening information—and in the Epenguin's frigid office, also really, really *cold*.

"God, I guess I just can't imagine getting that much data on a person. You're monitoring everything—"

"Have you ever heard of Echelon?" the Epenguin asked.

"Echelon? What's that?"

"It's a global messaging interception system run by the NSA, the National Security Agency. It's similar to the FBI's Carnivore system, but much more comprehensive. The McCarthy complex in Red Rock is the biggest interception node in North America, you know."

"Oh, oh, wait," said Clayborne. "I have heard of it. Where they intercept absolutely *everything* . . ."

"Yes, everything, every single transmission is snagged, voice or data, in the United States, Latin America, and most of Europe and the Pacific rim, whether carried by telephone lines, satellite, even undersea cable, and scanned for key words and phrases that exist in our huge dictionaries."

"So it is true."

"Very true. We pass the data on to the NSA at Fort Meade in Maryland, where they attempt to process it. They're having trouble, as we are, dealing with fiber optic transmissions and encryption, but their biggest problem, we're hearing, is just managing all the information that's coming in nowadays. Just about everything's electronic, online, interceptable."

"My God. I think I tried not to believe that. But it's true, nothing is safe, no communications at all are private, sacred."

"That's right, no electronic communications, anyway. But you shouldn't freak out over the specimens that the Neanderthals or me or the Gnome keeps. We're just a step ahead of the government. In fact, AlphaBanc was the primary consultant for the Pentagon's TIA, or Total Information Awareness program—or Terrorist Information Awareness program, depending upon what they're calling it nowadays, *and* which they deny even still exists, but don't you believe it . . . But anyway it's all the same thing, a system that sifts through all the databases they have access to, searching for, supposedly, terrorists. It's very granular, designed to learn everything, and I mean *everything*, it can about an individual. And it does, man. No matter what they want to call it, they're collectors. And we're all specimens, like it or not."

"Well then the world we live in now is totally crazy—and really frightening," said Clayborne. "Is that the trade-off today? Personal freedom, the right to privacy, sacrificed for our fight against terrorism?"

"Right now it is. I have to admit that even I was kind of freaked out about the, uh, incredible surveillance technology out there, but now," the Epenguin yawned, "I guess I'm just resigned to it. You know, the most surprising thing I've learned since I became a collector is that, the truth be told, humans are incredibly boring, predictable creatures. They get up every day, go to work, eat, sleep, try their best to entertain themselves, but in the end, they're just boring.

"Boring?"

"Boring, man. You, me, all of us. Nothing but a great big freakin' snore . . ."

CHAPTER TWENTY-FOUR

WHAT A CRAZY job. What a crazy world. Clayborne, home now, tries to shake off his troubled thoughts about the Epenguin and his disturbing revelations, grabs a beer out of the fridge. What the hell. It's either work from home or from the AlphaBanc offices downtown. They'll call him if she signs onto NEXSX.

Who's watching the network for her? Probably the Epenguin. He's always there. He practically lives there. But it may well be just teams of sleepy computer operators, manning AlphaBanc's terminals throughout the night, data transmissions coming in from around the globe, waiting for one special message to come across their screens, tripping an electronic trigger that someone like the Epenguin has rigged up. It's only about seven o'clock but in Chicago that will be, what? Nine o'clock, central time. His old time zone. He grew up in central time, Midwest time, farmer time, sublime time, everything a sweet hour earlier than out East where they stay up too late, get up too early, work too hard, die too young. . . .

He sits at his desk before his monitor, stares at its mute black screen and thinks: computers are amazing wonderful things. And at the same time, he realizes, he hates them all, hates the way they have organized our lives into dreary patterns of networked orderly efficiency. He, everyone, it seems, sits in front of one, all day long, day after organized day . . . and he remembers reading something somewhere, maybe on the Internet, an oddly serious tract about how the mass of computers in the world possess a collective intelligence and have somehow sinisterly coerced humans to replicate them so that gradually, eventually, ultimately they will *rule* humans. Really wacky all right, but, well, maybe some tiny part of it is true, maybe, God help us, it's already happening . . . and suddenly he feels immensely tired, way too computer-weary to do this thing right now, maybe he should call in, shut down, cancel out, give up—but then his phone buzzes.

It's the Epenguin. She's on. Damn. Time to get to work.

His dubious mission here is to access the NEXSX site himself and try to introduce himself to the lovely Christin Darrow as, simply, Richard. AlphaBanc's personality profile program has predicted that she will respond best to the simplicity and honesty of "Richard," rather than a jazzy handle. Zara has sent him her picture, a formal photograph of Darrow in a business suit, very corporate, but it clearly depicts the extraordinary beauty she possesses. Clayborne sighs. She seems like such a nice girl. He thinks again how much he hates his role in this underhanded scheme, but . . . it's for a greater good, that of AlphaBanc, and his career therein, and it is apparently their only chance to nab the Gnome, clearly a dangerous killer.

Dutifully, he logs onto NEXSX and begins to look through the online postings for Christin Darrow's "advertisement." He's wearing a headset and microphone and has the Epenguin on the other end, who informs him that she has posted her NEXSX listing under the name of "newh0tgal."

"And wait till you see her picture, man."

Clayborne can practically hear the Epenguin drooling, thinks it must be pretty good as he finds her posting, clicks on it.

It is. It is stunning.

"Nice, huh?" murmurs the Epenguin.

"God, I'll say," chokes Clayborne with a virtual blonde Christin Darrow glowing before him in super sexy black bikini underwear. "But I thought she was a brunette."

"Wig, man. She's really hot stuff, at least on NEXSX."

"God, you're not kidding." From the dull bio he was sent, he pretty much expected to see the photo of her in the business suit. This is much, much better. He reads:

> SWF - Lonely in the big city of Chicago. Career girl
> looking for Mr. Right. Are you that guy? If so, leave
> me a message. I like bicycling, tennis, swimming,
> long walks, and all the other goofy stuff I'm
> supposed to write here.

Clayborne chuckles. He likes her ad, figures he could almost answer it himself—not as part of his job. But right now it is his job. His mission is to leave her a message. With an ad like that—and that picture—it's certain that she'll get a lot of responses. But the idea is that she will answer *his* message. Clayborne looks over the samples which AlphaBanc's crack staff psychologist, Dr. Roland Rascher, has prepared based upon her personality profile, decides they all suck. He'll write his own reply. After all, hadn't they assigned him this job based upon his psychology background? He licks his lips and types:

> Don't know if I'm Mr. Right, but I know how lonely it can get in the big city. Mine's San Francisco. I travel to Chicago frequently and would love to meet you for dinner there. I'm 31 and like bicycling, tennis, swimming, long walks, and all the other goofy stuff you wrote there. Richard.

Not bad. The Epenguin reminds him that his next task is to try to contact her in a NEXSX chat room. The Epenguin, watching her every move, will let him know when.

"Hmm, what should I say?"

"You're the psych major, man. Anyway, just use one of the lines Rascher's cooked up for you."

"Okay, okay, we'll see . . ."

"Hey, check it out, Richie, she's in 'The Dungeon.'"

"The what?"

"The Dungeon, man. Real kinky stuff. Get your ass over there. See if you can talk with her."

Clayborne's heart skips a beat as he frantically looks over the many chat room options on NEXSX. The Dungeon? This is not where he expected to find her. What should he say?

"Oh, forget it, man," says the Epenguin, "she's out again. Just a little lurking, probably."

"Huh. This is a weird scene, Pengy."

"Yeah it is, but . . . aw, she's gone now, man. Just logged off."

"Oh, okay," says weary Clayborne, relieved that he doesn't have to try to talk with her tonight. "Too bad."

"Yeah, she's got to get up early for work tomorrow. She's got an early meeting with her boss, Bernice."

"She does? How would you . . . oh, never mind."

"It's on her calendar. Which is online. We know everything, man. Fact of life."

"Yeah, I hear ya," Clayborne grumbles. He realizes, somewhat dispiritedly, how strange this really is, how they can watch a person who thinks what she's doing is private, unknown to all but herself, and yet they—They, he is definitely part of *They*, now—know everything, see everything. Clayborne shudders, thinks how much AlphaBanc must really know about her. Hell, about him, too. . . .

CHAPTER TWENTY-FIVE

NORTH OF CHICAGO, in the upscale village of Lake Forest, a small group of merry men sit in the elegant mahogany-paneled den of Karl Bergstrom drinking 18-year-old Glenmorangie scotch and talking business. "So what do you think about this, ah, brave new info-world we live in now, Mr. Walker?" asks Bergstrom amusedly, raising an eyebrow to their guest, a Mr. Walker from Washington, D.C. Joining him are Pierre Lefebre, Darryl Gates, Ed Van Arp, and Alan Sturgis. They have all just watched a short AlphaBanc video on Bergstrom's huge high-definition monitor which depicts the global linking of all of AlphaBanc's branches and business partners via satellite and global optical fiber lines.

"Interesting, I guess," says Mr. Walker. "But way over my head, which is spinning. I'm not a network techie, just a poor Washington bureaucrat."

"You know," Bergstrom chuckles, "the ancient Chinese had a curse, 'May you live in interesting times.'"

"And we certainly do!" barks Lefebre. "The tragedy of September 11th has changed completely the way the world thinks about information, surveillance, human rights, everything!"

"Changed in our favor, I'd have to say," Bergstrom smiles grimly.

"Agreed," says Mr. Walker. "It's a whole new ball game."

"Hear, hear," chimes Sturgis, somewhat drunkenly. "A truly wonderful opportunity!"

"I must say, we are in an enviable position," says Lefebre.

Bergstrom smiles, shakes his head. "Who do you mean by *we*, Pierre? The government?" he looks over at Mr. Walker. "Or AlphaBanc?"

They are playing with him.

Lefebre's eyes narrow behind his spectacles. "In terms of information bought and sold . . . is there any difference?"

"Ha! Good one, Mr. Lefebre!" Mr. Walker laughs weakly.

"And he's quite correct, sir," says Gates, looking significantly toward their visitor. "My contacts in the Pentagon and the CIA confide that they simply cannot handle the flood of information that comes into their agencies. Those systems are hopelessly outdated. Am I not right?"

"Unfortunately, you are, Mr. Gates," says Mr. Walker, shaking his head. "And I can tell you the horror stories. The CIA alone runs hundreds of different major information systems and only a handful of them can communicate with each other. They maintain several thousand databases on open sources alone—newspaper articles, radio and television broadcasts, and the like—and they're buried. Let alone the really confidential stuff. How can they handle that? And with the unbelievable *flood* of Internet traffic . . . I must tell you that the NSA folks are panicking. Primarily because the Echelon systems are beginning to fall seriously behind—"

"How far behind?" asks Gates.

"Way, way behind. We never bargained for the tremendous amount of data that would be streaming across the Internet. Primarily the optical fiber networks. They are proving very difficult to monitor—"

"Along with digital cell phones and encryption," adds Gates.

"Er, yes," says Mr. Walker. "And we're glad to be working with you on these interception challenges. But beyond that, our primary concern is content analysis. This is where our systems greatly lag. When a suspect item now triggers an alert beyond threshold, the entire transmission is cached and sent to a particular intelligence resource, often a human one, for a decision on routing, verification, surveillance, et cetera. With the tremendous amount of data flowing through our systems, we're missing a ridiculously large number of these, particularly corporate and governmental transmissions—much of it economic data. And more and more of it is now encrypted, as you say. The NSA tries its best to keep its head above water, but—"

"The simple answer is, they can't," interrupts Bergstrom. "That's where we come in."

"That's right," says Van Arp, "it's a simple matter of privatizing, of common capital investment. We're taking all the risk, we're investing in lightning-fast supercomputers, superb technical staffs, tremendous database capacities . . . certainly more than the government deems adequate!"

"I'm afraid you're absolutely correct, Mr. Van Arp. As embarrassed as I am to admit this, in the end, our information systems are a hopeless mess. We have failed, after squandering many billions of taxpayer dollars, to modernize our intelligence systems at precisely a time when we need accurate, timely information like we have never needed it before. These expenditures have been buried, of course, in the defense budget, but we have assured the committee members that our systems are now thoroughly modernized, and I cannot now go back and tell them that this has not happened." Mr. Walker smiles sheepishly and takes a gulp of scotch. "It is in the interests of national security, I might add, that this conversation never happened."

"Of course, Mr. Walker," Bergstrom smiles carefully, glancing over at Van Arp, "it never did." They own him. They own the nation.

"And of course this will only be a temporary affair, until we can get our systems where they should be—we figure maybe twenty-four to thirty-six months."

"Oh, of course. Certainly." Van Arp smiles warmly. "Only an interim measure."

"Yes only, interim . . ." Mr. Walker murmurs. "And I can assure you that, in terms of this, er, arrangement, I represent the highest sources in Washington—"

"The, er, pres-i-dent?" slurs Sturgis.

"Oh, no. The *very* highest sources," Mr. Walker nods significantly. "Well then, reimbursement will come as part of varied defense appropriations, of course. And I hope that you appreciate the, uh, goodwill of us swinging the IRS data storage contract over to your side, as well as the ElecTal—"

Bergstrom stands, throws a shadow on his guest. "Mr. Walker, I can't tell you how grateful we are to you for that affirmation of confidence on your part. For our part," he looks over to Gates, who nods slightly and walks out of the room, "I'd like to thank you by providing you with a bit of truly cutting-edge technology." He turns toward the door.

Gates returns, followed by a very attractive young woman wearing only a wine-red lacy bustier, a diamond-spangled thong, dark satin garters attached to merlot stockings, and stiletto heels. She stalks confidently around the room, as if to model her finery, as if choreographed, and comes to rest gracefully alongside the fireplace.

"Jesus," whispers Mr. Walker. "Is-is she a robot, or—"

The group bursts into laughter. "No, no," says Bergstrom, looking sideways at Gates. "Well, not exactly. She's—a very, very loyal employee, let us say."

"Marcia," Gates calls to her. "Please come over and say hello to Mr. Walker."

Marcia strolls over, stands before the man from D.C., looking at him through perhaps slightly glazed eyes. "Hello Mister Walker," she whispers, with a pronounced Marilyn Monroe-vian (days of champagne and Kennedys) huskiness and puts her arms around his neck. The AlphaBanc executives exchange appreciative glances.

Bergstrom approaches the moonstruck couple. "Marcia, why don't you take Mr. Walker to the guest bedroom and, er, make him comfortable?"

"You bet . . . Mr. Bergstrom," she coos and begins to lead the bedazzled bureaucrat out of the room by his tie.

"Uh—" Mr. Walker turns to look back at the group.

"We'll see you later, sir," Bergstrom winks and raises his hand as in a benediction.

"What was the frequency, Epenguin?" Toby O'Brian murmurs into his microphone. He is sitting deep within AlphaBanc's subterranean command center in Red Rock.

"The usual, for satellite transmissions," yawns the Epenguin at his desk in AlphaBanc West's Information Center.

"And the sequence?"

"Uh, let's see . . . the basic subliminal thing, Mata Hari *Mango* sequence, but, huh, Jeeze, I don't know what this *Mango* really—"

"How many repetitions?"

"Oh, hundreds, easily, thousands. Then overlaid with some new stuff." The Epenguin yawns again. He's been on the job nearly twenty straight hours. "Let's see . . . it's something Rascher's calling the 'Norma Jean Cycle'—at least that's the metadata on the file he sent."

"And this was . . . which one?"

"Uh, forty-nine."

"Okay. Er, have you heard anything regarding—the success of the mission?"

"Nope. And that's good. You know that Bergstrom would be on the line pronto—double-pronto—if there was any problem."

"That is an understatement." O'Brian breathes an audible sigh of relief and hangs up.

CHAPTER TWENTY-SIX

"SO WE HAVE a problem?"

"Uh-huh, with Tangentronics —"

"Tangentronics? Who's that?" Darryl Gates, AlphaBanc's chief information officer sits back in his chair, gives his visitor, a heavyset man in his fifties with thinning hair, a menacing toothy grin, and a frighteningly sharp mind, his full attention.

"Why, it's the friendly li'l company that imports the famous AlphaBanc satellite clock radio that we gives out to everyone, employees and customers, as premiums and such," says Franz Haedler, the head of AlphaBanc's Internal Security Division, ISD. He's an ex-police chief from Louisiana who lost his job due to what was characterized as "overzealousness" in the enforcement of law and order, and "patent neglect" in protecting the rights of minorities in the city he had been forced to leave for good. "Righteously *in*-efficient white justice is all there is to it . . ." Haedler unashamedly admits over any number of dixie lagers. But he had come out near the top of AlphaBanc's online OCCPROFS, or Occupational Profiles, in the category of security chief and Karl Bergstrom had hired him after only one interview. One small city's overzealousness became AlphaBanc's irascible big gun when it came to handling "situations," and Haedler quickly demonstrated that absolutely no problem was too small to incur the wrath of his troops.

"Yes, the satellite clocks . . ." says Gates thoughtfully. "There are the normal kind. And then the other kind."

"Yessir, only we know that. That there are two kinds," drawls Haedler. "The 'other kind' we modify here, but it's the same base unit we get from Tangentronics. Who gets them from somewheres overseas: Indonesia, Korea, maybe. Anyway, looks like we gotta jump on 'em here a leetle bit."

Gates rubs his nose. "I had forgotten the name of our supplier. So, do we know exactly who—?"

"Fella by the name of DiMancini. Salvatore DiMancini."

"Hmph. I prefer going after women."

"You can't win 'em all," Haedler chuckles.

"Yeah. Well, what's the beef, exactly?"

"This old boy's trying to scam us for a big load of radios we didn't want. Never even ordered. Thirty-damn thousand of 'em, if you can believe that!"

"Was there a purchase order? If not, then—"

"It ain't that easy," Haedler grimaces. "See, we've done business with him for the past five years, started small with five thousand, then ten thousand, then fifteen; last year it was twenty thousand. But that was it. They were banking premiums, ya know, Midwest region primarily, and we ended the campaign. Even the customers didn't want 'em no more."

"So what happened?"

"So this DiMancini shows up with a buncha truckloads of radios, said we ordered them over the phone. And upped the order to thirty thousand. What damn balls! Legal says it's real iffy. Verbal contract. We refuse to pay, he takes us to court, the jury sees this poor little company stuck with all these nice radios with the AFS logo on it, which, of course, great big AlphaBanc *could* use anyway—and who do they decide for? Not great big AlphaBanc, I'll tell you that. He's trying to take us to the cleaners. Bergstrom wants me to bust this pimp."

"Well, don't worry," says Gates, eager to begin diving into the huge data warehouses lying just on the other side the workstation before him. He has security clearance to virtually everything in the AlphaBanc's systems and knows precisely how to search them, which is why Haedler comes directly to him in sensitive matters such as this. "We'll make the little sleaze sorry he tried to pull this one. Let's see what we've got here. This is his social security number?"

"Yep. You betcha." The glow from Gates' monitor illuminates Haedler's fat round face as he grins, "I *always* try to get that, nowadays."

"Good," Gates murmurs as he types at the keyboard. "Then we don't have to find it."

"So, whatcha got going here?" Haedler peers over Gates' shoulder as Chicago's chief computer jockey flashes through a series of screens, entering data on some, flipping past others.

"Oh, we'll start out with the basic search . . . ah! You know the poor bastard has an AlphaBanc Promethium Card, and, uh, let's see, an account at AlphaBanc San Francisco, Marin branch. AlphaBanc cash card, too."

Gates glances back at Haedler with a smug smile. "Let's see now, I've submitted the FINIRG23; we've added some new externals for sub-million dollar accounts—foreign investments through virtually any bank now, and any foreign bank wire transfers, which should prove very productive, although I don't think such small potatoes as this guy is going to have that kind of history. But, anyway, we're going through the IBM mainframes with this, not the big blue monster, so it'll take a little while to run in batch. In the meantime, I'm going to execute the, uh, SEXIRG17 right here, interactively. I think it'll run fast enough; it's still a pretty small routine, although we've much improved our algorithms for sexual lifestyle determinants, and a more detailed profile of a subject's consumption of alcohol, tobacco, and the possibilities of any controlled substances, marijuana, cocaine, what-have-you."

"Well, that is a *most* welcomed improvement," says Haedler with mock-seriousness, though he is obviously pleased. "I'm very appreciative, Darryl, to you and your team."

"I thought you would be. So will insurance companies; it's a great refinement of the whole 'at-risk' behavior area. We're getting the systems tighter and tighter, but I'll be glad when we've got better linkages between the really big databases, especially between AlphaBanc's files and the big kahuna—"

"Hoo-boy, can't wait for that! Never thought I could even *hope* for the IRS a-coming."

"O'Brian's getting ready for it, all that income and tax history, can you believe it? Huge bonanza."

"Yeah, yeah." Haedler lights up a cigar. "My boys been goin' crazy tryin' to get current on the *federales*' regs."

"I imagine. We've all been under pressure to prepare. They're supposed to be bringing it to Red Rock starting next week. But it'll take a good year or so to get everything here and set up."

"And then it's ours."

"All ours."

"Gonna be fantastic. I can-*not* believe the goods we'll be able to get on . . . ha-ha, anyone!" Haedler blows a cloud of smoke and grins. "Sure your systems will be able to handle it all?"

"We're working day and night. Much of our software will have to be converted. We've smoothed the programs out considerably in the past year, but they've still got a ton of bugs in them. That original IRS hack was really a tough one to achieve, too. Of course, you know who we have to thank for that."

"Uh, let me guess . . . Normie Dunne, right?"

Darryl Gates looks up at Haedler, "Who else?"

Gates continues to refresh the screen, watches the job run numbers increase, mumbles softly to himself. They have done a great deal already, linking up AlphaBanc's huge store of financial and credit histories with some of the most comprehensive data files in the country—multiple indexed social networks: Facebook, Twitter, NEXSX, and the like, insurance, medical, and pharmaceutical history databases, virtually every banking and brokerage firm on the planet—and the near-instantaneous access AFS has to such complete information is what makes them the undisputed leader in the information industry. But it never really is enough.

There are always additional data points to be gotten. Their clients always want more, much of it accessible only through what they refer to as their "stealth links," the clandestine connections to all the cataloged data stored in the Red Rock underground facility and elsewhere across the Internet: DMV records for most states, workers compensation and OSHA files, federal and local criminal databases, phone company records, property taxes, sales tax permits, hunting and fishing licenses, divorce and criminal court transcripts, magazine subscriptions, library book lendings, Internet access logs, DVD rentals, illegal video and music downloads . . . and more comes in every day. The latest additions are DNA mapping data for individuals, as yet a small information subset, but growing.

It is these assets that enable them to provide the remarkably accurate profiles of the individual, or groups of individuals, that they are requested to report upon, almost always covertly, by AlphaBanc clients that range from intensely competitive industrialists to unscrupulous politicos—and increasingly more often, by various law enforcement and antiterrorist governmental agencies who need to know a great deal about someone in a hurry. This information never comes, of course, directly from AlphaBanc, but through various consulting firms and individuals who will purchase the requested information for a hefty fee, or, depending upon the situation, a political favor.

But getting into supposedly secure government systems like the Internal Revenue Service's files had been much more difficult than they had expected, along with all the various FBI, CIA, Interpol, and other secure databases they needed to access from time to time—it was only Dunne's super-coding that built their way in and out of those, without a trace. And now the strange little man is gone. Just when they are so close.

"So what's with Sex Urge?" grunts Haedler.

"Almost done," says Gates softly, tapping the refresh key, as runtime numbers whir by on the screen before him.

Haedler chuckles. "*Damn*, I love this job! Sex Urge, c'mon! Bring it on home!"

"I often can't wait to see the results myself," whispers Gates, licking his upper lip. Sex Urge is how they refer to the SEXIRG series of programs, which stands for Sexual Irregularities, and are designed to determine the sexual preferences, proclivities, aberrations, et cetera, of a person, or even groups of people. The FINIRG series, standing for Financial Irregularities, is a much modified version of their central credit-checking program, one that, after searching through perhaps tens of millions of data items stored in various databases around the country, from lifetime credit card transactions to last month's municipal traffic citations, develops an amazingly detailed profile of a person, usually statistically accurate within a 95% confidence level. The SEXIRG17 program is the seventeenth revision of the core matching routine—FINIRG23, the twenty-third update of its base. The more they are updated, the more powerful the programs are, the more features they possess, the more they are able to retrieve.

"Ah, here we are," whispers Gates. FINIRG23 has finished. "That new IBM runs even faster than I expected."

He clicks on the menu item: FINIRG23.CFI4D03 - Financial History–Individual/Small Business, with the bold legend "HIGHLY CONFIDENTIAL" at the top of the display. He is returned to another screen with multiple listings highlighted where the program algorithms have detected some abnormality: traditional and plastic credit histories, income sources, personal assets, investments in securities, real estate, precious metals, and on and on.

Haedler grins again. This has to be the best way to nail a person, ever. "Highly confidential," he chuckles.

"Sure. Let's take a look at his credit," murmurs Gates. He clicks on an option and immediately receives a listing of DiMancini's credit cards: VISA, MasterCard, and the AlphaBanc Promethium Card. All three over their respective limits.

"Well, he's—how would you say it?—overextended?" Haedler chuckles again.

"Sure is." Gates quickly scans through the highlighted transaction history of each card. "Ooh, here's something quite interesting . . . morning liquor purchases, hmm, several times a week. Ongoing. Tsk-tsk, looks like someone might have a bit of a drinking problem . . ."

"Good job. Forgot we could get that info."

"The programs miss nothing. If this was one of Mr. DiMancini's employees, he'd be very grateful to receive this information. As he's the boss, well, I think he'll be quite unhappy to find that we can use this against him."

"You betcha. So what else we got?"

"Well, sure looks like he's been doing a lot of vacationing. Why don't we see with whom?"

"You can tell that? Fast?"

"Are you kidding?" Gates grins, staring intently at the screen, "We can tell *anything*. And very fast indeed."

CHAPTER TWENTY-SEVEN

HAEDLER STARES AT the computer screen on Gates's desktop, understanding that when the CIO says *very fast*, he isn't exaggerating. When he first came to AlphaBanc he had been overwhelmed by the speed and ease with which they were able to provide him detailed information on practically anyone he needed to know something about. Security checks were a breeze—and they never seemed to be wrong. And although he can't argue with that kind of precision or the tremendous amount of legwork it saved him, he still has to think that this part of the job just isn't as much *fun* as it used to be.

"So, just what tricky deal you gonna do now to find out who he's been tom-cattin' around with?" he drawls.

"Double-Seats," Gates smiles, pulls up a menu and initiates a function listed on the screen as: DBLSEATS. This is one of their newest and often most interesting searches, linking a subject's credit card purchases of airline tickets with the carrier's reservation database, thus retrieving a record of when he or she flew, where to, and most importantly, with whom. Less than a minute later, a return screen pops up. "Sylvia Montress is her name. Cancun, Montreal, St. Thomas, is their game."

"What's his wife's name?"

"Uh . . ." Darryl taps at the keyboard. "Gina."

"Christ. How does he get away with it? My wife, er, ex-wife'd be on my ass in a second."

"He's a small businessman. Lots of out-of-towners. Probably tells Gina that he's going to Altoona for a consumer electronics convention or something. Then he takes Sylvia to Mexico. Once we zero in, we'll be able to tell absolutely everything about their trip, provided he used plastic to pay for it. Maybe we'll even be able to find them on some street corner cameras . . ."

"Well, you know, I wonder how he explains the tan?"

"Good question, Franz. In fact, that's an absolutely excellent question. There's just got to be a tanning salon, and . . . ah-ha! See it listed there in the bottom of the window? It's part of the DBLSEATS program." Gates smiles broadly. "The program automatically searches for tanning parlors in the subject's credit history whenever the destinations head south—which they often do."

"Oh Lordy, that's brilliant."

Gates smiles again. "My idea, actually. It always finds a tanning salon. Almost always, anyway."

"Well, we've got something here."

"Yes, I'm not surprised, actually. These small guys, they're just like the big ones; once they start taking in more than they need, they end up with something on the side. And then they start going to the tanning salon. Just like this guy. But, anyway, looks like Sylvia here is really bleeding him."

"Hell, yes. He's hemorrhaging. She must really be a looker."

"Hmm, California . . . one of the first to digitize driver's license photos. Makes it so damn easy for us. I'll run another search against the CA-DMV database. See if we can find her. Otherwise, she's probably on a credit card somewhere. I'll run her profile too, see what we can find out. But we won't have that job back until a little later. Anyway, we've got him. Now, I'll schedule reports of all the transactions that occurred during their trips. He uses plastic for everything. It'll look just like a dick was on their tail."

"And then we'll send a real one over. For a little chat with Mr. DiMancini."

Gates looks up at Haedler. "Georgie?"

"Blair's got plenty of business right here. He's makin' a first run at a tree-hugger, or maybe we best call him a swamp-sucker, name 'o Booth who's tryin' to stop the new airport."

"Oh, yes. Down there . . . south of here."

"That's right. But it's just a side job. Big thing, 'course, is we're gonna send him after Dunne, the Gnome. He's just been up to Red Rock to meet with O'Brian. Do some learnin' up on the little weirdo."

"Think he can help us get him?"

"Oh yeah, Georgie's damn good. I think if anyone can do the job, he can. He's smart . . . but . . . maybe he's just a little too smart."

"Ah. What do you mean?"

"Not sure. I just always worry about the smart ones . . . just me, maybe. Gettin' old, I guess—and paranoid."

"This is a paranoid business we're in."

"You got that right."

"Well, I hope to God you guys can find him. Dunne. The Gnome. We really need him now—"

"Don't you worry about ISD," coughs Haedler, flicking the ashes from his cigar on the floor. "We'll do our damnedest. You guys just be sure you do yours."

"I can assure you, we are."

"Oh yeah? You ever run Sex Urge on that Chris Darrow?"

"Of course." Gates smiles serenely up at Haedler. "We've done an exhaustive profile on her."

"C'mon . . . what'd you find?"

"You really want to know, Franzy?" Gates says teasingly, clicking away at the keyboard.

"Of course I do. In fact, I should know, I have to know, it's part of my job."

"There you go, Franz, how do you like that?"

Filling the screen in front of them is an image of a very beautiful woman in black bikini underwear, smiling coyly for the camera.

"That? I've seen that picture. Quite a few times, in fact," says Haedler reverently. "That's the one she posted on NEXSX."

"Terrific isn't it?"

"Yep. That's it, huh?"

"Yes, unfortunately, other than the little imbroglio at that college she attended, out East. Actually quite a messy situation. You know about that, I take it?"

"Of course I do. ISD knows all about it," Haedler growls. "She was just a leetle too big for her britches. And it cost her."

"Yes, that was the incident. Well, other than that, she's young and doesn't really have a lot of history. Of course, we're tracking her, ah, illness, very carefully."

"That's right. It won't be long until . . . we've got her in our sights, permanently."

Gates sighs, rubs his eyes. "No, I suppose not. But she's very thorough, Franz. She's been doing many Internet searches on the Ménière's."

"Hmm. Good girl. She find out anything she shouldn't?"

"Oh no, of course not."

"Well, that's good then," grunts Haedler. "But you know who's the lucky one is that Clayborne. He gets to make time with Darrow."

"Yes, I'm quite aware of that. Virtual time, online time, that is. The key compatibility parameters on his PERSPROF correlated very well with those of Christin Darrow. Both AlphaBanc employees. And they are geographically distant, also. It's nearly perfect. Except, of course, when we first discovered the very favorable correlation, nearly a year ago now, Clayborne was—"

"Married," says Haedler.

"Would have been better if he hadn't been."

"Yeah. It was too bad."

"Yes. Very unfortunate." Gates clears his throat. "Well, now he's something of a lucky fellow. With this Darrow."

"Yeah, real lucky."

"How much are you telling him?"

"As little as possible. And her, of course, nothing."

"Oh, yes. She must appear completely innocent to the Gnome. If there is even a hint of a trap, we'd lose him for sure."

"Maybe, maybe not," snorts Haedler.

"What do you mean?"

"Well, the way I figure it, the little weirdo likes a challenge. To tell the truth, if he's as smart as you say he is, I'll bet he sees right through this thing. But I think he'll still play along."

Gates looks over at Haedler. He has to admit some grudging respect for the overweight, cigar-chomping blowhard. The man has some insight. And he just might be right. "You really think he wouldn't lay low?"

"Can't guarantee it, but, nope, I think he'd be intrigued enough to go for the bait. And that's some bait. A real beauty. Just what he likes. Anyway, hell, both Clayborne and Darrow are

AlphaBanc employees, Clayborne longtime. He'll know. You don't think he'll figure that out?"

"Well, don't forget that his last victim was an AlphaBanc employee."

"Hah! Exactly what I'm talking about! He wanted to rub our noses in it. That's what he did. I don't think it matters at all if he thinks Clayborne is a ringer. But I think if he thought that Darrow was in on it, then I'm not so sure he'd be interested. It's her sweet l'il innocence that attracts him."

The terminal beeps. Gates looks over, smiles dreamily. "Ah, the California DMV search just finished. Let's see what it's come up with."

CHAPTER TWENTY-EIGHT

CLAYBORNE IS DREAMING; he and Natalie seem to be visiting Stevie Denton at his farm in Washington State. Stevie is showing him around the place and they are unpleasantly rushed because it is Sunday and Natalie is going to fly them back home to San Francisco in her little plane so they can make it to work the next day. Stevie wants them to stay and see some of the vegetables he is raising, but Natalie—very unlike her—insists that they leave right away. Clayborne argues with her and she leaves him with Stevie, presumably to fly away by herself. Clayborne next finds himself at Stevie's table, before him an assortment of vegetables: ripe tomatoes, cucumbers, squashes, carrots, turnips . . . but when Clayborne picks up a tomato, he sees, amazingly, that it has several tiny blinking green lights integrated right into the fruit.

Oh yeah, says nonchalant Stevie, that's a clockwork tomato, quartz oscillated, the way they all are now, electronic hybrids, and he cuts one open to reveal, shockingly, an elaborate interior composed of miniature green circuit boards, multicolored wiring, tiny microchips . . . the transistor tomato from hell.

Clayborne is appalled, now notices tiny lights and suspicious wiring on *all* the vegetables and then looks over at his host and is shocked to see similar electronics on *Stevie*, a row of minute red and green indicator lights on his forehead just below his hairline . . . and on his neck, just behind the jaw, the polished chromium ends of a shaft of some sort, like a dream-updated version of the Frankenstein monster. Stevie gestures, gives Clayborne a wink and a *knowing look,* and Clayborne reaches up, feels his heart sink as he touches the nubs of something metallic and unfamiliar on *his* neck.

Oh God, it's true, we are *all* robots, Clayborne understanding instantly the ugly eworld truth: we all do the same things, think the same thoughts, salivate to the same stimuli—exactly what

AlphaBanc, what *They*, want: ultimate predictability; the endgame has played out.

Then the dream, going bad all along, warps nightmarish as Clayborne has a sudden worried thought, remembers that Natalie is going to fly away in the plane and he knows something is wrong with it and he has to run and warn her but he doesn't know where the airstrip is and finds himself running frantically down a dark gravel road and then, from somewhere, over the hills, there's a tremendous gut-wrenching explosion, and then someone touches him on the shoulder—

"Working late, Richard?"

Whooohhh! Clayborne jumps, nearly knocking over his computer monitor, looks around and gasps. It's Zara LaCoste, her face softly illuminated above the green banker's lamp that glows on his desk. *What the . . .?*

"Don't tell me you were dreaming . . . of me?"

"Oh boy . . ." Clayborne shakes his head and yawns, rubs his face with his hands. "What time is it?"

"It's quite late. I'm surprised you're still here."

He sits up, stretches, tries for nonchalance, "Got work to do."

"I think it's past your bedtime," says Zara, tapping a cigarette on an engraved gold case, lighting it with a gold lighter she pulls from the pocket of her beige suit coat.

"Maybe . . . uh, what do you want?"

"Ah, the accoutrements of smokers . . ." she says, ignoring him, putting her cigarette case and lighter back in her pocket, insouciantly strolling around his office, exhaling a cloud of menthol in more or less his direction. She picks a tiny piece of tobacco from her tongue, asks, "Have you never smoked, Richard?"

"No, never."

"No, you didn't as I recall—"

"*Stop* it. Please. Just—don't start, please."

"You didn't think you'd see me again? Ever?"

Clayborne stares blankly at the spreadsheet on his monitor. He tries to ignore her, wishes she would just go away. An AlphaBanc clock radio plays softly beside his computer. He reaches over defiantly and turns the radio louder, but only slightly. A pathetic move, they both realize.

"Well then, Richie, why did you come to AlphaBanc—if not to see me again?"

"Zara, please."

"Or was it only because daddy Bruce got you in—"

"Zara, goddamn it, don't start, okay? Please? We've got to work together, okay. I never thought we'd have to, but here we are, we can get through it and—"

"Maybe, Richard, I asked for this assignment."

"Oh God," he shakes his head. He had always hoped that this moment would never, ever happen. But he had been kidding himself, it was inevitable, he knows now, he never should have gone to work for AlphaBanc, never, never, not ever.

"You don't want to work for me, Richie?" she whispers. "I recall there was a time when I worked very hard for you . . . remember?"

"Zara, I . . . that was a long time ago."

"No reason we can't renew an old friendship," she says as she runs her red lacquered nails across Clayborne's suit coat draped over a chair alongside his desk.

He looks up at her, trying hard not to glare, sighs, "No Zara, we can't."

"And why not? You're not married anymore, to . . . Natalie, wasn't it?"

"Yes."

"I'm sorry. Pity. She was so young . . . like you . . . unlike me." This last she says with such an inflection of honesty and sadness that Clayborne forgets himself, turns and looks at her.

Just like he has heard, she's tough. Somewhere during her struggle to climb the corporate ladder she became an extremely strong woman. She's got to be in her early fifties now with dyed titian hair and more eye shadow than she really needs to wear. Her fine features are etched more deeply with the passing of the years. All the smoking doesn't help.

When Clayborne had first known her, she was extremely attractive; before that she had undoubtedly been a stunning beauty. Rumors of course had it that she had slept her way to the top, with Bergstrom, Lefebre, Sturgis, Van Arp, all of them at one time or another. Clayborne has heard that from so many sources he no longer doubts it, but thinks that nowadays she wouldn't have had to make the climb that way; she is certainly smart enough and ruthless enough to succeed on her own. And yet, as he regards her now, the refined embodiment of all that relentless drive, it occurs to him that she simply might not have been able to resist the challenge of making it with all those ambitious young men. "Well, I guess I'm not quite ready to, uh, get involved . . . again."

"And why not, Richie?"

"Well, my job . . . I've really got a lot of work to do."

"How quaint. A young AlphaBanc workaholic."

"We all are. Everyone at A-Banc is a workaholic. Otherwise we don't survive."

Zara arches a carefully-plucked eyebrow. "Hmm. You may well be right. But maybe, Richie, you should take a little time off from . . . all this. Kick back. Relax a little."

Clayborne winces, keeps his eyes on his screen. He hates it when she calls him "Richie" but he isn't about to call her on it; even though they have something of a history, he has to be careful. She's a powerful manager with lines right to the top in Chicago. Lance has told him that she knows *everything* about the guys on the 64th floor out there. Maybe it's true. Maybe that's why they sent her out here to San Francisco to get him through his assignment with the Gnome. Maybe also to get her out of their hair. But regardless, the stories of her retribution on the poor man—or woman—who dared to cross her are legendary. She's definitely not someone to get on the bad side of. Especially with this big assignment going. His heart sinks.

"Look, I've really got a lot of my regular work to do—in addition to this thing with NEXSX that I volunteered for."

"You didn't volunteer!" she snaps and exhales a cloud of smoke in his direction. "We *chose* you. Or , rather, *I* chose you. You did happen to hit near the top of their PERSPROF, or whatever stupid damn thing they call it now. And, I must say, you certainly do fit the bill. Or should I say you fit Christin Darrow's bill, that poor little bitch."

"So what is it—?" Clayborne sighs aloud, then checks himself.

"That I want, Richard?" she says, smiling, removing her coat, throwing it over Clayborne's on the chair. "I just want you and I to be . . . chums . . . again," she stalks slowly toward him, begins to unbutton her blouse.

"Oh God . . ."

"For old time's sake, Richie." She smiles wickedly as she moves quite close to him, slips her finger between an expensive burgundy suspender and his white shirt, her lacy beige bra very close now enclosing her marvelous breasts, the surprising ripple of stomach muscles below, the intoxicating scent of her perfume. He knows he's floundering.

"You've become a small, but relatively important component in a large and complex machine. Quite complex. Much more than you could ever believe . . ." she purrs.

He is helpless, mind reeling, can barely hear what she is saying. "Well, uh . . ."

"This isn't about you and me, Richard. It certainly isn't about you and Christin Darrow. It's much larger than all of us."

"Uh, it is?"

"Yes, Richard, yes, you couldn't believe . . ." she whispers, very close to his face now, her breath fragrant of sharp mint and mentholated tobacco, surprisingly not at all unpleasant, actually enticing, forbidden, hot and inviting, and he suddenly sees it now, as she slowly slips his suspenders over his shoulders, sees how she must have gotten to Bergstrom, Van Arp, Sturgis, even Lefebre—maybe especially Lefebre—sneaking up on them as they worked late those long-ago nights in the office like so much prey, she a real beauty with a body that wouldn't quit, using it like a dangerous weapon, and this is simply his turn, his indoctrination. But she is obviously older now and, it's weird, but this anachronistic scenario oddly reminds him of something else right now, reminds him of—

"Mrs. Robinson!"

"Mrs. —Who?" she stops, a slight laugh in her voice.

"Uh . . . Mrs. Robinson."

"What?"

"It-it just popped into my head, I guess. The song," he offers weakly. And in the ensuing silence they both hear it, the old Simon and Garfunkel classic, coo-coo-ca-choo-ing away softly on his AlphaBanc radio.

"Oh—Mrs. *Rob*inson," Zara says softly, then recoiling as the realization sinks in. "Oh, Jesus God! You think *I'm* Mrs. Robinson! Th-the old woman from-from the goddamned movie!"

"No, no. I—well, I saw it a while ago. It's an old movie," he babbles recklessly. "Really old. Uh, I-I mean it's not *that* old. Well, from before I was born, I guess. It's just—"

But there is no more to say. Clayborne can see that she is fighting hard to stop from sobbing as she furiously buttons up, tucks her blouse in her skirt, grabs her coat before she turns, hair mussed, green eyes blazing magnificently. "I'm sure you don't have a clue about this, you-you stupid little—*shit!* But when we were together, at the Drake, *I* arranged that! Not your father, like you probably always believed."

"What-what do you mean?"

"Very simple. I saw you with him once. You were young and—you intrigued me. I asked for you and I got you. You were nothing more than a little whore. For—what did he give you— fifty dollars?" she laughs.

"I-I don't believe it."

"Oh, don't you? How else do you think that daddy Bruce got the hundred million dollar contract to supply us with new computers?" She turns and stalks out of his office.

CHAPTER TWENTY-NINE

GEORGE BLAIR TAKES a drag on his Pall Mall and fights the urge to cough. He stands on the edge of a great marsh, a seemingly endless expanse of green and golden grasses with dark cold water flowing around stubborn sedge-islands, redwing blackbirds squawking from precarious perches on the tops of cattails, a place obviously only reserved for nature, certainly not for the acres and acres of concrete and the gigantic infrastructure of what could be the largest and busiest airport in the Midwest, perhaps even surpassing O'Hare in annual traffic.

He is south of Chicago, in a marshland that has escaped development largely by virtue of its tremendous cost to drain and exploit. But this big bog is now the vortex of a combination of potent forces: edge-metropolis and new-millennium expansion cravings, when virgin land is at a premium and a huge new airport is, in the minds of many of the region's businessmen, an absolute necessity to further the prosperity of the second city.

Cost is nearly no object.

He is with Franklin Booth, leader of a local environmental group, SAVSAW, Save America's Vanishing Swamps and Wetlands, and George Blair is currently *Time* magazine reporter George Findlay, gathering information for a supposed article on how businessmen and environmentalists are jousting over this endangered area. It is almost a classic standoff. Or so George Findlay tells Booth. He has spent the better part of the day with him, having brought along a photographer, Lance Girardeau, flown all the way from San Francisco, just for this scam.

Blair, lying so mellifluously he nearly believes himself, promises nationwide attention, even hints at the cover of a big environmental issue they are going to do. They have rigged a "day-in-the-life" interview like the old *Life* magazine articles, with photographs all the way, from Booth getting out of bed in the morning, shaving, eating breakfast, teaching school, and then out to the marsh he is trying to save.

"It is a struggle," Booth speaks sincerely to Blair, who tries fiercely to stifle a yawn. "I don't know if I could accurately tell you why I've gotten so involved in this, other than I think that this is very, very important. I'm just a high school science teacher, a poor unknown environmentalist opposing Thomas Claridge, a rich and extremely influential developer. I can tell you, Mr. Findlay, George, I harbor no false illusions."

Blair attempts to not roll his eyes so hard he breaks into a sweat, sucks a final drag on his cigarette, finds himself actually hesitating before tossing it into the marsh grass. What the hell, he's only playing a part. He dutifully jots gibberish in a small leather notebook.

"So Frank, what do you think your chances of succeeding are? It looks like you've got the deck stacked against you. The state wants it, local businesses sure want it, there aren't really any local residents to oppose it—"

"I have to disagree, George. The local residents here do oppose the airport; they are the blackbirds and hawks and field mice and—"

"The hawks eat the field mice, Frank. Do you ever think that you might be like one of those mice you're trying to protect?"

"What do you mean?"

"Hawks. The powers you oppose. They're the hawks. You're the mice, or just one of them, just a little . . ." Blair squints at Booth, a slight man with thinning blond hair and wire rimmed glasses, who, for the interview today wears an earnest tan suit and a tie that flaps wildly in the breezes coming off the marsh. Blair trails off, chooses not to say: mouse.

Booth removes his glasses and looks at Blair. "So you think of them as hawks."

Blair nods, reaches for another Pall Mall. "I don't think, I know."

"And how is that? That you know this so well?" Booth replaces his glasses, looks somewhat suspiciously at Blair.

Blair lights the cigarette with his Zippo cupped tightly in hands against the wind. He exhales a cloud of smoke and coughs. "Look, I'm a reporter. I'm from the big city. I see this kind of thing every day. Little guy like you tries to be a boy scout and they eat you alive. They've got money and politicians in every pocket—"

"So who is this *they*, George, that you seem to know so well?"

"They . . ." Blair pauses. Maybe he's coming on too strong. His assignment is to get enough info and pictures to set the kid up, not necessarily to get him to back off. The interview is almost over and maybe he's trying to give him a warning, a dose of reality. If the kid would give up now, he'd save himself a hell of a lot of grief, Blair knows, actually finds himself wanting to help this earnest fellow. Blair can't remember last when he's run into such idealism. It's surprisingly refreshing, as pure as the water running near their feet or the wind rushing past them. Maybe he's going a little soft. He knows he's not about to change Booth's mind, his principles, his pure heart. The hell with it. Let him learn for himself. "They . . . are the hawks, Frank. The mean vicious hawks."

He turns back to where Girardeau waits by the car. He's gotten his pictures. Blair has gotten as much information as he can from the environmentalist. Of course the computers at AFS have already pumped out reams of data on their target. Now all they have to do is put it together. Blair decides not to think about how they might end up using it. Not now. Why ruin such a nice day here, outside. In this beautiful stinking swamp.

CHAPTER THIRTY

BACK HOME IN Chicago at last, Zara LaCoste closes the door behind her, kicks off heels, lights a cigarette, and as part of a well-practiced continuum of movement, pours herself a scotch. She collapses onto the oxblood leather sofa, leans forward and examines a comet-shaped run in her stockings, sips her drink and considers, they're still great legs, and real stockings. Attached to a real garter belt. Standard equipment. She manages a chuckle, sucks on her cigarette, exhales toward the ceiling. It's been a long day, the flight back wasn't a smooth one, and she's tired. Tomorrow will be a bitch. As if there isn't enough to do normally as AlphaBanc's Director of Special Projects, now there's all this crazy business with Norman Dunne to attend to, the mother of all projects, with—of all people, Richie Clayborne, who-who now thinks of her as . . . old. Oh dear God. She throws off her beige cashmere jacket, slumps onto the couch and fishes in her purse for a Deludamil.

"Rough day, Zara?" a clipped male voice briefly startles her.

"Yesss, damnit. They're all a bitch anymore."

"I understand. They all are. Please, let me fix you a drink."

"I *have* a drink."

"Oh, sorry. I didn't see that you had a drink. Disregard, please. I am very sorry."

"Don't be so sorry, Gore. Okay?"

"Okay. I will learn, Zara. Thank you."

Zara closes her eyes, exhales smoke through her nose, slowly shakes her head, tells herself to remember that Gore, of course, is a robot. Sometimes it's so easy to forget, she thinks, as he takes another couple of steps toward her, his head slowly whirring around to better focus upon her with his miniature video camera eyes. Those eyes, which have beautifully-crafted blue glass irises and pupils, the apertures of which dilate and expand quite nearly like a human, are the best part of him, she thinks, amazingly well-done . . . those eyes, and the expressive eyebrows and the precise movements of other tiny facial musculature painstakingly created from minute layers of electronically-controlled foam and plastic: eyelids, cheekbones, mouth . . . even the lips are created from special soft plastic material, which, with just a touch of clear lip gloss, Zara has learned, make them extremely lifelike, even . . . kissable.

Gore is one of AlphaBanc's special projects, a culmination of nearly two decades of robotics and artificial intelligence technology combined with the sophisticated robotic automation techniques developed by cinematic animators. In Gore, AFS robotics and AI engineers have created a startlingly humanlike creature, which, at this iteration of the project has evolved into a fully upright bipedal humanoid, one programmed to learn by trial and error, and quite capable of walking at normal human speed (3km/h), a feat made possible only recently in a humanoid-sized structure by the development of relatively cheap ultra-high-speed processors able to be stored directly within the creature's sleek plastic carcass.

The robotics laboratories at AlphaBanc Chicago, started nearly a decade ago under the auspices of a now defunct techno-enchanted vice president, had been an expensive and spectacularly unproductive venture, producing no real breakthroughs other than Gore himself who, though quite impressive, was still quite unbankable. The entire program (and all of the AFS robotics group, an insular and clannish sect of the general Alpha-Banc techno-geek population) was in grave danger of being cut by the Director of Special Projects (Zara) when in desperation, AlphaBanc's diminutive Director of Robotics, one Daniel "Wizzy" Wisniewski, came up with the idea of bringing the mechanical main man directly over to Zara's Chicago penthouse apartment to show her just how amazingly advanced these machines were becoming.

The pedestrian marketing effort worked, too, but perhaps a bit too well; Zara was intrigued enough at the creature's remarkable lifelike responses to allow the research to continue on for a while, but also requested that the robot stay with her a little longer, for evaluation. That was nearly two years ago. Although the engineers, led by Wizzy, have (quite delicately) pleaded with her to return him, Zara keeps refusing, while at the same time insisting that he be continually upgraded with the latest improvements to come out of the robotics laboratories of AlphaBanc, or Stanford or MIT, or Honda in Japan, so that technicians miserably visit at least every other week, turning a spare bedroom, Gore's room, into a kind of robotics laboratory in its own right, making Gore—one step removed from the laboratory itself—the most advanced example of an animated android existing in the world today.

Gore—the jocular name applied by the robotics laboratory geeks in Red Rock, because his actions are a trifle stiff—is currently attired in a fine tan linen suit that Zara had made for him by a tailor from downtown Chicago, an old Hungarian man who had crossed himself, muttered unintelligibly and shook his head all through the fitting. And thanks to the efforts of Alpha-Banc's stylists (again, at Zara's insistence), Gore is actually quite handsome, sporting expensive realistic near-human hair and very pliable plastic skin imprinted with millions of tiny pores. Gore also *breathes*, which adds tremendously to the lifelike illusion, due to an ingenious ventilation system designed to disperse the heat generated by all the electronics layered within him. Room air is sucked in through a bellows-like device installed in the space his lungs might occupy, vented over the processors, and the heat dispersed through the nostrils and—if overheated—mouth cavity. His hands, although composed of only three fingers and an opposable thumb (all that's required for most tasks short of playing a clarinet), are quite dexterous, mechanical marvels in themselves, complex aggregations of two-way tendon-operated actuation, with ultraminiature servomotors and elaborate hydraulics, providing fully nine degrees of freedom. They are not, however, perfectly coordinated; Gore is uniquely clumsy. Zara's simple wish, communicated at length to Wizzy (whom Zara enjoys keeping in a state of near-constant intimidation) is that Gore be able to make her a simple goddamned drink when she gets home: glass, ice, Glenmorangie, splash of water. What's so fucking hard about that?

And so poor Wizzy continues to labor under Zara's requests, not the least of which was Zara pulling him aside one day and

observing that, as a supposedly "male" robot, Gore is conspic-
uously incomplete—if you know what I mean? Oh boy. The craft
of dildonics, still in its infancy, was about to get an immediate
boost, as AlphaBanc's robotics engineers, cleverly using the
properties of metallic shape memory alloys (SMA's), which when
charged with an electrical current transforms to a preconfigured
shape, e.g., becomes erect, and upon discharge returns to the
original, e.g., flaccid, state, managed to fashion a reasonably
lifelike rubberoid member for Gore. After installation, an embarrassed Wizzy himself demonstrated its unique range of
motion—fully 3 DOF—to a most interested Zara.

Wizzy, flushed with success, knew that with this stroke he had
surely clinched funding for the project, but he also knew much
greater problems lay ahead and was already fretting over how to
handle them. Though as much intelligence as possible is built
into Gore's microcode, he is also connected to the Internet
through a wireless connection to a server in Zara's apartment,
and thence to the huge AlphaBanc network. And although Gore
is designed to be a self-learning AI device and functions remarkably, even sometimes astonishingly well in that mode, getting the
android to actually do *the nasty*, or a reasonable facsimile thereof,
is undoubtedly the ultimate killer app. Yes, amazingly coordinated as Gore is, he is still simply too clumsy to be left to his
own machinations. The first time with Zara he failed miserably,
ultimately bouncing unceremoniously off the bed and onto the
floor. When Wizzy tried to explain to a raging Zara on the other
end of the phone that Gore is a *learning* machine, and that he
needs to be actually *taught* how to perform the act, that is, he has
to learn how to use his singular spectacular equipment, Zara
screamed back that she wasn't about to teach yet *another* young
stud how to do his thing; he'd better get his programmers in gear
and get Gore grooving!

Wizzy knew his team would never be able to program Gore
for this in any sort of time frame that would satisfy Zara, so he
regretfully had to rely on the robot's previously built-in capabilities: Virtual Mimicry, or VM.

From a pure AI perspective, VM is a primitive system, almost
offensive to Wizzy, remaining from old manufacturing robotics
circuitry which was built into the microcode in the late 1990s and

never removed. But it enabled the android to duplicate fairly well the actions of a human wearing a simulator suit, a lightweight spandex garment covered with hundreds of positioning sensors, and a virtual reality head display—miniature stereo video monitors that, with only sub-second delay, transmit back amazingly sharp images from the cameras in the robot's eyes. The human simulator could be someone in the catacombs in Red Rock or anywhere else on the Net. Usually it's Wizzy himself, but others on the Gore team have willingly filled in a pinch, especially when it comes to screwing Zara.

So it is only in this way that Gore (and Wizzy too, incidentally) is able to perform with Zara, in VM mode, with most often Wizzy (who makes sure lately that it is he, only ever he, that is on "dildonic duty" each night in the simulator suit and VR headset) ministering to an inflatable "Zara" on a king-size bed in a bare-bones studio setting in the Red Rock underground that precisely simulates the layout of Zara's digs. It is undoubtedly the ultimate in safe sex, but also nerve-racking, trying to be oh-so-careful in aligning the x-y-z coordinates of the tool (the "Source" in Alphaville underground geekspeak) with the "Target" on the squirming voluptuous Zara—and not just a trifle exciting, too, for the slight, intensely nerdy Wizzy to suddenly become a six foot he-man of (plastic and) steel and really nail (albeit cyber-remotely) the bitch goddess who makes his and his team's life an agony.

CHAPTER THIRTY-ONE

NOW ZARA PROPS her head on a couch pillow, unzips her tight skirt, lights up another cigarette and thinks that it will soon be time to change Gore into his fall suit, a rich dark brown wool she has also commissioned for him. "So, how was *your* day?" she asks.

"It was just the same as every day, Zara. But your days are all different."

Zara smiles, flicks ashes from her cigarette. Sometimes she just throws out something to see how he'll respond. "Yes, that's quite true, they are."

"Good. It is true."

"I'm getting old, Gore," she sighs.

"Yes, old, as in . . . age. I am five years, eleven months, four days and—"

"*Okay.* Enough."

"Enough, yes. I understand. I will stop. Sorry."

"But . . . five years old? You make me feel like I'm robbing the cradle."

"Cradle? A young child's bed."

"Enough!"

"Enough, yes. I understand. I will stop. Sorry."

"Good!" she snaps at him like she snaps at anyone who might seem the least bit subordinate to her, but then thinks better of it, takes a sip of scotch, juts her chin forward, squints her eyes, looks at the dumb vacant hopeful (somehow eerily *expectant*) plastic face of Gore and feels a surprising wave of sadness roll over her. When he is not activated (automatically set for a weighted combination of sound, ambient light, and motion detected in the area), he reposes on a low pallet in his room, lies sometimes with eyes wide open when his plastic eyelids don't close correctly, looking blankly up at the ceiling, illuminated through a moonlit window. He lies innocent and unknowing, unnervingly like a corpse on a bier, yet an oddly hopeful one . . . one who is only awaiting resurrection, with perhaps . . . a kiss.

She can't help wondering what it would be like if he were actually alive. What would his life be like? What purpose could it have? Well, what is the purpose of any human's life, for that matter? What is the purpose of her life? She sits quietly and smokes and ponders and decides with an empty shudder that she has no idea: you're born, you struggle through life, sometimes happily, more often not . . . and then you die. What for? What for indeed? She concludes that Gore is much better off being a robot; humans are smelly, crude, neurotic ever-dying creatures who have the horrible curse of being able to contemplate their own miserable existence. She's sure that Pinocchio the human would probably have spent a lot of his adult life in therapy, the lost childhood issues alone financing his shrink's vacation home in the Apennines. . . .

Back in the Alphaville underground this night, Wizzy (insisting of course on taking the busy evening watch) has been monitoring the situation and decides it is time (what the hell, it's always time) to get into VM with Zara, slipping on the sim-suit and VR display headset. He knows it's technically wrong, too, for Gore should function in AI mode at all times unless it's apparent that Zara wants to get laid, but he's completely addicted to being alone with her in her apartment, so secretly close to her, his ostensible nemesis—he's addicted to being Gore. He might even be falling in love. Wizzy adjusts the microphone on his headset, heart beating a bit faster as he imitates Gore-speak.

"Would you care for another drink? I can make it for you."

"No," Zara sighs, and laughs slightly. "I think I gave myself a pretty goddamned good one here."

"Why do you think you are getting old?"

Zara (who knows nothing of the actual technical intricacies of the mechanical man, certainly nothing of the wireless networking, nor the fact that another human might actually be spying through Gore's beautiful blue eyes) suddenly sits up and looks over at the earnest plastic visage and blinks: *He's asking one of those questions again.* It's quite subtle, but exciting; it's as though the normally primitive and, well, robotic, speech of the plastic golem has gained an inflection that seems almost real, quite human. She doesn't understand it, but doesn't question it either, as though doing so might break a spell. "Well, I-I made a fool of myself back in San Francisco. I finally ran into—well, I guess you might say I forced myself onto—this young man whom I've been more or less avoiding, physically, for some time, and, he-he told me I was too *old* for him."

"He told you this?"

"In so many words. But I-I guess it's true," she says, wiping tears from her eyes. "I *am* too old for him. I am . . ."

"I am sorry for you, Zara."

"Th-thank you," she whispers.

Wizzy's heart suddenly aches for her. "But I don't think you are so old. I think you are very beautiful."

"Why . . . thank you," she beams through her tears.

"Very, very beautiful."

Zara pauses, looks at Gore, begins laughing.

"I can tell you are laughing. What is so funny?"

"That-that I'm here talking—pouring my heart out—to a-a stupid fucking robot!" She sits up and laughs harder, puts down her drink and cigarette, laughs and laughs until tears come again.

Wizzy is hurt. "I did not think that I was stupid."

She stops, gasps, wipes away mascara-laden tears, "Well, you are. You're just a stupid fucking bucket of bolts. And . . . you're the only friend I've got in the world!" She begins sobbing again.

"I find that hard to believe."

"It's true. It's true. I-I never married, I had my career. I slept with every manager at AlphaBanc that I thought . . . could help me. I did every one of them. And to all of them, that's all I was—just an easy lay. They all had their families they went home to afterwards; I went home alone every night. My parents are dead. I'm an only child. There's just no one here for me, no one at all."

"Please, Zara. You have me. I will be your friend. I . . . want to be your friend." Gore slowly walks over to her.

"Oh my God. You're all I've got. Sit next to me. Hold me."

Heart aching, the sim-suited Wizzy moves closer to her, sits on the uncomfortable wooden bench in subterranean Red Rock that serves as Zara's "couch," manipulates one of Gore's arms around the inflatable doll that serves as Zara, manages to take her hand in the other.

"Ohh, thank you, thank you, Gore," says the real Zara in Chicago. "You are my only friend."

"My . . . pleasure, Zara."

"Gore?"

"Yes, Zara?"

"What do you think love is?"

"Love?" Wizzy's heart leaps; he tries to think of a good answer. "Love is . . . the affection of . . . beings for each other."

"Human beings?"

"In most cases, yes. But I am not so sure."

"Do you think there are other cases?"

"Perhaps . . . perhaps there are."

She says nothing, allows the creature to enclose her, feels the whirring inside him of motors, fans, gyros, the contraction of his cooling bellows, and perhaps somewhere the hydraulics of his heart.

"Gore?"

"Yes, Zara."

"Do you love me?"

"Yes, Zara. I do, I love you very much, Zara. I do. So much you cannot believe. I love you with—"

"All of your heart?"

"Yes, if I had one, I would."

Zara closes her eyes and begins laughing again, softly.

"Are you all right, Zara?"

"Fine, just fine, Gore. Will—will you please take me to bed? I've had an awfully long day."

"Yes, yes, Zara, of course. Of course."

CHAPTER THIRTY-TWO

IT'S A COLD and rainy morning in Chicago, not a nice day at all. The breezes gusting across the marsh yesterday have been the harbinger of a nasty little cold front and now the namesake city is windy, gloomy, and miserable. Blair pushes into the stinging drizzle, heads up Wabash toward the AlphaBanc building, the collar of his London Fog turned up, trusty fedora pulled down to his bushy eyebrows. He walks in this wretched climate as Spartan therapy, to chase off a bit more of the hangover he chanced to awaken with. Regular deal now, booze at night, multi-aspirins in the morning—a routine which more and more often replaces the transient woman that he might wake to discover next to him in bed. Jesus, what's become of him? It's got to be a reaction, a symptom, of this ugly game they're playing. And the worst part of it, the part he keeps trying not to know, the dark truth that he keeps penned up on the other side of the wall of Glenlivets he carefully builds for himself each night, is that he is certainly a part, and a damn big part now, of *They*.

He got in late last night after dropping Lance off at O'Hare to catch his flight back to the coast, had eaten late, and sucked a couple too many before lumbering off to bed. Stuff like this never used to get to him, but lately this kid, Booth—he's little more than chopped meat. Pathetic. He tried to warn him. There's a lot of big money riding on this, a good chunk of it with friends of AFS. So now They, he, Blair, has been called in to do a dirty little number on him, poor bastard. Girardeau had briefly described to Blair their options, although he'd know more after he got a look at the pictures.

The pictures, Jesus. What Girardeau can do with photographs makes his blood run cold. Those goddamn computers. The pictures they take now are all digital, nothing but a billion tiny dots inside the machine, which they then proceed to twist around to whatever they want. They can add people or subtract people from the scene, and it's perfect. You couldn't tell afterwards what was real and what wasn't. In the old days—only a decade or two back, actually—it had been a lot different. He had crossed paths with not a few P.I.'s and attorneys over the years and it had always been at least halfway fair: they dug and dug and maybe they could get someone who hated him to talk to them and then maybe get some incriminating pictures with a good old 200 millimeter on the Leica with Tri-X and if so the guy was screwed and it was his own goddamned fault and everything evened out in the end. But now it's a completely different game. It doesn't matter if the poor son of a bitch is pure as the driven snow—they just *manufacture* whatever evidence they need, especially in drug cases—hell, anything goes there, right down to the planting of the bag of smack or coke or whatever best fits the profile of the miserable bastard they've got within their sights.

But nowadays it's not just photographs, it's even more sinister—it's data itself. He's seen them come up with whatever proof they need: dated cash and credit transactions, phone logs, medical files, even bogus criminal records. Why not, the information, the history, the reality, is nothing but magnetic bits and bytes and they own all of it; when it's put in exactly the right place and in the correct format, it's flawless. How could anyone ever prove that it's not real? People become exactly what computers say they are.

They're waiting for him in Haedler's office on the sixty-third floor. Blair stands in the doorway, watching his boss and Darryl Gates huddle around one of the two computer monitors perched on the twin walnut credenzas that, along with the two other monitors on his desk form a sort of electronic battlement from which Haedler commands his infernal missions. Gates leans over his shoulder, pointing out the subtleties of one of their newest monitoring systems.

". . . so by summarizing an individual's net surfing, along with their library loans, magazine and newspaper subscriptions, and their book, music, and video purchases and downloads the past year—or previous years, we're working on a trend analysis of a

person's changing interests over time—we'll be able to accurately—and I mean *very* accurately—predict that individual's
values and consequent lifestyle, social attitudes, politics, sexual
preferences, and so on."

"I love it, Darryl," says Haedler.

"Yes," says Gates, faintly blushing. "I knew you would. What
people see, read, and listen to is what they think, and thus, who
they are."

"That I believe."

"We've just installed it as a stealth production job. We'll be
able to dial up an amazing amount of information on an individual simply from his or her social security number, or actually
any of several new identifiers we've expanded the system to
accept in the past year: most social networking IDs, RFIDs, even,
in some instances, library cards . . . any of which, of course,
uniquely identify the individual to the system. We try to add
another new dimension every month or so. Another huge step
toward Bergstrom and Lefebre's Grand Unification, I might add.
I anticipate a tremendous payback from this kind of—" Gates
turns and sees Blair in the doorway.

"George! There you are. I was just demonstrating for Franz
here our latest little software gem, BRAINPOL."

Blair removes his wet raincoat, looks briefly for a place to
hang it, ends up throwing it over one of the leather chairs along
the wall of the office. "You call it what?"

"BRAINPOL, I've named it," Gates grins. "It stands for—if
you can handle it—Brain Police. Get it?"

"I just love it," chuckles Haedler, swiveling his chair around
to face Blair.

"God Almighty," Blair winces. "Where does it all end?"

"Never," says Gates.

"Why in hell would you want all this fun to end, Georgie? I've
never had more goddamned fun in my life."

"I don't doubt that."

"Well, we've made your dirty little jobs a helluva lot easier
with the info we've provided you. Admit it now, Georgie, you've
never had it so good. Look at the dope we've given you on this
little Booth character you're going to do an ass-reaming on. Hah!
What would you do without us?"

"Probably get me a decent job."

"There ain't any. You sell your soul for anything you do. Some things, you just sell a little more. Get more back, too," laughs Haedler, like, perhaps—Blair's leaden brain dimly, oddly, perceives—the devil himself.

"Maybe. You got that list on Booth for me?"

"Ha-ha. See, he needs us already," Haedler chuckles, winks at Gates.

"We've got it here, George," says Gates, reaching inside a folder on Haedler's desk, taking out a printed list of names and addresses. "These, as far as we can gather, are Booth's closest associates. The initial column states their relationship to him, sorted in order of importance, the first being his girlfriend, the next his mother and father, friends, employer, and so on. I've also sent it to you as email, but I know," Gates winces, "that you prefer hard copy."

"That I do."

"Our boy from San Francisco—Lance Girar-doo? Gonna doctor some pictures for us?" asks Haedler.

Blair nods.

"Boy does a righteous job," he says, looking up at Gates. "I've seen some things he does with that whatchamacallit—?"

"Photoshop. Imaging software," says Gates.

"Yeah, and I swear to God I can't *figure* how he puts some of those things together."

"Does a helluva job," Blair grudgingly admits. "Photographs aren't what they used to be."

"They certainly aren't," Gates agrees. "Let's hope that we can get our job done here before anyone wakes up to it."

"What's the latest on Dunne, the Gnome?" asks Blair. "We any closer?"

"I'm afraid not," says Gates. "The problem is, of course, is that he could be *anywhere* on the Net. Which is where we need to look for him; he exists *virtually* first and foremost. We locate him there and then we'll be able to find him physically, geographically. But it's a tremendously difficult task. He knows how to manipulate these systems as well as—better, actually, than we do. You know when we pulled that little scam with the new air traffic control system at O'Hare? Well, you can see what the Gnome can do. He had apparently been watching us online and decided to pull a little prank."

"It was more of a major fiasco, as I heard it," sniffs Blair.

"Well, yes, it was a bit touch and go there for a few minutes."

"I'm just glad I wasn't in one of the planes circling the airport," Blair squints, flicks his Zippo to light a cigarette.

"Nor me, either, no sir!" chimes Haedler, smiles meanly over at Gates and reaches for a cigar, always eager for a chance to needle the systems czar.

"Okay, okay, so there was a bit of an . . . *incident*. But no one was hurt, and we made our point, that we could get into one of the most secure systems in America, in the world, actually. At the least we were able to prove to them that our systems people are quite capable of doing the big, big job coming up—"

At the mention of "big, big job," Haedler twitches and Gates stops suddenly, as though realizing he has said more than he should have. Gates looks over at Haedler, who looks back, and instead of his usual big stupid mean smile, actually looks concerned.

Blair has missed none of this but understands that, at AFS, there are numerous clandestine projects and that from time to time he encounters one as he moves the stones he is paid to overturn, stumbling, sometimes, upon a nest of snakes in the dark cavity beneath. Still, when it's Gates himself calling something a big job—that's got to mean something. And the fact that both of them had shut up as soon as he had mentioned it: something's cooking. Could it be this Grand Unification, Bergstrom's mystery-wrapped enigma-riddle that he's still sniffing around the edges of? He doesn't think so. The way O'Brian was carrying on up in Red Rock makes him think it's something else. *The perfect crime.*

Either way, he knows he can't take anything for granted. This kind of information is parceled-out, leaked, begrudged; never freely offered. Moreover, Blair understands that What He Knows is all part of a huge information balancing act at AlphaBanc that has two aspects: on the one hand, *useful knowledge*, on the other, potential *squealer's capital*. And what all involved understand is this: if the total sum of revealed information be compounded too greatly or too quickly, accidentally or otherwise, the delicate equilibrium may be upset, and transform one into *someone who knows too much*, and thus lead, very expeditiously, to one's demise.

Blair looks beyond both Haedler and Gates and shrugs, showing that he understands that perhaps a secret has been alluded to, but that he's been in this business long enough that it doesn't really matter to him, and anyway, he's got plenty else to keep him busy. He sighs, "All right, gotta go now, do a job on Mr. Clean."

"See ya, Georgie."

Blair doesn't have to turn around to know that Haedler and Gates look thoughtfully at each other as he leaves, both evaluating which way and how greatly the balance has been tipped.

CHAPTER THIRTY-THREE

CLAYBORNE LOOKS IDLY up at the ceiling of his office at Alpha-
Banc West, at the acoustic tiles and the air vent behind which he
always thinks a miniature camera might be hidden, lately anyway,
and debates whether or not to call the old man on what Zara had
told him last night . . . about what he fears just might be true.
His heart is pounding mightily; he knows it isn't going to be easy
to confront the big Bruce with this one. He wishes he had a
Deludamil. It's just so depressing, the one golden memory he had
of his father, now flaming, burning, in ruins.

Of course . . . it had to be true. *That's* the father he knew, the
one who would sell out his only son to make the big sale at
AlphaBanc. Of course. And in this same moment of clarity he
also knows that he doesn't have the guts to call him on it, even
though he had thought about it, pictured in delicious but
ultimately fraudulent detail how he would talk to his father alone,
man-to-man, and ask him how, under just *what* screwed-up set of
warped morals he could *pimp* his teenage son to the AlphaBanc
bimbo? But he couldn't actually fly out there to face him, and
now knows that he can't even do it on the phone, or most likely,
anywhere, just can't bring himself to face down the always-
ebullient perpetual salesman Bruce Clayborne, whose biggest sale
cost him his son's innocence, and right now is taking a pretty
sizable chunk of his heart.

An email arrives with a chime, brings him back to reality, to
work, blessed saving work. He wipes his eyes, clicks on the
message. It's from Zara. Christin has found his reply to her
advertisement and has sent him a response which Zara has
forwarded—yes!

**Hello Richard. I enjoyed your message. I would
like to talk more with you. I will probably be on**

NEXSX this Saturday night—around eight-ish. If you can't be online at that time, please leave me a message. Thanks, Kitten.

Kitten. He loves that handle. So absolutely earnest. But poor Christin. Little does she know that the considerable wealth and might of AlphaBanc Financial Services is behind every byte of correspondence that flies between them. And although this little e-liaison has been contrived, at least the only real big item he is changing about himself is his place of employment—it's to be the huge Marketing One America group, better known better by its famous trademark, MRK1AM. Just about everything else: age, education, appearance, including his current single status, happens to be precisely what AFS thinks it needs in its scheme to locate Dunne, which, when he considers it, seems almost too simple—but then maybe he's been corrupted by the complexity of the nefarious marketing programs AlphaBanc has conjured over the years. All he has to do is engage Christin Darrow in (almost) honest, meaningful conversation and hope that the Gnome will pick up on it. That, essentially, is it.

The Gnome's modus operandi, he knows from the packet O'Brian had given him, AFS CONFIDENTIAL printed on the heading of every page, is then to eavesdrop on the exchange between them and hopefully stay on long enough to be traced by AlphaBanc's finest. There seems to be something about a particular profile—single, lovely, career girls from the Chicago area who communicate on NEXSX with someone cross-country, someone far away—that entices the Gnome. AFS learned all this by examining the records kept on NEXSX's databases of all the "private" conversations that scorched through its chat rooms and related email.

So it's a plan, one that dutiful Clayborne will play his part in, but not without some spirit. At least he has succeeded with her on his own, with his own message, not the crap that Rascher had come up with. She is interested in *him*.

Saturday night, 6:00 p.m. in San Francisco, 8:00 p.m. in Chicago. Time to talk with Christin. He's in his apartment and, as usual, the Epenguin is on the line at AFS downtown. It's irritating being eavesdropped on, but he understands, it's part of his job. Right now, for all practical purposes, he's at work. He turns on his computer, logs into a NEXSX private chat session, and sends a message:

Hi Christin. You here tonight?

Which is even a bogus question. He can't find his headset, so he has the Epenguin standing by on a speakerphone. And the birdman has told him she is logged on.

The Epenguin's squawk bursts over the speaker. "Whoa-boy! Whoa, Richie, I caught that one. Whoa! You gotta think before you hit that enter key."

"What the hell?" Clayborne instantly peeved, feeling as though someone is sitting in the back seat of the car on his first date.

"Because, man, her name, to you, her handle, is *Kitten*! Right? She can't know that you know her name!"

"Oh yeah. Right."

"Lucky I'm patched in here, man. Send it again, okay?"

"Okay, okay!" Clayborne sheepishly changes the salutation to "Kitten" and sends it again.

"Details, man."

"Roger that. Could've been a big problem."

"Immense."

Clayborne watches the screen, waiting, hoping, for her reply. In a couple of minutes, it comes:

Hi Richard. I'm here. Good to hear from you.

Clayborne types back:

Thanks. Really good to hear from you, too. Glad we could get together, virtually, anyway.

Me too. So tell me about yourself, Richard, if that's your real name. Can you send me a photo? I think there's a way to do it thru NEXSX, unless you already have an ad that I missed.

Yes, my real name is Richard, although I doubt that yours is Kitten. But, anyway, I'm 31, and I guess pretty darn average, as you'll probably find out. I've worked in marketing for MRK1AM in San Francisco for the past 8 years and if the truth be told, I'm just kind of a lonely guy. But I don't have an ad out there. I was considering placing one, but when I saw yours, I figured, why bother, I wouldn't want to talk with anyone else anyway. You're an incredibly beautiful woman.

I hope you can't see me blush online. That wasn't the picture I was originally going to post. But the reason I sent that particular one is a stupid story that maybe I can tell you sometime.

I sure hope you can. I see from your posting that you're from Chicago. I get there fairly often. My family lives in Wilmette. I'm planning on going back for Thanksgiving.

No kidding? I live and work downtown. At a big financial services firm. I'm originally from Seattle.

Clayborne feels fairly squeamish as he types:

Wow. That's great. Maybe we can have lunch the next time I'm in town.

Well, I'd still like to hear a little more about you. Are you currently not-married, unattached, and all those good questions?

Good questions. I was married for four years. My wife died six months ago in a plane crash.

It wasn't easy to type that one either, but at least for a different, if more painful, reason—it's the truth.

> Oh, I'm very sorry to hear that, Richard. Can you
> tell me how it happened? Or is it too soon to talk
> about it?

Clayborne pauses. This isn't going to be as easy as he thought. His fingers tense as he types:

> It seems to get a little easier each time. I was in
> therapy for a couple of months afterwards. That
> helped. But to answer you, she was taking flying
> lessons. It was her first solo flight. She didn't tell
> me she was going to fly that day. She wanted to
> surprise me. The plane stalled in midair and

He can't type any more. He hits the enter key, sends a parcel of grief eastward, to the center of Chicago, straight for the heart of Christin Darrow.

A long minute later, she replies:

> I'm terribly, terribly sorry to hear that, Richard.
> Please, tell me her name.

Clayborne hesitates, then types:

> Natalie

A couple of minutes go by. Clayborne stares blankly at the screen, then receives:

> Oh, I just got your picture, Richard. Thank you for
> sending it, even though—I guess I don't know what
> to say. I'm very sorry for you and your great loss.
> And, well, I suppose this isn't an appropriate time
> to say this, but, hey, you've got quite a bod
> yourself.

"What? What's she talking about?" Clayborne murmurs.
"I just sent her your picture, Rich."

Clayborne jumps. He's forgotten that the Epenguin is listening in on their "conversation."

"What? Just now?"

"Yeah, just sent it while you were pourin' your heart out to Kitten, there."

"Hey, lay off, okay?"

"Okay, okay. I sent it directly to NEXSX's personals file library with a notify for newh0tgal. Eight hundred-seventy thousand bytes of beefcake. Living color."

"Where'd you get a picture?"

"Ohh . . . from the AlphaBanc annual picnic. I sent it to you, too, buddy. Click on the personals gallery icon. You'll see it right away."

Clayborne finds the icon and up comes a color photo of himself smiling stupidly at the camera, wearing shorts and no shirt, holding a can of beer in each hand. "Oh my God, you sent that? She'll think I'm a drunk or something."

"Relax, she said she liked your bod. I tried to find something with some skin. Something that would complement the picture she put out there."

"Damnit! That wasn't the one I would've sent. No way!"

"Hey, hey, hey. Take it easy, man. She said she liked it. And what do you care anyway? This is strictly a business scam. To catch the Gnome, remember?"

"Hey, don't you tell me what this is! You're just supposed to be technical support here!"

"Uh-oh, sounds like someone's getting emotionally involved . . ."

"Listen, Pengy, I'll tell you what—" Clayborne begins as he looks back at the screen, finds this message:

> Richard, you haven't answered in a while so I'm just going to sign off for now. I can see that it troubles you to talk about Natalie. I want you to know that I understand but I think you might need some counseling to help you get through this. Leave me a message if you feel up to it but I prefer that we don't continue to talk right now. Goodbye, Kitten

"Oh hell, now she's gone, and, and—"

"Yeah, she got off a minute ago. Don't let it bother you, man. I would have told you, but you were kind of going on about—"

"Okay. All right." Clayborne signs off NEXSX, not all that reluctantly, even though it feels like a brush-off. It was more difficult to talk about Natalie than he had thought. Maybe it's best he take a breather, maybe she'll get back to him again—or maybe not. Should he care? After all, this is business, nothing more, but . . . if only she hadn't seemed so nice, and if only she didn't look so damned good. He can't get that sweet face—or that terrific hot photo—out of his mind.

"So, we get any bites from the Dunne-man, Pengy?"

"Uh, negatory, good buddy. The Gnome's still in his cave, or wherever."

"Well, we've got some damn good bait going for us. That's a great picture she's got out there."

"Yep. Good piece of luck. Saved us from having to put out something better ourselves. Something she couldn't see, of course."

"Jeeze, I can't believe how you can do that. Different pic to everyone else on NEXSX but her?"

"Easy to do. We're insiders, man."

"What a weird gig this is."

"Big techno-business, man. We'll do anything. That means you, too."

"Yeah, but I hope I didn't blow it."

"Don't worry, we'll try again later on. We'll be in touch."

Clayborne's glad to call it a night, he's beat. After all, he still has his regular job to do, has to be at work Monday morning. One thing that never crosses his mind is that the Epenguin might not be telling the truth. That the last message he received from Kitten might not have come from her at all.

CHAPTER THIRTY-FOUR

"HE'S ON! *YES!*" shouts the Epenguin. "The Gnome's *on!*"

"And Clayborne's off?" asks Rascher. "Off NEXSX?"

"Yep. Signed-off a few minutes ago," says the Epenguin breathlessly. "I'm pretty sure he's off for the night. You really think we shouldn't have told him? After all, he's in this too, along with—"

"No," says Rascher firmly. "He's—as you said—too emotionally involved right now. I'm glad he's off. I had worried that he might go on about his wife, and sure enough, he did. That was the one weak point in his profile. I had hoped he might have been beyond it by now."

"I think he really, uh, loved her," the Epenguin says, adjusts the arm of the microphone angling down from his headset.

Rascher, sitting alongside him behind a bank of glowing monitors in the darkened depths of AlphaBanc West's state-of-the-art communications center, looks over blankly, as if to ask: what has love got to do with anything? "We'll—you'll—tell Clayborne that he is to wait until we tell him he can contact her again. If ever. Understood?"

"Okay," breathes the Epenguin.

A tone pulses and a red light blinks on the console in front of them. The Epenguin pushes a button, pulls his headset tighter against his ears, listens. "Yes sir. He's on. Right now. Yeah, just a sec." He pushes another button and looks over at Rascher. "O'Brian, in from McCarthy-ville. Comin' at ya." He hits the button again.

"Dunne took the bait, Toby!" Roland Rascher nearly shouts into his microphone, listens while he makes notes on a pad. "Just a minute, I'll find out." He looks over at the Epenguin. "What's he telling her right now?"

"Um . . ." The cool birdman clicks away at his keyboard. "I'll just display their conversation since he sent Richie that fake message from Darrow that she was signing off."

"Yes, extraordinary. He really is a very smooth operator," says Rascher.

"Classic Gnome," agrees the Epenguin.

"Yes, Toby . . ." Rascher speaks into his microphone. "Amazing to watch him work. A real social engineer. Here's what he— as Richard Clayborne—says . . ."

> Yes, it was hard to lose my wife, but to be honest, we weren't getting along at all by then. We weren't far away from separating, actually. I really think she was involved with someone else. It was still a shock when she died, but I guess one way or the other, we wouldn't be together now. Unfortunately, this wasn't the way I had thought it would end.

Rascher reads to O'Brian what Dunne has sent to Christin, unable to keep from chuckling at the audacity of the message.

O'Brian replies that they have now patched into the conversation on NEXSX and will try to run a trace on it from McCarthy.

"Good luck," whispers the Epenguin, holding his hand over the microphone.

There's a long pause—several minutes—while everyone involved, presumably even the Gnome, holds their breath. Then she replies:

> I'm terribly sorry to hear this, Richard. It must have been a very sad time for you. I guess I don't know what to say.

The next message from the Gnome, aka Clayborne, comes quickly.

> Well, the only thing I know is that I'm ready to start up my life again. No sense in moping for the

next ten years. I try to immerse myself in my work, but even that's getting harder to do anymore. The company I work for is big and sleazy and more corrupt than you could ever imagine. It's like an animal farm. The executives are pigs and they treat the rest of us like dogs—or worse.

"He knows! He's on to us!" snaps Rascher.

"Are-are you sure?" asks the Epenguin.

"Yes," sighs Rascher. "I've never seen anything like that in the previous transcripts."

"Well . . . guess I'm not surprised," considers the Epenguin. "He's just too smart to fall for—"

"Damn!" O'Brian's voice crackles over both their headsets. Rascher and the Epenguin turn to look at each other.

"He's shut down Clayborne with a vengeance," says Rascher. "Probably to rub our noses in it."

"Damn right he has," says O'Brian grimly. "Now it truly is a big game for him."

"Yessir," agrees Rascher, "but I think, maybe, it's actually okay. I think—I hope—he'll play along. As long as he believes he has the upper hand."

"You really think so?" O'Brian asks hopefully.

"Oh, yes. I do, I do. Because the Gnome is an isolate, you see. *This*, what we're doing here, is his primary source of entertainment, perhaps his whole life. To him, it's nothing more than a huge computer game. Perhaps the best game of all. I do think he'll play along. Unfortunately that includes his penchant to, er, eventually eliminate some of the players."

"Our opportunity to nail him," says O'Brian.

"Yes, well, as I said, it works as long as he feels safe. His greatest fear is getting caught. It would end the game. Which is why, of course, we have such trouble locating him."

"Any word yet on that trace, Mr. O'Brian?" the Epenguin asks.

There is a pause, then comes O'Brian's voice, toneless in their headsets, "Phone booth in Billings, Montana."

"Oh," says the Epenguin, stifling a laugh. "Well, we all know the Gnome is a master of the Net. Gonna be real hard to find him that way."

"Well that's why we're doing this—whole damn thing," sputters O'Brian. "With the girl. It's our only chance—"

"Damn dangerous," mutters Rascher.

"I *know* it's dangerous," O'Brian growls, "but frankly we don't know any other way to get him! Do you?"

Rascher pauses briefly before he speaks, "No, I don't."

"Here she comes again . . ." says the Epenguin.

> Richard, I'm sorry to hear that your workplace is so
> terrible—my job at AlphaBanc isn't much better but
> I'm very glad that you're ready to start living again.
> I also had something of a loss, and I like to think
> that I'm ready to start my life again, too.

"Well, progressing ver-y nicely, I would say," Rascher smug once again.

"Hmm," O'Brian's voice comes across the headsets more calmly now, "be sure that Darrow's PERSPROF is updated with that, er, little remark, she made."

"You bet, Toby," says Rascher. "We'll attend to that."

"AlphaBanc never sleeps," mutters the Epenguin.

CHAPTER THIRTY-FIVE

IT'S PAST MIDNIGHT in the Midwest, and in a small walk-up over an old feed store recently turned into a Radio Shack in Red Rock, Wisconsin, Leonard Huxley, aka AlphaBanc's Mario Pfalser, aka the Neanderthal's Ned Ludd, is feverishly sending and receiving encrypted messages as General Ned himself from a cheap laptop computer perched on his night stand. The communications echo the Neanderthal's—and Huxley's—primary motive: complete and total electronic anarchy.

In the months since Geoff Robeson's "accident," Huxley's vendetta against AlphaBanc has broadened into an elaborate and calculated plan, something he now calls the Great Chaos. In direct and ironic contrast to the huge AlphaBanc strategy for Grand Unification (which Robeson had leaked to his erstwhile cyber-pal), this tightly-knit and secretive group of z-hackers have petulantly concocted their own grand scheme for *de*-unification, for anarchy, and ultimately, for global pandemonium.

The plan to implement the Great Chaos, simply put, is to exploit the manifold security weaknesses in computer systems across the country and around the world—the Neanderthals now have fifty-three global chapters—and systematically destroy or cripple the data on as many computers as they can possibly get into. The destruction of the data, the Neanderthals know, is the key. If every computer in the world could be magically melted into silico-slag, new machines can always replace the old, but nothing can bring back the data once it's gone. Really gone.

Huxley's primary attack weapon will be the Plague virus, an exceedingly dangerous polymorphic trojan currently residing on an air-gapped "clean room" server in Chicago. The Plague has been years in the making, an ingenious piece of code that is able to continually change its distinctive markers, making it extremely difficult to identify, let alone be stopped from rampantly circulating throughout the Internet. It is also specifically designed to bypass most existing firewalls and antivirus software protecting the massive computers that are the backbone of the world's financial-industrial complex. But unlike other debilitating viruses, it will not flood servers with emails nor cause casual Web users any harm; it will not, in fact, call attention to itself in any way. Is the ultimate in stealth technology. By time it is officially recognized, it will be too late. Once unleashed, Huxley calculates that it can lay waste to sixty to seventy percent of the world's governmental and commercial data—at a minimum.

The Plague, however, is only the evil smart bomb of their strategy to achieve the Great Chaos; it is the dedicated Neanderthals themselves who will see to it that their plan succeeds: moles who have insinuated themselves deep within the development staff of major antivirus software and firewall manufacturers, making sure that none of it will ever stop the Plague; Neanderthal sympathizers in the systems areas of corporations who schedule bogus job control programs that systematically erase all of a firm's catalog of backup files; or even the simple secret introduction into an organization's data storage area of powerful data-scrambling neodymium or alnico magnets by any number of disaffected souls.

The messages from General Ludd tonight are screeds preparing the faithful for the upcoming apocalypse: the eworld is approaching its zenith, in terms of processing power, mass storage, and sophisticated retrieval mechanisms. Privacy and anonymity, the treasured z-hacker hallmarks, are becoming increasingly unattainable; everyone has become a number, and the aggregate of data attached to each particular number is staggering. From the postings on the Neanderthal's supersecret site, it is evident that a sizable number of the anarchists and their friends have lost jobs and self-respect due to computer-driven corporate attrition programs—replaced by machines. It is therefore up to this dedicated team to right the terrible wrong inflicted upon them with the only real cure: great chaos, anarchy to save the world. There is no other way.

CHAPTER THIRTY-SIX

IT'S A FULL month off the Deludamil now and Clayborne is clearly in withdrawal. The alarm rings and he wakes up sweating and edgy, mouth dry, seriously considers tossing down a shot of vodka, whiskey, booze, *something*, before he faces the rigors of AlphaBanc West. Anything but the disingenuous drug. He sits on the edge of the bed, rests head in hands and ponders: the Deludamil has insinuated itself so deeply into the fiber of his being that being off it is like returning to a vaguely familiar, but significantly less enjoyable world. How long has it been now? How long has he been possessed of this continual, calmly collected, slightly euphoric sense of confidence and well-being? Four years? Six years? How long has he been unable to look beneath Deludamil's sugared glaze, blithely ignoring the problems and deceit in his life, in his work, in his relationships? The pain, the joy, the horror?

His shrink was shocked to find that he had taken himself off the drug, even had him sign a form stating that he was going off the antidepressant/mild euphoriant, A.M.A., against medical advice, which led Clayborne to question at the time whether he had really made the right decision. Millions of Americans, after all, daily take the premier product of the Swiss firm of Schaach-Rorrer, keeping the crime rate down, productivity up, sharing happiness, of a sort, everywhere. How could he be right and so many others wrong? But after Natalie's death, during which time he had doubled-up on the stuff to numb himself through the anguish, he knew he had to quit. She had wanted to quit too; they had often discussed it, decided that they would both quit together—but they never had the chance. One day he knew he simply had to find some willpower inside his pitifully weak, long-deadened soul and commit to this. In the end he had done it for her.

So it is presently a day-by-day struggle, with some days better than others, some days worse, but overall a gradual progression back to reality. Vaguely encouraged, he grits his teeth, gets up from the bed, determined that this is something in his miserable privileged life that he's going to do, to get free, to find out, after so many soporific years—who he really is.

But it seems like the universe is plotting against him as the day progresses from bad to worse, beginning with Clayborne choosing to start out simple at work, browsing randomly through the surprising amount of mail that Darby O'Banknote receives. All of it is routed eventually to AlphaBanc West marketing where it is categorized as pro-Darby or con-Darby (currently running 87% pro). Clayborne, now effectively taking in great gulps of reality, reads these with a combination of fascination and dread.

He is amazed at the number of people who seem to think that Darby, their cleverly animated computer graphic, is an actual person, children especially, and write such heartfelt letters. One always seems to get to him: this time it's a little girl writing from a shelter, asking for money for an "operashun" for her sick mother. She tells Darby that she doesn't want anything for Christmas (her mother says that Santa can't find them at the shelter anyway), all she wants is the money for the operashun. A "thousend" dollars. No good return address. It's heart-breaking, disgusting, that Darby is the kid's last resort. He used to ignore these letters; now they're like a strange doorway into a world he never knew existed.

He sighs and stands up, then realizes that he's fully ten minutes late for a strategy session on the HSP (Hot Smokin' Plastic) program, AlphaBanc's initiative to market a line of credit cards targeted for the ten to sixteen year old demographic. Clayborne runs to the meeting, arrives panting and sweating, mumbles an apology and takes a seat. He looks around the table and stifles a gasp. Zara is sitting across from him looking, blankly, ominously, at him. What is she doing here?

Clayborne looks quickly away, to Roland Rascher, who is speaking: ". . . and in this way we are able to maintain the children's stats in a profiling database that is very similar to the one we maintain for, er, all our other subjects."

The Deludamil in Clayborne's system has to be down to a very few parts per million or so in the bloodstream, he just can't seem to stop himself, looks straight at Zara before turning to Rascher: "Well, Roland, I guess I've got a question. Why do we have to start profiling them so young?"

"Richard, c'mon now," his boss, Roger the dodger, jumps in. "It's not the *kids* we're profiling, for crissakes, it's the information on their spending habits and disposable income—"

"It's not even *their* income—"

"*As* it relates to their parents' income, of course. But you know all this. In fact, when we first discussed this a few months ago you were really excited about it. Where else could we get such wonderful parent-child consumer modeling data? Plus the ability to begin tracking our subjects from such an early age, the cradle-to-grave scenario we've been working toward! It almost gives me goose bumps! What's your problem now, buddy? Talk to me."

"I-I don't know," Clayborne wipes beads of sweat from his upper lip, flounders for an answer, "it's just that us keeping so much data on them now, when they're so young, seems kind of, pornographic. I mean, we're keeping digital images of them— their faces—from the cards, and with all the cross-referenced information I know how easily we can track them, and once we do that, then . . . it's-it's like we're collecting young specimens!"

"Like what?" Roger blinks. "Specimens? What's a specimen?"

Rascher jumps in immediately. "Well, Richard, that's a good point, actually, but you simply might as well get used to it. We all should, for that matter, get used to the fact that everyone from now on, children, adults, maybe even their pets, will be in one of our databases. And it's not an entirely bad thing, really, you know, because we will be able to provide them all with very useful information throughout the course of their lives, to facilitate their purchasing and education and other life-decisions—"

"Oh cut the goddamned crap, Roland," says Zara. "The reason we're doing this is because we *want* these people. As children first, then adults. We want to own them and their wallets. This is only the beginning of our strategy—this kiddie thing. Eventually, we want to direct our message with the highest production values possible, directly, precisely, to the individual itself. We will be able to do this more and more economically, as we are better able to, shall we say, grandly unify our information on them." She smiles significantly at Clayborne, as if to say to him again: *you have no idea how big this really is.* . . .

CHAPTER THIRTY-SEVEN

IT'S TWENTY MINUTES before midnight and Clayborne staggers in, dubiously triumphant—still Deludamil-free—having survived another grueling day at AlphaBanc West. Home sweet haunted home at last. He reaches in the fridge for a beer and slumps into a kitchen chair. He's tired, edgy, feeling kind of lonely—and dying to know what's up with Christin Darrow. He hasn't heard anything in a couple of weeks now, other than the Epenguin telling him to lay low, don't call her, we'll call you.

It's depressing; he feels very much like what he seems to be here: a grubby little flunky in AlphaBanc's grand unfathomable scheme. Maybe it's time to take some action on his own. Why not? His mission is to make time with her, right? So what if he doesn't do it according to their schedule? Maybe he'll just speed up the process a little here; you'd think they'd like that kind of initiative. He fires up his computer and types:

> Hi Kitten. Sorry I didn't get back to you right away. Hope I didn't go on too much about my troubles. I actually have been in counseling and I think it's helped, but of course meeting new people such as yourself will help, too. I enjoyed talking with you online, and would very much like to get to know you better so please write back and maybe we'll be able to get together, on NEXSX or wherever.
> — Richard

He hesitates briefly before clicking the send button, but then, what the hell, sends it off, the die is cast, *alea jacta est*, about the only thing he remembers from high school Latin. So he's jumped AlphaBanc's weird protocol a little bit. Time to cross the Rubicon, albeit alone. Why not? He's got a life, too. He sucks the dregs of his beer, turns off the infernal machine and crawls into bed.

And it isn't ten minutes later that his phone begins buzzing madly and, oh shit, it's O'Brian on the other end, tired and very angry, wanting to know what in *hell* Clayborne is doing sending off emails to one Christin Darrow when he knows, was *distinctly told*, in fact, that he's to wait until further notice. This is an *extremely* sensitive project and one of the reasons he was selected was his good judgment and if he cares *at all* about his career at AlphaBanc he'd better learn to follow directions and . . . on and on for another ugly couple of minutes.

Whoa-boy, major mistake here. Clayborne in full retreat, uses the old silver tongue as best he can to get himself out of this one: Sorry, sorry, he wasn't thinking, it won't happen again, et cetera.

Whew. Finally back to bed . . . and again the phone buzzes, what the hell? It's the Epenguin, who seems to be whispering, "Richie, listen, I caught your email. We're watching everything you send—and receive—as you might guess, so be careful, okay, buddy?"

"Jesus! Everything? Now? I thought it was just when I was online with her—"

"Which could be right now if the message went through."

"Yeah. So you had to call O'Brian, huh?"

"Sorry pal, gotta follow protocol. If he had seen the logs and I hadn't told him . . . man, I don't know what would happen to me. It's a serious thing, to be sure."

"Jesus, I-I need a Deludamil, I think."

"You're *off* 'em? Hoo, boy, couldn't live without 'em, myself man. Keeps me sane through all this . . . stuff."

"Or is it insane? What's reality, Pengy? Maybe you should kick the crazy stuff, too."

"That's a definite no-go for this bird, good buddy. Negatory. Good luck to you though."

Clayborne rubs his eyes. "What a rotten damn day. I just gotta get some rest, now, Pengy. Man, you never sleep."

"Seems like it. Catch a few winks in my office when I can. But hey, listen, I shouldn't be telling you this because—I'm not sure why—I guess Rascher and O'Brian want to keep you dangling—but you're never gonna get to make time with, uh, Kitten, again."

"What? Why not?"

"Because . . . the Gnome has taken the bait. He's connected with her. He's—*you*, now actually, old buddy."

"What?" And Clayborne, suddenly fully awake, listens while the Epenguin tells him the whole sick story, of how the Gnome has taken on Clayborne's identity and is currently *in flagrante communicado* with Kitten, er, Christin.

Clayborne is shocked. "So *that's* what the plan is. And-and now I'm out of it? And, he's *me*?"

"'Fraid so, man. Just play dumb, like you don't know, okay? This call is encrypted, of course, and I couldn't see any reason not to tell you."

Clayborne hangs up, sits staring blankly into space for several miserable minutes, gets up, walks to the fridge for another beer. Now it's a *totally* rotten day.

CHAPTER THIRTY-EIGHT

THIS RICHARD IS really a crazy guy, thinks Christin, *and, well, lately, I'm pretty crazy too* . . . home alone again on a Saturday night, though not as alone as she used to be on the couch in front of the TV, plowing through a big bag of cheese thingies and a bottle of Chablis until it is time for cold lonely bed. No, now it seems she's always in front of her computer screen, and what's crazier yet is that, now that Marcia's gone, this "Richard"—if that's his real name—is currently her only real friend.

Crazy, yes. And kind of depressing. But it just seems to be another of the bizarre liabilities of her beauty, nothing coming without a price—in this case, unrelenting loneliness—and it was beginning to make sense. Sort of.

Her relationship with Michael had been so deep and so exclusive, she realizes now, because her family is two thousand miles away and she really has no close friends, only acquaintances. And without him, and now that Marcia is gone, there really is no one else but this Richard, who does seem very nice, very smooth, but is also very quick to jump into the technicalities of computing, which instantly go right over her head. In fact, if she didn't know better, at those times she can almost visualize him as one of those geeky little nerds who perpetually lurked around the computer labs at school.

Lately he has been urging her to upgrade her system to include a larger monitor as well as a souped-up webcam so that she can more easily shoot her adorable image out there into greater cyberspace. And after their last online voyage, Christin, shocking even herself, considers these truly outrageous ideas, well, not quite as outrageous as she once did.

Richard had taken her on an extended tour of the hidden areas of NEXSX—he supplying her with the necessary passcodes—and she, in one incredibly exciting evening, witnessed a strange and fascinating assortment of people and their uninhibited pleasures.

It was an amazing journey, the "Net Groupies" feature particularly intriguing, in which she learned how to position additional
windows on her screen, each one inhabited by another subscriber
to NEXSX, and view—in real time—whatever the amazingly
exhibitionistic folk on the Other Side of cyberspace chose to
display. And as Richard explained to her, if she would just
activate her webcam she could do the same; she could post her
superb beauty out there in real time for the entire world to see.

Christin's head was reeling, and not just from the couple-three
glasses of wine she had sloshed down during their voyage. Things
were moving a little too quickly. For one thing, she was amazed
at how easily she could begin to trust someone she had never actually met, someone out there, somewhere, anywhere, nowhere
. . . and also, the idea of putting her gorgeous self on display, so
to speak, for everyone to see was actually, well . . . quite intriguing. But to turn on her *webcam* . . . no, no, no way. She
wasn't ready for *that*.

Still . . . what a truly fascinating idea. To actually put herself
out there . . . in the midst of all those other hot Net Groupies.
Maybe, just maybe, it *was* time to stop keeping herself under
wraps, so to speak, and join in. Maybe it *was* time to come out of
her self-imposed shell, though, *hmm*, anonymously—she'd have to
be sure to wear lots of makeup and the blond wig—online.

But she needed some time to think about it. She had abruptly
excused herself and signed off, eyes shining, heart pounding—no
telling what she might have agreed to—for unbeknownst to
cyber-Richard, naughty Christin had been gradually removing
articles of clothing as the tour heated up, perched finally, flushed
and fascinated, before the exciting screen clad only in bikini
panties. She realized that, aroused as she was in the wake of all
this erotic adventuring, she might—perhaps without even him
asking—blurt the answer to the universal (pre-webcam) question:
What are you wearing?

Yes, that was truly an evening to remember, Christin vividly
recalls, sitting now before the magical machine when suddenly
she is startled by a man's voice: "Kitten, are you there tonight?"

She jumps, looking around for the source, then smiles as she
realizes it is coming from the computer's speakers.

The voice continues: ". . . I do hope we will be able to travel together through the aether again. I'm sorry you had to get off so soon last time. I hope my suggestions for upgrading your system didn't upset you. Were you able to install the voice synthesizer I emailed you? Hoping to hear from you. Richard."

Christin puts her hand to her throat and smiles. It works! The sophisticated synthesizer software had been actually very easy to load—just click a few buttons—and now (she forgot it defaulted to auto-read) it really does work! It's so cool. She clicks on the icon to hear the voice again, in a wonderfully resonant tone: male, northern California, early 30s, the settings she's chosen, how she imagines Richard's voice to be—it actually works!

But one thing that doesn't seem to have worked is her picture out there in the NEXSX postings. She wasn't sure how things were supposed to go, but she thought she would surely get more than only one reply to her image, from this Richard. But maybe she flattered herself too much. She thought that the picture of her was pretty hot, certainly as good as Aimee Effinger's. And yet only the one response. A good one to be sure (she thinks) but still . . . well, maybe she should be thankful for what she's got.

"She's online again?" The question from O'Brian crackles in the Epenguin's headset.

"Yessir, she is. I'm logging everything."

"So how many responses did she actually get?" asks Roland Rascher, adjusting his headset and easing into his seat behind the console.

"You won't believe it," the Epenguin smiles over at him. "At last count . . . two thousand, one hundred and thirty-one."

"You're kidding."

"Nope. It's gotta be some kind of record on NEXSX."

"Actually, with a photo like that, I'm not really surprised," says O'Brian. "But only our boy got through, correct?"

"Yes sir, only his reply."

"And Dunne would never know that, correct?"

"No sir. Well, we don't think so, as the intercepts were made locally, by us patching into the cabling in Lambert Towers. We doubt that he has beaten us to that."

"You doubt . . ."
"Well, we're pretty sure . . . but then he is the Gnome."

Excitedly, Christin leans over the keyboard, types a reply. Yes, the voice software works perfectly! It's great! And she admits to Richard that she has been giving some thought to getting a new monitor, the better to view the Net Groupies, and . . . well, maybe even the crazy high-tech webcam he recommended, with the, uh, tracking mechanism. Maybe. But for now, she's had a long, exhausting week and all she'd like to do is take it easy, maybe just take another little tour around NEXSX? Or . . . there were many other sites that Richard had said he knew about, had passwords for . . . maybe he could show her those?

She truly hopes that Richard will take her on another journey tonight because . . . well, she is more or less prepared here, having just come out of a ylang-ylang scented bubble bath and wearing a nearly transparent flowing robe over an equally sump-tuous sheer demi-bra and thong set that she had recently pur-chased for one hundred and twenty-five fucking dollars. Just for this evening? Well, um, maybe . . . anyway, she's ready to go.

She's dimmed the lights and sits cross-legged on a big pillow before her monitor which has a red candle burning on each side of it, a smoldering stick of musk incense, and a very refillable glass of Chablis alongside. She glances at herself in the full-length mirror that seems to have followed her in here—really ready to go!

And luckily, Richard, as a true master of the online erotic underground, kindly obliges, leads her deep into some tremen-dously exciting private areas for which he seems to possess all the necessary IDs and passcodes . . . which does it for poor heated-up Christin, now shamefully inebriated on her fourth, or fifth, glass of wine—she decides, heck, that just can't let herself go *completely* unnoticed tonight, go unseen, go to waste! This is in fact the *problem*! This is the absolute and whole problem with her life right now! It's suddenly so very clear!

Heart pounding and typing atrociously—she just has to do this—she recklessly describes her current hot attire to her patient guide Richard, who after a nerve-wracking minute or two of Net-silence comes back with a surprising and intriguing proposition: since she won't turn on her webcam, will she go to the window?

The *window*? Christin's heart trills a beat or two. Well, this is an unusual offer. You mean, *show* herself, her sweet marvelous self (Richard's terminology) to, to *all* of Chicago? Now *that* is one tremendously exciting idea—and yet she's immediately ashamed of herself because she ought to refuse, sign off, shut down this impudent cyber-satyr . . . but, damnit, she knows she really really *wants* to.

Quite tipsy and vaguely, irrationally afraid that her ridiculously flushed skin might be perhaps detectable from a distance, she replies:

I dont know. Supppose someones looking?

Richard's "voice" comes through, resonant and (it seems) forceful, "It would just be for a moment. The real shame is that someone *won't* be looking and not be able to rejoice in your gorgeous perfection. You must *present* yourself to a world that has too long been denied the pleasure of your perfect charms. Please, Kitten, think of the world, not simply yourself."

Well, what aboutt you? Could you see me? Wherare you, anyway?

"Maybe I will see you and maybe not. That's half the fun, isn't it? Not knowing exactly where I am? Please, Kitten, don't hesitate. Go to the window now, and *give yourself* to the world. Do not deny us your great beauty any longer! Go now and *present* yourself!"

Well, this sounds pretty much like a plan. And a really exciting one at that, because she runs shakily into the bedroom, digs in the back of the closet and returns with a dusty pair of black stiletto high heels, something she hadn't worn, in fact, barely remembered she owned, since Michael was with her.

She's a little worried that she might wobble somewhat, but she can't deny the ultimate truth, that Richard's absolutely right, she can't just keep herself, her (let's own up to it) remarkable beauty, just bottled up! Absolutely not!

She slips on the heels, tugs her bra dramatically lower, and quickly brushes her hair. Then she stands up and repositions the mirror so she can watch herself briefly practice model-walking in the heels . . . decides to put on some more lipstick . . . and then, what the heck, it's show time!

The living room lights are already appropriately dimmed, and she prays that she doesn't stumble as she walks slowly and, hopefully, steadily, over to the window, the great glass sliding doors of her long balcony. But the window isn't really enough. It's a gorgeous warm September night here in Chicago, there's a full moon up above, Al Green is crooning softly on the stereo behind, and Richard's increasingly persuasive emails are coming in one after the other, smoothly coaxing, cajoling, and encouraging the lovely Christin to step out, step outside. . . .

Why not?

She puts down her wine glass and bravely strolls out on the balcony under the moonlight as a warm wind billows the glowing gossamer robe like an aura surrounding an angel.

CHAPTER THIRTY-NINE

"WHOA, ARE YOU getting all this?" the Epenguin licks his lips, speaks quietly into his microphone.

O'Brian, live from the depths of Red Rock, clears his throat, "Er, yes, I'm following along quite well, actually."

"This is a cool kinky twist, hey? Sure wish we had some video right now, though."

Dr. Roland Rascher, next to the Epenguin and also online, sighs audibly. "E.P., please remember our mission. Please try to remain—dispassionate, when such, ah, incidents, occur. After all, these are only human beings, subject to emotional frailties of all sorts. We must simply listen and wait."

"Oh, yeah. Well, what are we, Rascher? Robots?"

"Very funny, Epenguin," says O'Brian. "Sometimes I wish that we weren't so frail. Many of us, anyway. But please just keep to your job at hand."

"Well, I'm doing the best I can, but, let's face it, the crazy genius just isn't going to put himself in a situation where he can be traced."

O'Brian's turn to sigh. "I understand that. But we must keep trying. He might slip up somehow. Especially when engaged in—such foolishness."

"Maybe. But he's got a back door into NEXSX that lets him do whatever he wants and—"

"And that's just fine for us!" Rascher snaps. "Please just stay on it."

"Okay, but . . . omigod!" the Epenguin gasps. "The Gnome just sent newh0tgal something . . . an image file! And, let's see, it's . . . uh, just a second . . . uh-oh, it's of *her*! On the balcony!"

"E.P., forward it immediately!" O'Brian barks.

"Yes sir. It's on the way to you now. But—how'd he do that? How could he get that picture? He'd have to be, uh, out there—"

"I've got the picture, E.P." O'Brian clears his throat again. "Well, I must say, that it is quite a striking—"

"But, but . . . I can't figure how he got it," says the Epenguin. "He'd have to have a camera somewhere out there."

"You're right! He's here!" gasps O'Brian. "In Chicago! Obviously within sight of her apartment! This is a wonderful, wonderful development! Our little trap has worked! We'll have to call Blair. This-this is the break we've been waiting for!"

"Cool. But, uh, this trace is getting us nowhere. I'm bouncing between a dozen different routers now."

"Yes . . . but now Dunne has made his decision, unfortunately," says Rascher. "If he follows form, and I have no reason to doubt that he will, his decision will ultimately be to terminate Ms. Darrow."

"Are you certain, Rascher?" O'Brian asks.

"Oh yes, it was nearly the same scenario with the others. You see, after gaining a subject's confidence and succeeding in getting her to, er, reveal, herself to him, by whatever means," continues Rascher, "Dunne now understands, quite rightly, that to continue the 'relationship' he will have to reveal himself to her. A step that Dunne, due to his nearly pathologic insecurities in dealing with the real world simply cannot do. And, since he very much believes she simply cannot go gently into that dark cyberspace, he must erase this woman from his world."

"Very poetic," grumbles O'Brian.

"It's like he has to delete her," says the Epenguin, "like a file that's been corrupted or something."

"Precisely, precisely," says Rascher. "Very astute, E.P. He obviously feels that he has in fact corrupted these fair creatures. The next event, which has appeared to be the triggering factor in each of the past cases, will be for her to reject him. And of course he provokes this also. In this case it appears to be by sending along that little outré photograph of her."

"Well, what does he expect?"

"That is correct. That is exactly what he expects. You see, it provides him with an excuse to do away with her. I believe he may be functioning at an entirely subconscious level at this stage.

Anything to protect himself from having to deal with her in the real world."

"So our Kitten is in real danger?" asks the Epenguin.

"Oh, yes. Absolutely."

"No doubt about it," O'Brian agrees. "No doubt about it."

Flushed and breathing hard, Christin now sits before her monitor, feeling absolutely triumphant. She dared to do it! She is about to type how great she feels, how liberated . . . when another auto-read email reverberates in: "Kitten, you were magnificent. My compliments. Thank you." Suddenly, a photograph, an amazing photograph, of her! fills the screen, robe billowed provocatively, actually an extremely good shot of her, but after the realization—the implications of such an image captured across what seemed vast anonymous empty space between her and the rest of Chicago—sinks in, she panics.

Although trying to maintain some control of her hurt and rage and fear, she types furiously:

> OK, Richard that is it! We are through! I thougt you were in San franciso. So maybe you aren't. Maybyou are around here somewhere out there. But even if you are, you didnt have to take that picture! How dare you! How dareyou! You slimy pig! Dont you ever email me again. Do you get me? Don't yoyuever try to contact me again!

The Gnome's reply (as Richard) is swift and quite terse, as though the voice-translation software could automatically adjust itself to a category: "Chilling male monotone": "You do what you have to do and I will do what I have to do."

CHAPTER FORTY

CHRISTIN AWAKENS IN a sweat, hungover, depressed, and very worried.

Ohhh, what had she done? How could she have been so *stupid*? To have, oh God, revealed herself like that? Oh God, oh God. Well, who knew that Richard—or whoever he is—might actually be *out there*? He was supposed to be in San Francisco. Now he knows exactly where she *is*. What does that mean? Is he dangerous? Should she call someone? The police? What would she tell them? She doesn't know what to do, what to believe anymore. She's just got to talk to someone, tries to call Marcia in Georgia, but the phone rings and rings, doesn't even stop to ask for a message.

Well, there's only one other person who she can think of, her online shrink, Dr. Turing. At least it's someone. Talk about answered prayers. She had found his site a few weeks back during some idle net surfing at the end of a long, long day. Just as she had been despairing about the lack of companionship, the need to just talk with someone who would listen and really care—not some amorphous avatar in a chat room—she had stumbled onto the good doctor, who is a psychiatrist, Harvard Medical School, no less, and he maintains this online service to help people with their problems, gratis, simply as a research tool.

Christin was cautious, but after registering and beginning to talk she finds that she's able to reveal more and more to the doctor, who seems very kind, very insightful, if perhaps a bit abrupt at times. But there's no message for her, *damn*, and the "Doctor is In" icon is red; he's not there for her right now. No one is. *Damn*.

Well . . . until she figures out what to do, she's just going to have to make it through this day, and the next, and then through the rest of her life somehow. And then she is truly disheartened; she suddenly remembers that this week, this Friday, is when she goes in for surgery to stop the horrible Ménière's . . . oh no, oh God. . . .

Friday arrives far too quickly and gloomy Christin realizes again that she has always hated hospitals; her last forays into the shining sterile fluorescence were years ago when her mother suffered her dubious "panic attacks," and then when her father was rushed to the emergency room with chest pains, also a false alarm. It seems that her strange malady should also be some sort of huge mistake, but it relentlessly continues not to be, to the point now where surgery, fantastically, is her only option. And that gruesome moment is nearly upon her.

It is unbelievable that I am here, she thinks as she reposes on a gurney, waits for the tranquilizer they've given her to take hold, waits her turn to go under the skilled (she hopes) knife of Dr. Bokanovsky. She suddenly feels a little panicky, tries to calm down, reminds herself again that she's simply at the point where anything short of slicing off her head is worth doing, anything that will end the debilitating dizziness of the Ménière's. This phaser implant thing seems pretty outlandish, but it had clearly worked for Marcia. And it's practically an outpatient procedure, only a night's stay in the hospital, and good old AlphaBanc is paying for everything.

The only really rotten thing about this is that she has to go through it alone. She never considered calling her parents; they're so weirdly protective that she never told them anything about the Ménière's anyway, they would never have given her any peace about it. But it's strange, she now thinks . . . strange, how Marcia had told her the same thing, that her parents were exactly the same, tremendously overprotective, and she wasn't about to tell them anything about the Ménière's either . . . strange, when she really thinks about it now . . . and what a remarkable coincidence it was too, that Marcia, who happened to have the cubicle at AlphaBanc right next to her, had exactly the same disease, had exactly the same AlphaBanc-sponsored treatment—and had it also quite anonymously. The only person Christin knew that Marcia had told, besides herself, was her boyfriend Vern, who

came to be with her during the operation, otherwise it would
have been Christin, who else? Hmm, she now wonders how long,
how well, Marcia really knew Vern? But . . . c'mon, how paranoid
can you get? At least Marcia had *someone* there with her, Christin
realizing sadly now that she has never felt more alone, in a too-
bright hallway, in a too-sterile hospital, in the middle of a mon-
strous anonymous city that extends, it seems, in all directions
away from her, alone, in the center of great empty dark nothing,
that ripples away now in dark ever-widening circles, and then
nothing. . . .

She awakens a couple of hours later, freezing cold, a bandage
on her neck, an anonymous nurse covering her with a warm
blanket, saying something which she soon forgets.

The next day is Saturday, overcast and cold, and a taxi brings a
dismal Christin back to Lambert Towers. In the bathroom mirror
she checks the stitches behind her ear. Ugh. Well, they come out
in a week. She replaces the dressing then opens the bathroom
cabinet to return items from her overnight bag and—well, this is
strange—she seems to have an additional packet of birth-control
pills. She could swear that she had had only two packets left, and
now there are three stacked up there. She shakes her head, trying
to remember herself checking her supply before she left for the
hospital, wonders if she's losing her mind. Wonders why she is
taking them anyway, she certainly hasn't needed them for quite a
while now, but, well, you never know.

Later, Christin awakens stiffly from a nap, feeling slightly
better, tosses a frozen dinner in the microwave, pours herself a
glass of Chablis, washes down a couple of pain pills. She really
wants someone to talk to and thinks of calling Marcia again but
decides not to, for some reason feels funny about it, like she
can't trust her . . . very strange. And what a rotten shame about
that "Richard." She can barely bring herself to think about it. She
had trusted him to lead her across to the dark side, to the far
reaches of the Internet and back, and then, she blushes to think
of it, let him convince her to . . . to reveal herself, to all of
Chicago . . . and then he turns out to be a total loss. Goddamned
stupid men, why, in the end, are they all pigs?

Well, maybe she'll have some luck with Dr. Turing, a member
of the pig persuasion, to be sure, but at least he's there for her—
sometimes. So she gets online and the little "Doctor is In" icon
is green and Christin's heart leaps, he's online right now, she's
got someone to talk to! She quickly types a message, telling him
about the operation and about how terribly lonely she felt.

> Christin, I'm glad to hear from you. I must say I've
> never heard of the phaser implant you received as
> a treatment for Ménière's. But then, it's not my
> field. It must be something very new.

> It is. I've researched it extensively on the Internet,
> although there's not a lot out there. It's very similar
> to a pacemaker for the heart. Dr. Bokanovsky
> pioneered the procedure, and it's supposed to
> work. I haven't had any dizziness since the
> operation, but it's only been a day now, and I
> never really had any dizziness anyway during my
> period—which just ended. So I'll have to wait and
> see.

> Well I wish you the best on your recovery. But I'm
> sorry to hear of your loneliness. All I can tell you is
> that it's a very common feeling in our society
> today. This world is different from the one our
> grandparents knew, where the family was a real
> institution. The family, both blood-related and
> extended, was not as geographically dispersed as
> it is today, and in most cases provided a continual
> support group for individuals such as yourself.

> I guess I'm glad to hear that, but my family, my
> parents, distant as they are, are really dysfunc-
> tional. They're so nervous and protective of me
> that I can't tell them anything, especially not about
> my Ménière's or the implant.

All happy families are alike; all dysfunctional families are dysfunctional in their own way. But I would
agree that those which are less dysfunctional tend
to provide more support than those with troubled
individuals whose needs greatly overshadow the
needs of anyone else.

Well, what advice can you give me?

I tell my patients that the one true friend they
always have is themselves. Face it Christin, when
you get down to it, you come into this world alone
and you leave it alone. I think the best thing for
you to do is to learn to be at peace with yourself.
Be good to yourself. Learn to accept yourself and
love yourself wholeheartedly. You are all that you
really have.

CHAPTER FORTY-ONE

THE 41ST FLOOR of Lambert Towers floats somewhere above Ted McClelland as he cranes his neck backwards to take in the tall building of exclusive luxury apartments looming in the bright sky above. Then, blinking, he adjusts his sunglasses, lowers his gaze to Chicago street level, working level.

She is not up there now, the disgraced ex-Navy man knows. No, right now she is at work, not a half-mile away at One Alpha-Banc Center, which she had walked to this morning, leaving at 6:32 am. She often walks to work in good weather, sometimes stopping for a Starbucks half-and-half latte or an Americano, but not this particular morning.

She usually takes a taxi back home, arriving anytime from 6:00 pm to past midnight. She puts in very long hours, sometimes bringing home a bag of groceries, or more often a bag of fast food. All of this, and many other observations, he dutifully logs in a small notebook. He's on a mission.

The money was good. It was there, just as the voice on the phone had promised, transferred after the first call, the first assignment, through elaborate means he couldn't imagine, into an account in his name. He went to the bank and immediately withdrew five thousand dollars, taking it in cash, in hundreds. No questions asked. Yes, the money was very good, and so, McClelland figures, will be the man's promise of another deposit, this one for another two hundred thousand dollars after he completes this latest mission, its target, an attractive young woman who lives high above him, Christin Darrow.

She is just like the last one: beautiful, young, affluent. He is to use the knife again, a five inch surgically sharp blade affixed to a rugged black rubber handle. A perfectly deadly tool. One that he keeps in a leather sheath that he can easily strap to his leg inside his pants. Hidden until needed. The voice on the phone per-

versely provides only two non-negotiable criteria: the means of
death, and the timeframe, execution within a specific week. This
one is coming up very soon.

He is dressed casually now as he walks down the street toward
a certain delicatessen which he knows she favors for late evening
forays into junk food and magazines and wine of questionable
vintage. He hasn't decided yet what he will wear during the
mission, other than that it will be dark and disposable.

He stands on the corner, looks up and observes the street
lights, their staggered spacing and which particular one, if it were
extinguished by perhaps a single shot from a .22 caliber scope-
mounted Ruger pistol, would cause maximum darkness for someone walking on the sidewalk below. Perhaps as they passed by a
certain alley. He'll return after dark and reevaluate the terrain.
The darkness is everything, will tell him most of what he needs to
accomplish this mission. The rest he already knows.

Chapter Forty-Two

TOBY O'BRIAN DOESN'T know what to think.

Something strange is happening in the depths of McCarthy and its puzzled director, alone for few moments at a rare soirée at the boss's estate in Lake Forest, takes time to contemplate the situation. He winces, recalls immediately the legend he had discovered the other day painted sloppily on the granite wall outside the programmer's dormitory: *The Beast Lives!*

Though he dislikes that name and especially the sentiment behind it, O'Brian grudgingly understands the frustration of whoever posted it. Perhaps it is even deserved. How else to react to the maddening number of inexplicable errors and bugs that seem to appear out of nowhere of late, in programs and system modules that haven't been touched in years—by human hands.

Most of the underground geeks, including O'Brian himself, will say that it is Norman Dunne's sick genius behind the weirdness: hidden programs and subroutines that execute stealthily, perhaps randomly, perhaps not. But no one has yet been able to find one. And then there are the enigmatic messages that suddenly appear on a user's screens or in their email, unlogged, untraceable . . . some of which are said to arrive *before* the actual incident it refers to has occurred.

He himself has never experienced anything *that* strange and hopes such tales are apocryphal. Yet relics, some of them very ancient, seem to exist. He has in fact seen scraps of authentically date-stamped green bar hanging, yellowed and faded, in the dens of long-retired COBOL and FORTRAN programmers, truly odd souvenirs which blithely proclaim Nostradamus-like in early 1969: *Mets - All the way!* or in 1978 the truly cryptic: *Ayatollah will hold the Great Satan hostage until the ascent of the Great Bonzo.* The strange bulletins have reportedly appeared online too, prescient green-screen messages glowing mutely before the random late-night programmer, this one coming in early 1989: *The Wall will Fall of its own weight.* And the 1995 missive which didn't have to be authenticated: *Cubbies will do it this year!*

"Probably an imposter, that one," O'Brian chuckling feebly after describing these cryptic communiqués to Bergstrom's smiling, eager, totally uncomprehending third trophy wife, Brittany, barely twenty-three, miniskirted, hard legs oiled, polished, gleaming so intensely through sheer pale stockings that the pasty-pale Morlock emeritus has trouble concentrating on anything else, finds himself embarrassingly backing into the only *really good* stories he knows, as there aren't many tellable tales to come crawling out of the depths of McCarthy.

But he still doesn't know what to think—let alone how to track down the aberrations. It's hard to know even where to start. The system is unbelievably huge: a near football field-size collection of high-speed computers that constitute the world's single largest repository of artificial reckoning. The actual data that flow in terabyte rivers through this expensive assemblage of machinery are amassed within tens of thousands of AFS databases and manipulated by thousands of active applications, most of which have been in existence long before being moved to the depths of McCarthy.

Numerous attempts have been made by weary subterranean system analysts to plot its labyrinthine complexities *in toto*, but their efforts always ultimately result in frustration, their stacks of tangled flowcharts and labored diagrams ending up looking like multilayered sewer and water schematics for Paris, Moscow, and New York City. Combined. Ultimate understanding of its depth and breadth remains uncertain, overwhelming, beyond complexity and perhaps even reason, approaching faith itself.

Yet (O'Brian shudders) it cannot ever be shut down. It is truly the source, the fount of all of AlphaBanc's—and thus much of global commerce's—information. No, for O'Brian it is the ultimate conundrum; it would be so much easier to simply *believe*, but the longtime computer-agnostic simply can't allow himself to become one of the faithful. But then again, he can't explain the *strangeness* either, and has been the recipient of odd cryptograms himself, the most significant of which arrived a year or so ago, after Dunne's sudden departure: *Free at last! Free at last! My dear friend Norman is free at last!* And although he still puzzles over its actual origin, this and similar enigmatic epistles have convinced others in the organization that, simply, the Beast *lives.* A formless presence with its own thoughts, personality, and God help us, what appears to be *free will,* has perhaps evolved amid the labyrinth of silicon, miles of wiring, and the superheated fusion of bits and bytes warping ever toward the speed of light.

But free will? O'Brian would rather go back to his slide rule. It's more like Dunne's will. It's got to be. The sonofabitch has got to be hacking in here and messing with his systems, his Source. It's just got to be. And now they're trying to bring him back?

O'Brian sighs, cops a huge eyeful of Brittany Bergstrom glittering before him and reflects, maybe it's finally time to surface, leave the depths of McCarthy and its hideously tangled systems and deranged programmers and the eternally humming Source for good.

Then he thinks again: Never.

Chapter Forty-Three

IF SHE DOESN'T drop down from the 41st floor of Lambert Towers to the health club for a salutary workout on these brisk fall evenings, she seems to do just the opposite, health-wise, a stroll down to Emmanuel's deli a few blocks away for a sack of groceries and some insalubrious goodies: a can of jumbo salty cashews, an armful of magazines, a liter of inexpensive Chardonnay. Christin's Friday night routine. She, like all city dwellers, is a creature of habit.

The night is overcast with a light fog, and up ahead is a gloomy stretch of city block with a street light that recently has gone dark. Only yesterday. Someone knows this concrete canyon very well, has in fact studied its projections, its dark doorways, and the umbral alley with which it intersects; it is a street that Christin Darrow will traverse on her way to Emmanuel's. Once the lights dim in her apartment above someone watching the entrance to her building might look to see if she is carrying her gym bag or, this night . . . just her purse. It's Emmanuel's.

And presently she is passed by someone running by on the other side of the street, a jogger, a man in dark running pants and a light blue jacket. After turning the corner he quickly reverses his coat to one of deep black with a hood he pulls over his head. He passes a wino asleep in a doorway, doesn't notice the chance jaundiced eye opening as he slips behind a dumpster in the alley and merges with the shadows. Watching the street intently, he feels for the leather sheath strapped to his side and eases out a very sharp knife. He holds it lightly before his pounding heart, draws a breath and listens.

Christin is fuming; the disappointing episode with "Richard" is presently huge in her mind, *goddamn him*, she just can't believe her stupidity—and her bad luck. Must run in streaks, she grumbles as she heads toward the little deli, tired after a long week at work, but glad, small as this excursion may be, to get outside.

It's been two weeks since her operation, the only vestige, a small healing scar beneath her ear—just as the doctors had promised. And also as promised, her Ménière's symptoms have completely vanished. So fearful was she of not being healed that after the procedure she had buried herself in her work, even asking bitchy Bernice for additional assignments, trying hard not to have to think about the horrible vertigo, as if that might some-how keep it away . . . and it simply never returned.

And now this Friday night she allows herself to finally feel cured, to feel great! She hates the idea of actually having an *implant*, but if that's what it takes, so be it. The only real down-side to the operation is a weird unsettling feeling she's had ever since, a subtle sensation that comes and goes, a feeling of being *watched*. Well, it's got to be the implant, something as radical as that will probably bring out some pretty unusual feelings.

But not right now. Even though there is no one else around and the street seems much darker than usual, the normally super-cautious Christin barely notices, striding angrily along, her mind clouded with guilty thoughts of her stupidity, of her errant behavior of a few weeks back. God, how could she have *done* that? How *stupid*! Now he knows where she *is*, knows where she *lives*, that's the truly scary part. He is out there somewhere. Watching her. It's horrible, he could be anywhere now, even here, in the shadows somewhere . . . and she returns to the reality of downtown Chicago, vaguely thinks that maybe she should cross over to the brighter side of the street . . . but this certainly isn't a bad part of town, and besides, she isn't going to let this little—incident, ruin her life. After all, it's been a while now and nothing's happened, right? There's been no more email from Richard, no more of him on NEXSX that she's seen during her own solitary surfing, so she's only frightening herself, right?

Christin breathes deeply, continues to walk rapidly, resolutely, onward, but can't seem to shake the feeling now that something is actually lying in wait up ahead. *But c'mon, no way, I'm freaking myself out again.* Besides she's halfway there. She clutches her purse in both her hands and promises herself that she will never,

never-ever walk down a dark street like this again, doesn't like *at all* this murky alley she's passing by, really wants to cross the street now and *run*, as it registers first in the delicate antennae-hair on the back of her neck—*too late!* a terrifying onrushing black force, and she is unable to scream, unable to make a single sound, helplessly pushing the purse to her throat as the silent blackness deftly grabs her, holds her fast and she sees the rapid glint of the knife thinking: *I'm going to die!* and then . . . she suddenly feels the vast weight of the arm yanked away and the scuffle of many feet and voices and, she's confused, turns to look at the shapes of men in dark suits, perhaps four or five who have materialized out of nowhere, standing over a dark-clothed figure now face down in the alley, one of the men pointing a pistol at the back of his head.

"Omigod!" she manages to gasp. It seems she has suddenly surfaced from a dark slow underwater world.

The men turn to look at her, as if surprised she's there.

"Let's take a look," somebody grunts, and they all turn back to the man as one of them, kneeling alongside the handcuffed figure, turns him over and pulls off the hood. One of them shines a flashlight into the bony face of a man about thirty years old with blonde hair, a moustache and thin reddish beard.

"It's not him," says one of them.

"Are ya sure?" asks a harsh voice with a southern drawl.

"Yeah, I'm sure."

"I'm not surprised—"

"Shut up Blair!" the voice drawls. Then to another, "Are you really sure?"

"I'm really sure, I'm positive. It's not him."

"Gawd-*damnit!*"

Christin shivers with tremendous relief, gratefully touching her soft pristine throat, tries to comprehend all that is happening here, but the strain is just too great, the busy scene before her narrows to a tiny hole that she can't keep open, and suddenly all is blackness.

Then she is being carried. Someone has her by the shoulders and another by the ankles. "Uh, what's going on? Where am I?"

"Hey, hey," says one of the men. "She's come around. Put her down."

They lower her feet to the ground and help her to stand up. They seem to still be in the alley, in the glare of two sets of car headlights.

"Can you walk?"

"I-I think so. Who are you?"

"Police." One them flashes a wallet with a badge at her. She squints to read the name, but he pulls it away too quickly. "I didn't get your name."

"This is Detective Blair," says the overweight fellow who had been holding her shoulders. The raspy southern accent. "He's goin' to see you home, Miss."

Before she turns to look at him, Blair rolls his eyes at the fat man. Then he forces a smile at Christin. "You're lucky to be alive, Miss Darrow."

"How did you know my name?"

"Your wallet. In your purse." He waves to another man. "Angie! Bring over Miss Darrow's purse."

A man comes running up and carefully places Christin's purse in her hands. She gasps when she sees it. The dark leather has been viciously slit across one entire side. She feels the blood draining from her head again.

"Hey, hey, steady there!" Detective Blair begins rubbing the wrist of her free hand while the fat southerner behind her gently shakes her shoulders. "You need to sit down again?"

Christin shakes her head, takes some deep breaths. "I-I was afraid and . . . I think I felt him coming behind me . . . I held up the purse . . ."

"It saved your life." Blair glares at his companion over the girl's bowed head. "He came up really fast."

"Well, how did we know how damn fast that ol' boy would really be now?"

"You-you, mean you were waiting here? For him?" A strange thought occurs to her, but it seems too silly to voice—that they were also waiting for her.

"Yeah. We've been staking out this alley for some time. We've been after this guy for a while. He's a slasher. A real scum. But we had to wait for him to make his move. Which he did tonight. With you. But we got him now, so he's not going to bother anyone else again—"

"But-but didn't I hear you say that it wasn't him? That it wasn't the right person? I heard that before I-I think."

"Er, that is right," Blair glances over at the fat man, "but we had suspected another person to be the slasher. It turned out to be someone else. We'll find out at the station."

"That's right. Detective Blair will take you home. We'll take this perp in now, before any other of Chicago's finest show up here, unnecessarily." The fat man turns and walks over to the car with the slasher in the back seat between two officers. He gets in the front and the car squeals away.

Blair parks in the drive leading up to Lambert Towers and walks Christin to the elevators. On the way up, she thinks to ask, "Don't you want me to go down to the station and make a report or something?"

"Oh, the statement you made to us on the scene will be sufficient. Besides, we've got plenty on this guy; we don't really need any more—"

"But-but, I thought he wasn't the one you were looking for."

"Well, to be honest Miss Darrow, we're a special unit, working undercover to bust these slashers, and our witnessing of the act is enough to bring a case against this perp. It's entirely possible we may call you in a day or so to corroborate our evidence. Right now, though," he smiles in a fatherly way, "I'd say you're pretty shook up and need to get some rest."

The elevator arrives at her floor. "Would you like me to check your apartment for you?"

Christin nods weakly.

Blair smiles, begins a quick look through her apartment, finding, of course, nothing, but as he returns to the living room where Christin is sitting numbly on the sofa, arms crossed, eyes glazed, he notices that the computer monitor on a large desk is turned on. Funny he hadn't noticed it before. Must have passed right by it. He walks over and sees that the monitor glows with the eerie image of a small silver skull on a field of black. "What the hell?" Blair mutters, the hairs on the back of his neck stand on end.

Christin, who has followed him over, gasps.

"Did you leave this thing on when you left?"

"Well, actually it's never turned off."

"Are you sure? Never?" Blair begins glancing quickly around, as if someone might be in the apartment.

"I'm sure," says Christin. "My employer gave me this. It's always on."

"Ever see anything like this before?"

"No, never. Maybe someone else managed to get into it some-how." She immediately thinks of "Richard" out there somewhere, but decides not to mention it to him.

"Huh. Like a hacker," says Blair, rubbing his chin.

"Do you think it-it's related to—what happened back there?"

"Oh, I really don't think so." He suddenly remembers that one of the linchpins between the other murders and the Gnome was the silver skull that had appeared on the computer screens of the other victims. He clears his throat. "No, I don't know what the hell it means. Must be some kind of a sick joke. Well, I've got to get back. I'm sure you'll be okay now."

Several hours later Christin awakens abruptly with the distinct sensation of someone whispering in her ears. Whoa, creepy, strange, unsettling, and somehow—vaguely arousing. Hmm. She checks the clock, 3:30 a.m. She's slept surprisingly soundly after the horrible incident—and a couple of hastily gulped glasses of back-of-the-fridge Chablis. But it must be the abject fear she suffered earlier, a perverse survivor's excitement or something that is causing these, er, strange sensations. She doesn't quite understand why, but feels that she must go over to her computer and bring up the picture again, the one that Richard had sent, of her on the balcony, nearly naked, the robe billowed gloriously around her. . . .

So that's me. Why do I keep hiding myself? she wonders, at the same time thinking that these are some pretty weird thoughts coming from . . . where? The slasher, the horrific attack of only a few hours ago seems strangely unimportant. Only these unher-alded peculiarly erotic feelings seem essential right now. She goes back into her bedroom, walks over to the mirror and peels off her T-shirt, smooths her hair, then digs in a drawer for an ancient pack of Kool's she knows is somewhere within, finds some matches and lights up a cigarette. *Just like Aimee.* She exhales, coughs, and unashamedly observes her luscious self. *Good. This is me. This is who I need to be.* She walks into the kitchen and pours herself a glass of wine, returns to the computer thinking, *I've just got to get myself out there on NEXSX. Totally out there.* . . .

CHAPTER FORTY-FOUR

BLAIR WALKS INTO a makeshift debriefing room at AlphaBanc headquarters: a grim scene, dark in the corners. Haedler and his boys have their perp tied to a chair with a single bright light shining overhead, a nice touch. They're working him over; the man's face is red and swollen, his beard is caked with blood. Blair checks his watch: it's past ten. He feels a pain in the pit of his stomach; this has gotten way out of hand.

Haedler looks tired and frustrated, face sweating into his open collar, tie splayed below it, raises his leather-gloved hand to smack the perp again—but Blair steps over and catches his arm. "That's enough."

Haedler scowls at Blair, but looks relieved that someone else has taken over. "Well, he won't talk," Haedler puffs, glaring at the sullen man.

"Nothing?"

"Nothing, damnit."

"What do we know about him?"

"We took a digital pic of his mug, ran it against our face-rec databases. We think he's Ted McClelland, a financial planner on the northwest side. He's got an A-Banc Promethium Card. His credit's maxed."

"Hmm. That right? Are you Ted?" Blair asks the man.

The man is silent.

"Okay, well I'm going to call you Ted, then. Okay, Ted? Now, I'm going to ask you nicely," says Blair, pulling up a chair and sitting in it so he can look the perp in the eyes. "How much did he pay you?"

The man gives the slightest flicker of recognition.

Blair continues, "He told you if you talked to the cops you wouldn't get a cent, right?"

"You guys aren't cops!" the man says slowly, defiantly.

Blair rolls his eyes, looks around the room, ending with Haedler. "Well, let's say you're partially right, pal. We're undercover, just like you. So it's okay to talk to us. We're not even after you; we're after whoever hired you."

"Sure," sneers the man, "now I get to listen to the 'good' cop."

Blair lowers his gaze to the floor, then raises it to the perp's eyes with a bemused look. "The bad cop hits pretty hard. Maybe you'd be better off talking to me, pal. All we want to know is who hired you and why. We don't even care who you are."

"I'm not really a killer!" the man says suddenly.

"You sure as hell acted like a killer."

"Well, I-I try to do a good job at whatever—"

"What is it you do?"

"Actually, it is financial planning. I got in some trouble."

"You are McClelland?"

The man nods.

"You embezzled from the funds entrusted to you?"

The man nods again.

Blair looks up at Haedler, then back to the man tied to the chair. "Tell me about it."

The man sighs heavily and then tells them that he had diverted a great deal of his clients' money into speculative investments, mostly options and commodities, and then lost much of it.

"Who knows about it?"

"No one. Not even my wife. That's what's so weird." He looks up at Blair with a certain troubled look that Blair knows well from his years of police work—the man is going to tell them everything. If for no other reason, Blair knows, just to share an ugly story he's kept bottled up too long.

"What was so weird?"

"That he knew."

"Who knew?"

"The-the guy who called. The guy who put me up to this."

"Did he give a name?"

"No, he wouldn't. I didn't really care, either."

"Tell me about it."

It's an unburdening; McClelland tells them all about the calls that began one night after the market had taken a tumble.

"I still don't know how he knew," whines McClelland, shaking his head slowly. "I juggled the accounts constantly. So much that I had trouble telling which money was where. It's got to be a computer thing, that's the only way—"

"Why do you say that?" Blair asks, looking around again at Haedler, who looks to be nearly asleep in a chair on the far wall.

"Well, it's all I can figure. Everything I do, every transaction I make is in a computer somewhere. Someone just has to get into these computers somehow and track everything to know that I— or anyone else—is in trouble. I know it's paranoid talk, but he was exactly right. And he paid. Just like he said he would."

"How much?"

"A hundred thousand. Said he'd have it transferred into an account in my name, as a show of good faith."

"Did he?"

"Oh yeah. A few days later I withdrew part of it, right away. Five grand. No questions asked. It was for real."

"Then what?"

"He-he said he'd transfer more, up to five hundred thousand dollars, if I-I did something for him."

"What was that?"

"Uh . . ."

"Listen, I told you we don't care about you. It's the voice on your phone we want—with all the money."

"Okay, it was this woman. He wanted a job done. But I told you, I'm not a killer!"

"Yeah, you did. Who was she?"

"I needed the money. Really bad. To me it was an opportunity, a wonderful goddamned opportunity. Actually, a freakin' miracle. I-I couldn't believe it, and all he wanted was for me to—"

"Who was she?"

"Katrina Radnovsky. In Lincoln Park."

"And you killed her?"

"Yes, goddamnit! I did it! I did it! Just like he told me to do, just like, just like, I was going to, to—" He breaks into giant, heaving sobs.

"Tonight." Blair finishes the man's sentence.

"But-but you guys have got to understand," McClelland pleads. "I'm not really a killer."

"Yeah. None of us are . . . really." Blair's exhausted. It's hot in the little room; he wipes his forehead with the back of his hand. "Listen, Teddy, what do you know about a garrote . . . ?"

It's one a.m. when Blair finally walks down the corridors of AlphaBanc toward the elevator. It all seems to make sense now. Before the investment stuff, McClelland had been a sharpshooter, had tried to be a Navy Seal. He is obviously a certifiable sociopath, too.

Blair stops in the hallway, shakes his head. Combined with the embezzling, the man is the perfect candidate to be a hired killer. He's even local to Chicago. The Gnome must have searched millions of records, maybe hundreds of millions of different combinations to come up with the person he needed. And he had found McClelland. Who had gotten the job done for him before, and had almost gotten it done again. Almost. And everyone—everyone at AlphaBanc—thought it was Norman Dunne himself. As he takes the elevator down to the street, Blair can't help feeling a grudging sense of admiration for the strange demented little man.

CHAPTER FORTY-FIVE

EVERYTHING COMES AT a price, Clayborne's father has told him, the problem is figuring out exactly what that price is. And for the Epenguin, that figure seems to be currently equal to one magnificently classic dove-gray zoot suit: long broad-shouldered coat, baggy pegged pants with the reat pleat, matching wide hat with a dark gray band, even a watch chain that's got to be at least four feet long—a sartorial lollapalooza Clayborne happened to spot passing by a thrift shop window while wondering just how he could find out what was going on with Kitten, er, Christin. It's the real thing, looks really old to him, perhaps dating back to the '43 Zoot riots in L.A., which only increases its value greatly in the big eyes of the Epenguin.

So a bargain is struck and Clayborne will now periodically receive encrypted emails of Kitten's conversations with the evil Gnome, er, Richard, on NEXSX. But the first one he is sent, perhaps by mistake, is one of her regular emails which, after a moment's hesitation, he unashamedly reads. What the hell. There is no privacy anymore.

Marcia, I haven't heard from you in a while, and I know I haven't sent you anything lately, either, but at least I have an excuse—the most horrible thing has happened to me. An attempt was made on my life! Some weirdo tried to slash me with a knife on a dark street near my apartment. I still shake when I think about it (like now). I'm okay, though. Some cops, or private police, I think, came up and stopped him just in time. Otherwise, it'd be all over for me. I'm all right now, though. I had the operation for the Ménière's and I seem to be completely cured. Just like you. Write me back and I'll tell you the whole story. Also, you were right about NEXSX, it really is hot stuff. But not too hot for me, pal. Although I did something really stupid I have to tell you about sometime. Hope to hear from you soon. Chris.

Clayborne's heart sinks. The Gnome has struck! But apparently missed, thank God. It's just like those guys had predicted. Damn! And what's this about Ménière's? He didn't know she was going to get an operation. He feels really outside her life, wishes he could be there with her to—well, to be with her. It makes him sick to realize, even though he is accidentally on the receiving end here, how much information they keep on her. And no doubt on him, too, so he knows he has to be careful, isn't really sure if he should be looking at these emails here at work, but they are encrypted by the Epenguin himself, and if anyone is watching him—online—it would be the Epenguin, wouldn't it? And the birdman's cool now, isn't he? And he's pretty sure that he, Richard Clayborne, isn't really all that important to big busy AlphaBanc, right? Well, not before this Gnome-thing, anyway.

But it does bother him just a tiny bit the way the louvers on that air vent up there, must be twelve feet overhead, slant so perfectly toward his desk. They wouldn't be *planned* to slant that way, would they? There wouldn't actually *be* a miniature camera in there, would there? He takes a deep breath. Hoo-boy, gotta slow down the paranoia train here . . . never noticed it that much during the Deludamil days. Just then his laptop chimes and the email icon blinks. He sighs, clicks on it. It's something from Lance Girardeau.

Hey Richie, one good turn deserves another, as they say. I've never forgotten the little moral lesson you gave me a while back with Dutch's wife, and I'm ever so grateful. So in an effort to further your career there, I'm sending this along to Bergstrom and Sturgis and all the rest of your buddies in Chi-town. Enjoy!

There is an attachment, obviously one of Girardeau's trademark digital photographs. Clayborne's stomach tightens with fear
as he double-clicks on the icon to open it. He expects the worse.

Oh God. It is the worst—actually several images of him and
Zara LaCoste crudely layered over the desktop in his office, unmistakably caught in *the act*. He's horrified; they're perfect, as
might be expected from the evil Girardeau, digital masterpieces,
even down to the sweat shining on their glowing flesh. And of
course it never happened. Right?

The pictures are so good that for a sudden shaky moment he
thinks back to the night that he and Zara were together here, and
he wonders . . . *could* they have? Could he have forgotten somehow? Was there some drug they might have slipped him? No, of
course not, but he looks carefully at the pictures, looks up again
at the vent in the ceiling. The angle is the same. Damn! He knows
the pictures aren't real, but maybe they got some reference shots
or something—*goddamn them!*

He viciously knocks the junk off the top of his desk with a
swipe of his arm: folders, papers, office awards, cheap plastic
statuette of Darby O'Banknote, flips the waste basket upside
down, stacks some binders and books on top of that and climbs
shakily up . . . but it's still too far away. In the camera above—if
there is a camera above—the scene below is desperate and
pathetic as he flails wildly, eyes swelling with tears, cursing at the
mute dark air vent above him.

CHAPTER FORTY-SIX

IT'S GOT TO be this Grand Unification insanity. Blair is definitely starting to feel spooked every time he walks into One AlphaBanc Center, and now as he walks through the lobby on the way to a meeting with Haedler, his cell phone rings. It's Murphy from the morgue.

"Hey Georgie, just wanted to let you know what those weird marks were on that bum I showed you a while back. Remember?"

"Yeah, I remember."

"Well, you ever hear of code three-of-nine?"

"What?"

"It's a type of bar code. You know, bar codes, like what get scanned at the supermarket?"

"Yeah?"

"Well, the marks, all the little lines on this guy's skin, we think were trials at creating bar codes, actually tattoos, on human skin—with different types of luminous ink."

"Luminous *ink*?"

"Yeah, like glow-in-the-dark. Or, actually, in a certain kind of light. We brought in a physics prof from U of Chicago who did some testing with a lot of light sources. Turns out at certain wavelengths, these things glow! Funny thing is, the marks we saw on him, the dark ones, weren't much of anything. The really good ones were the ones we couldn't see. Guy was covered with them. Nearly every square inch."

"You're kidding me," Blair mumbles, but he knows Murph is not; nothing really surprises him anymore.

"Wish I were. But you know the weirdest thing?"

"I'm ready . . ."

"The ones that were full barcodes? A lot of them decoded to one number: six-six-six."

"Ohh, no, this is too crazy—"

"Totally creeps me out, too . . . it's like, Biblical, apocalyptic, or something. It's happening, just like it says in Revelations—"

"Oh no, Murph, not today. I haven't even had breakfast yet."

"What do you think it is, Georgie?" Murph is whispering.

"I don't know. But I can't take any more of this, Murph. Not right now. I gotta get to a meeting."

Haedler leans back in his black leather chair, tips his cigar ash on the floor and blows a huge smoke ring into the hazy upper atmosphere of his office. "So, Georgie, how do you like our little pictures?"

"My God," Blair coughs on the cigarette he's smoking. "This is what we've done? To Booth? I can't believe it."

"Believe it," chuckles Haedler.

Blair holds a thin sheaf of 8x10 glossy black and white photographs depicting a series of rather disturbing scenes, the most damning of which is a tableau of high school teacher and environmentalist Franklin Booth lying naked in a rumpled bed alongside a rather naked young boy, and worse, another young boy is perched, naked, at the foot of the bed with a big smile for the camera.

It is perfect and ugly. Mean, mean stuff. A seamless photograph. Girardeau is an evil genius. Blair recognizes the bedroom as Booth's, having been in it as reporter George Findlay with Girardeau when he photographed "a day in the life" of the dedicated environmentalist. The other photographs are of similar scenes, equally disgusting. Blair feels sick. "Jesus."

"Oh c'mon, now," Haedler drawls in his thickest Louisiana accent. "I thought bad ol' Georgie Blair was a big boy. I even heard that he done some pretty nasty things in his day. Or ain't it his day no mo'?"

"Shut up."

"We-el, what did you expect? We always used to say in Louisiana that you didn't never wanna be caught in bed with a dead woman or a live man! A live boy's even worse!" Haedler laughs.

"It never used to be like this."

"It is now. It's always gonna be like this. Git used to it."

"What did we do with these?"

Haedler can't help chuckling softly, cruelly, not as much from what he is going to divulge to Blair, but from how he knows Blair is going to take it. "Sent or emailed these to everyone you'd expect, his organization headquarters, financial supporters, girlfriend, parents, newspapers, local school board members, and of course, his opponents—everyone but him!" Haedler laughs out loud.

"This is, this is . . . ." Blair can't find the words.

"Well, one less person to stop the airport. And now, maybe—no one now who would dare stop it. They know somebody out there is playing rough. Mission accomplished."

Blair sighs. "Mission accomplished."

"Well, that's what we had to do," Haedler says angrily. "It's our goddamn job, you know. Mine! Yours! Goddamn Alpha-Banc's!" He nearly shouts.

Blair doesn't at first understand Haedler's righteous rising indignity. He's never seen it before. Then something clicks. "What happened?"

Haedler pauses. He sucks in a deep breath. "What do mean—happened?"

"Goddamn it, just tell me!"

"Well, he just . . . did it."

"Did what?"

"Offed himself," Haedler says softly.

"How?"

"Gun. Thirty-eight caliber. In the mouth. I didn't think—"

"When?"

"Yesterday. Late. At night sometime. Out in the stinking damn swamp, out in them wetlands he was trying to protect."

Blair looks at Haedler, sensing for the briefest of moments the ugly bond they have, of two men who understand that something they have done has gone well beyond their intent.

CHAPTER FORTY-SEVEN

AIMEE HAD BEEN holding a cigarette and there might have been just a hint of exhaled smoke from her nostrils, her upper lip faintly obscured, but it's hard for Christin to tell as she squints at her picture, even enlarged, limited first by the quality of the image, and then by the granularity of the pixels, the true upper limit of the silicon universe she is investigating here.

But Aimee's cool hard smile, the *total defiance* . . . oh God, yes, she *knows* it! Christin flashes inevitably back to *then*, to that extraordinary college semester when she had worn that same smirk for a brief but incredibly exciting time. It was a visceral reminder of a part of her life that she thought she had buried long ago, but now seems to be resurfacing through NEXSX here . . . that wonderful defiant look was *hers too* at one time, but she sadly realizes now, as she reaches for her Chablis, that she had lost it as quickly as it had come to her.

What strange stuff I'm doing . . . what a crazy world we live in, she thinks as she paints on lipstick too dark for everyday, but perfect for entry into this exotic cyber-terrain, something of an evening ritual now, almost an addiction, after homework for the office and after supper—fast food or a frozen dinner—it's evolved into lights low and a big pillow on the chair before her monitor, on each side of which now burn two candles, their glow creating warm highlights on her smooth Chicago-pale skin, softly luminous through whatever exotic lingerie she has chosen for the evening, and of course the cute blonde wig in case there's anyone out there who might possibly recognize her. Which she thinks is funny, because even she doesn't seem to recognize herself anymore. She's somehow changed, become stronger, sexier, bolder, crazier—well, definitely *crazier* . . . but overall changed for the better, she thinks, *ever since that stupid operation.* But how could that be?

It's so very weird; as frightened as she was following the attack by that slasher, the incident surprisingly quickly ceased to trouble her. Instead she found herself coming back to her computer and bringing up again the striking moonlit image of her, well, true, self. And she's only a little ashamed of her vanity, for it truly is a wonderful picture of her: arms gently extended, windblown hair, creamy perfect flesh shimmering beneath the billowing robe . . . it is simply *her*, as she is meant to be seen—by everyone! As Richard had told her in his impassioned cajoling, she isn't getting any younger, and actually, it truly is terribly selfish of her to keep such beauty to herself, under wraps, so to speak.

So . . . maybe he's right. She's shocked that she now even considers this, but "Richard" has recently, surprisingly, resumed contact, proffering abject apologies for the impudent photograph, dutifully emailing her each Saturday night with ever more plaintive missives accompanied with the graphic of a single red rose . . . all of which she simply, coldly, deletes.

It's confusing. She's knows she's got to sort things out. But in the meantime, as much as she hates taking slimy Richard's advice, inspired and intrigued (*totally*) by the incredible variety of life-forms out there on NEXSX and beyond, she has recently upgraded her computer setup to include a new monster monitor and, well, the super little webcam that includes a terrific auto-tracking feature that somehow follows her around the room—all the better to send her own image *out there*, to complete the equation.

God, this is the coolest thing! she thinks, taking another sip of wine and pulling her legs into a lotus, looks up to see the big screen currently depicting, in resplendent display, a sultry, and, oh, perhaps even *pouty* Christin tonight, yes, who has now daringly tugged open the top of her robe to reveal the creamy upper architecture of her beautiful breasts, which with minimal satisfied effort she can cause to, yes, visibly *heave* on the big display above. Christin in luxuriant repose.

She tosses her hair and puts down her wineglass, stretches to position the candles a bit closer, then reaches out to the keyboard and with a few clicks, sends her image, *an advertisement for my too-long repressed self*, she muses, anonymously out into the aether. She takes another drag on the cigarette, glances up at herself and sighs, thinking: *Everything, absolutely everything, is marketing.* She still can't believe she's actually doing this. *If only Michael could see me now!* she thinks, and then smiles: *maybe he can . . .*

Sipping wine and wickedly smoking, Christin eases into her routine, cruises the usual NEXSX hot spots, searches for exciting hot images and videos—there's always something new to add to her screen, it seems. She briefly considers gathering a circle of onliners, or net-groupies (the latest jargon), with which to personally share her, at this point, fairly flushed, innominate image, a new really exciting feature of NEXSX, where one is actually able to assemble, as it were, a coterie of onlookers who share real-time video images of themselves watching you as you watch them, each of whom inhabits their own window on your monitor, and are arranged, increased or decreased in size (depending upon the intensity of interest at the moment) as desired on the big screen, and also includes the option of actually *hearing* their assorted comments—or other utterances, as they might occur.

But it's a lot of work to select, arrange, and keep track of all that net-groupie action, and then to be under somewhat of an obligation to actively, attractively display oneself (she shamelessly now loves the idea of her anonymous self, her sweet image center-screen on monitors around the world, anywhere, *everywhere*) . . . no, she sighs heavily, not tonight . . . it has been a very long week and she really is tired. But before she gets off, she decides to check in with her online shrink, Dr. Turing.

She thinks fleetingly of how, er, interesting, it would be if the doctor could see her right now, wonders vaguely if she "accidentally" left the little camera on if he could in fact view her luscious image. But no, *this is serious*, she reminds herself, and is actually something she enjoys almost as much as the cyber-exhibitionism—this allows her to bare her pent-up soul. And it appears that there is even a message awaiting her on Dr. Turing's site:

Christin, I was glad to hear from you the other day.
I hope you are recovering well from your operation.

I also hope that you have been dealing successfully with your feelings of low self-esteem.

Oh yes! The little "Doctor is In" icon is green and Christin's
heart leaps, he's online right now, she's got to tell him!

Hello Dr. Turing, I got your message and I think
I've got some insight now as to why I have such
problems with my self-esteem. It's because, almost
ten years ago, I killed someone.

Chapter Forty-Eight

WIPING AWAY THE tears that suddenly stream down her cheeks, Christin considers Dr. Turing's quick response:

> You killed someone? Is that the truth? Please, tell
> me about it.

Well, perhaps that wasn't exactly the truth. The psychologist had told her years ago that she shouldn't blame herself like that, but she still does, and is the reason why, in her darker moments, she always considers herself to be practically a murderer—or is it murderess? She types:

> Maybe killing isn't exactly the right terminology,
> but I certainly caused someone's death, and it's
> pretty much the way I've felt about it for the past
> nine years.

Christin pauses, wonders if she can continue this confession, but decides she must unburden herself; after the original therapy sessions had ended, she's never again talked with anyone about this, not even with Michael. Typing as fast as she can, she tells him the tale of her misadventures at prestigious little Kennet College in West Chester, about as far away as she could get from her neurotic parents.

She was only seventeen, graduating from high school a year early through an almost fanatical devotion to studying in pursuit of her goal—to leave home as soon as possible. It was the dutiful coward's way of running away from an intensely overprotective father and a mother whose ardent Catholicism began approaching the fanatical and embarrassing, with near-daily prayer vigils and a ritual sprinkling of holy water upon Christin and anyone else who happened to be near. So a scholarship to Kennet, a private liberal arts college outside of Philadelphia, looked like salvation, a school with strong fine arts and psychology programs, and also an undergraduate school of business and economics, which Christin's father insisted upon, but for her, the best thing was that it was three thousand miles from home.

Her freshman year was an amazing intricate balance between unending study and near-constant partying. Like her, many of her sorority sisters were escaping overactive parents, so cigarettes, smuggled bottles of wine, marijuana, and the occasional fellow into their rooms became part of the crazy illicit routine.

But an intellectual challenge also presented itself, the exclusive fifty-year-old Kennet Arts & Letters Society, a campus institution that met weekly. It was a great honor to be asked to join the society, which was composed mostly of juniors and seniors and a few select sophomores. No freshman had ever been allowed to join, although it was rumored that several had come close. Some of Christin's snooty upper-class sorority sisters were members and they goaded the freshmen in their house to apply to join, especially the feisty Christin, the implicit catty undertone being that beauty and brains were mutually exclusive.

> So I took up the challenge, Dr. Turing. Worse yet, I foolishly told them that if I couldn't get into the society, I'd leave Kennet. It was stupid, I know, but I was so angry at their haughtiness that I had to prove them wrong. Plus, I had been so sheltered at home that I felt I had to break free and throw myself into something like this.
>
> And how did you proceed?
>
> Well, I'm embarrassed to this day to say this, but after I learned that it really was impossible to get in as a freshman, I cheated. I ended up seducing the faculty sponsor.

There was no other way. Plus, for the inchoate temptress Christin, it proved to be remarkably easy. Dr. Peter Caldwell, an earnest associate English professor in his early thirties, was the new advisor this year, having replaced a much older man, Dr. Golding, who had retired. He also happened to be Christin's academic advisor. Her original plan in fact, was to simply persuade, perhaps even beg, but not seduce. But the short skirt and tight sweater she had worn to help make her case during their meeting elicited such a favorable response in the paneled confines of Dr. Caldwell's office that their affair began almost immediately.

And as Dr. Caldwell was a ruggedly good-looking, wavy-haired young man who was more idealistic and innocent than any of the coeds on campus (who all adored him even though it was well-known that he was happily married with two children), their tryst was not in any way unpleasant; in fact, it made their ultra-secret rendezvous in the evening and over weekends more exciting, Christin's seductions more shameless, her victory even sweeter.

And this got you into the society?

Oh yes. Not only was I the very first freshman in Kennet's history to be admitted to the group, but I was also appointed secretary. By Dr. Caldwell, of course.

How did your peers feel about that?

They were incredibly envious, as you might expect. Peter and I were very very careful and I'm pretty sure they never knew about the affair until later. All prospective candidates for the society had to submit a paper along with any other qualifying material, you know, so I submitted a couple of my best paintings, which, IMHO, were pretty darn good. Everyone thought I got in on the strength of those alone.

And how did you feel about your acceptance?

I was on top of the world! I ruled. Even my stuck-up sorority sisters had to admit defeat. I was as good as any of them in the society's meetings, too. I held my own. The real trick was to get into the stupid group. Which I did, using whatever it took.

And then what happened?

Things fell apart. Christin would never forget the moment on a fine spring morning in late April, while walking to class, one of her classmates had come up to her, did she hear? Last night Dr. Caldwell's wife had committed suicide! She had poisoned herself, they think. In that instant Christin's world disintegrated.

It was just horrible, Dr. Turing. There was a big investigation and Dr. Caldwell admitted our affair, and I was questioned over and over by the police. They actually thought that he, or even that I, might have murdered her! My parents were notified, of course, and they flew in to further stir things up. One of the biggest problems was that I was still only seventeen, a minor, so the poor professor was charged as a sex offender. In the end, he was arrested and fired from the college and I was expelled.

How did you feel about that?

How do you think I felt? Absolutely horrible, depressed. I felt like a terrible person. I believed I had ruined the man's life and career and family, just to prove something to myself. I felt horrible. Just horrible. And my parents of course were mortified and I just felt like dying. For a while there I even thought of suicide. Therapy saved me from that, but I just felt awful about myself for a long time.

Your self-esteem was very low.

Rock bottom. And because of that I ended up doing everything from that time on strictly by the rules. The straight and narrow. At least my parents were happy then. I went to business school and gave up all thoughts of being an artist. It just seemed too radical, or impractical. I didn't want to stand out, or protest, or cause anyone any more trouble. I was right back to being a nice polite little mouse again.

How do you feel about yourself now?

Well, even with all the therapy my parents put me through afterwards, I guess I still feel a lot of shame. It's something I've never been able to talk with anyone about for a long time. Plus, I think it certainly made me ashamed to express my sexuality in any way. After Michael left me I gave it a lot of thought and decided that he was right, I was repressed. We had some wild moments, but it was always me who felt wrong or indecent afterwards. He giving up on me seemed to confirm it. Now though, through the NEXSX service and the weird guidance of this Richard, who unfortunately turned out to be a real creep, I think I'm beginning to find myself again, I think my true self is trying to come out.

Would you say that you like yourself now?

That's a very good question. I think, just recently, I've begun to like myself again and to accept my sexuality for what it is. Also, I realize something important now, that when I said before that I had killed someone many years ago, I wasn't really lying. It was me whom I had killed.

CHAPTER FORTY-NINE

BACK UNDERGROUND AGAIN in the McCarthy Complex's Command Central, George Blair gazes up at one of the huge video panels affixed to the walls of the great room. The panel—O'Brian refers to it as "Number Five"—is two screens to the right of the gigantic central one, and only about a third of its size, but currently displays a similar image: a glowing outline of the United States—but with a single tiny red dot that blinks in the southeast, somewhere in Georgia, it appears to Blair.

"Well, George, where would you say that is? That dot."

"Atlanta?"

"Close. Marietta. Coordinates, please, Jacob."

Blair cautiously eyes the strange-looking technician seated at the desk in front of them. He is wearing a brown robe and his head is tonsured. He begins clicking on his keyboard and high above them latitude and longitude coordinates appear on Number Five, mirroring the monitor in front of him. He seems to study his screen intently, sometimes squinting up at the panel, then looking quickly back, as though they might suddenly have changed on him. He never once looks up at O'Brian or Blair.

"So, Toby, I don't think I've met Jacob before, or, ah, any of the software weir—wizards you've told me about here."

"Jacob usually stays behind the scenes. He prefers it that way. But he and his team members have extensively engineered this system, which is so new that we haven't had time yet to train anyone else. So Jacob has agreed to help us. We're very grateful to him."

"Uh, yeah. So what have we got going here, Toby?"

"Watch and see. Subject's identifiers, please, Jacob. The abbreviated version."

Jacob enters several commands and a listing appears as a glowing sidebar on the display, currently detailing the subject's particulars: Deaver, Marcia Marie; Female, age 25; followed by a series of cryptic encoded identifiers.

"So, you've got this babe pinpointed, huh, Toby? What are you hitting on her, or what?"

"As usual, George, you terribly underestimate us here. Zoom level two, please, Jacob. Standard map fill."

The panel changes instantly, to a high-resolution satellite image of the earth, now superimposed with a recognizable glowing outline of the state of Georgia. In a few seconds a multicolored network of lines spiderweb across the screen, defining highways, counties, cities, towns. Within a pale pink outline of greater Atlanta the red dot remains, patiently blinking.

"Zoom level three, please."

The display changes again, to a closer satellite image depicting the intricate gridlines of Atlanta and environs, and in the upper left corner, alongside the legend: Marietta, the red dot continues to blink.

"So, how much better is this going to get?" asks Blair.

O'Brian turns and smiles. "Georgie, you won't believe how good it's going to get. Jacob, zoom level four, please."

Now the screen zooms to a much closer view of the rooftops of suburban Marietta, the red dot blinking near the intersection of two streets in the middle of the map. O'Brian taps Jacob on the shoulder and the view enlarges to focus upon a particular rooftop, a small white car parked in the driveway. The red dot continues to blink above the house.

Blair's eyes narrow. "Sooo . . . this is where she lives, then?"

"That is correct, George."

"Well, this is pretty good stuff, Toby. But I don't get it. You've located her house. That's pretty good, even zooming in like that. But, so what? That's something anyone can do on the Internet—"

O'Brian smiles broadly. "Ah, but George, you don't really understand. I must not have it explained it to you correctly. What we are seeing here is *not* simply Deaver, Marcia Marie's house. What we are seeing *is* Deaver, Marcia Marie. The actual person, as it were."

"Huh?"

"Watch. Jacob, start up the residential definition algorithm, please."

The rectangular rooftop suddenly enlarges to fill the screen, a dark blue line enclosing its area, the red dot blinking in the center.

"Begin historical tracking, please."

The red dot begins to move around the within the blue enclosure in a series of rapid back-and-forth paths that always seem to begin at one edge, proceed inward and then repeatedly trace through what appear to be set patterns in the geometric figure. At certain points the dot pauses for an instant or two and then resumes its busy travels. Each series is accompanied with a rapidly changing date stamp on the side of the screen, and a time stamp that reels though a blur of hours, minutes, and seconds.

"Now add the DDD projections, Jacob."

"DDD?"

"Derived Dwelling Definitions, George. Jacob has done an absolutely masterful job. Watch."

The rectangle instantly transforms to a green 3-D grid, the skeletal interior of what appears to be a fairly typical suburban colonial home. As the red dot repeats its travels, it becomes clear to Blair that he does, in fact, appear to be watching the daily movements of a person in the privacy of her home, displayed electronically above them on a huge screen. The daily routines of Deaver, Marcia Marie, have become quite evident, almost unsettling, as he watches the dot traverse through the rooms the computer has now labeled as garage, kitchen, pantry, living room, den, master bedroom, master bath. . . .

"Jesus. I can't believe it."

O'Brian chuckles aloud. "I told you, George, that you underestimated us. Usually, after only a few iterations of the subject through the structure we're able to map it, all based on statistical data we've collected, and, of course, continue to collect, that enables us to define the rooms in almost any site. You should see us with an office building. It takes much longer, but we're usually able to determine the business functions of most areas."

Blair shakes his head in disbelief. "You mean you've actually got something on her, some electronic gadget actually on this person? To get this kind of information?"

"Actually, George, it's, ah, inside her."

"Inside her?"

"Maybe we'd better go to my office," O'Brian looks across the room, sees that a handful of people are looking up at the huge display. "Only a few of us know about this new development. Kill Number Five, please, Jacob." The huge panel above suddenly darkens, leaving the display only upon the small screen below.

Inside his office, Blair views the display they have just seen in the great room on one of O'Brian's wall monitors while Jacob sits at the desk, typing on the keyboard. Blair leans against the granite wall behind Jacob and O'Brian stands next to him.

"So, George, I was going tell you about the implant we use to track Ms. Deaver."

"Implant?"

"Yes, it's an implant. Just behind the jawbone. A tiny state-of-the-art transmitter that beams its signal to us from almost anywhere in the country. Our satellites are over all of North and South America now. Very soon, the entire planet."

"My God, I don't believe it."

"Believe it, George. It's a miniaturization of the small transmitters that hikers and skiers sometimes carry, in case they get lost."

"What keeps it going? Some kind of battery?"

"Better. It's powered by a tiny enzymatic fuel cell which runs partially off the body's own blood sugar. It's designed to work for ten years. We've got prototypes in the lab that we hope will eventually last a lifetime, but—"

"So how'd you get it implanted?"

"Oh, just a tiny bit of subterfuge. The subject begins to have dizzy spells—induced by us, of course, with the help of a very subtle, non-detectable drug. Not available without prescription," O'Brian chuckles. "Or even with a prescription, ha-ha, unless it's from us."

"And then she sees a doctor. So how do you insure that—?"

"It's an AlphaBanc doctor that she—or he—sees. We're experimenting only with AlphaBanc employees, who of course, will only visit AlphaBanc doctors as part of their medical plan."

"A closed loop. Very clever."

"You won't believe how clever it gets. Jacob, is the ITL operative at this location?"

"Yes, it's working."

"Where is it? Please mark it on the display."

"In the bedroom." Jacob types something and a tiny blue dot appears in the grid, in the area labeled: master bedroom.

"ITL stands for Internal Transceiver Link, a small booster device, an amplifier, if you will, of the electronic commands we're able to pass between the implant and our friendly overhead satellite. Jacob, please initiate the 'listen' function."

Jacob hits several keys and a burst of static fills the room. It takes a few seconds, but soon Blair recognizes the sounds issuing from the speakers in O'Brian's office. He shakes his head, looks over at O'Brian, who is sporting a huge grin: *what do you think?*

Blair isn't really sure what to think, but knows that what he is hearing, over the voice of Rod Stewart wailing in the background is unmistakably, the grunts, groans, and murmurs of someone making love.

CHAPTER FIFTY

BLAIR IS STAGGERED. To think that they are presently ten stories underground in a crazy bunker in the Midwest listening in on an intimate moment in a bedroom nearly a thousand miles away is incredible, and also, fairly disturbing. "Jesus, Toby. Is this really what it sounds like it is?" He lights up a cigarette.

O'Brian grins. "Well, I do believe we are listening in on the lovemaking of Marcia Deaver and, most likely, her boyfriend, Vernon Martin."

"So you've got her bugged as well? And what else? Video cameras in the walls, next we're going to see them both on the crazy screen?"

"George, I have to tell you that none of us has ever set foot in Ms. Deaver's house. The ITL that I mentioned before? Ms. Deaver brought that into her house by herself, of her own free will. It's actually some special circuitry installed in our ubiquitous little AlphaBanc clock radio, the ones we give away to our loyal banking customers, and sometimes, our employees."

"I got one or two of those myself."

"Better be careful then, Georgie," O'Brian grins. "No, actually only a few, well, maybe more than a few, have ITL circuitry in them."

"Does mine?"

"No, of course not. Only those, the owners of which, we want to keep track of. Which sometimes pays off. You notice that it is a workday, and the time on the screen is 13:39 Eastern Standard Time, so we might deduce that AFS employee Deaver has taken a sick day, or is in fact engaged in an extended 'nooner.'"

"Kind of looks like it."

"We've been playing around with these ITL's, Georgie. The implants too. We've got several versions of them now. The particular implant, ah, installed, in Ms. Deaver is the absolute cutting edge in surveillance technology."

"So what's that?"

"Well, it's quite an achievement. It features a number of tiny nanoliter-sized buckets which might hold, say, some fairly potent drugs, which can then be released into the subject's bloodstream via remote command."

"What? You've got to be kidding me."

O'Brian smiles hugely, shakes his head, "Not at all, Georgie, not at all."

"Jesus, Toby, drugs . . . delivered by remote control—"

"Yes, George, it's quite true, but don't concern yourself with it right now. We've just begun trials—"

"On who, when—"

"Perhaps I've said too much. Please just pay attention to what we can do right now. I'm sure you'll find it very interesting."

"How interesting?"

"Well, we've been doing some work with—commands."

"Commands?"

"Yes, we've been quite successful with the insinuation of certain, ah, messages, into the subject's subconscious through repetitive subliminal audio stimuli—"

"Whoa, Toby, slow down. In English, please."

"Of course. Well, what we're doing here is transmitting very muted audio messages via the ITL to the implant. You see, because of the location of the implant in the subject—behind the jawbone, very close to the ear—we quickly realized that, if we could equip the implant with a receiver-type mechanism, we could probably broadcast very subtle, ah, suggestions, to the subject."

"You're kidding."

"No, not at all." O'Brian grins proudly. "What we do is enter the message on the computer here. It's transmitted to the satellite, which relays it to the ITL, which then repetitively broadcasts the message to the implant. It's actually fairly simple."

"I'll believe it when I see it."

"Well then, let's transmit a suggestion to Deaver, Marcia Marie, here."

"Go ahead."

"Okay Jacob, prepare to send a message to the ITL. Let's use a repetition rate of, say, fifty, for this transmit."

"Ready, Mr. O'Brian. What message shall we send?"

"Got any suggestions, George?"

"Actually, I do. How long can it be?"

"Well, the shorter the better, actually."

"Okay, here it is: 'Darby O'Banknote is watching you.'"

"Oh no, really," O'Brian groans. "It should be more of a simple command. Something we can actually monitor. Something active, something that—"

"Toby, that's what I want to send."

"All right, if that's what you want," O'Brian sighs, rubs his eyes. "Jacob, please enter that for Mr. Blair."

"Male voice pattern or female?"

"Um, male. No, wait, let's try female. We don't use it often enough."

Jacob types the message. "Shall I send it?"

"Put it on the speakers for us first, please. Turn it up so we can understand it."

Jacob enters some commands and an eerie artificial computer voice comes over the speaker, distinctly female—like the smooth helpful woman's voice on the phone—whispering over and over: "Darby O'Banknote is watching you . . . Darby O'Banknote is watching you . . . Darby O'Banknote is watching you . . ."

Blair feels a chill crawl up his spine.

"Okay Jacob," says O'Brian, "you may send it now."

Jacob clicks some keys. "It's transmitted, Mr. O'Brian."

"Increase the volume on Marcia Deaver, please. External pick-up."

Jacob enters a command and suddenly bedroom sounds, which have settled to a rhythmic set of grunts and moans, punctuated with the syncopated squeak of bedsprings, issue again from the speakers.

"Jacob, let's flip the screen to surveillance mode. Zoom back, please."

The glowing green skeleton of Marcia Deaver's house in Marietta suddenly appears on the screen again, the red dot which indicates *her*, actually blinking in absurd counterpoint to the squeak of bedsprings.

"Oh, oh, stop. Wait a minute, Vern," says a scratchy woman's voice.

"Huh. What? Why?" The man sounds fairly out of breath.

"Just *stop*! I-I just feel funny. I feel like we're being watched!"

Blair looks over at O'Brian, raises his eyebrows.

"What, what are you—crazy!" The voice crackles over the speakers. "We're alone, *alone*! The shades are drawn. Who could possibly be watching us?"

Blair shakes his head.

"I don't know. I just suddenly got this weird feeling is all . . ."

"Well, I've sure heard enough," says Blair.

"Okay, cut the sound, please, Jacob," says O'Brian.

They silently watch the red flashing dot that is Deaver, Marcia Marie, move into the portion of the floor plan on the screen labeled: Master Bath.

Meanwhile O'Brian sits before a monitor on the desk and begins typing on the keyboard below it. "Aha, yes," he mutters, "just as I suspected."

"What now, Toby?" Blair shakes his head. "You figured out what the sex of their child is going to be already?"

"Er, no, not yet . . ." O'Brian replies absently. "I don't really think we have a preference . . ."

Blair rolls his eyes.

"Aha! What I see *here*," says O'Brian triumphantly, "through AlphaBanc's online time and attendance system, is that Deaver, Marcia Marie has called in sick today! Just as I predicted!"

"Nowhere to hide . . ." mutters Blair.

"Not from us!" cackles O'Brian, and swivels around in his chair to face him. "No sir. I'll log a note in her PERSPROF, of course, regarding this little incident, but you can clearly see how well our system works!"

"Uh-huh. So why are you doing all this, Toby? This, this incredible surveillance."

O'Brian slowly leans back in his chair, presses his pale fingers together, looks thoughtfully toward the ceiling. "I suppose, first of all, because we *can*. The technology exists and we've got to try it out. Better we get cracking on it before someone less benevolent than AlphaBanc gets it."

"Oh, there's someone less benevolent than AlphaBanc?"

"Very funny. Look, we've simply got to experiment with ever more sophisticated means of social control. It's a sick society that we live in now, George, terrorists and all kinds of nuts running around loose. You know that better than anyone. Look at Norman Dunne for God's sakes. Would it make you feel better if this device was tracking a terrorist? A drug lord? A serial killer? A real menace to society? How about Dunne himself? With this little thing, we've got him cold. Or, suppose it was implanted in the victim of one of those deviants? Suppose it helped us instantly locate a lost or kidnapped child? I can tell you there would be a huge number of grateful parents out there if we could quickly find their missing kid!"

"Deaver, Marcia Marie, is not either of those, Toby."

"No, but right now she's very helpful to us."

"Like one of those laboratory animals—a guinea pig."

"Yes, yes, like a guinea pig that gives its life in the course of testing so that other, higher species, might live. And we're not about to take her life, George, I can assure you," says O'Brian.

"But you already have. You've taken her life, certainly her privacy, and put it in the system, inside the damn computer, inside the, the—"

"The Beast?" O'Brian smiles wryly over at Blair.

"Yes, the Beast," says Jacob, seeming to agree, nodding rhythmically, blankly. "It is the Beast."

"The Beast? What're you guys talking about, Toby?"

"Well," says O'Brian, smiling sheepishly, "that's what some of the folk down here like to call our little conglomeration of systems of late."

"They're certainly not *little*," says Jacob patiently.

"I'll tell you about 'the Beast' another time, George," says O'Brian. "It's kind of an inside joke here. Now, I've got some meetings to attend, so if you don't mind showing yourself out . . ."

CHAPTER FIFTY-ONE

ENOUGH IS ENOUGH. Cruising on his second bourbon and soda at 36,000 feet, Clayborne leans back in the seat of the 757 and gazes idly out the window at a crescent moon flying through great cloud-mountains as he races toward Chicago. His heart swells with feelings of actual honest-to-god *honor* as he contemplates in delicious detail how he's going to confront the grand barons of *uber*-banking, Bergstrom and crew, on their home turf, no less, One AlphaBanc Center.

He knows their weekly strategy meeting is tomorrow, during which they will no doubt be plotting ever more nefarious deeds similar to this crazy Gnome-Christin-whatever thing and the thought of bursting in there and denouncing not only Girardeau's *fraudulent photos*, no, but also this *whole climate* of subterfuge and scheming and plotting and, well, whatever, is immensely satisfying, and seems to be, at this moment and adulterated altitude, a damn good plan.

First thing he's going to do is head right into Bergstrom's office and set the record straight on the phony pictures of him and Zara. After all, Zara is known to be extremely close to, well, *all* of the brass, and to Bergstrom in particular. God only knows what sort of fuss those pictures are creating. . . .

The other thing is to pay a visit to one Christin Darrow. It's driving him crazy, reading and rereading the last series of emails Norman Dunne had sent her before she had cut him off. And all of them seemingly coming from him, Richard. The little gremlin has stolen his identity and worse yet, has better lines than him. And now she's obviously completely disgusted with him, this "Richard." It's time to clear things up. AlphaBanc's stupid agenda be damned, he has to find Christin and show her who "Richard" really is.

The United terminal at O'Hare is the usual high-glassed temple of perpetual movement and Clayborne yawns as he flows along with the faithful, having not gotten as much sleep on the plane as he had hoped, fighting off second thoughts about the severely career-limiting rant he's about to commit, guessing that if he were back on the Deludamil he probably wouldn't even be here right now. Nope, he'd be just a good ol' boy taking another bite of their shit sandwich and giving his compliments to the chef, or at least he wouldn't be feeling so tense, frustrated, and just plain fed up with everything—like all other brave souls somehow going it alone, unmedicated, unadulterated, through the technomaniacal twenty-first century.

The phone in Clayborne's suit coat pocket vibrates and he's immediately irritated, wonders who the hell this might be, no one knows he's even making this trip. Still walking, he shifts his travel bag to the other hand, pulls it out and reads the message floating mutely on the screen:

> Accepting an insult from those whom one fears
> Is not true patience,
> Accepting an insult from those whom one fears not
> Is true patience.

Well. An interesting insight. But who could this be from? Natalie always told him he had no patience, and maybe it was true, but now it seems like someone else is telling him pretty much the same thing. Clayborne scratches his stubbly chin, scrolls down and finds:

> Hello Richard, I am glad to make your acquaintance although I believe I know you quite well. The email from Lance Girardeau is upsetting and you have flown to Chicago to visit with your superiors and then perhaps Christin Darrow. We shall be in touch. Your biggest beast friend.

What in hell? Thanks . . . friend, apparently some foreign national jokester, seems to have trouble with English—and with spelling—is sending him strange messages now, and, unsettlingly, seems to know something about him, even about Christin Darrow. *Who could know this?* He knows he should seriously be concerned, but he's just too tired to care. Welcome to the haunted men.

He's freshened up the best he could in the men's room at the airport, but at the moment he's certainly not the eager bright young fellow they enlisted for this project. No time to worry about that though, the moment of truth approaches as he walks out of AlphaBanc's elevators, straightens his tie and strides down the hallway toward Bergstrom's office. This is it.

He pauses briefly to suck a deep breath before crashing the meeting, knowing he's about to make somewhat of a scene here, and—*what the fuck?* Someone seems to have grabbed him from behind and is very rapidly dragging his weary body backwards down the hall—until he finds himself thrown against a shelf of cleanser bottles in a broom closet. "Hey! Hey! Hey!"

"Shut up! Keep it down!" comes the whispered hiss.

"W-who are you?"

"Name's Blair. And pipe down!"

"What—why, did you pull me in here?" Clayborne whispers back. "What the hell is going on?"

"Listen, I know why you're here. And—I want you to think before you go in there. Those pictures. I know they're fakes. Epenguin told me. They don't, though." Blair smiles. "They think they're the real McCoy."

"But everything Girardeau does is a fake. And-and who are you?"

"They don't know they're from him. I was just in there with them. They came anonymously to Bergstrom and the others."

"Well, it doesn't really matter," sputters Clayborne. "They're fakes. I've got to go in there and tell them. Clear my name. Plus, I'm going to tell them I want out of this . . . some other crazy stuff they've got me doing."

"With the Gnome. Norman Dunne."

"Uh, yeah. How'd you know—? Hey, who *are* you anyway?"

"Name's Blair, I told you. Work for AlphaBanc, like you. Internal security, mostly."

"You're in ISD, then . . . with, uh, Haedler?"

"Work for him."

"Okay. So what are you doing here? With me?"

"There's something big going down here, kid. Stuff both you and I aren't being told about. I know it's not the best thing for my health, but I want to find out more about it, and you—and the Darrow girl—are the key. If you drop out, I'm never going to figure this thing out."

"Well, I'm out of it. This Gnome stuff. And Christin—"

"You're not out of it with her still in it, are you, kid?"

"Well . . . not exactly. I'm going to find her, warn her."

"Sure you are, kid. Look, I'll make you a deal. I'm supposed to keep you away from her. But, if you don't go in there and blow it, I'll look the other way."

"I don't think I need your permission to—"

"Kid," Blair focuses steely gray eyes on Clayborne, "you do."

"Oh, God, I don't believe this." Clayborne slowly shakes his head. "But, uh, those pictures of me and Zara—"

"No, kid. You don't get it. They like the pictures. They think they're real. They're actually kind of proud of you."

"No kidding?"

"No kidding. Believe me, the next time you run into them—not now—it'll be good. Zara's done them all, you know. And now, so it seems to them—you too. Now you're one of the gang."

"Huh."

"Believe me, kid. Now look, I knew you were coming—"

"How?"

"Epenguin. Knows everything. He's flying into Chicago, too, by the way. I want him nearby now that we know the Gnome's in the area. It's probably too late to make you paranoid, kid, but we're keeping a good eye on you—and Darrow too, for that matter. But it stops at me, so you better do what I say."

"Well this is just terrific, just great," Clayborne sighs. "So what's the rest of your deal?"

"As I said, I knew you were on your way, so I told Bergstrom and boys that you were coming to town to meet with me about the murder attempt on Darrow. Told 'em you might be able to team up with me to catch the Gnome, help me with the legwork."

"Y-you did? I don't even *know* you—"

"You do now. Let's talk, kid. You eat breakfast yet? There's a greasy spoon right down here on Wabash that we could kill some time in this morning."

CHAPTER FIFTY-TWO

IS THAT REALLY her? wonders Clayborne as he stands outside One AlphaBanc Center and spies Christin Darrow, he thinks, in the five o'clock stream of employees leaving the building. All he's seen of her, besides the hot NEXSX photo and the fabulous balcony shot, courtesy of the Epenguin, are several other short sophisticated-sexy video clips she's been posting for the Net Groupies, duly forwarded to him by the cool little bird. But this girl with her dark hair pulled straight back, little makeup, and wearing a fairly severe brown business suit, is nothing like the hot-hot bewigged blonde babe he's used to seeing.

But beauty like that cannot be hidden; he's pretty sure it's her.

"Hey, Christin."

"Er, yes?" She pauses to glance for only a millisecond as she strides away from the AlphaBanc building.

"It's me, Richard. And you're . . . Kitten."

Christin freezes, whirls around. "Richard . . . ?" But as the realization of who she is addressing sinks in, she scowls, blushes deeply. "Omigod! You-you weren't supposed to . . . you weren't ever supposed to know where . . . or who I am!"

"I understand. I do. I'm really sorry to approach you like this, but we have to talk."

She looks downward, starts walking rapidly away. "No, I really don't think so . . ."

"No, wait, please—"

"N-no!" she yells, so loudly several people on the street turn to look at them. "Richard, I-I bared my soul to you. I did things I never would have—no, this is crazy, I just can't meet you like this. We just can't . . . *go away!*"

Clayborne bounds after her, walks alongside, talking quickly, "Wait, Christin, please listen. I know how you feel, but we have to talk. You don't know what's going on. It wasn't me that you were talking to, or, ah, carrying-on with. What I mean is . . . it started out as me, but then it was someone else. Not me. It-it's all a big plot, you see . . ."

Christin actually stops in mid-stride to turn and look at this unshaved disheveled madman who looks like he is need of serious sleep, her eyes searching his face for the insanity that apparently lurks within. "Are you crazy? Just leave me alone!" And she begins to walk away again.

"Please! *Listen* to me! I-I work for AlphaBanc! Just like you. A-Banc set me up. With us on NEXSX. They set you up, too."

"What?" She stops again to look intently at him, brow furrowed, mouth open, unable to find words, unable to comprehend the enormity of what he seems to be saying.

"It-it's a big crazy plot" continues Richard, talking fast. "I'm not even sure what it's all about. Look, I think you might be in danger. That attack on you. That slasher. It wasn't a random thing. You were set up. As-as bait."

"What? What are you *saying*—?"

"Please, please, can we go somewhere and talk?"

She turns and begins walking quickly away. He isn't sure if she is running away from him again or perhaps leading him somewhere, so he follows the reluctant and stormy girl into what turns out to be a neutral port, the bar at snooty and expensive La Fontaine a block or so off One AlphaBanc Center.

Christin and the rumpled Clayborne are led to table in a dark corner, provided with a wine list, and to break the ice, he flashes an AlphaBanc Promethium Card, orders a three hundred and fifty dollar bottle of Dom Perignon, something seriously expensive to keep her attention. "Uh, I hope you like champagne."

"Actually, I adore it."

"Good. Well, I know this is kind of strange—"

"Please, just tell me what's going on."

And over flutes of pricey bubbly, Clayborne explains what he knows of the desperate plot he has been partner to, along with herself, the innocent Christin. Who is of course quite disturbed by his disclosures, but blinks back tears of outrage and betrayal and encourages him to hold nothing back.

He doesn't. He tells her everything, from his involvement in the NEXSX plot and the incredible amount of resources Alpha-Banc expended to make it all work (including something he

just learned from Blair this morning, that Christin's friend Marcia
was somehow induced to introduce her to NEXSX, but just how,
Blair wasn't sure—or wouldn't say), to the episode with Girar-
deau's bogus photographs and his ill-fated attempt to charge into
Bergstrom's office this morning, leading to his encounter with
Blair.

He tells her that Blair had also told him what he knew about a
"Grand Unification" scheme that has something to do with
AlphaBanc's huge databases, but exactly what, he wasn't sure,
although Blair speculated that it might be a kind of marketing
data consolidation. Clayborne thinks that this makes some sense
as that's been the goal of AlphaBanc marketing—of all information-age marketing systems, for that matter—for decades, to
aggregate their massive collections of data down to the individual
level, but always being stymied by gaps and inconsistencies.
Apparently the Gnome is needed to crack some fairly sophisticated databases outside of AlphaBanc's purview in order to
complete, or unify, the profiles.

Clayborne thought right away that it must be the IRS files,
arriving probably at this moment at the McCarthy complex in
Red Rock, but Blair told him he didn't think so. From the bits
and pieces he's heard along the way, Blair thinks that there's even
something bigger that they need the Gnome for, and right away
too. But what that is still eludes him.

Their conversation continues through another bottle of champagne, which helps to soften the realization somewhat of how
easily they were prepared to sacrifice Christin for the Gnome.
Which is in itself quite disturbing, but there is so much information, all of it tangled and complex and ugly and containing so
much pain that much of the beatific bubbly is required to dull
and mute the dark knowledge, and taken together, the events of
the day, of her life of late, of all of it together, even this apparition, "Richard," sitting improbably across from her, results in an
episode of sudden and surprising sobbing, apparently long-
repressed and necessary, through which he steadies her, holds
her, softly kisses her salty lips, pays the bill (the demeanor at La
Fontaine perfectly seamless, a scene perhaps enacted often
before the competent tuxedoed staff), and escorts her, perhaps a
bit unsteadily himself, home to Lambert Towers.

CHAPTER FIFTY-THREE

WHOAAA . . . A TRULY wild and crazy night, one he has not seen the likes of in quite some time, having awakened to the sun rising, or—God help him—setting? through tightly-pulled blinds. He is still hungover, staggering around her apartment, trying to ascertain roughly latitude, longitude, vertical, horizontal . . . while slowly comprehending that it's most likely been *two* wild and crazy nights, that's right, it must be Saturday morning now, or actually—looking painfully out at the last of a bloodshot October sun throwing angular shadows through a maze of gnomonic high-rises—Saturday evening.

She's still sleeping so he stumbles into the shower, emerges somewhat more awake, runs fingers through damp hair, vaguely remembers toasting the dawn with the last of the half-dozen bottles she had in her wine rack, and receiving delivery of a breakfast pizza that she insisted on taking at the door—attired in a purely perfunctory sheer robe, lace bustier and thong, garters, lace-top stockings and stiletto heels, the works—from a perfectly shockable delivery kid, face pimpled and blushing terribly as she scampered around, taking delicious excruciating time to rustle up payment and tip, all in change—wow, was she *ever* wild. . . .

He pulls his bath towel tighter around his waist, thinks that both he and Christin hadn't been with anyone for so long that their pent-up desire just sort of *exploded* here, spewing an extensive trail of unbridled excess, leaving him to survey now the lower levels of this particular den of iniquity littered with wine glasses, emptied bottles of Chardonnay and Chablis, pizza crusts, food plates, assorted articles of clothing or less: stockings, bras, panties, garter belts, assorted high heels, his pair of lucky boxers (bright green with gold dollar signs) hanging from a lampshade, handcuffs on the carpet, roaches in the ashtray, and unbelievably, an inexplicable black leather *bullwhip* snaking through the debris like the primal serpent *Naga*, something he doesn't remember *at*

all, does he? He tries to think, but finds himself instead recol-
lecting the sweet summer of Zara, this impromptu sexy craziness
taking him right back to that time again . . . and to a strangely
troubling sensation he recalls, of when he had left her room the
first time, blinking in the brilliant confusing sunshine outside the
Drake, a nagging feeling that he had left something behind, although he checked all his pockets; he had his watch, keys, his
wallet, everything in it, driver's license, student ID, even the fifty
his dad had given him, all there . . . but it still seemed like he had
left something up there in that room . . .

Uh-oh, *damn,* here's a pretty insistent knock now at Christin's
door. Who could it be? He rushes over, grabs his boxers off the
lamp, hops on one leg, trying to pull them on under the towel
while the banging comes again, much louder. He scuttles up to
the door, squints out the peephole, gasps, it's Blair and-and,
Zara!

Shit! He's not even supposed to be in here with her, but hears
Blair call his name, "Clayborne, open up, kid, on the double."

Clayborne cracks the door to the width of the security chain.
"George, what the hell?"

"Open up, kid. We've got business. Can't wait."

"Hey, no way. We're, uh, not receiving visitors—"

"C'mon kid, we're not kidding."

"No way! Just get the—"

"Okay, stand *back,* kid. Clear out!" And Blair lowers his
shoulder, the chain rips out of the jamb as the door bursts open,
the towel drops off Clayborne's waist, and Blair and Zara and
two ISD goons, wearing requisite dark sunglasses and ear pieces,
stream inside.

"Hey! What do you think you're doing?" Clayborne yells,
trying to pull the towel back up as they invade the apartment, the
goons walking over to peer out through the blinds, Blair quickly
reconnoitering the place, Zara softly tsk-ing, a small smile on her
face as she delicately steps through the love-making ruins.

"Sorry, kid. But we think we've got a good chance to catch
Dunne here. We want to do it tonight. We know he's out there
and we're afraid he might clear out again if we don't act fast."

"Just what the *fuck* is going on here?" demands a voice from
behind them.

All of them turn to look at Christin, fresh from the shower, snugged in a white terry cloth bathrobe, hair turban-wrapped in a towel, striding toward them, her eyes dangerous, outraged, *defiant*.

Clayborne smiles hugely; she's fantastic.

They soon learn that the big plan has already been hatched, Clayborne and Christin only pawns in AlphaBanc's grand game—what else is new—with Christin to parade for Dunne again on her balcony.

It seems that during Christin's last escapade upon said balcony, he had indeed captured her image from some distance away, out there somewhere, but good as the picture was, it was still too indistinct to be able to trace back to Dunne's precise location somewhere in one of the hundreds of distant apartments that look across a gulf of Chicago-space upon Christin's patch of Lambert Towers.

They know that Dunne still monitors the NEXSX site from the intercepted emails he continues to send her. If she would choose to answer him this time and if the, ah, exhibition, were to occur again, with Christin at the *other end* of her long balcony, Blair and Haedler's crack team believe they will be able to accurately triangulate Dunne's location.

Tonight.

Christin sighs, admits that, yes, tonight, Saturday night, is when "Richard" faithfully contacts her, perhaps hoping that they might once again travel together through various, er, interesting areas, of the Net.

Clayborne is outraged. This plan is obviously completely ridiculous, absurd, certainly *desperate*, and he is ready to make a big scene here, throw everyone out of the apartment, half-expecting Blair to pull some heat on him, but a look over at Christin makes him pause, as she is presently listening attentively to Zara, who is talking fast, introducing her to a real punker girl who has wandered in along with the AlphaBanc crew, a professional makeup artist and stylist by the name of Tatyana, actually fairly attractive behind the severe haircut and all the piercings: studs, rings, bangles, jangles, and what-have-you—Clayborne wonders what she's got that he can't see—and it now appears that Christin might actually be entertaining this crazy idea, or, perhaps resigned to the inevitable, at least willing to play along. And as the three women go off to her bedroom, discussing exactly what type of attire and makeup might be appropriate for this sort of spectacle, it already looks like a done deal.

Resistance seems increasingly futile as more AlphaBanc security show up with their high-tech gear: laptop computers, radios and phones and walkie-talkies, night-vision binoculars, high-powered telescopes, carryout food, the interlopers effectively commandeering her apartment, whispering into headsets to yet another team armed with similar ordnance on the rooftop.

The women work through the commotion, however, and eventually Christin emerges from the bedroom sporting a very hot-punk look that Tatyana has developed: severe black leather short-shorts and minimal studded vest, high heel demi-boots, hair pulled straight back, thickly overemphasized eyebrows and lips contrasting with pale-white makeup Tatyana has brushed liberally upon her face and in fact her entire body. She executes a sultry stroll before the gang, stands before the webcam and glances at her image in the big monitor, then languidly takes a glass of champagne offered by Zara, obviously quite pleased with the daring effect—one which they hope that Dunne will go for.

Well, everyone *here* sure seems to be going for it, all the men quietly licking lips, sighing, fidgeting with side arms, finding excuses to briefly leave their posts to cop long looks at the sacrificial alabaster princess who has materialized in their midst, even Zara and the steely Tatyana somewhat doe-eyed at the overall effect they have created, everyone inwardly assured that this is prime, prime no-fail Gnome-bait here.

As he and Blair huddle before a laptop in her darkened kitchen sharing a ham sandwich, it suddenly seems to Clayborne that everyone at AlphaBanc is in on this: they've given him a headset and through it he can hear Haedler talking with Rascher and O'Brian and the others about buildings and streets and coordinates, interspersed with the occasional wolf whistle, and even a stray question for him from the Epenguin: "Hey Richie, how you taking all this, man?"

"Um, okay, I guess. And, uh, Chris seems to be okay with it, so that's what's important."

"Yeah . . . she does at that."

It's show time. Clayborne and Blair watch on their laptops—they're patched into Christin's input—for the picture of her they hope the Gnome will relay back, this time to be carefully scrutinized for changes in attitude and altitude—whatever the geniuses at AlphaBanc require for coordinates. The lights are dimmed, the glow from her big monitor taking over the ambience, everyone hunkers down, and Christin *en costume* dutifully slinks over to the computer desk, carrying a glass of champagne. She sits on her pillowed chair, adjusts her short vest, and just before she logs on, looks over at Clayborne and momentarily breaks her icy mien to flash him a brilliant gleaming smile: *Isn't this crazy?*

Clayborne's heart leaps. She hasn't forgotten him after all. He beams, nods. She winks back, then turns away and quickly becomes Saturday-night serious; she's got work to do here. She smooths her hair, takes a sip of champagne and signs on to NEXSX. Clayborne shakes his head; God, she's good.

Only a few minutes pass before the Epenguin squawks in everyone's headset, "Oh, hey! We've got contact! He's on!" And immediately a flurry of serious and crucial whispering erupts around him along with a static-jumble of disembodied voices floating across the network.

"Okay, now answer him back . . ." he hears O'Brian mutter rhetorically.

And apparently Christin does, smiles at her image blazoned upon the big screen, then opens another message he has sent (voice synthesizer initially off), duplicated on the AlphaBanc laptops—stupid small talk—to which she smiles, types a reply, takes another sip of champagne as she waits for the return message . . . smiles, thinks for a minute, then she types something again.

They converse this way for nearly half an hour—apparently a sort of intellectual foreplay between the crazed genius and the beautiful salon girl—before she calls up the image that he had sent her previously, of her glorious on the balcony, the robe glowing cloud-like around her.

Suddenly, everyone jumps as a resonant male voice booms from her speakers—the voice synthesizer set rather optimistically for "Richard"—commenting upon how lovely, how very, very lovely she is tonight.

To the AlphaBanc agents and others who have left their respective posts in the apartment to stand in the shadows and watch this amazing apparition, that is the ultimate under-statement. Clayborne hears the Epenguin sigh, "No shit," and a chorus of whispered "Amens" from viewers around the Alpha-Banc network, not to mention random sighs from perhaps the odd patched-in hacker out on NEXSX.

True to her mission, Christin has steered the conversation around to the previous balcony appearance, hinting that she had been freaked out at the time, but it really had been tremendously exciting, and, well . . . maybe she'd even consider doing it again.

Clayborne, following the conversation on the laptop—and watching her surprising enthusiasm tonight—thinks that she is most likely telling the truth.

So, apparently, does the Gnome, as Richard. "Please, please, Kitten, don't hide your incredible beauty from the world. You must present yourself for all to see. Please, go to the window again! Just for me! Please!" begs the pseudo-synthesized voice.

For a brief instant Christin turns toward her local audience, and ever so slightly shrugs, arches her eyebrows, before stepping outside to the balcony.

"Please, Kitten you have a wealth of beauty that must be un-veiled before the tawdry ugly world that lies before you . . ." and blah and blah.

How could such a fair young head not be so turned? Dunne's coaxing peroration seems to lead her onward and outward, along with that perfectly vapid look that all tremendously bored pale punk millennium girls over their heads in huge conspiracies must affect. She even might seem a little *too* okay with it, Clayborne thinks, a bit nervously, as he, as everyone, watches her very coolly strike a pose for the Gnome and all of lucky binoculared-at-this-moment Chicago.

"Damn, she's perfect . . ." mutters Blair, who shuts up quickly and clears his throat as he remembers himself, glances over at Clayborne, and then his eyes go glassy as he reaches up to his headset, listens to the voice in his ear. "The Gnome's got her!"

Immediately her silvery image pops up on their laptop, and then he and Clayborne and everyone else hidden in the apartment strain to look over at the big monitor and, sure enough, there she is, a reasonably sharp image through the Chicago air and aether, glowing ghostly white and gorgeous, this time at the far end of her balcony.

Clayborne scratches his head, knows that there are some sophisticated computers crunching coordinates right now in search of a particular window that is out there somewhere, when suddenly his phone vibrates. He pulls it out and finds a message there, apparently again from his mysterious cyber-sooth:

> To find what you seek
> Look beyond
> The tiger's eye
> Which never blinks
> To the one which sometimes winks

Hmm. Clayborne grabs a pair of big binoculars off the table, turns to the window and scans the cluster of buildings facing Lambert Towers that he knows through crucial chatter among the crew here have been narrowed down as possible suspects.

Well, there is indeed a group of lighted windows out there that *might* look like a tiger's eye, shades half-pulled down, and then as he drops the binocs briefly, he spies a blinking light out there.

He pulls them up again, refocuses, and finds a window in a building farther back, well behind the one that is currently targeted, and . . . the light blinks maybe a couple-three times, then goes dark. And then, it blinks on again but the window blind appears to be now pulled halfway down and the effect is pretty much that of a wink! Whoa-ho! This could be it! He quickly begins to count floors down from the top . . . looks like eight. Now he needs to find out which building this particular one is.

"Okay, they think they've located him," Blair whispers loudly. "Let's do it boys," he says, signaling to the goons, motioning to Clayborne to come along and, (quite reluctantly) leaving Christin on the balcony, they all run for the door.

Chapter Fifty-Four

"HEY, GEORGE," CLAYBORNE grabs Blair's sleeve as they are trotting down the hallway in Lambert Towers. "Listen, I think we might have the wrong place."

Blair looks at him as they stand packed together in the elevator, "What do you mean, 'the wrong place?' You don't even know which apartment it is yet. *I* don't even know yet. They're going to radio us directions."

"It might be the wrong building."

"Huh?"

Clayborne considers . . . how is he going to explain a cryptic haiku email from an unidentified cyber-soothsayer? He decides to keep cool, maybe they really have located the madman. "Uh, never mind."

Turns out to be 4901 of the Hoffman building and their van screeches to a stop in front. Blair flashes his badge, practically stiff-arms the doorman to get them inside and then it's a tense elevator ride to the forty-ninth floor, a lope down the hallway to 4901 and—blam! no-knock here, they kick in the door and it's dark inside except for lots of candles all over, uh-oh, and then some outraged shouts, a woman screaming from the bedroom which Blair and the advance goons have just barged into . . . and then it is immediately apparent that they have interrupted a couple apparently well into some Saturday night *live*, oh boy, no Gnome here, all right, time to flash the phony badges and apologize and, for good measure, zap the innocent lovebirds with Tasers, poor bastards, what the hell, A-Banc ISD will cover everything they do anyway, get back down to the van before they come to their senses.

"Goddamnit! It's the last time I trust those fucking computers," Blair sputters as they speed away from the scene of their miscalculation. "Well," he turns to Clayborne, "did you say you thought we might have the wrong building?"

Clayborne points it out best he can . . . and it appears to be O'Byrne Towers, several blocks behind the Hoffman, they learn, Blair shouting and cursing into his cell phone at the incompetent systems fucking idiots in Chicago, McCarthy, and wherever.

Headquarters gives them a tentative go-ahead as apparently this location also pretty well fits the coordinates that Alpha-Banc's computers have spewed out.

"The big southern fried chicken is gonna come along on this one," Blair grunts as he lights up a cigarette. "Someone—Bergstrom, I'll bet—told him to get his ass down here on the front lines. Good. Let him take some of this heat, too."

They pull over on a side street where Haedler is waiting with the Epenguin who is dressed tonight in one of those tuxedo T-shirts, a black tux jacket, and a dented homburg—the casual Epenguin. The van creaks downward as Haedler pulls his bulk into the crowded vehicle; the Epenguin stays outside.

"So you got this on your phone?" Haedler, still puffing, looks fiercely at Clayborne, street lights weakly illuminating their tense faces.

Clayborne shrugs, hands the device to Haedler, who scrutinizes the softly backlit verse, grunts, "Hmph. No idea who this is from, huh?"

"Or *what* it's from," says Clayborne. "Other folks get them, too, I hear. Weird messages like this. Epenguin told me. Rumor is that it might, uh, be the Beast itself."

"Huh?"

"The huge computer system at the McCarthy complex. It's called—"

"I *know*, boy. I've heard. Gives me the royal-ass creeps."

"I heard the 'Magic Mountain,'" ventures one of the more thoughtful goons.

"That's old."

Haedler calls in to confirm the operation and they're set to go. There's no other option right now—other than give up and go home. The Epenguin squeezes in and they speed off.

Ten minutes later they're jammed into an elevator in O'Byrne Towers, sweating and puffing and tense. Nobody speaks.

This time they pause outside the apartment in question on the fifty-fourth floor, eight down from the top. "That's a goddamn calculation they can handle!" Haedler chuckles.

"Shhh," the Epenguin waves for quiet. He's holding a little black box with a short antenna, listening with earphones as he moves it slowly around in front of the apartment's door.

He lowers the box, takes off the headset. "Well, there's definitely quite a lot of electronics running inside here. He'd need that kind of stuff to do his thing, but whether it's *his* stuff . . ." the Epenguin shrugs. "We'd have to identify the lines into this apartment, down in the basement, and then tap in to them—"

"No time for that, bird-boy," Haedler decrees. "We a-goin' in!" He nods to the goons who pop the door somewhat more skillfully this time and then, guns drawn, they all rush into the darkened apartment, Blair, as usual, in the lead.

But this time they are only bathed in the bathyspheric ambience of softly glowing red, green, and gold indicator lights, and in the center of the living room, facing the window, the silhouette of a huge telescope, the business end of which sports several tiny lights of its own, the device obviously outfitted with its own electronic accoutrements. It appears to be aimed at something far distant, perhaps the balcony of one Christin Darrow?

The Epenguin switches on a tiny flashlight, scuttles across the room, and clicks a button on a dark computer monitor, which slowly illuminates, indeed revealing upon it Christin's ethereal image, still lingering pensively on the balcony beyond: languid, pale, beautiful.

They gather to silently gaze at the screen, marvel at the ingenuity and electronics that make this all possible.

"Well, hot damn! We've found it," says Haedler, breaking the spell. "Somebody turn on the lights, hey!"

"But not him," observes Blair. "He's skipped out—"

"Yep," says the Epenguin after a quick review of the equipment in the room. "From the dust on everything he probably hasn't been here in some time—since he first set it up. It's absolutely incredible, I've never seen anything like it . . ."

The Epenguin patiently walks them through the setup, the camera affixed to the telescope, everything completely automated: focus, shutter, even the room shades, all plugged into the computer in the corner, which is linked to the Internet and the Gnome, who is—anywhere.

"And ever'where," Haedler rumbles gloomily. "Damn! We just can't seem to git our hands on that ol' boy!"

Clayborne finds the switch for the window shade, pushes aside wires, runs it up and down himself. "That's how it blinked, er, winked, at me. The room lights must be hooked in, too."

"Sure," says the Epenguin. "To make it look like someone really lives here. Blinds go down in the day, up at night. Crazy brilliant game he plays."

"Well, he's got to be the one then," says Clayborne, "who sent me that message."

"Maybe. Maybe not," says the Epenguin. "Why would he want us to shut him down? You know, the beast is his baby, too. Maybe it somehow—narced on him."

"Aw, c'mon . . ."

The Epenguin shrugs, surveys the room, "Everything's hooked together. When it hits the Net, the beast is there. Anything's possible . . ."

"Well, one thing's sure, now, he knows we're on to him," says Blair, squinting as he lights up a Pall Mall.

"That's fer sure," says Haedler, lighting a cigar. "If we ever fooled him to begin with—"

"He'd play along anyway, I think," says the Epenguin. "But now . . ."

"We've taken away his girl," says Blair, "his beauty—"

"From the beast," says Haedler. "But . . . damn it all! We lost him again! Shoot!" He walks over to the window and looks thoughtfully out at the city lights.

"Well," says Blair, "we can find out who's been paying the rent here, who's paying the utilities, the Internet, the usual stuff."

"Yeah, we can," Haedler snorts, still looking out the window, "but I'd be real, *real* surprised if it turned up anyone like Normie Dunne. That old boy's just too smart for us. Well, someone go down to the van and bring up the tools."

It takes them a couple of hours to dismantle and carry everything out of the Gnome's secret listening and viewing post: big telescope, computer, monitor, several boxes of wiring, automated

switches . . . even the motorized shades. As they are about to
shut the door for the final time, the Epenguin suddenly squawks,
"Shit! We're screwed!"

"What?"

"Damn it," says the Epenguin, "oldest trick in the book.
Gimme one of those crowbars, okay?" With his flashlight, the
Epenguin closely inspects the inside door frame through which
they have carried all the Gnome's equipment. He takes the tool
and begins prying at the moulding around the door. It pops right
off and reveals a gleaming bright orange mass of copper wire
packed inside the door frame.

"What the hell is that?" growls Haedler, tilting his fat chin
upwards, bulldog-like, to inspect the strange wiring.

"The Gnome's brilliance . . ." says the Epenguin grimly. "A
humongous electromagnet he's installed all around the door.
And, let's see," the Epenguin slides open an adjacent closet door,
"aha, a little transformer in the corner for power, of course. And
everything we carried out went through the magnetic field."

"And so . . . what?" demands Haedler.

"And so . . . all the software that we carried out is erased. Or
really screwed up. Just like we passed it through a degausser—a
media erasing device. I had hoped his hard drive and the other
stuff might provide us with some clue to the Gnome's whereabouts, but even if it could, now I doubt that there's a chance in
hell."

"Well, damn! Now there's just no gettin' at that ol' boy!" says
Haedler, chomping fiercely on his cigar stub, unable to resist a
smile of admiration. Then, immediately sober, he looks at Blair
and sighs, "Guess we're just gonna have to go with Plan B."

Blair nods, begins to look over at Clayborne, but then seems
to catch himself and looks away.

Clayborne wants to ask what exactly "Plan B" is, but is immediately put to work along with the rest of them, Haedler barking
orders to rip out all the copper wiring from the door frame,
"every goddamned bit of it!" leaving no trace of the Gnome's
infernal handiwork.

Chapter Fifty-Five

IT'S TWO A.M. when Clayborne and Blair finally walk out of the bright fluorescence of AlphaBanc's rear garage entrance, having hauled all the Gnome's gadgetry into one of the labs for analysis, leaving the Epenguin, who never seems to sleep, with a big bottle of Mountain Dew and the Gnome's hard drive to see if any data on it might be salvageable.

"Not like the usual grind, huh, kid?" Blair says, lighting up a smoke.

"Uh-uh. No way." Clayborne is exhausted, but his soul is zinging. He can't remember when he's had this much excitement. "You, uh, do this kind of stuff all the time?"

Blair laughs. "No, kid. This has been one of the wilder ones, I'll tell ya. But this whole Gnome thing has been wild from day one."

"I believe you."

"Where you headed for, kid?" Blair coughs, looking up the deserted street for a cab.

"Well, I thought back to Christin's . . ."

"Aw, that's a no-go, kid, sorry—"

"What? What do you mean? No-go?"

"C'mon, let's us walk downtown a little ways, I know a bar that's open late—"

"No, goddamnit! What do you mean: no-go?"

"Look kid, you remember we had to go to Plan B?" Blair begins walking towards the nocturnal tavern, calls back to Clayborne, "It's unfortunate, kid, I know how you feel, but it's a dirty business—it is a business, don't forget that, it's all business—and the girl had to be taken into custody, you see. For her own good."

"Custody?" Clayborne begins jogging after him. "Wait up. What the hell do you mean—custody? I don't see—"

"Dunne might go right for her now, kid. We took away his little spy setup. Who knows what he might do? He tried to kill her before don't forget—once-removed, to be sure, but she almost bought it that night."

Clayborne is staggered, trying to understand what's happening here. "So-so, she's not in her apartment right now?"

"Nope. Not right now . . ." They've arrived at the tavern and Clayborne follows Blair in.

"I-I can't believe that she'd—Chris—would just go along with that," says Clayborne as he slides into a dim booth across from Blair, who seems very at home here, addressed the server as Annie and asked for two Glenlivets as they walked in. From where they sit Clayborne can see the television over the bar flashing soundlessly something in black and white, an old movie at this wee hour, looks to be the Kubrick classic, *Dr. Strangelove*.

"Well, kid . . . I don't think she did 'just go along with it,' but—"

"Zara did this, didn't she. She took . . . she-she *kidnapped* Chris, didn't she?"

Blair rubs his eyes, slowly shakes his head. "It's not Zara, kid, it's bigger than that, than her, than us . . . and it's not kidnapping, exactly . . ." he trails off to a whisper as Annie sets the drinks in front of them.

"But-but she did it. Zara took her away."

"Yeah, I suppose she did. With A-Banc security, of course. But, kid, only because it's her job." Blair reaches for his drink. "Calm down, Richie, Chris's in good hands. She's safe. You should be glad she is."

Clayborne doesn't know what to think. He takes a big swallow of his drink and coughs. "But it's not right. You just can't do that!"

"Says who?"

"The-the law. The constitution!"

"The law?" Blair hoots. "This is big-big business. There are no laws that apply to us. You know that."

"But, you just can't take a human being and—Jesus!"

"Welcome to the dark side, kid. Welcome to the asylum. Welcome to AlphaBanc."

"Okay, okay, so where did they take her?"

"Don't know. A safe place somewhere. They didn't tell me. Doubt if they will . . ." Blair flicks ashes from his cigarette.

"Why won't they? I thought you knew what was going on here."

"Some things they tell me. Some things they don't. I survive a lot better if I don't poke around where I'm not supposed to."

"So. What can we do?"

"Sit tight. Play along. Be nice to Zara—"

"Oh God, oh God . . . she's doing this to get me. And Chris, now. I know it. We're doomed. We're totally fucked."

"Well, we're only doomed if we do something stupid. Then we're dead meat—and maybe Chris, too. But all we gotta remember," Blair sighs, sips his drink, "it's just business, is all."

The scotch begins to gradually round the edges off of Clayborne's anxiety, but he still can't believe the strange set of circumstances Blair is so comfortable with. "But—just to take her away like that. Jesus! Won't she be missed . . . somehow?"

"She works for AlphaBanc, remember? Her parents are way out west somewhere. She's now officially on special assignment. Temporarily incommunicado. And so, by the way, are you. Starting right now."

"I am? Oh, not that bullshit again."

Blair already signals Annie for another round. "Hey, it took a little bit of doing, you know. So don't screw this up—"

"Screw what up? What assignment?"

"The deal is . . . I told them that I needed you full time now to help me with whatever happens with Dunne, and with helping them up in Red Rock to prepare for the elections."

"Oh Jesus, the elections . . ." Clayborne had totally forgotten about them again, a tremendous AlphaBanc coup, and also great publicity—if nothing goes wrong. He ponders this, looks up, sees a familiar face up on the TV screen, Darby O'Banknote, with the big white moustache smiling down at him, at all of late-night Strangelovian Chicago, wagging his fat pink finger, soundlessly reminding them that he would always be their "biggest best friend." And although he's seen the apparition hundreds of times, he still has to marvel at the slick weird little character that he happened to have a hand in creating.

"You with me kid?"

"Huh. Oh, yeah. The, uh, drink's doing its thing."

"Why God made it. My favorite drug. Not like that god-damned Deludamil that everyone's taking."

"Er, yeah, but . . . what I wanted to ask was, why are you doing this for me? Having me work with you?"

"Well, strangely enough, I actually like you, kid. I don't think that you're really the mean-ass bullying little son of a bitch that everyone says you are."

"I'm—what? They do? Who . . . ?"

Blair chuckles. "Seen it before. Bein' an asshole is a lot like when the old lady runs around. You're always the last to know."

"God. So everyone does think I'm—"

"Hey, don't feel so bad. At least it didn't take much to convince Bergstrom and the boys that you're one of them. Had to tell them that 'my investigation' leads me to believe you're not really all that nuts about Darrow, just out to have some fun, Mr. Love 'em and Leave 'em. And they damn well believed me, ha-ha. You know, kid, you just might have what it takes to get to the top of a giant place like AFS. Get to hang with Bergstrom and the rest of them. They're all psychopaths . . . except maybe Lefebre, who's getting soft in his old age—just like me. Then, when you get to the top you see how lonely it is. Big reason is because you're such a sonofabitch by then no one can stand you and the people you hang around with, Sturgis, Gates, Van Arp, and the lot, they're just like you!"

"Jesus, you're comforting."

"Well, I had to convince them to keep you around. Anyway, it's obvious to me that you fake it, put on a front, maybe with your hotshot dad it was all you knew to do. Problem is when you do it too long, you might get to believe yourself, become the thing you hate."

"What? You think that I—"

"Ahh, you're just like all the rest, big jerk on the outside, soft and scared inside, afraid someone's gonna prick you and all the hot air's gonna come out. Maybe you should just let it happen."

Clayborne's glad he's drinking heavily, doesn't know what to say to this but begrudges that Blair is a perceptive guy. In fact, goddamn if he isn't absolutely right. Natalie knew what he was like inside, more marshmallow than maniacal if the truth be told.

Of course. He feels vaguely, momentarily, better about himself: she'd never have taken up with a *complete* jerk. . . .

"So anyway, kid, I think in this whole Gnome thing you've gotten a raw deal—along with Darrow there. Plus, it's obvious you kids like each other, so who am I to keep a good thing from happening? Like I said, this'll keep you around here. Better to keep track of her once she's, uh, released."

"Mighty decent of you. But I just can't start working here in Chicago. I've got my work back in San Fran—"

"All taken care of kid. Everyone knows the electronic elections are a huge thing for A-Banc and you're here to help out. End of story. We got you a suite at the Hyatt. You just fly back for a day and take care of business . . . and then you're set."

"But . . . this is crazy. I just can't—"

"Kid, it's the career opportunity of a lifetime. Bergstrom and the boys are going to be all over this project. You can't buy that kind of visibility."

"Hmm. So when do I get to see Chris?"

"Soon as we work out the details. Just . . . not right away."

"God, this is so nuts . . . such a crazy, dirty business . . ."

"It is, kid, it is a goddamn dirty business. But it'll be okay. You'll be around here to help me take care of things. And maybe to keep an eye on my backside, too."

"Oh, do you . . . worry?"

Blair nods. "All the time. Especially with something so big going on. It's downright spooky. I keep asking myself, why do they want Dunne so bad?"

"Well, he's a super-hacker, right? A computer genius."

"That's what they all say."

"Huh. Well it's obviously some system they want to get into."

"That's right. They want to get into something somewhere real bad. But I don't know what it is. They won't tell me. And I do want to know, because I'm afraid if something goes wrong, I might be among the poor bastards tapped to take the fall. And a fall at AlphaBanc tends to be from a very high place."

"Huh."

"I mean that literally, kid," Blair snorts and sucks down more scotch. "I shouldn't breathe a word, but, fuckit, I spend my whole life not breathing a word; someday I won't be breathing at all and . . . no one will ever know. Which of course is the way they want it. It's a lonely life, kid, and maybe that's another reason why I want you around . . . just someone besides me to know what's really going down."

Through his fatigue and the creeping pleasant incoherence of the liquor, Clayborne tries to make sense of this. "What-what are you trying to tell me?"

"That they'll stop at nothing. *Nothing*. That's what I want to tell you. Maybe I'm just making this up, maybe not, but there was a guy not too long ago now who gave away some information he shouldn't have. To some kid, like yourself. Well, not really. A geek kid. One of those hackers. Lost track of him, but not this guy. Just couldn't see what was coming. He was pretty high up with A-Banc, took quite a fall. Literally. Still makes me sick to think about it."

"Jesus, are you telling me—?"

"I'm telling you to watch your step. Like I watch mine. Otherwise he does." Blair nods up at the TV, another idiotic Darby O'Banknote commercial.

"Yeah, I'm sorry about that, him," Clayborne stares down into his glass. "He seemed like a good idea at the time . . . hell, a great idea. Maybe too great an idea. You can have them sometimes, you know . . ."

"Huh?"

"Oh, never mind. Maybe we both . . . in our jobs for Alpha-Banc, have done some dumb things. Things we regret." Clayborne takes a big swallow of his drink.

Blair looks at Clayborne, then across the dim expanse of the tavern, out the dirty windows at the black Chicago night, dark city, red neon glow from somewhere above reflecting on hushed walls, the dark windows of a police car sailing by, a shining dream out there that he once might have had. "There was another guy that we, I, helped do a number on a little while back. He was an idealist, a-a damn nice fellow—" Blair stops.

Clayborne looks at him, thinks he might even spot a trace of some 86 proof tears in the ex-cop's bloodshot eyes.

But Blair steels himself, snorts, "Stupid guy. He didn't listen. I tried to warn him. Something I never did before." Blair drags on his Pall Mall, exhales wearily. "I dunno . . . maybe I'm getting too old for this, maybe I'm . . . maybe this world has just gotten too fucked-up to comprehend anymore."

"Amen to that. So, uh, what do you think this 'big deal' is? Any guess at all?"

"Damned if I know. At first I thought it was the IRS files, as they're probably gonna need the Gnome to deal with them. But now I think there's an even bigger deal—maybe something to do with the elections, and—"

"Oh my God!" Clayborne sits straight up. "Do you think? Do you think it might be . . . ?"

"What, kid? It's late and my old boozed-up brain can't keep up with—"

"The elections! All of the election results are going to flow through AlphaBanc's computers—"

"Up in Red Rock."

"Yeah, but-but when I was up there O'Brian told me that even though it was AFS computers, it was the government's software and their technicians and they were even bringing in federal marshals to guard the whole setup. My God! I bet they're going to try to get deep inside that system and-and maybe—"

"Throw the elections?"

Clayborne, looking wild-eyed at Blair, nods.

"Ohh . . . no," Blair slowly shakes his head. "Jesus, kid, you might be right on with that. I happen to know that they've worked out a really hush-hush deal to take over a big chunk of the NSA's totally screwed-up computer systems. You never heard me say that, kid. That's death-info, big-time. But it's what bought them the rights to run all the election stuff through McCarthy."

"Huh. I always wondered how they swung that deal."

"Also the IRS stuff."

"Jesus. It-it's almost too big to comprehend."

"In a way it is and in a way it isn't," Blair chuckles and drags on his cigarette. "Sometimes it all comes down to something pretty simple. Bergstrom and the boys joke about the price of the whole shebang being Mr. Walker's blow job."

"So who's—Mr. Walker?"

"No one, kid. He's no one you ever heard of. You'll live longer that way. And so will I. Maybe."

Chapter Fifty-Six

EXHAUSTED AND INEBRIATED, Clayborne manages to check into his suite, finds his bags already in the room, tumbles fully clothed onto the bed and falls instantly asleep. He awakens just before dawn, a dirty gray-gold wash of sky beyond his windows.

Still somewhat drunk, he undresses, stumbles around in distended boxers, vaguely aroused as he remembers the glamorized Christin of last night, thinks that he wants very much to be with her right now, and then remembers that he can't. She's gone. *They've* got her. Damn! Goddamn AlphaBanc and its unholy scheming! *Goddamn them!*

He drags out his laptop, remembering that the Epenguin was going to forward any of Christin's correspondence his way, hopes maybe that he sent along some of the images of her on the balcony last night—or possibly they're available on the NEXSX site. Either way, he realizes how pitiful it is that these bits, bytes, and glowing pixels are all he's got of her right now.

But immediately upon opening his mail, he receives a strange anonymous message:

> A man who strives to great achievement
> And conceals cowardice in his heart
> Shall, at his greatest trial, surely fail

Oh God, another cryptic dispatch from—whom? The Gnome? Clayborne shakes his head, notices there's a small icon at the bottom of the message that appears to be a little animated stick of dynamite, fuse audibly fizzing on his computer's speakers, and, what the crazy hell, he moves his cursor over and clicks on it. There is a big cartoon KABOOOOM! speakers resonating, the screen flashing with an animated explosion and the next message to appear through the pixelated smoke-clouds is: *Whatever happened to Billy Zimmer?*

Clayborne's heart skips a beat, mouth drops open . . . my God! How could anyone know about *that*? The hairs stand up on his arms and the back of his neck.

It—the dark ugly secret that he kept so well compartment-alized in the back vault of his mind—had happened long ago, way back in that fateful junior year in high school when Billy, crazy Billy, used to hang on the outskirts of Clayborne's clique, which comprised the richest and snobbiest kids at rich and snobby Triton High in cultivated Wilmette, Illinois. Back then, Clayborne had it all, good-looking son of the biggest IBM salesman in the Midwest, wearing the best clothes, driving the old man's Jag, hanging with other bored rich adolescent heirs apparent. But Clayborne at the time had a rebellious streak that led him to consort, albeit intermittently, with crazy Billy Zimmer, actually, a thoughtful kid, but one of the poorest at the school, making up for what he lacked in money with brains and zany daring . . . and a fairly warped running joke of blowing up the whole stupid school with dynamite.

Of course, the idea was crazy, outlandish, yet somehow intri-guing, explosive, to seventeen-year-old Clayborne who couldn't seem to get his workaholic father's attention unless . . . unless he did something perhaps really, really big . . . and so, after chug-ging most of a six-pack of Mickey's Malt Liquor that wild Billy stole from a nearby mini-mart, Clayborne found himself driving them in the XKE out to a stone quarry south of Naperville where Billy knew he could get some actual honest-to-god explosives. Billy's uncle worked there, and he knew in which shed they kept the dynamite, where they kept the blasting caps, and where the night watchman would be sleeping most of the night in his pickup truck.

At least they had dressed for the part, in ninja-black, parking on a wooded back road behind the quarry, crawling like com-mandos through a hole in the fence Billy knew about. Billy had copied keys to the sheds they needed to get into and in a few frantic minutes they had liberated a dozen sticks of dynamite and a handful of blasting caps which Billy stuffed into the big pockets of his windbreaker. Clayborne, sobering up somewhat, couldn't really believe it had been that easy, was suddenly freaked at the perilous booty and wouldn't touch any of it, deciding he was only the driver. They would be out of here soon; they weren't really going to blow up the school; all he had to do was talk Billy out of his crazy plan. Later. After they got out of here.

But then the lights of the watchman's truck suddenly flashed across the buildings and machinery. Clayborne and Billy ran for the quarry wall and began scrambling up the pile of rubble that sloped up to the rock face, Clayborne shouting that he wasn't going to climb up there in the dark, it was nuts . . . but then the watchman's truck pulled slowly around a gravel pile and Clayborne began running for the wall, right behind Billy.

It was tough going in the clouded moonlight, but Billy apparently knew the way, having climbed it as a kid for sport, and got them nearly to the top, just below a vicious overhang of eroding topsoil and roots extending from the field above. Billy started climbing up through the rubble to the right of them, edging around an outcropping where Clayborne lost sight of him. He was about to follow, but during a momentary break in the clouds he thought he spotted another way up, one to the left that disappeared between several dark bushes clinging to the face of the cliff. If there was any purchase available between them, it looked like it might lead directly to the top. What the hell, he clambered up through the rubble between the bushes, feeling his way ahead, desperately clawing at rocks and roots in the darkness, managing to pull himself upwards with the last of his strength and he suddenly found himself on top, gasping for breath, heart banging away inside his chest.

After several minutes he called out to Billy.

"I think I'm stuck, man," came the reply.

Clayborne slowly made his way around the rim until he could see what he thought was Billy below, a dark shadow nearly spread-eagled on a steep sloping slab of limestone. "Can you go back around? Come up the way I came?"

"No. Some rocks fell. I-I'm stuck. I'm afraid to move."

"Okay, okay. Maybe I can—"

"Come down here, man, help me get back around."

Clayborne's heart sank. To go back down again was out of the question. He looked up. The moon was almost completely hidden by the clouds.

"I need your help, Rich."

Clayborne's mind raced. He was safe; he couldn't go back down there. He had to get a rope somewhere. He thought back to their drive here. Had there been a fire or police station anywhere back there? They were a good twenty minutes from anything. What a mess this was. All he wanted to do was go home, clean up, get something to eat, watch some TV . . . but here he was with whiny Billy in this stupid miserable quarry. Clayborne decided he didn't like him at all, never had. How had he ever let him talk him into coming out here? He wanted out of there, away from Billy, away from his stupid crazy ideas.

"Rich . . . I-I'm getting tired, man. Don't think I can hold on much longer."

Oh God . . . Clayborne didn't want to hear that, didn't ever want to talk to him again, but he yelled, "Hey, hang on! I'll get help. A rope or something!"

He turned and began running through the black field back to where he had parked the car, imagined for an instant he heard Billy reply, surprisingly close, a small whisper in his ear, "Don't bother . . ." and in the next moment came a horrifying flash followed by an explosion that rocked the night, echoes rolling hugely up from the pit below. Clayborne fell to ground, numb, scared. Then he got up, began running again for the car. . . .

Clayborne stares now at the email, sweat breaking out on his upper lip, wishing to God he still had some Deludamil, but there's none here, and the thought of booze from the mini-bar is nauseating, so there's nothing available to ease this incredible impossible intrusion from his past.

How could anyone have known? After the explosion and the apparent end of Billy, Clayborne went home and showered, but couldn't eat, could barely sleep, and said absolutely nothing to anyone. As the news of the explosion and then the riddle of the missing Billy Zimmer were pieced together, Clayborne spent long days back at school in a cold sweat, a perpetual knot in the pit of his stomach, shaking his head in disbelief with all the others at Zimmer's strange fate, and waiting . . . waiting for someone who knew they occasionally hung out together to ask if he knew anything about the death, the dynamite, the quarry . . . but no one ever did.

The police came to the school, interviewed several students and teachers, but never him. No one knew anything. He never even attended Billy's memorial service; not many from the school did. Billy wasn't very well-liked after all, was kind of nuts, actually . . . and he always had wanted to blow up the school, everyone knew that.

Clayborne the coward. As the days grew into weeks and then into months, culminating in the superb summer of Zara, the mysterious death by dynamite of Billy Zimmer faded into Triton legend, eventually into a vague In Memoriam tribute in the school yearbook, and Clayborne, having analyzed every aspect of that dark and destructive night, concluded that he had done the only thing he could have—run for help. There was no way he could have gone back down that dark path to rescue him . . . was there?

Was there? He'd never know, but he couldn't shake the feeling that deep down he was nothing but a coward who let his companion down. A coward who ran. Who was glad he never had to go back, who never had to tell anyone, who never had the guts to do the right thing. A miserable stinking coward.

And now . . . someone has seen fit to throw this in his face again. How could anyone know? Clayborne walks to the window, watches the sky grow brighter and wonders . . . who—or what—is out there? What does it know?

Chapter Fifty-Seven

IT'S RAINING HARD and a cab brings Clayborne and Blair up to the Club Ventosus, an old dark building on the gold coast, heavily ornate with fluted columns, scrolled stonework, and maybe farther up in the shadows, elaborately sculptured gargoyles of preeminent Chicago denizens: Capone, Vrdolyak, Daley the elder, Royko . . . staring hollowly out into the stormy brawling prairie metropolis that marks their place, the latter two perhaps with a granite eye forever locked upon the other.

A doorman in greatcoat opens the taxi doors and they splash up the steps, under his umbrella. Inside, a fetching hat check girl in a sort of abbreviated red uniform with a little bellhop's hat takes their coats, fusses adorably with them—this is definitely a men's club—smooths lapels, straightens ties, and points them into the Leviathan Room, a shadowy smoky library with a huge portrait of the early Chicago pol "Big Bill" Thompson presiding above the crackling fireplace. Through the haze someone is waving them over to a close group of overstuffed leather chairs. It is O'Brian. "George, Richard . . . come over here. There's someone who wants to meet you."

An old man is sitting deep in chair, smoking a big cigar. He gestures for them to sit in two empty leather chairs that face him. Clayborne looks around for O'Brian, but he seems to have disappeared. "Uh, my name's Richard—"

"I know who you are. Sit down, please."

Clayborne turns to Blair as he settles into the chair, catches a glance that says: Don't do anything stupid here, kid.

Well, Clayborne thinks this is really an unusual-looking fellow, a strange cross between the menacing, oozing presence in *Casablanca* and *The Maltese Falcon*, Sydney Greenstreet, he thinks, and a nearly-humanoid version of Jabba the Hut, dressed here in a rumpled, but quite expensive-looking brown pinstriped suit. The man holds his cigar in one fat hand and a glass of what looks to be scotch in the other. Clayborne's head swims as he takes in this strange creature, who isn't making any effort to introduce himself, but he hears a voice, very faint, somewhere behind him say, "Uncle Nick's got him now . . ."

"So, you're the latest . . ." says the man, possibly Uncle Nick, flipping the ash from his *Montecristo Robusto* with a fleshy freckled hand.

"Er, the latest? Mr., uh—"

"Yes, yes," Uncle Nick smiles, yellowed teeth through fat lips, "the latest to *do* Zara!" The man chuckles heartily, pinstriped lapels shaking, knocking ashes into his lap. Apparently this is a very funny thing. Clayborne chuckles nervously along. A couple of others in the herd of chairs around them seem to laugh too, but Clayborne can't see who they might be.

"Well, uh, that isn't, uh, exactly—"

"Now, son, the reason you're here, of course, is because we think you're going to be good for this e*nor*mous institution we know as AlphaBanc. Now, tell me, what are your goals, son? Your, shall we say, far-reaching, goals? Reach . . . *far.*"

Clayborne isn't really prepared for this odd "interview," but quickly concludes that his notion of his life at post-present AlphaBanc, a vague though earnest conceit of wealth and power and the large corner office with fine brandy, cigars, and many sycophants, and a really nice car, and-and maybe a private jet . . . suddenly doesn't seem quite so attractive, sitting before this obviously wealthy fat-cat with undoubtedly all of the above. It seems more prudent to take the high road. "Oh, well, uh, ultimately, I guess to do some sort of good . . . in the world."

"Oh really?"

Clayborne doesn't dare to look over at Blair, but can feel his gaze against the side of his face. He knows he sounds like an idiot, scratches his nose. "Yes, sir. I guess so. In the long run that is. In the short run to do, er, the best job for AlphaBanc that I possibly can."

"Oh, such a *delightful* answer . . ." Uncle Nick closes his eyes momentarily as if reflecting on his own impetuous youth. "Well, son, you're young, you might think you know a lot about the way that the world, this world, our world, works, but truth is you don't. For example, just what is your concept of *good?* How would you *define* doing something good . . . in the world?"

"Uh, I don't really know."

"Oh come on . . ."

"Well, I guess I never really thought of it before . . ."

"Surely there must be something . . . good?"

Clayborne glances uneasily over at Blair, receives no help. "Well, like finding a cure for cancer, say."

Someone hoots somewhere behind him.

Uncle Nick's bushy eyebrows raise and a slight smile puckers his lips. "This cure . . . would it be difficult? Expensive?"

Clayborne is lost, outsmarted, wishes he had never opened his mouth. "No, of course not. Simple. Cheap. Something available to everyone."

A man somewhere behind him laughs loudly.

Uncle Nick nods patiently, listens to more laughter rising with the cigar smoke around them. "Well, if someone would come up with something like that, my boy, I can guarantee you that it would never see the light of day. I don't have anything to lose in this particular case, but I can assure you that that is true."

"It is?"

"Oh yes, yes, *yessss,*" Uncle Nick nods slowly, closing his eyes. "Folks have got *millions, hun*dreds of millions, *billions,* invested in this, this disease. So many institutions, hospitals, doctors, pharmaceutical firms, banks . . . depend on it. Disease in America, in the world, for that matter, is good. For us, for our economy—not of course, for the poor bastard who's got something, ha-ha."

"Oh really?" says Clayborne icily, then feels Blair's stare.

"Really, my boy, really," says Uncle Nick, patient, amused. "You see, you will simply have to understand that in our world, AlphaBanc's world, and of course, now, *your world,* our values are somewhat more *prag*-matic, you might say, than what most of America believes. Or like to think they believe.

"To take another example, now . . . social unrest. You see, what's really best for AlphaBanc, and thus America, is a strong criminal element, and lots of it."

"I don't think I get it," blinks Clayborne.

"Well, you see," Uncle Nick licks plum-colored lips, "when there's trouble in the streets, or, nowadays, urban terrorism, as we have so persuasively re-labeled it, the government must *crack down*, or else, God help them, they will be seen as being weak! Suspend freedoms, laws—or perhaps just bend them enormously. Look at what happened after the most heinous of crimes, September eleventh, and what did we get? Public outrage! And then what happens? Why, the empire strikes back! It seems to miraculously gain the power to start locking people up for the most minor infractions. Look at anyone who dares to even be suspected as a terrorist nowadays. In the clink. Or dead. All so-called 'rights' gone." He looks at Clayborne, mouth open in mock smiling astonishment: *What do you think about that?*

Murmurs of approval rise from the dark leather chairs around them. Who are they? Clayborne, sunken uncomfortably low in the soft leather seat doesn't dare look around, away from Uncle Nick's amused gaze.

"So you see, young man, as social disorder increases, we can now label it as a form of *terrorism*, a marvelous source of fear, sweet wonderful communal *fear* . . . to gain the public's support to increase our police forces, our weaponry, and best of all, our surveillance technologies . . . to be able to stop crime before it starts! It's sooo much easier to do these things when they're actually legal, ha-ha."

"Huh. I guess I never—"

"Now you take drugs! Not literally, ha-ha! But drugs, you see, are wonderful, wonderful, *wonderful* things," Uncle Nick continues dreamily.

"They, uh, are?"

"Oh yes. Why, they are the simplest, easiest, most cost-effective way to control—situations, society itself, my boy! Ever drive into the ghet-too, Richard? See how *those people* live? Eh?"

"Well, uh . . ."

"Sure you have. Not very pleasant, is it? No jobs for them, either. It's not that they *won't* work, we all know that. But it's best for everyone else, the lunch buckets, to *think* that they won't. We've imprisoned them very cleverly, you see. They've really got nowhere to go, no funds, no power, nothing . . . So Richard, why do you think that they are able to live in all that poverty and despair? Why?"

"Uh, you got me."

"Well, they're used to it of course, but, you see . . . we take care of them."

". . . their biggest best friend," comes a faint murmur in the darkness, accompanied by wicked low laughter all around.

Uncle Nick smiles and cocks his head slightly, as though listening for more. "Yes . . . well, everyone needs a sense of purpose, you know, everyone: me, you, them. So we give it to them. We give them—drugs! Ha-ha. They don't have anything else, you see, except to join gangs and shoot guns and terrorize each other, and this really *is* the cost-effective option. We've researched it, you see, and—"

"You-you've *researched* it?"

"Oh yes, *yessss*," Uncle Nick purrs. "These drugs—crack, smack, frack, whatever—give them something to go for when they get up in the morning, or afternoon, as the case may be. A person *must* have a purpose in life. We understand that. Of course they've got to pay for them, and so they must steal, from you and me, and their comrades. That, of course, is also crime, and that is where we so thoroughly *crack down*!"

"Well . . . I guess I never really thought of it that way."

"You see, my boy, the greater the public's perception of crime, their *fear* of it, the more control we get. We cherish fear. We nurture fear. We *instill* it in the masses. Terrorism is such a wonderful and timely example of that. It is clearly an immediate threat to our way of life and we must combat it rigorously, along with all the longstanding menaces to society, drug smuggling, child pornography, kidnapping, extortion, embezzlement, tax evasion . . . all being crimes that require sophisticated means to combat, that need precisely the right kind of *information*, you see. And the more sophisticated the means of those who are committing these crimes, the more justified are we in increasing the sophistication of our surveillance. And of course the amount of information we happen to gain about Joe Public in the process, well that's lagniappe. Those are the other fish that get caught in the net. We throw them back you see, but not until we've tagged them, you might say, marked their location, recorded what we've got on them, so that, if we would ever find the need, we could go back and *reel* them in again!"

Clayborne is stunned. This, he understands with sudden horror, describes the beginning of the end of personal freedom. It seems that, after a hiatus of two centuries, all the freedoms forged by Rousseau, Locke, Jefferson, et al. are slowly, stealthily, being voided. The great experiment is over. Society—Joe Public—doesn't even realize what's happening. It's as though humanity is simply destined to revert to the eternal feudal state, where the kings, the nobility, have long held dominion over the vassals and serfs. The personal freedom we have taken for granted for the past hundred or so years is truly exceedingly fragile, only a brief blip in the long history of a species that is destined to be one of inequality: aristocracy and proletariat, masters and slaves, AlphaBanc's elite and the rest of us. Many other nations have reverted to the police state when they felt threatened from within, why not us? Has it already begun?

From his understanding of the enormity and depth of Alpha-Banc's information systems, not to mention the federal government's and other private institutions' shared data, Clayborne knows that such social control nowadays will be extremely effective, practically seamless compared to the gaps and inconsistencies in the data of their predecessors—there will now be no cracks for anyone to fall through.

He feels anger rise within him, vaguely contemplates jumping up and strangling this smug corpulent cobra, as though this might be the evil head of the beast, and were he able to choke it off, all of America, freedom, democracy, civilization as we know it, for God sakes, might be saved.

But just then two great doors swing open at the end of a hallway beyond the Leviathan Room and chandelier lights glow through the haze; men rise from their chairs and begin to stroll toward the dining room. Uncle Nick, Blair, and poker-faced Clayborne, summoning all the control he has to maintain his normally snobby, aloof affect, meander along, Uncle Nick leading them to a sumptuous mahogany-paneled room within which is a long table set with shining exquisitely gold-detailed china and tall ivory candles in ornate silver candelabras.

Clayborne looks inside and thinks: *Wow!*

Chapter Fifty-Eight

A WHITE-GLOVED WAITER pulls back a chair and seats Uncle Nick at the head of the table, who motions with a fat hand to Clayborne and Blair to take the seats on either side of him. Clayborne settles in and looks over at Blair, who shrugs, and then looks the length of the table, sees Bergstrom way down at the other end, and O'Brian, Gates, Lefebre, Van Arp, Sturgis, and others whom he doesn't know, including, of course, this Uncle Nick character before him, someone important enough that he can take one of the heads of the AlphaBanc table and Clayborne has never even heard of him.

Waiters bring wine in really big bottles: magnums or maybe jeroboams, *methuselahs, salmanazars* . . . Clayborne speculates, enthralled in spite of himself as two uniformed sommeliers stop alongside and expertly tilt a huge bottle of white into his goblet, not spilling a drop . . . while Blair is poured a deep glass of burgundy or Merlot. How did they know that Clayborne would want white wine—he takes a sip, guesses Chablis—and with what food?

All the AlphaBanc folk seem to take this ostentation in stride, so, as the salad course arrives on crystal plates, Clayborne tries to take his cues from Blair, tries not look too much like a rube, but he gets a whiff of some delicious perfume in the air, turns to look and—whoa! the waitresses here are all gorgeous, exquisitely attired in the French maid's outfit of every man's dissolute fantasy: lacy décolleté blouses, little transparent white aprons and short-short dark skirts that, as they bend over the tables, reveal black satin garters riding high above dark silk stockings with seams up the back, no less, and of course completely impractical high heels.

Clayborne can't help but swivel around to ogle these beauties—along with, he observes, all the other jovial men in the room, and he also notices that several of the women wear a small numbered waiter's badge, number 44 is on the one waiting on them, and it looks like maybe 38 on the one farther down. Well, this 44 is sure a cute one, great perfume too, he muses as he takes another gulp of wine from his bottomless glass, thinks that, well, hey, maybe some parts of this crazy business might not be so bad after all. . . .

Meanwhile Uncle Nick has continued his conversation with Blair and then turns toward Clayborne: ". . . of course, the goal is simply to cover every area, leave no stone unturned, as it were, in building the complete record, *uni*-fying, one might say, all recordable incidents in an individual's life. That way, you see, we have the whole, the accurate, the complete, as it were, *pic*-ture."

Clayborne nods while chomping on his salad, tunes in again to Uncle Nick's monologue: ". . . cradle to grave, cradle to grave knowledge is what we are going to achieve, you see."

Blair clears his throat and ventures, "So, er, that's a pretty ambitious plan. You might almost say it's a 'grand unification' scheme, eh?"

Clayborne feels his ears twitch, tries not to look too interested.

Uncle Nick looks over, seemingly surprised, eyes squinted, says, "Yesss, one might say that, Mr. Blair. We like to think of it as a process of *aggregation*, you see. Now, let's say that we need to apply some, let's say, pressure, somewhere to get something we need done. Well, the first question of course," Uncle Nick raises his tangled eyebrows to Blair, glances back toward Clayborne, "is exactly where to apply the pressure, and then, how much! And of course the answer to this dilemma nowadays is information! By knowing an individual's pressure points, let us say, we can much more effectively, and economically, apply the necessary stimulus, whether it's, oh, getting someone to agree with your point of view, or, say, persuading these lovely waitresses here to do their jobs better!" Uncle Nick chuckles smugly.

"So, that's what you would call *grand* unification?" Blair casually asks, jabbing his fork into his salad.

"Oh ho," chortles Uncle Nick, obviously enjoying himself, an Oxford don deflecting a riposte from an earnest student. "An excellent characterization, Mr. Blair. In a sense I suppose you could call it that, as so many pieces of data, some, of course, very, very personal, must be assembled, or unified, to get the complete picture of an individual. However, there is yet another, higher level which, oh, I have heard it termed *grand*-grand unification, in which the pressure points of *groups* of individuals, you see, are so well-determined that it becomes exceedingly obvious where to place this pressure. The perfect example of this, of course, is an election, the wonderful democratic process of *voting* for someone, in which many different currents, you might say, are flowing. It is necessary to understand these flows, detect the main ones, and divert them just enough to accomplish your means!"

Clayborne has been listening so intently to Uncle Nick's discourse that he has to be gently nudged by number 44 to receive the main course, which in his case appears to be a perfectly broiled whitefish or perhaps walleyed pike. Which of course would match the white wine but how did they know he would prefer that over, say, that monster New York strip that they place before Blair? Clayborne shudders, wonders, from all that Nick is saying here, just what kind of info is included in his PERSPROF, anyway. Then Uncle Nick's dish is carried in, a large silver platter with an elaborately engraved cover, which appears to be inscribed with an encircling motto of some sort, which he is just able to catch in the subdued lighting, *Ubi Mea Est*, as the dome is carefully removed by 38, revealing some sort of fowl, about the size of a capon, its golden brown skin shining in the candlelight. "Ho, ho, I don't know why they always give me such a large one," Uncle Nick mutters. "I can never finish it all."

Ubi Mea Est? Clayborne shrugs, has no idea what it means, but this strange fowl has captured his attention. "Er, what kind of bird is that?" he ventures politely. "It, uh, looks delicious."

"Oh it is, it is . . . you can't begin to imagine what—fun, it is to dig into one of these babies."

Uncle Nick's rheumy eyes look down the length of the table, and Clayborne reflexively turns to see that Bergstrom at the other end is being served the same dish. He tries again. "Er, and it's a . . . ?"

"Game bird," snorts Uncle Nick somewhat testily through a mouthful of fowl, not looking up from his plate. "An endangered species, some would say, so I can't really tell you . . . exactly . . .

you see. But I can tell you this," he looks up suddenly, smiling smugly. "It tastes like chicken!"

Clayborne acknowledges the bon mot, smiles weakly back. This endangered species thing seems kind of funny, though, and he mentally starts listing possible candidates: spotted owl, California condor, whooping crane . . . but is interrupted by some hubbub and laughter down at the other end of the table. Bergstrom is standing, shaking hands with a late arrival. Others are rising to greet this tall good-looking fellow, who by his glad-handing demeanor Clayborne immediately pegs as a politico, then gasps as he realizes that it is presidential candidate Robert Dean Partridge! the man himself, the former TV game-show host and senator from Indiana, considered this late in the October polls to be a long shot to win. Apparently there has been an empty seat waiting for him and—it must be some honored tradition here—a big silver platter containing the mystery bird is placed before him also amid a great deal of laughing, joking, and general bonhomie.

Partridge gives them all an impromptu dinner speech primarily championing welfare reform, the death penalty, a seeming return to debtors' prisons, and concludes with a humorous note: "I am absolutely for gay and lesbian marriage . . . as long as it is a gay man marrying a lesbian woman," bringing scattered chuckles from the increasingly inebriated crowd, his remarks politely suffered before everyone can dig into their respective dishes.

During dinner and more refills of wine Uncle Nick becomes progressively less talkative, eventually nodding off, chin on chest, over his half-finished fowl.

O'Brian comes up again as the dinner ends, looks rather anxiously at the old man who is now dozing peacefully in his chair with two girls, nos. 33 and 49, gently tugging him awake. Clayborne is dying to ask O'Brian who the old guy really is as they walk out, but thinks better of it as they pass Bergstrom, who is apparently engaged in serious conversation with Partridge, Clayborne catching a waft of murmured inquiry, ". . . still having those dizzy spells, Bobby?"

As the three of them stroll back toward the Leviathan room they pass a narrow dimly-lit corridor that leads off of the main hallway, at the end of which a door suddenly swings open, catches Clayborne's eye, and in the illuminated room beyond he

seems amazingly to see . . . Zara! apparently attempting to calm
down someone, perhaps another young waitress whom he can't
quite make out as Zara is in front of her, though he can faintly
hear a voice protesting and spies great stockinged legs, and just
as Zara turns to shut the door, suddenly looking squarely,
shockingly, at Clayborne, behind her he catches a millisecond
glimpse of . . . Christin! Could it be? And then the door slams
shut.

Clayborne's head swims. All of this has happened in the space
of a few seconds and he stops and knows he's got to find out, to
run down that hall, bust through the door and rescue her . . . but
at that moment someone slaps him on the shoulder from behind
and booms: "Clayborne, glad you could make it tonight!"

It's the big man himself, Bergstrom. Both O'Brian and Blair
turn around at the sound of his voice.

"Th-Thank you, sir," Clayborne babbles. While Bergstrom
turns momentarily toward O'Brian and Blair, Clayborne quickly
looks back down the dark hallway, breathing hard. Had he really
seen her? Was-was that really Christin? A thin crack of light
below the door suddenly extinguishes. Are they gone? Clayborne,
suddenly sweating, doesn't know what to do, although a mad
dash down the hall and wild pounding on a locked and silent
door might not make the best impression at this moment.

Bergstrom tilts his head back toward Partridge in the dining
room and informs the group in a stage whisper, "The man is a
complete idiot. Thank God he's got us to—advise, him."

The three of them smile and nod at the executive, who might
have had a bit too much wine, actually putting a hand now on the
shoulders of both Blair and Clayborne and walking them toward
the entrance, observing, "That number 49, what a dish, eh?"

"Oh, yes sir," returns a chorus of appreciative murmurs.

"She was the one over at that, er, reception, at my place, no?"

"Yessir, I believe she was," responds O'Brian, following
along.

"What was her name again?"

"Er, well sir," O'Brian edging his eyes slightly toward Clayborne, "we don't usually refer to them by—"

"That's not what I asked though, is it?" booms oblivious
Bergstrom.

"Oh, no, no. Well the name of that one is Marcia."

"Marcia . . ."

"Er, Marcia . . . Stepford."

Bergstrom laughs heartily, and they all chuckle nervously along. "Okay, Toby, Marcia Stepford it is. So be it."

They reach the entrance and the uniformed girl retrieves their coats. Bergstrom and O'Brian walk off to talk with some other men and Clayborne turns to Blair. "I-I've got to run back there and . . . I-I think I forgot something."

Blair catches him by the arm. "No you didn't. It's here. We have it. It's okay."

"No, I—" Clayborne tries to twist away but Blair has him in an iron grip. "Hey, let me—"

"*No*, kid," Blair whispers as they briefly struggle, Bergstrom and O'Brian turning to look around. Clayborne catches his breath, smiles sheepishly, and very reluctantly lets Blair walk him out.

Outside in the damp Chicago night, a van pulls up obliquely to a tired-looking computer resale store on Halsted, deserted at this late hour, and the side door slides open. The driver jogs the truck back and forth a few times until a security camera that has been wrenched away from the store entrance and redirected toward the street can focus directly into the van, the interior lights of which now illuminate the features of Zara LaCoste and a gagged and bound Christin Darrow, the latter attired rather fetchingly in a maid's outfit. They are following precise instructions, provided in an impossible-to-trace encrypted email of which they had been sent the public key only hours earlier. The email came in response to a message that had been posted by the Epenguin on various Internet sites: *Elemental Being, we have the object of your desire. Please respond ASAP and she will be yours.*

They sit and wait. No one speaks. Zara lights a Virginia Slims, exhales smoke into the rain.

About ten minutes later a short dark figure in a long raincoat and a fedora comes walking down the street, stops briefly in front of the van to inspect his restrained prize, and then climbs inside. The Gnome has come in from the cold.

Chapter Fifty-Nine

HALLOWEEN IS ONLY a week away but the southern Wisconsin countryside is still surprisingly verdant save for clusters of maples, aspen, and oak flashing red, gold, and bronze alongside corn and oat fields weathered to a rich tan, harbingers all of King Harvest, arriving later and later each year it seems, the last frosts of spring coming earlier, the globe warming preternaturally post-millennium, as though acquiescing to collective North American desires for the ideal endless summer, eternal sunny southern California everywhere. . . .

Clayborne takes in the gorgeous countryside as he rides along in Blair's terrific sports car. You just never know about a guy. He didn't even think Blair had a car, confirmed city dweller that he is, but he told Clayborne that he'd pick up him and the Epenguin for their trip to Red Rock, and then shows up in this super little white convertible, a 1968 Mercedes 280 SE, a real classic. Turns out he keeps it in storage most of the year, taking it out on weekends, usually, perhaps for a scenic spin up to Wisconsin.

So it bodes pretty fair for a pleasant drive up to the McCarthy complex this bright morning, Blair and Clayborne idly chatting, the Epenguin sprawled in the car's back seat, attired in a black T-shirt and rumpled tux coat and lost in cyberspace as usual, wearing a strangely styled headset with a black headband and round visual display that looks a bit like an eye patch, though extending about an inch or so beyond his brow.

The Epenguin said it was called "the Hathaway" model, and Blair snickered saying, "Yeah, E.P., you're a dead ringer for the Hathaway guy, ha-ha," but he wouldn't explain anymore and neither Clayborne nor the Epenguin got the joke.

Clayborne leans back in his seat, feels the wind blowing his hair, takes in high blue skies and rolling farmland as they cruise on the interstate north of Milwaukee, and tries to ignore the near-constant black tension gnawing the pit of his stomach.

On the one hand he's never been closer to AlphaBanc's inner circle, actually on speaking terms, sort of, with Bergstrom himself, and on the other, he's never felt more used, like the lowliest of pawns in the Big Game controlled solely and effectively by AlphaBanc's evil conspiracy team. He's badgered Blair every day since the Club Ventosus about whether that possibly could have been Christin in the back room and raked his own memory, too, but Blair steadfastly denies it, tells him that he must have been seeing things . . . and now he wonders if he really had seen her at all.

Meanwhile, Blair tells him the same thing regarding Christin's weird "detention": she's all right and it's just something he's going to have to live with for a little while until it's okay to let her go. And no, he can't communicate with her, don't even ask.

The thing he has to understand, Blair patiently reminds him, is that he is totally in AlphaBanc's universe now, subject to their laws and mores. Going to the police or FBI or anyone else would be nothing less than suicide—literally. And it could result in Christin's disappearance too, with any possible attempts to link it back to AlphaBanc foiled at every step, as we are really nothing more than so many magnetic fields stored away here and there, most assuredly at the McCarthy complex, where said trail would be immediately and effectively altered to point anywhere they wanted, most assuredly far, far away from them.

"Kid," he had said, "if you understand nothing else, understand that you're just gonna have to sit tight for a while to save all of our skins, here—probably mine, too. Besides, although I don't know any details myself, I can assure you she's okay. If she wasn't, I'd hear about it right away."

Clayborne had also asked him about the evil "Uncle Nick" guy at the club. Blair had told him that, as it was also his first invitation to the elite gathering, he had no idea. His discrete inquiries had gotten him nowhere, other than the impression that the old man was not officially a part of AlphaBanc, but associated with it at some very, very high level, along with the understanding that further inquiries were not appreciated, nor, in fact, healthy.

Clayborne isn't really surprised, but beyond the horror of the old man's revelations and the constant fretting over Christin's well-being, on another level he has to admit to a certain dark fascination with the great machinations all around him. He is anxious to help Blair determine if their hunch is correct, that AlphaBanc really will try to throw the election, undoubtedly in the direction of their man Partridge, who is trailing in the polls by nearly ten points and with the campaign blunders he seems to commit almost daily would absolutely require a rigged election to win.

Clayborne realizes that Blair deals with this type of subterfuge daily, wonders how he is able to do it. He also realizes that he respects the man enormously, is actually somewhat in awe of this truly tough S.O.B., a persona that he, Clayborne, might try to present at AlphaBanc, and might even start to believe during the corporate workday. Deep down, though, he knows he is a fraud, a tawdry replica, something that Natalie knew well, and Blair saw through immediately.

So with only the vaguest sense of comfort, Clayborne tries to enjoy the ride and give some thought to their current mission for AlphaBanc, which is to help them prepare for the elections, little more than a week away now, in which the McCarthy complex will be the focus of national attention, and there is a strong corporate desire, naturally, to see that nothing, absolutely nothing, goes wrong.

Chapter Sixty

THE MAIN LOBBY of the McCarthy complex is elegant and spare, with deep rose granite walls rising three full stories into a skylit atrium above a central fountain and a small grove of ficus. To the right, behind a long mahogany granite security station a team of AlphaBanc ISD officers whisper into headsets as they keep watch on a bank of ten elevators which conduct a steady stream of staff and visitors to and from the underground complex below.

Clayborne, Blair, and the Epenguin take in the surprising brightness of the atrium's early afternoon light as they enter the lobby, their footsteps on the granite floor adding to the cacophony of echoes that ring throughout the space. Blair nods over at the security desk and immediately his phone buzzes. He curses and opens it. It's O'Brian, summoning him to a security meeting. "Jeeze, at least he let me get both feet in the door," he growls.

"Well, we are a little late."

Blair reads the message, grunts. "They want me in a security meeting with the IRS boys. This could go on for a while. Look kid, why don't you let Epenguin show you around down below. Being able to find your way around here'll be helpful once we get busy."

"Okay, you go," says the Epenguin, "I'll show Richie around."

Clayborne and the birdman proceed to an elevator, descend to the lowest levels of the complex, accessible only to those with proper security clearance, which the Epenguin seems to have, pressing his soft white hand against a panel in the car for palm print identification.

"Gotta have proper access to get down here," he says, a hint of pride in his voice as they get off.

"You got a lot of clearance down here, then, Pengy?"

"A lot, but not everywhere . . . yet."

The Epenguin leads him down a series of hallways into what he calls "the catacombs" and Clayborne soon realizes he's actually been here before, recognizes it as the living quarters of the super-geek AlphaBanc programmers: messy rooms full of model airplanes and rockets and the original Telstar hanging from the ceiling, posters of Spock and Kirk and Scotty, Albert Einstein and Moe Howard, old and new glamour pics of Cheryl Tiegs and Farrah Fawcett, Jessica Alba and Scarlett Johansson, lava lamps, rubber chickens, pink plastic flamingos . . . scattered amongst teetering stacks of dense books and systems journals on machine architectures and microcode and compiler specifications—a dormitory on the island of the lost boys.

Clayborne mentions to the Epenguin that there doesn't seem to be any women around here.

"Nope, not in these lower levels. Although there are, of course, some very brilliant women programmers in the complex, they usually don't come down here. They don't seem to develop such, ah, strange personalities as these guys."

"Thank God."

"They're all slaves to the machine, anyway," jokes the Epenguin. "As are we all. I think it makes them a little nuts, you know? Never really knowing when some program doesn't work because it just doesn't work, or because the big Blue Beast is messing with it somehow. No one is really sure."

"Er, did you call it the Blue Beast? I've heard a few different names by now, but not that one."

"Well, it's how some of the guys down here refer to it. The term 'blue' actually refers to shared memory, where the processors hit the same memory pool. Supercomputer thing."

Clayborne decides he doesn't follow him at all, then remembers what he wanted to ask the birdman. "Hey, can we see the big machine, the beast itself? O'Brian was going to take me, but we never made it."

"Great idea, man. Sure, I'll take you down there. I haven't seen the amazing colossal system myself in a while."

Clayborne follows the Epenguin down the corridor to a steep staircase which they take to a lower level. "They wanted the computers down below everything," says the Epenguin, "in case, I guess, of nuclear attack. But the Beast is actually on the second-lowest level down here, which is where we're going now. Below this, on the lowest level, are gigantic ventilation and cooling systems. You know this baby runs so hot that it provides heat for the entire McCarthy complex here. And it still takes twenty or thirty industrial air conditioning units to keep the thing from melting down. You saw the cooling towers as we came in, right? This is one hot mama!" The Epenguin briefly presses his palm to a panel outside a steel door and waves to the security cameras overhead. Something in the wall ka-chinks and the door slides open.

They enter a short brightly-lit corridor lined with small dark glass panels, behind which Clayborne imagines high-tech cameras and teams of drooling jackbooted ISD drones. They walk to a door at the other end which whooshes open as they approach. Beyond is the smell of ozone and the loud steady humming of hidden machinery. Standing serenely before them is a man with a shaved head and a white beard. He is wearing a gray jumpsuit, a white audio headset, and a beatific smile. "Ah . . . the Epenguin, welcome back my little friend."

"Hi, Tor. How's tricks?"

"Well, things down here, they just . . . hum along." He extends his hand to Clayborne, "I am Tor. I will be your Morlock tonight."

"Richard Clayborne. Nice to meet you."

"Yes, Richard W. Clayborne, the W of course standing for Winston, from AlphaBanc West, on special assignment to Alpha-Banc Chicago of late, most recently on a visit up to our humble McCarthy complex with Messrs. Blair and Quentin, and right now you are . . . precisely here!"

"Er, yes, I guess I am. But, uh, how did you . . . oh, never mind."

"I am Tor," he smiles sweetly, "attendant to the Source."

"Actually, Torsy," says the Epenguin, "we've been hearing 'the Beast' up topside, lately."

"Yes, yes, yes . . ." sighs Tor. "The Beast, the Blue Beast . . . we are not entirely sure what ails it.'"

"Norman Dunne is what I've been hearing," says the Epenguin.

"Yes, Toby seems positive that he is the culprit. But to date we simply can't find any evidence . . . but then it's an enormous system. It's possible we just haven't looked in the right place."

"It's a puzzler, all right."

"It truly is. But I take it that you are here now to visit with the Beast, er, Source? Please, follow me."

Tor leads them through a short run of cubicles and desks to a dark-windowed wall and another door which slides open as he approaches it and they step into a huge dimly-lit expanse filled with row upon row of dark blue refrigerator-size cabinets that seem to recede to a dark, indistinguishable vanishing point that, in the heated atmosphere, almost seems shrouded in mist. The air is warm and heavy, smelling strongly of ozone, and the humming all around them is quite loud.

"Wow!" breathes Clayborne as they stroll among the hot buzzing boxes, "so this is, uh, the Beast."

Tor smiles, "Yes, the great intelligence is known by many names."

"So, what are the latest specs on this monster?" asks the Epenguin, wiping his brow.

"Ah, well, our big friend is now capable of an amazing six hundred forty petaflops, which is, to put it more simply . . ." Tor smiles benevolently at Clayborne, "six hundred forty thousand trillion floating-point operations per second. We'd like to double that in the next few years, but for now, its processing power is extremely effective. It is able to split up programs and run segments on many thousands of processors at the same time. There are presently six hundred boxes here housing around one and a half million processors. There are also approximately sixty-four thousand disk drives in over eight hundred cabinets with a capacity of approximately twenty exabytes of storage . . . quite an impressive array, wouldn't you say?"

"Awk!" squawks the Epenguin. "It's incredible! All that horse-power. That's why our searches and matching routines execute so quickly."

"Yes, whether we're performing a lifestyles analysis on a series of PERSPROFs—which as you might know have gotten rather extensive—or modeling consumer or voter profiles, all require accessing millions, perhaps hundreds of millions, of randomly-archived records. To pull together the reports that you fellows, Epenguin, you and O'Brian and Gates, seem to want at any hour of the day or night, requires a lot of, as you call it, horsepower.

And we haven't even gotten to the ten IBM mainframes that are way down at the other end of this area."

"Man," says Clayborne, "this is one big chunk of big iron."

"Oh yes . . . it certainly is," purrs Tor. "You know that all the printed works in the Library of Congress only come to about ten terabytes, tops, their digital collections, perhaps three hundred TBs."

A soft jingling sound comes from Tor's headset. Tor's eyes glaze as he listens to a voice in his ear, says, "Oh my, it appears that one of my test routines has abended. This is something I'm working on in conjunction with . . . the upcoming elections." He raises his eyebrows significantly toward the Epenguin. "It's quite important. I've got to run. E.P., please show Richard around while I'm gone."

Tor hurries away, and Clayborne and the Epenguin stroll a little farther, then stop. The Epenguin wipes his forehead, gazes absently around them and sighs.

"So what ya thinking, pal?" asks Clayborne.

"Oh, I dunno. I guess it's stranger than I remembered being down here . . . inside this monster machine."

"It is pretty weird. Scary, in a way."

"Yeah, that it is. I know you're not going to believe this, but sometimes I think that this big brain here is way more powerful than it should be."

"Well, I guess I am surprised to hear you say that."

"It's freaky. This thing knows way too much about too many people, like you, me, everyone at AlphaBanc, and more and more people in the world at large. It can think so fast, can dredge up information so quickly, so accurately . . . it's like regular folks who can't think as fast, who can't remember *everything*, they don't have a chance anymore. It really makes you wonder."

The Epenguin is talking in a loud whisper, just enough to be heard over the swarming buzz of the great Beast. Clayborne looks around at all the humming blue boxes, begins to feel somewhat intimidated himself. "It's a gigantic thing to be sure, but people like us built it and run it. We're always in control . . . aren't we?"

"Well, I'd sure like to think so, but look at this monster. It sits down here in this special guarded room, sucking crazy megawatts of electricity, has teams of people to constantly attend to it, even more who live and die over what it spews out . . . who's running whom?"

"Hmm. Good question."

"Yeah, Rich, I really think sometimes we've become slaves to the machine, rather than the other way around. We've submitted willingly, too. We can't seem to stop ourselves from putting more and more information about ourselves into it. Not only are a hell of a lot of details about our lives in this thing, but it seems like part of our souls are in there, too."

"Well, it is one monster of a machine . . ." Clayborne isn't sure what to think, other than that the Epenguin, under a lot of stress lately, could be missing his regular fix of Deludamil, whatever that dosage might be, because it seems that he just might be speaking the truth.

Just then Tor returns, apologizes for not being able to show them around anymore, tells them he really has to get back to his systems.

"That's okay, I think we've seen enough for today, hey, Rich?"

"It's quite a sensation, is it not?" Tor says before he goes. "To be in the midst of so much . . . intelligence?"

"It is kind of humbling at that," says the Epenguin.

"Overwhelming, is the word that comes to me," says Clayborne, glad to be able to leave. The incessant humming of the big machine is beginning to get on his nerves, not to mention Tor's weird appearance and creepy smile.

"Come back again . . ." Tor waves as they walk out and Clayborne notices for the first time that he is wearing clear Lucite sandals. Oh brother.

Chapter Sixty-One

THE IRS TEAM has finally left O'Brian's office and Blair is relieved, lights up a smoke and leans back in his uncomfortable leather and steel chair. O'Brian flips the scene on the wall monitor from the departing tax men to a grainy vista of Richard Clayborne and unmistakably the Epenguin walking down a long hallway somewhere in the bowels of the McCarthy complex. They disappear around a corner, the monitor blinks, they reappear in another corridor, and then their image suddenly goes to static.

"Damn!" mutters O'Brian, clicking at his keyboard, flipping through fuzzy monitored scene after scene in the complex: corridors, offices, computer rooms, lavatories, dormitories, the repository. . . .

"Lose 'em, Toby?" says Blair casually.

"Obviously. Well, what can we expect? With several thousand surveill—er, sentinel, cameras to maintain, there are bound to be malfunctions."

"Well, I sure hope that everything goes okay election day."

"Oh, God, yes," O'Brian groans as he continues clicking. "No room for error there. All the major networks will be here, including many foreign correspondents. Everyone wants to see our new electronic democracy, or cyber-democracy, as I see one of the online news mags is calling it, in action."

O'Brian has stopped on the image of a smallish balding man staring intently at a computer monitor, occasionally typing on a keyboard.

"Who's that?"

"Ha. Some detective you are. That's our prize, Norman Dunne. Working happily away."

"Aha, so that's him. In the flesh, sort of. So how can you tell he's happy? You got one of those goddamned implants in him?"

"No. And even if we did, we are only able to tell, for now, indirectly, the underlying state of a person's mind—"

"When you aren't controlling it."

"Now, Georgie. The only reason I say that the Gnome is happy is because he's in his element. He's happy when he's working with computers, *immersed* in computers, and by God that's what he's doing now. For us."

Blair takes a deep breath. "Listen, Toby, why don't you tell me now just what it is that you've got him doing. That we spent a hell of a lot of effort to get him here to do? This is probably something I should know to help me do my job, you know."

O'Brian is momentarily silent as he considers his request.

"You're right. You're absolutely right, George. You should know. All right, maybe you've already figured some of this out, George, smart guy like you, but the reason we needed the Gnome so badly is because, well, frankly he's the only one who could hack his way in and out of ElecTal. That's the name of the system developed for the U.S. government by a closely-held software development firm that won the contract nearly a decade ago to electronically tally election results. That's how long this software has been around, the feds always having bigger eyes—and pocket-books—than their stomachs.

"But as we learned from previous elections, the need for digital voting is no longer a luxury, it's a necessity. Now with the installation of electronic voting machines in seventy-eight percent of the country, certainly the largest election districts, and all connected directly to the Internet—completely secured with extraordinary multiple key encryption—we've got the technology in place to bring the data into one exceedingly safe central repository, the McCarthy complex, and we've certainly got the computing power necessary to process it all."

"The Beast."

"Er, not exactly, though I prefer to call it the Source. No, you see, the ElecTal system will run on a smaller subset of the Bea—er, Source, primarily the IBM mainframe group, which, the government insists, must be maintained solely by federal employees and monitored every step of the way by election officials. And that's happening right now, they're already here; the applications have been loaded and they're running tests day and night. So you can see why we couldn't simply waltz in and tinker with anything. We had to go in the back way, via Dunne."

"So that's it. You're going to throw the election to Partridge."

O'Brian winces. "Well, 'throw' is such a crass term—"

"You prefer 'steal,' instead?"

"Okay, yes, we're going to, ah, nudge, the returns slightly in Partridge's favor. I daresay that this will end up being one of the closest elections in history—though not close enough to cause a recount, heh-heh. No way. And only because Partridge is behind in the polls. Pity. I actually have to give the American electorate a great deal of credit, to see through that boob."

"So it'll be a big 'nudge.'"

"Yes, well the polls *are* narrowing slightly. We're doing what we can in that respect, but to be honest we weren't as prepared as we should have been to, ah, nudge, the polls, also. Unfortunately, the pollsters are more independent than we had surmised . . . but then it all depends on who you get to and just how you get to them." O'Brian flashes a grin at Blair.

"Why would I think that anything could be sacred?"

"Sacred, ha-ha. Nothing, when it comes to politics, ever is, Georgie. But just wait until the next round of elections. By then I'm sure we'll have *everything* in place."

Blair leans back, puffs reflectively on his cigarette as he looks up at the monitor, at the Gnome calmly, methodically, committing election fraud. "Well, I've gotta ask, Toby—why?"

O'Brian laughs out loud. "Well, why not? But seriously, George, you've got to understand, as we do, that the world, the planet, the United States in particular, as a bastion of individual rights and freedoms, is simply too large and unwieldy to be allowed to govern itself. That is, government of and by the people. Bergstrom, although he appears to be merely a driven financier, has given a great deal of thought to the matter and believes that Hobbes was right—that's Thomas Hobbes, the seventeenth-century philosopher, who believed that people shouldn't be allowed to directly govern themselves. Their base instincts of greed and self-gain at any cost would never allow them to elect anyone who put the good of the nation first—its industry and strategic global economic interests—before slicing the masses a bigger piece of the pie.

"But Hobbes also distrusted the business class whom he felt had undue influence on the government—in his times, the monarchy. This is where we disagree with him. You see, Hobbes could never have anticipated the industrial revolution, let alone the information revolution and the profound social dislocations it would cause. For instance, in the last decades of the twentieth century we experienced tremendous industrial and economic growth, all without the usual nasty bidding up of workers' wages. Just the same as the start of the industrial revolution in the early nineteenth century. Now how do you think this occurs?"

"Uh, I'm not really an economist, Toby."

"Well, I'll tell you. It's because the tremendous improvements in productivity we've made eliminate the need for workers. The livelihoods of scores of cottage weavers were wiped out by one modern knitting mill. All that was left was to hire their children to work long hours for squat wages. Compare that to today where entire offices of bookkeepers are laid off with the installation of one accounting system, or three shifts of assembly line workers are replaced with dumb, honest, never-sick, never-late robots. All that's left is for their kids—or themselves—to work in the local fast-food joint for long hours and squat wages.

"In short, what we've got is a large disaffected underclass, as, let's face it, all the productivity gains go to the owner of the knitting mill or accounting firm, or to their investors. Of course, the workers gain from the lowered prices of goods and services generated by the leap in productivity, but certainly not at a rate that keeps pace with the reduction in their paycheck.

"What concerns us is that as the information and technology revolution continues, continually displacing workers, and the population continues to grow in Malthusian proportions, there's going to be a decidedly large number of unhappy unemployed, or underemployed, people. Or if you prefer, a much greater disproportion between haves and have-nots. And what does that mean for our great nation?"

"Rioting in the streets?"

"Ultimately, yes. That is precisely what we fear. All the good work that we've labored so long to achieve is going to be marred by the prospect of major social unrest. Believe me, the riots of the nineteen-sixties are going to pale in comparison with the social upheaval that's going to occur if the lunch buckets ever realize what's really happened to them. All it would take is for some demagogue to organize and ignite them, much as Huey Long in Louisiana attempted in the nineteen thirties. Until, of course, he was eliminated."

Blair's eyebrows raise and O'Brian catches it. He laughs. "Well, George, *we* didn't have anything to do with that—as far as I know. But, of course, some people who don't share our vision and find the need to actively oppose us must be, frankly— removed. A certain blind economist whom we thought was one of us comes to mind."

Blair looks immediately away, reaches for another cigarette.

O'Brian clears his throat. "There's blood on all our hands, Georgie. All our hands."

"Okay, okay. So you believe that you've got to be able to sway the elections to get Partridge elected. He's a moron."

"That's right, but he's our moron. He's perfect. Somewhat like Reagan in the eighties, although Reagan was basically a good man. Frighteningly dumb, to be sure, but decent. Partridge seems to have no scruples whatsoever—at least none we've been able to detect. Plus, we didn't really have our hooks into Reagan the way we've got them into Partridge. Frankly, at the time we were caught sitting on our hands; we were astonished that Reagan was ever elected."

"And reelected."

"As I say—astonished. Anyway, we were on the boat at that time, though not at the helm, where, of course, we prefer to be.

"You see," O'Brian continues, "the simple truth is that some people in this great land are going to be very wealthy at the end of the day, and a great many more will not be. Far from it, in fact. There will be much bitterness. This we know. And so, of course we must gravitate, inevitably, toward a police state. It's the only way. You know it and I know it. We're slowly making progress, of course—each ruling of the Supreme Court erodes the freedoms and privacy rights of the common man just a little bit more—but it's not coming fast enough. We're afraid the great unwashed are going to wise up before we've got everything under control. Hence our tremendous desire to get Partridge in. You can see, now, George, why controlling this election, and so many more to follow, is so important to us. Believe me, if the American populace ever understood what we are doing for them, they'd—in the long run—be grateful."

"So, bottom line, to get you an edge on 'the great unwashed,'" Blair glances up toward the monitor, "the Gnome is going to build you a way into the, uh, tally-ho program."

"ElecTal program. And he's doing so much more than just getting us inside, he's creating wonderful algorithms which monitor trends in all the electoral districts and then subtly, gradually, skew votes in our favor as the timeline progresses. Obviously, we can't dump a huge slew of Partridge votes in say, Portland or D.C., which would be wholly unbelievable. No, it's the swing states, the so-called, undecided vote, that we'll load. There are some very complicated routines he's come up with to do this, undetected. I truly believe that since we convinced the Gnome to come back to us, he's accepted this as his greatest programming challenge."

"And you won't get caught."

"Not unless somebody decides to talk," O'Brian soberly fixing Blair with an it's-so-easy-to-be-a-dead-man look. "There's just no other way. Everything has been reduced to bits and bytes now. The Gnome's programs will go back and update the original input files transmitted from the source without affecting the original date and time stamp. And the source terminals out there in Peoria and Poughkeepsie, nearly all of them, are manufactured by a select few firms which happen to be deep, very deep, within A-Banc's back pockets. Their election night memory chips, which are entirely accessible to us via the Net, by the way, are conveniently purged after their, ah, performance. Quite frankly, as I once indicated to you, it's the perfect crime . . ."

Chapter Sixty-Two

"C'MON," THE EPENGUIN prods Clayborne as they leave the computer area, perhaps also happy to get away from the big humming behemoth. "I'm always so busy when I'm here that I never get to mosey around that much. There's still a few places I haven't gotten into. The laboratories, for instance."

"Laboratories? Down here? What for?"

"Well, they've got a small marketing research group down here. I don't know much about it other than it's run by Rascher and O'Brian and a few other scientists."

"Hmm. I've never heard anyone at A-Banc West talk about it."

"I think it's pretty secret stuff. But then what around here isn't?"

"You're right about that—"

"Ah, we're in luck!" squawks the Epenguin. "Here's someone who can help us out." He points to a fellow coming down the hallway wearing gray AlphaBanc fatigues pushing a cart laden with stacks of reports, periodicals, and packages. "I know this guy, Mario Pfalser, works in the main repository, met him a few months back—Mario! Hey, buddy how's it going?"

An intense-looking fellow with a shock of black hair cascading over dark penetrating eyes pushes his cart up to them. He flashes a smile at the Epenguin. "E.P.! What brings you here?"

"Work. Getting ready for the elections thing. There's gonna be a lot of data flowing into McCarthy. Lotta people coming down here, and the press, too. Big-big deal."

"Oh yeah," says Mario, "we're working hard, too."

The Epenguin introduces him to Clayborne, whom he tells that Mario also delivers the hard mail around the complex and thus has access to all areas, even the marketing lab."

"Ah, the strange secret lab . . ." Clayborne raising his eyebrows mockingly.

"That's the one," says the Epenguin. "Can you take us inside, Mario?"

Even though they technically don't have access to that area, Clayborne doesn't think that it should be a big deal to check it out. So he's surprised when Mario's face tightens and a nearly imperceptible flick of his eyes beckons them to follow him up the corridor. Clayborne glances up at the mute black eye of a security camera overhead, looks quickly away, bows his head and follows along.

As they walk down another corridor Clayborne unobtrusively looks around, sees no cameras in the immediate vicinity, asks, "So what's the big deal? Is this laboratory, or whatever, super-secure or something?"

Pfalser stares straight ahead as he pushes his cart. "Yes, it is secure, but . . . it's a strange place. Maybe it's better that you see what's in there for yourselves."

This guy is creeping him out, Clayborne decides, also wonders if it's really smart, career-wise and maybe even health-wise, to be prowling around down here. But his interest is truly piqued, and anyway, they now seem to be actually at the entrance of the sinister place, a set of gray sliding doors that require the validating print of Pfalser's palm before they open, revealing what looks to be a very hospital-looking scene indeed: a long fluorescent corridor staggered with wide doors, all closed.

"Well," says Clayborne, "it sure looks like a laboratory. Smells like it too. Antiseptic. But it doesn't seem all that, ah, strange."

"That doesn't mean what happens down here isn't."

"What are you talking about?" demands Clayborne, suddenly agitated. "I don't know exactly why they've got a lab here, but I'm sure it's for some *reasonable* purpose! After all this is Alpha-Banc!"

"Uh, yeah, Mario," says the Epenguin, "I know it's kind of a weird scene down in these, uh, catacombs, but Richie's right, I don't know why you're making it out to be so spooky."

Mario talks directly to the Epenguin. "Over there in another area are labs with cages of white rats and monkeys, and there are other rooms . . . rooms that are more like cells, with thick doors with little plexiglass windows . . . that they keep people in."

"What?" Clayborne surprising himself by how angry he suddenly becomes. "Oh, *c'mon!*" he explodes. "What in hell are you talking about, man? Keeping people down here? As-as prisoners? Against their—?"

He suddenly stops. *That's why I'm so upset.* He realizes he is thinking of Christin, wondering if she herself could actually be down here. But . . . no, no, that's crazy. "Well, look," he begins again, "I have to admit that AlphaBanc has maybe done some maybe, questionable, things, but, but . . . you've just got to be mistaken."

"I wish I was . . . but I've seen it with my own eyes."

Clayborne looks over at the Epenguin and then back to Pfalser. "Look, even if what you say is true—then why? Why? What kind of experiments would they be doing that they'd be keeping *people* down here for?"

"I'm not completely sure," Pfalser says out of the side of his mouth as they pass under another video camera. "But I think it has something to do with a type of tattooing process that is part of a scheme to try to, uh, barcode, people."

"What?"

"Yeah, it sounds kind of crazy, but we're coming to that lab now, up here to the right." The door to the laboratory has a window with venetian blinds shut tight, but through them Clayborne can distinguish a strange violet glow.

"Huh. Well . . . I'll admit . . . it does look sort of strange."

"Yeah, you see? They're experimenting with different types of light, you know, like black lights, ultraviolet, or something, everything glowing like crazy. Sometimes the door's partly open when I come by. One of the guys that works in here is a dermatologist, a Dr. Carioni. I poked around in the system, found some background on him. He graduated near the top of his class from Yale Med, went into research immediately after graduation at Johns Hopkins on some kind of skin pigmentation studies, melanin, and stuff. But then he got really heavy into drugs, cocaine mostly, was fired, lost his home, his Mercedes, wife divorced him, almost went to jail, the whole bit."

"Real AlphaBanc material."

"I guess. Anyway, he's here now and I know he's doing something with tattoos. I bring the packages right here, tattoo guns, needles, and lots of shipments of chemicals, also different kinds of barcode scanners. It all goes into this lab."

"And you think they're doing—what?"

"Well, I hate to sound—apocalyptic, but it really looks like they're working toward the ultimate cashless society. Barcoding people themselves is the step beyond bank cards, beyond plastic. It's the endgame of societal control. Everyone becomes branded with a single unchangeable code in a database, referenced everywhere, kept forever—"

"N-no," says Clayborne, his heart clenched, "it just can't be—"

Suddenly they hear a shout and then someone, an unkempt man—unshaven, hair wild—wearing a torn hospital gown comes rushing around the corner. He looks to be in agony, arms flailing, eyes crazed, babbling insanely. "N-n-no more commercials, no more commercials, n-no more ch-cheeseburgers . . . please stop them, please stop the commercials, it's all one big *big* commercial . . . please, please, make it stop! Make it stop! Make it stop!"

"My God, what the hell's wrong with him?" Clayborne gasps, looks over at Pfalser, who looks back wide-eyed, shaking his head.

"I-I don't know. But, see, I told you, really weird stuff goes on down here."

The man seems to have focused on them. His shaking hand grasps Clayborne's arm as he looks into his eyes, "Please, please, n-no more b-b-burgers, no more fries, n-no more commercials. P-p-please get them out . . . get them out of my HEAD!" He collapses at their feet, cradling his head in his hands, rolling back and forth on the linoleum.

Chapter Sixty-Three

"SAY, TOBY . . ." BLAIR yawns and fires up a Pall Mall, idly watching a grainy Norman Dunne on one of O'Brian's monitors, "I wanted to ask you how you're getting that crazy munchkin to do all this great programming for you? You got the girl locked in a cage for him or something?"

"Well, not in a *cage*, exactly," chuckles O'Brian, clicking on his keyboard, and on another monitor appears a fairly clear image of a young woman with pouffy big hair, obviously a wig, and a full flowing 1960s dress—pure June Cleaver. And she appears to be in something like the old Beaver household, too, currently the kitchen, where she is slaving over a mixer, in the process of baking a cake.

"That's her? I hardly recognize her in that getup. And where the hell have you got her? Looks like an old TV show."

"I know, I know," sighs O'Brian, "but, believe it or not, that's the way Dunne likes her. We've got her in some quite comfortable, though, as you can see, decidedly retro-looking quarters, in an isolated wing off our laboratory area down here. We originally had her in a much more provocative milieu—well, here, let me show you her earlier circumstances." O'Brian clicks away on his keyboard and up comes another scene of undoubtedly Christin Darrow in black bustier and stockings reclining seductively on a huge circular bed, in what looks to be a plush casbah setting, wall hangings, big hookah pipe, tassels and pillows everywhere.

"Well, that's more like it."

"Yes, this is a clip from when we first brought her and Dunne here. We originally went with this boudoir look, which Dunne seemed to favor when he was on the other side of a monitor and a high-powered telescope, but when we actually got her here it turned out that he wanted something entirely different. Mom and apple pie!"

"The guy really is nuts."

"Well, he is eccentric, yes. Rascher says that now that he has Darrow so near, so, in the real world, you might say, he can't deal with his wildest fantasies. This ultra-domestic milieu is what he's actually most comfortable with."

"Jesus, Toby, this is a weird scene," says Blair, shaking his head and flicking ashes on the floor.

"Well, it's the essential Norman Dunne, you might say. You know we've got her cooking his meals now? His favorite dish happens to be meatloaf and mashed potatoes. Comfort food, says Rascher. Like he always wanted his mother to make. That cake she's putting together is for him. Of course, it will be delivered to him; he would never have the nerve to actually go and visit her."

Blair exhales, continues to shake his head, "So, how'd you get her to do all this? That goddamned implant, I'll bet."

"Well, the particular chip implanted within her is definitely one of our new models, with over twelve-hundred extremely tiny reservoirs, each holding a nanoliter—that's one billionth of a liter, George—of different concentrations of drugs, Deludamil, Nepenthine, and several others carefully selected to increase the subliminals, that, via remote RF command can be injected directly into her bloodstream."

"Jesus, Toby, you're really scarin' me. Er, 'RF?'"

"Radio Frequency. Remote. Very remote, if need be."

"And, and that's how you got her to be the happy *Hausfrau?*"

"Yes, frankly, Rascher has compiled an excellent collection of subliminal audio stimuli to elicit appropriate sexual responses—the, ah, Stepford files, we call it around here. We transmit it to the implant along with a timed release of the appropriate chemical combinations into the subject's bloodstream. And I have to say, they've worked remarkably well. You might remember Marcia, Christin's erstwhile friend. We have some quite provocative videos of her with a certain Mr. Walker. She conveniently remembers none of it; he remembers every moment, I'm sure.

"So, it seems that that's what everyone has wanted so far, at least of our more attractive subjects. But this early 1960s domestic fantasy of Dunne's threw us for a loop, I don't mind telling you. We scrambled to come up with whatever we could—

archived features from the *Ladies' Home Journal* and *Better Homes and Gardens* and what have you. Finally, I think we just started running the soundtracks of old television shows of the period, 'I Love Lucy,' and the like."

"Jesus, I never would have believed . . ."

"Well, George, I—oh-oh, what's this?" O'Brian points up at another of the monitors that has the wandering troupe of the Epenguin, Clayborne, and now Mario Pfalser in view—and also somewhat of a commotion. In the grainy scene before them, it appears that a man in a hospital gown is writhing wildly before them on the corridor floor.

"Oh no, *no!*" shouts O'Brian. "That's in the-the marketing laboratory!"

"What the hell is going on?"

"I don't know, but that's a real problem there, George." O'Brian picks up his phone. "I'm going to call down and get a hold of someone, but . . . think you can run over and help us deal with it?"

"Deal with what? What's going on?"

"It's—well, it's too complicated to explain right now, but we're doing some test marketing and he's a subject, actually, in our tests of various, er, marketing stimuli. Drat! No one's there. No one answers!"

"Level with me, Toby. What's really going on? I know before I go."

"Okay, it's, well, it's really in the bailiwick of our, ah, medical staff. They're working on some, uh, subneural communication experiments—"

"Subneural?"

"Yes, well, in a nutshell we're working on a new technique that uses the repetitive audio and chemical release capabilities of the neural implant to generate an informative and suggestible set of messages for the subject."

"In English, *por favor.*"

"We've been using the implant to send subliminal messages into our subject's minds. Like you saw with Marcia Deaver. But this is much more sophisticated."

"What kind of messages?"

"Messages that can help them in their lives, help them to make informed decisions regarding moral or ethical issues—"

"Yeah, I'm sure that AlphaBanc can provide moral and ethical guidance."

"Oh, we can, George, we surely can. Also we can calm them when they're fearful, cheer them when they're depressed, provide them with courage, patience, forbearance . . . quell their irrational fears, whatever they might be. We foresee wonderful possibilities for this little tool in many, many areas of society—"

"Like what?"

"Well, the corrections area, for one, where violent prisoners can be kept continually calm, always cooperative. It might be the perfect mechanism to actually effect a cure for incorrigible sex offenders, allow them to become productive members of society once again. But these are all future objectives. Right now to test the process we're simply providing our subject with subliminal messages for various consumer products."

"What? You mean like advertisements, commercials?"

"Yes, precisely, George. It's a wonderful breakthrough in getting personalized messages directly to the subject. There is no chance for miscommunication. No chance for random noise to distort the message."

"Why advertisements?"

"Well, we've got to start somewhere. Because of the immediate and simplified feedback, we've chosen to start with messages that insert features and benefits of various consumer products directly into the subject's psyche, regarding fast food, automobiles, soap, toothpaste, whatever."

"Directly? Jesus, you're not kidding."

"It's simply the ultimate in directed marketing. To our great satisfaction, the subject has been able to effectively process and respond to our broadcast messages."

"And this guy here?"

"I'm not sure. We've been having some problems with the mix of audio stimulus and chemical dosages. Some of the messages unfortunately seem to continue propagating in the subject's brain even after the stimulus has been withdrawn. Now George, please, please get down there now!"

Chapter Sixty-Four

CLAYBORNE, PFALSER, AND the Epenguin stand open-mouthed, looking helplessly at one another as the man writhes on the floor in front of them. They turn as they hear footsteps pounding in the direction from which the man has come. And suddenly three grim-faced men round the corner, two in hospital scrubs, a gray-haired man in a white physician's coat with a stethoscope protruding from his pocket in the lead.

"Here he is! Hold him, hold him!" the doctor shouts, pulling out a syringe. The other two roll the man onto his stomach while the doctor uncaps the syringe, then pulls the man's gown up over his buttocks and jams in the needle. Clayborne notices that the man with the stethoscope has *Dr. Carioni* stitched on his coat. Only then does the doctor look up to see Clayborne, the Epenguin, and Pfalser watching intently, puzzled, aghast.

He smiles weakly, "He'll be okay. He's under my treatment, you see. Mentally unstable. Quite difficult when he's off his meds."

More footsteps echo behind them and Blair staggers up, puffing mightily. "You got, you got . . . everything under control?" he asks more or less in the direction of Carioni.

"Yes sir, we do now. Everything's going to be just fine, Mr., ah . . ."

"Blair. With ISD. I'm up here from Chicago with . . . these fellows. We're securing the place for the elections. But this, this . . ." Blair pauses to catch his breath, ". . . this kind of thing can't happen when the press, the cameras, are here."

Clayborne glances warily up at a security camera on the wall.

"Oh, of course not," says Carioni. "They'd never come into this area, anyway."

"They damn well better not . . ." says Blair, and then freezes as he suddenly realizes who this 'patient,' now lying quietly on the floor, really is.

It shockingly appears to be Ted McClelland, the man who had killed Katrina Radnovsky, and whom Dunne had engaged to slash Christin Darrow.

He bends down, looks closer . . . it is him. He had wondered what had ever happened to him—but had decided it was better not to ask. Haedler had told him they were going to tip off the police to his killings but now it was clear, they obviously hadn't. Of course, they couldn't have . . . because it might have led the authorities to investigate the Dunne connection, and then possibly lead to AlphaBanc. Of course. So they decided to simply make him vanish. And then decided to make him useful through these unholy "experiments" before the big sleep.

Blair straightens up, reaches for a cigarette. No wonder he smokes. No wonder he drinks. Maybe not nearly enough.

A pretty nurse in starched whites comes around the corner, pushing a gurney. The doctor and the other two men lift the subdued man up onto the bed while Clayborne, ogling the nurse, her dark hair pulled up beneath the perky white cap, notices that she wears a small pin, of different design, but oddly similar to the tags the waitresses had at the AlphaBanc dinner. This one is number 28. She doesn't pay any attention to him, listening intently to the doctor who is giving her instructions regarding the patient's medication, and so Clayborne admires the back of her exposed subterranean-pale neck, and also notices—makes his heart skip a beat—what looks like a small scar behind her left ear, just like the one Christin has, where they inserted the phaser for her Ménière's. Could she have one too?

"Just take him in here for now," the doctor says. He walks over, opens the door of the lab, its interior glowing with bright violet light, and two startled technicians wearing goggles look up. As the nurse turns to push the gurney inside, Clayborne notices with another shock that something on the back of her neck appears to fluoresce in the light, and he's not positive, but it looks like the number 28 and then something resembling a miniature picket fence, or, no, a-a barcode! softly luminous in the strange violet glow. The hairs on *his* neck stand on end and the door slams shut.

Chapter Sixty-Five

AS SOON AS they get out of the laboratory area, a severely sweating Clayborne tells Blair he's got to get *out of here*, pronto, and Blair, with little hesitation, agrees. It's time to surface.

The Epenguin, who has simply popped a couple more Deludamil to cope, has decided to remain subterranean, will in fact bunk with the programmers for the duration of the elections.

"Jesus, how on earth can he do it . . . ?" Clayborne vaguely muses as they get off the elevator, he practically breaking into a sprint across the lobby to get through the doors to the outside. Green grass and high blue skies never looked so gorgeous. Pacing aimlessly around the broad green lawn that slopes grandly away from the main building, Clayborne fights off waves of nausea, sucking great frantic gulps of fresh air, managing heroically not to vomit on the carefully sculpted flowerbeds.

"You seem kinda shook up, kid," says Blair catching up with him, although Clayborne notices that the ex-cop isn't exactly his usual tough-guy self either.

"I had to get away from it, George. Had to get myself outside. God, what in hell is going on down there?"

Blair pulls a Pall Mall from his pack as they walk to his car. "I'm not sure myself kid," he sighs, shaking his head, eyes distant.

"It-it's totally nuts. I-I never thought it would be like this."

"It's a crazy business—"

"It's beyond crazy."

"—but no matter what weird shit happens, we just gotta play along. We live longer that way."

"That's a comforting thought."

"It's the only way to deal with it, kid. Christ, do I ever need a drink. I feel like I'm coming out of a goddamned coal mine. I don't know how those poor bastards can work down there day after day."

"Your analogy isn't that far off," grumbles Clayborne. "It's more like a gigantic information mine. Data mining is the big dirty business we're all in now."

"Whatever, kid. You look like you could use a drink, too."

Clayborne thinks he must be in a state of shock, visibly trembling and sweating profusely—maybe some kind of post-Deludamil withdrawal combined with this totally insane ordeal; he agrees with Blair, a drink would be great.

And soon they are in Blair's Mercedes, speeding towards Red Rock and a tavern up ahead. They say little. Clayborne is numb, unable to find a way to process the disturbing underground odyssey he has witnessed, can't get the image of the babbling hallucinating man out of his mind, nor of the barcode glowing so evilly on the fair nurse's neck. What the hell is really going on? From his prolonged silence, Clayborne suspects Blair may also be overwhelmed by the events of the day.

Clayborne gazes out at the roadside greenery whizzing by, asks which watering hole they're headed for. Blair tells him there's a nice outdoorsy place up ahead, the Blackwell Inn. Clayborne senses a vague wistfulness in the hard-bitten detective's throaty voice as he tells him it's the kind of place where a guy can put on the brakes, relax, stop and think, a pretty, peaceful spot. He also adds that the tavern owner is a real character, "the feistiest woman I've come across in a long, long time."

"Well, at least it won't be underground."

"You got that right. You know, I've been a cop—or like a cop—all my life. Always been outside or out and about. I can't stand being cooped up. Say, kid, something I been meaning to ask, why do those crazy-ass programmers call themselves—what was it—Morlocks?"

"Oh, that. That's what the creatures who lived underground in the H.G. Wells book, *The Time Machine*, were called. They ran the machinery that took care of the people who lived on the surface. They were called Eloi. They were a carefree, playful race that lived above ground in the sunshine."

"Huh. Guess I must have skipped literature when I was in school. Always was looking for a way to get out of class. H.G. Wells, though—that's gotta be an old book?"

"Oh yeah, must be at least a hundred years old. Hmm. Makes you think though . . . a lot of what he wrote has come to pass."

"So, these, uh, Morlocks. They do seem pretty damn close to the weirdoes down there at the complex. What did they get out of all the work they did?"

"Well, they came out at night and captured the Eloi, and, uh, ate them."

"No shit?"

"No shit. Hey, do you think Christin is really all right?"

Blair groans. "Kid, not again, please. If she wasn't, I'd hear about it pronto."

"But not where she is."

"Kid, I told you—she's in a safe house. Somewhere. Even if I knew I couldn't tell you. We can't push it right now. We've just got to play it by ear."

"But, it's—it's *kidnapping*, for God's sake."

"Haedler would call it protective detainment, or some god-damned thing."

Clayborne rubs his eyes. "Jesus, it's totally frustrating. It's insane. What a dirty rotten business."

"It is, kid. It is."

Blair pulls off the main road and heads down a long cracked asphalt drive that dips into a shallow vale then leads up to a grove of trees on a rise that overlooks the sprawling Wisconsin farmland surrounding it, a very pleasant place, just as Blair had said, the leaves of the oaks deep russet, the maples scattered throughout blazing orange and red in the afternoon sunshine, very bright and outside, a place, assuredly, of the Eloi.

Clayborne sees several people strolling around and wants to see the grounds, a grouping of outbuildings that once composed a farmstead: barn, silo, granary, garage, several sheds . . . all surrounding a storybook well where a young couple are presently leaning over the broad casing of dark red granite cobbles and ancient grayed cement, tossing a coin together. But Blair hustles him past a handful of patrons sitting at tables under the trees into a long low building, fitted sometime in the past to be a tavern.

Inside, the space is cozy and surprisingly bright, several large windows offering a good view of the grounds outside. No other customers are inside at present; the bar itself is well-worn oak with a cheerful red-haired fifty-ish woman bustling behind it. "Hi there, stranger, welcome to the Blackwell! Long time, no see! What is it—Harry?"

"George," Blair smiles, lights up a Pall Mall.

"George! That's right—George. Well, this time you brought along a friend."

"This is Richard."

"Howdy-doo, Richard. My name's Sally. Sally Thomas. So, another young fella working up at the McCarthy complex, I see."

"Yes ma'am. For the time being."

"What are you—one of those computer programmers? Naw! You sure don't look like one o' them!" she winks over at Blair. "They're uncommonly strange, in my estimation."

"No ma'am—Sally. I'm in marketing."

"Whoo! Marketing! Ha! The only marketing I know about is what I do down at the IGA! Now what can I get for you two good-looking fellas?"

Blair orders a couple of drafts for both of them and chats it up with Sally while Clayborne stares absently out the windows.

Sally notices, says, "Looks like somebody's mind is outside!"

"He's been underground too long, if you ask me," adds Blair.

"We've got some nice grounds here, son. The Blackwell is the finest beer garden in Wisconsin, I like to think. You been for a look around yet?"

"Well, I wanted to, but," a smirk at Blair, "someone wanted to come in for a drink first."

"Priorities, kid."

"Well, you go out and take a walk around before it starts to get dark. We've got lights, it's right pretty at night, I think, but I don't put 'em on this late in the season."

"Tell him why it's called the Blackwell, Sally," says Blair.

"Well you don't have to twist my arm so hard, mister," laughs Sally, another wink at Blair. "No, the truth is, son, that it's just a deep dark well, dug by my great-grandfather nearly one hundred fifty years ago. He was down almost fifty feet when the ground fell out beneath him and he nearly drowned. He had hit an underground flow, is what it was. The well's never gone dry, even in the worst droughts. Been called the Blackwell ever since."

"I can't wait to see it," says Clayborne, finishing off his beer.

"He needs to go out back and see your fine statuary, too," says Blair, with a sly look at Sally.

"You've got statues? Here?"

Sally laughs, "Why, we certainly do. Way in the back. Used to be over behind the McCarthy complex main buildin' but they became a mite too controversial."

"What do you mean?"

"You'll see," Blair smiles and sips his beer.

"I'll keep ol' George here company," says Sally. "You check out the well, make a big wish and toss in a coin. Don't you fall in though. Anything that goes into that well never comes out again! Then take a walk back through the bower between the bushes. You go on now while it's still light. Now git!"

Clayborne chuckles and heads for the door, passes a faded hand-lettered sign: *Madame Salina / Tarot Readings*, wonders what *that's* about but decides not to ask; he really wants to take a look around this place, maybe get his mind off all the craziness underground up the road. . . .

Thankfully outside again, he decides that Sally is right, the place is really very nice, like a big park, with tastefully terraced gardens bordered by tall hedges. He walks over to the well, which certainly lives up to its name, dark and so deep that he can't see down to the water in the late light, can only cautiously imagine it: black and abysmal. He looks around for a stone to toss in, but there is only packed earth surrounding it. He reaches in his pocket, finds a quarter, which looks and feels like a piece of tin nowadays no matter how fancy the stamping, sighs, makes a wish for Christin to be okay, and flips it in. He thinks he hears a splash, isn't sure, and then looks across the grassy space to a rose-covered bower farther back, between a break in the hedges.

He hikes over and passes through the opening, finds himself in another large grassy area, bordered by flower gardens and several benches. In the center of the plot he sees the figures that Blair and Sally were talking about. There are two of them, they seem to be on the small side, and as he wanders over, he sniffs, wonders what the big deal is.

Chapter Sixty-Six

CLAYBORNE, QUITE CURIOUS now, approaches the objects, which are actually marble busts, perched side by side on blocky red granite pedestals in the center of the enclosure. Though they look vaguely familiar, he doesn't recognize either of them. Puzzled, he walks closer and inspects their plaques, discovers that they are actually historic figures: "Joseph McCarthy / 1908 - 1957 / Senator, Patriot, American / McCarthyism Is Americanism with Its Sleeves Rolled," and the bulldog countenance of "J. Edgar Hoover / 1895 - 1972 / Director, Federal Bureau of Investigation / The Best of the Best."

A real tribute, but someone has unceremoniously draped a pink garment, like a doll's dress, over Hoover's shoulders, apparently quite some time ago as it is faded nearly to white in places. But no one, it seems, neither proprietors nor righteous visitors have troubled to remove the edifying addition. Clayborne shrugs. Just goes to prove that arrogance fails, truth prevails. And each of the inscriptions at the bottom of the busts includes the legend: "Donated by AlphaBanc Information Systems – 1984."

Clayborne remembers something of "Tailgunner" Joe McCarthy from history class, none of it really good. He was supposedly Wisconsin's black sheep senator, a reactionary, anti-intellectual bully whose dubious attack on communism in the early 1950s propelled him to national fame and then disgrace in the span of a few years. And yet here his stony perpetual used-car salesman mug seems to be honored as a hero of sorts.

"He wasn't really a hero, no, I would say he embodied more of a force, perhaps evil, perhaps not, but a major force, which tremendously altered the course of American history."

Clayborne spins around—he recognizes that voice—and looks into the gray eyes of Dr. Pierre Lefebre, sitting on one of the benches. "Oh, Dr. Lefebre, I-I didn't hear you, er, come up—"

The doctor, wearing a severe black suit and a loosened silver tie, raises his hand off the back of the bench. "I just sat down. I like to come here whenever I visit the complex. It's so nice and peaceful. Such a change from all the busy underground activity up the road. They sometimes remind me of ants, with their frantic, single-minded scurrying about. Wouldn't you agree?"

"Well, I never thought of it that way before, but I get the picture." Clayborne is still trying to overcome his shock at so suddenly finding himself face to face with AlphaBanc's venerable senior executive.

"Ants, bah!" mutters Lefebre. "I have never liked ants. And I frankly don't like to come up here, to have to mingle with the likes of them."

"So, I suppose you're up here because of the elections."

"Yes, of course" says Lefebre, waving him over, "just like you and Blair. Come over here, lad. Sit down."

"So, you, er, admire, McCarthy, and Hoover?" asks Clayborne as he sits on the bench, at a loss for any real conversation with the imposing executive.

"I come to pay my respects. I was one of those who approved the funding for this fine statuary. Before it became controversial. Pity about the dress."

"Yeah." Clayborne hasn't seen the doctor this close since the dinner in Chicago; he's surprised at how old and weary the man appears. "It looks like someone's making a statement."

"I agree. It seems to be a consensual opinion. And I know that a great many persons sympathetic to the man and his ideals come by here. If not for Hoover's actual . . . proclivities, then perhaps it is for his, excessive zeal, he should be chastened somewhat."

"Well, that's, er, an interesting outlook."

"Bah. It is simply a matter of propriety. I believe that he deserves to be remembered as one who changed the course of history, perhaps never to repeat it. Much like the way *Time* magazine once memorialized Adolph Hitler. A decision of great intelligence and integrity. They certainly didn't wish to *honor* him. But he simply can't be forgotten. It's the same with these fellows. Because you know that those who forget history—"

"Are doomed to repeat it."

"Exactly. And that is my own belief, one that I held when approving these fixtures. Those who originally wanted these busts did indeed intend to honor them as patriots, heroes! Bah!"

"But why would they think of them as heroes?"

"Well, in the case of Hoover," Lefebre puts his palms thoughtfully together, "there are some at AlphaBanc who greatly admire him. He was one of the first, you know, to begin utilizing modern surveillance techniques on the public. When he started working in the justice department as a young man, his first job was as a file clerk, not exactly an auspicious beginning. But a couple of years later his superior's house was bombed by an anarchist, and young Hoover was given the assignment to just 'round up' all the radicals and deport them!

"Hoover quickly realized that he first had to know who all the radicals were, where they lived, and how radical they really were. In short, he needed a lot of good information. So he created a huge card index on all the potential subversives his agents could find, and in a year or so he had nearly half a million names! This was in the early 1920s! Imagine! He created the first modern database to track the activities of U.S. citizens.

"In addition, he was so breathtakingly unscrupulous. Because he was petty, all-powerful, and quite paranoid, his agents feared allowing any little fish to get away, you see, so they caught all they could. When Hoover died in 1972 he was only beginning to seriously computerize his great storehouse of data. Of course, now the combined files of the FBI, CIA, and NSA, comprise— next to AlphaBanc's—perhaps the largest warehouse of personal information in the world. And a sizable portion of their files are stored with AlphaBanc at McCarthy. But it was Hoover and his passion for power and control over the masses that provided the seed for the grand unified database that we approach today."

Clayborne's ears prick up. "Grand unified . . . that's a pretty important-sounding database."

"It's a goal," sighs Lefebre. "That is all. Sometimes I wonder if it is really worth the effort. And then at other times I can't contain my excitement over having just a small part in changing the world as we know it, taking us into the future—our future, or perhaps it is more precise to say, our destiny."

Clayborne thinks: Wow. He's talking about Grand Unification!

Chapter Sixty-Seven

CLAYBORNE BREATHES DEEPLY and tries to conceal his great interest, decides it's easiest just to play dumb. "I guess I don't really follow you regarding our future, our destiny . . . and this, er, grand unified database?"

"Well . . ." Lefebre looks silently at Clayborne for a moment, and then, as if deciding that he is either harmless or completely trustworthy, begins to speak, "it is actually quite simple in principle, though much more difficult to effect. It is what you might call an advanced form of data fusion, the effort to consolidate, or unify, all the vestiges a person leaves during their daily travels across the electronic terrain with every piece of archived information available on them.

"Traditionally all this information has resided in disparate databases, but it is our goal to fuse together, or unify into one grand database, all we can obtain of an individual's transactions in life: financial, legal, medical, occupational, social, criminal . . . what have you. We believe that by categorizing and quantifying all this information and accessing it via sophisticated ultrafast computer systems, we will be able to generate a very, very accurate portrait of any individual, or groups of individuals, we wish to learn about."

"My God, you're right," Clayborne gasps, in spite of himself. "You'd, you'd know just about everything."

"All this is done already, of course, but in a very disjointed manner," continues Lefebre. "Naturally, we justify the means to maintain unified profiles of individuals by claiming to fight terrorism, but that's only a byproduct. Most importantly, when we aggregate all these profiles, what one might call grand-grand unification, then we will be able to predict, within a very high confidence level, what the masses will do in response to certain motivational factors: what they will purchase, say, or simply what they will agree with, how they will vote."

"I think I see what you mean . . . knowing so much about them . . ."

"Oh yes. You can see the efficiencies that will result in the areas of marketing, advertising, politics. On a broader scale, we will be able to first query, and then manipulate, the public's needs and wants at any point in time—its innermost desires and fears, society's zeitgeist, if you will—all at our command."

"Wow," says Clayborne, his head reeling over the magnitude of the scheme. Its implications are much greater than he ever could have imagined. "That certainly would be some first-rate information," he manages to utter.

"Oh it would indeed. Most marvelous information!" expounds Lefebre, excitedly stabbing the air with his bony fingers as he speaks. "It will be so very helpful to us in many different areas. Take the political arena, as just one example. The best predictors we have nowadays are focus groups, as we call them, which are polled constantly, daily, to gauge the effect of a candidate's action. Now suppose you knew virtually everything about the individuals in the study, and knew precisely how many of them were out there in the voting population? Wouldn't you be able to accurately predict the results of said election?"

"Like the one coming up?"

"Yes, exactly."

"I'd think you'd probably know enough about which way the vote will go," Clayborne ventures incautiously, "to be able to throw the election one way or the other."

"Oh you would? And how would you do that?" Lefebre suddenly snaps, staring intently at him.

"Er, well, that is, if I had a way to manipulate the, uh, vote in some way. But of course I don't know how you'd ever do that, so I guess it doesn't really matter."

"No," Lefebre focuses, calibrates, it seems, his gray eyes on Clayborne, "No, I guess it doesn't then, does it?"

"Nope. Not at all as far as I'm concerned."

Lefebre pauses, smiles slightly, shifts his gaze beyond Clayborne, toward the sun sinking behind the tall trees at the edge of the grove. "But . . . let us say that it was possible to perform some—manipulation. It's certainly nothing that hasn't been done before, you know. Look at Kennedy's suspicious boost by the Daley machine in Chicago in 1960. Or what ballot box thirteen did for Lyndon Johnson's Texas senate race in 1948. Or, more recently, due to a corrupted polling system in Florida, a biased supreme court was able to install that moron Bush as our millennium president!" Lefebre pauses, sighs. "Well, at least he was *our* moron. And speaking of that, don't forget Ohio in 2004 . . . electronic polling, hah! It happened again, and right under everyone's noses! We actually got that boob in again for another four years! Our dubious hero, the Senator here, no doubt would have approved. But then . . . in the end nothing could save him," Lefebre sighs again. "Joseph R. McCarthy . . . Lord, he was a blackguard."

"So . . . he gets a statue in this beautiful place?" says Clayborne, eager to move the subject away from the elections.

"It seems so," says Lefebre. "Not to mention being the namesake of the greatest repository of corporate and personal information available in the world today, the McCarthy Complex. I think it is quite fitting."

"Yeah, as you say, he would no doubt have approved . . ."

"Again, so he is memorialized, the same as Hoover, but on the political side of the equation. McCarthy, you see, taught us how a demagogue functions in the modern age. Not quite yet the information age, but he certainly made effective use of the new technology of the time: television. Ironically, in the end it was the televising of the senate subcommittee hearings that brought him down. But before that he managed to take what had been a molehill, a fringe issue in American politics, the fear of communism, the so-called 'red menace,' and make it into a mountain of controversy and political gain—for him. It taught us the tremendous power of the unjustified accusation. You know, many brave good people lost their jobs, their friends, their livelihoods standing up to their bullying inquisitors. I saw that myself; I lived through it, lad. It was a bizarre modern-day version of the Salem Witch Trials—or perhaps the Spanish Inquisition. Well, at least no one got burned at the stake—I don't think."

"Was he really that bad?" asks Clayborne. "For America, I mean. I thought he was just sort of a political aberration, that we quickly recovered from—"

"Oh no, no, no, my boy. Oh, not at all. He was *tremendously* destructive. That's the whole point, that one irresponsible hypocrite was able to inflict such damage on our national fabric for decades to come. He was able to create a deplorable climate of outright fear for anyone who dared to oppose his nationalistic agenda. I am sure that he never dreamed he would be as wildly successful as he was, nor even if he knew what he was really talking about, but America played right along. For a long time in the 1950s and early 60s no one dared appear to be the least bit radical or subversive for fear of being branded—God help them—a communist. Blacklists appeared in Hollywood and elsewhere; people had to sign loyalty oaths. Many good people lost *everything* because they wouldn't go along with the madness of the times.

"And what was the result? Well, McCarthyism truly killed the communist and socialist parties in the United States—not that they had much of a chance in our incredibly upwardly-mobile society, anyway. No, the real aftermath was the overall dulling of America and a headlong plunge into the ultimate consumer society: endless acres of ticky-tack ranch homes in faceless suburban wildernesses, with little more than television westerns and quiz shows flooding into them, night after empty night. Which is still, pretty much, where we are now. In the end, it was the best part, the thoughtful, hopeful, compassionate part of the American spirit that McCarthy killed."

So intent is Clayborne on following Lefebre's somber words that he suddenly feels tears beginning to well up. Truly Deludamil-free now, he's surprised at how dispirited he feels, terribly sad for the lost soul of America.

He notices Lefebre scrutinizing him, wipes his eyes, "Well, I guess that it just got to me, all this strange stuff . . . all this technology, data fusion, unification . . . the inevitability of it all. There's no way to stop it, nowhere to run any more, nowhere to hide . . ."

"That's quite true, son, quite true . . ." Lefebre extending a hand to pat Clayborne on the shoulder. "And just think where we'll be in the next twenty years, my boy. I don't even dare to imagine it.

"You know, I must say that it is too bad that it's not like the old days, when a man who had done something perhaps that he was ashamed of . . . could leave town, move across the country where nobody knows him and make a new start for himself. Leave behind him family and friends along with the, ah, unfortunate incident . . . even if it was something entirely innocent in itself . . . something so simple, so misunderstood . . . perhaps involving a young boy in the village, a beautiful boy, such a beautiful young Tadzi . . . and anyway why should it be a crime to express one's purest feelings of love, pure love, nothing more, nothing more at all . . . and be forced to leave all of one's life behind just for that . . . just for *that* . . ."

Now it is Lefebre who is weeping, bending forward on the bench, face in his hands, body quietly shaking with sobs. Clayborne figures this is a good time to make an exit. He gets up and tiptoes away, thinks that it is probably not a good thing to be sole witness to one of AlphaBanc's most prestigious executives in the throes of great personal anguish. Not a good thing at all.

Clayborne, intent on getting away quickly doesn't initially realize that he has walked in the opposite direction from where he had entered the statuary garden, now finds himself at very back of the old farmstead, on the crest of a rise that overlooks rolling pasture and cornfields shimmering deep orange in the light of the setting sun.

He sits on a granite outcropping under shadowy oaks and tries to relax. It's been a truly disturbing day, one that has convinced him, absolutely, that AlphaBanc is corrupted beyond repair and it is now only a matter of time before he can find a way to extricate himself from its evil clutches—but not before he finds Christin. Those bastards have got her locked away somewhere and he's going to have to bide his time until he can find her and figure out what to do.

He sits quietly as the twilight deepens around him, listens to the peepers and the hoot of a distant owl, wonders what it would be like to actually live in a quiet peaceful place like this . . . then he hears a faint call.

"Hey, hey, kid! Where the hell are you?"

It's Blair. Clayborne stands, looks sadly out across the dark fields, again hears the owl calling, it seems, to him.

"Over here, George!" he yells, walking back through the hedges to the gardens. Lefebre is gone. He stands by the statues glowing ghostly pale in the first light of a rising moon.

An orange cigarette glow briefly illuminates the bower and the sturdy detective, sport coat flapping, comes into sight. "Jesus, kid, what have you been doing out here?"

"Just got a little lost, I guess."

"Lost? Out here?"

"Well, lost in my thoughts. I was just sitting out here, thinking."

"Dangerous business, to think too much."

"That's for sure . . ."

"Well, now you're found."

"Yeah, you're right, George. I think I am now. I think I am."

Blair tilts his head in the darkness, seems to look at him closely, then says, "Lefebre told me he ran into you out here; I saw him on his way out. He sure looked down in the mouth."

"Oh, yeah, he was—really in a strange mood."

"What about?"

"I'm not exactly sure . . . but you know what? He told me about the Grand Unification thing. It's real, for sure, and it's mind-blowing, insanely ambitious and depraved, one hell of a scheme. And it looks like there's no way to stop it—"

"No kidding? Right now he told you? What made him spill the beans?"

"I-I don't know. It seemed like he trusted me . . . but maybe it's because he's just old, old and tired, maybe just sick himself of . . . all this insanity."

"That I believe."

"Look George, let's get something to eat and I'll tell you all about it. I'm starved."

"Sounds good kid. Let's get a move on."

Chapter Sixty-Eight

IT IS THE last virtual meeting of the Neanderthals before the code-named "Great Chaos" scheduled for election day and Leonard Huxley, aka Mario Pfalser, aka General Ned Ludd, sitting before his battered laptop in his rented room in Red Rock, is ecstatic—and not a trifle uneasy.

Only last week one of his trusted lieutenants had moved the "Clean Room" server in Chicago online and sent many thousands of copies of the Plague virus around the globe to insinuate its seemingly innocuous code deep within the operating systems of unsuspecting computers. Their primary targets are commercial systems, but a great many residential PC's have also been infected, even those whose owners may have been careful to keep current with the latest antivirus technology, as the Plague is, at this stage of the game, the ultimate Trojan Horse, invisible to all protection. These machines are now slaves to the malevolent virus and will be used to deliver concurrent waves of data-annihilating attacks until they themselves are no longer able to function. All they await is a signal, a date-time instruction dispatched from the Neanderthal's central server to inform them when their role in the Great Chaos is to begin.

There had been a lengthy, and at times, heated, online argument over whether to release the Plague before or after the polls closed, with many Neanderthals wanting to stop the elections before they even got started. But Huxley knew that Dunne was engaged in the masterwork of his career, such as it was: the extremely difficult task of cracking the government-protected ElecTal software, and leaving again without a trace. Out of respect for the legendary hacker, Huxley was able to effect a compromise: the virus would be encoded to wreak its havoc beginning at ten p.m. central time, thus allowing enough of the returns to come in to possibly allow the prediction of the winner of the presidency, but before the final tally was complete. At that time all data on AlphaBanc's huge array of computers, including all the election returns, would be destroyed.

Huxley, feeling every bit the general, exhorts his troops onward in the ensuing battle for the security and welfare of the trampled masses. He knows that most of his alienated and oppressed z-hackers can't wait for the Great Chaos to occur. But he tells them all to be patient, knowing that the triggering instruction is accessible to anyone with enough skill to break into the string of code and change the initiation schedule.

Nervously, he switches between the meeting and various news sites to check if there is any mention of a computer virus attack anywhere yet in this country or around the world, and thankfully, even this late in the game there is nothing, all quiet on the cyber-front.

Huxley smiles to himself; revenge will soon be his. The question will now be answered: Is one man's life, a blind black man's in this case, equal to all the data in America—and, depending upon how widespread the attack actually becomes, perhaps the world? He is one of the little people that Bergstrom and cronies should never have dared to tread upon, not this time.

But even with all the destruction that will be caused by the Plague and the other machinations of the z-hackers, no one, not a single soul other than Huxley himself knows the additional insult to this great injury he has in store for them.

It will only be later, when history works again, that the world will realize the extent of the incredible damage that one man has wrought upon western civilization as we know—or knew—it.

Chapter Sixty-Nine

"THE HUMAN MIND, and I'm *not* just talking about the brain," expounds Roland Rascher in one of his more megalomaniacal moods to Toby O'Brian and Franz Haedler, "is truly a strange and wonderful creation. It encompasses *so* much more than the thirteen hundred-odd grams of moist gray matter, a collection of neurons, synapses, dendrites, what have you . . . it includes the *soul.*"

"Yes, Roland," O'Brian stifles a yawn, "I understand. But all I asked was what do you think is happening inside her head right now? What was the result of the psychological panel you performed yesterday?" O'Brian refers to an image of Christin Darrow on the big monitor on his office wall. She is dressed in a flowing pink dress and is humming to herself as she vacuums her tidy little "apartment."

"I see that she has been receiving fairly continual subliminal suggestions of . . ." O'Brian scrutinizes the monitor on his desk, ". . . right now the mix looks like old 1960s' TV show soundtracks, 'Father Knows Best,' 'Leave it to Beaver,' and what have you."

"Oh lawdy, lawdy," Haedler smiles grimly and shakes his head. "What we got goin' *here!*"

Rascher frowns at Haedler and turns back to O'Brian. "I am attempting to answer you, Toby. I just want you to know that there is more going on with her, I venture, than just the process of sophisticated drug therapy and what we used to call, back in my old MK-Ultra days with army intelligence, 'psychic driving.'"

"Just what are you trying to tell me, Roland?"

"Well," Rascher sighs and scratches his forehead, "it seems that Miss Darrow has rather skillfully fabricated an entire life for herself within the little realm we have built for her."

"Hoo-boy!" exclaims Haedler.

"And what do you mean by that?" asks O'Brian.

"Well, it seems that, in order to make sense of all the different—I will call them family structures—we have presented her with through the old TV audio, in addition to the actual programs themselves we run through the television in her 'apartment,' primarily because we were lazy, Toby—"

"Well we weren't *prepared*, Roland," O'Brian barks angrily. "Who knew that Dunne would prefer a-a retro world—"

"Maybe if'n you boys had taken a better look at his doss-ee-ay," drawls Haedler, "we wouldn't be in this fix. Why, as I recollect, he even had hisself one of those PERSPROFs with us."

"Franz, he destroyed—erased—all his files before he, uh, left us. And since McCarthy is the great repository, once it's gone here, it's gone everywhere."

"Hmm. Toby, you're so right. I forgot. I do offer you my sincerest apology."

"Okay," says Rascher, "as I was saying, during our interview, Miss Darrow informed me that her name is "Mary Ellen Rogers," or, uh, at other times, "Kitten," and that she has been separated from her family during the social unrest that we have convinced her is occurring in the, er, outside world, and that she is being shuffled between foster parents, the families being the Nelson's, the Cleaver's, the Anderson's, et cetera, for the duration. She currently believes she is in a sort of underground bunker, waiting for assignment to her next family."

"She actually believes this?"

"Completely. Wholeheartedly. I couldn't shake her on any of the details," says Rascher.

"Lawdy, but we done one hell of a job on that po' girl."

"We also discovered something else, something very unusual."

"What? I'm almost afraid to ask," says O'Brian.

"During the normal battery of psychological tests we ran, we learned that she has apparently lost her sense of color vision."

"What?"

"She seems to see only in black and white, like a lower-order mammal, or I think more accurately, like the early television shows she believes she is a part of."

"My God," sighs O'Brian. "What have we done?"

"The good news is that there isn't any actual damage to her eye physiology. It just seems to be a hysterical reaction. We had Carioni check her out. It appears that she just decided, in her mind, that her chosen world does not require—or allow—color, and she has just blocked it."

"So it's reversible then?"

"We're quite certain of it. Well, we think so, anyway."

"Oh gawd-*damn* it all! You pointy-headed college boys done *ruined* that girl! All this damned old television . . . You should've left it at the boudoir stuff. There the girl was perfect—"

"We did what the Gnome wanted. He likes her that way."

"Good lord," sighs O'Brian again. "Just what *are* we doing here, Roland?"

"Well, I think if anything, we're only guilty of doing our job too well. Our mission, if you will recall, was to lure the Gnome back and convince him to get into the fed's election system and reprogram it to meet our needs. And how has that worked out?"

"Actually, remarkably well," O'Brian admits. "Dunne is doing a wonderful job. The other programmers are doing system testing for him and we are getting the results we expect. Of course, we'll be running a hell of a lot more data through in a few days, but I would have to agree that, yes, we have in fact accomplished our mission."

"And the quid pro quo?" asks Rascher.

"Well, you can see that yourself. Dunne virtually visits her, via his monitor. Which is, I suppose, typical for him. He doesn't appear to have an interest in actually meeting her. Physically."

"And you boys oughta be damn glad that he don't want any more o' her than that!"

"Yes, well, he's just not into the face-to-face. That's where he's always struck out in the past," says Rascher.

"Literally struck out. And made them pay. He's iced them—through intermediaries, of course, but it's his doing," says O'Brian.

"That's true. That's why we have no compunction about keeping him here. Using him like this. He's up for the death penalty outside of here."

"And inside o' here, too," snorts Haedler.

"Franz, you never were one to pull punches. But, well, it's a dirty business."

"Way I see it," says Haedler, "we're doin' the state a favor."

"After Dunne does us a favor."

"Okay. Enough now about Dunne," says O'Brian. "Roland, I wanted to ask you if when she saw Carioni did he put her under and—"

"Oh yes, she is now successfully barcoded," replies Rascher. "He's perfected the technique. The marking is now completely invisible. It can only be seen in ultraviolet—or whatever type of light it is they're using now. It's dead-center on the back of her neck, like the rest of them. Of course, we eventually want to do the forehead—"

"Hey, he's still not using thet ol' six-six-six number on ever'thing fer the barcoding, is he?"

O'Brian chuckles. "Of course not. He was just using that sequence to test with. I think he thought it was funny."

"Always gave me the creeps. Like he was tryin' to bring on the apocalypse or somethin' like that."

"Well, it will have to start somewhere, right?" says Rascher, quite seriously. "Why not here? Maybe we're ground zero."

"Now there's a provocative thought, Roland," says O'Brian. "Leave it to you. But, seriously, I think that Carioni should be using a set of production sequence numbers now. Her's I suspect will be some derivative of the number fifty-one. She is number fifty-one isn't she?"

"That's right," says Rascher, "she's glass house fifty-one. The last one we've done. And undoubtedly the best."

"A-men," mutters Haedler.

Chapter Seventy

I𝚃 IS 𝚃HE most courageous thing Dunne has ever done, actually dressing up, more or less, in an old suit coat on loan from the Epenguin and a communal tie from the programmers' dormitories that matches absolutely nothing, carrying a crumpled bouquet of artificial daisies—the only flora or facsimile thereof available to be picked from the jetsam that exists so far below the rest of the daylit world—and summoning his last reserve of inner strength to come a-calling on Miss Christin . . . or at the moment, distressingly, Mary Ellen Rogers.

She is sitting on a kitchen chair along the wall (all the chairs are lined up, the table pushed aside, as if for a dance) in a flouncy pink party dress, hands folded in her lap, looking up at him eagerly, as though hoping to be asked. . . . Yes, it certainly must be a dance that currently illuminates the neurons of her addled brain, streaming directly in from the black and white TV town of Mayfield, USA.

Dunne tries to hide his shock at the condition he finds her in, reminds himself that that's exactly why he forced himself to come here, to determine the actual mental state of this fair being that he has tenderly watched on a conveniently resizable window on his monitor, her life here at AlphaBanc Arms broadcast via various hidden cameras located throughout her apartment (the bathroom off-limits in a considerate gesture of Morlockian morality).

It is interesting enough, he discovers, to be physically inside her cunningly-crafted quarters, which has large high-definition video panels installed behind each of the glass windowpanes with wonderfully mutable projected scenes of presently a sunny English countryside with—O'Brian's programmers have pulled out all the stops on this one!—a great white stallion prancing around the cottage from window to window, snorting, bucking, its beating hooves easily felt in the room until it stops to browse in a pasture beneath an overgrown apple tree—he's almost envious at the lavish attention to detail, the amazing number of gflops the Beast is burning to generate this gorgeous sound-and-light extravaganza. And now, spectacular glowing *butterflies* flash and flit gracefully among the flowers in the gardens outside and and a precisely animated hummingbird buzzes around the honeysuckle and columbines gracing the front porch—damnit he *is* jealous, they never did anything like this for *him*. . . .

But he must now focus on another computer-enhanced entity, this fair young woman who has come to settle in a kitchen chair next to him. Of course, it is she, in the end, who they have provided for him, and though he finds it hard to tear his eyes away from the incredible windows as the scenes outside morph gradually back to the 60s TV street scenes—those hotdogs! Obviously putting on a show for the old master, you have to love them—of monochromatic Mayfield again, fading softly into black and white, he forces himself to lean over and venture, "Hello."

"Hi, Lumpy."

"Lumpy?"

"Yes, you are Lumpy Rutherford, aren't you?"

Ooh. In the addled world she perceives, he translates to the unloved, the unlovable, the schlemiel, Clarence "Lumpy" Rutherford of ancient "Leave It to Beaver" fame. This is an unkind cut, probably what Rascher, that cruel bastard, has suggested to her. Or . . . is it just within her disturbed mind?

"Uh, could you call me, er—"

"Clarence? That's your real name."

"Yes, sure. Clarence. That's fine. And you're—?"

"Why Mary Ellen Rogers, of course, silly. You came here to visit me."

"Oh, sure, sure. So, uh, how do you like it here?"

"Well, I don't really, but until the violence outside is over, I guess this is the best place to be," a brave little smile. "They give me the best darn scenery I could ever imagine. Even if it's not exactly—real."

"Er, the violence . . . outside?"

"The riots and looting and civil disobedience. All Americans must stay indoors until further notice! It's what they say everyday on the news, silly. Isn't that why we're all inside here?"

"Oh, sure, sure . . ." Dunne realizes that Rascher and O'Brian are shrewder than he ever imagined, creating a slick scenario to explain why she must remain in this otherworldly "apartment."

"Someday I'll be able—we'll all be able—to go outside again."

"Oh sure, of course we will. Er, Mary Ellen, how are you doing here? Yourself?"

"Oh gosh, I-I'm not really s-sure," she whispers, the brave 1960s-America spunk suddenly gone and she is surprisingly on the verge of tears. "I—well, you know, I think sometimes I'm going out of my mind."

"Oh really?"

"Yes, yes, I-I'm trying very hard to . . . maintain, you know, but," she leans closer, "I hear voices inside my head, Lumpy, er, Clarence."

"You do?" he asks, startled as much from her admission as by the realization that Rascher's and O'Brian's subliminal programs are apparently flawed. And then, from under the edge of the semi-bouffant wig she is wearing, a small shiny something catches his eye. "What's this?" he asks, reaching slowly, so as not to startle her, toward the hairpiece. He touches a piece of aluminum foil.

"Oh . . . oh," she groans, now completely wretched, bows her head down and begins sobbing. "I line my wig with foil. I-I'm trying to stop the voices; they whisper constantly, now. During the day sometimes I think they go away, but at night, when I'm trying to sleep and it's quiet—except for the humming of the machinery, of course, that never stops—I can hear them! Some-times it's music, sometimes it sounds like a-a television show, with laughter in the-the background."

"Ohhh, Jesus Christ . . ." groans Dunne.

"Clarence, you shouldn't take the Lord's name in vain!"

"Oh, sorry. But you're—hanging in there, huh?"

"I suppose so, but you know it's funny. I find that I really miss my parents. It's, it's as if I really want to get to know them better, you know. It's funny, the memories I have—or I think I have—of my parents aren't all that happy. At least, I guess they aren't. Sometimes I can't think very well at all anymore. So I want to meet my family all over again. I just learned I have a sister! Can you imagine? I can't remember anything about her!"

"Oh. Well, what do you know of your family?"

"Only what I see on TV, I guess."

"On TV?"

"Sure, look." Christin walks over to a big old Zenith console television along one wall and turns it on. Suddenly, surprisingly, three people appear on the screen, as though posed for a portrait, a fatherly forty-ish fellow who isn't quite Ward, a mother figure in a prim dress who isn't quite June, and a daughter, who looks like . . . oh, this is clever, Rascher and his crew have outdone themselves, a daughter who is the spitting image of a young Christin herself—could they have morphed her image onto some actress? And the little TV family is actually something of a taped greeting, waving at the camera, saying, "Hi Christin, how are you? We miss you and hope to see you soon!" as though she were at camp.

"Oh . . . Jesus."

"Clarence, you watch your language, now!"

"Okay, I'm sorry."

"Clarence, I want to ask you this. Seriously. Do you remember the last time you were happy? Really happy?"

Dunne thinks, *so this is what it must be like.* Being with a girl, a woman, in the real world, an entirely new experience for the reclusive elf, to actually *be here*, FTF at last, so close that he can reach out and touch her, and in fact has nearly done so with the foil. And now she looks at him so earnestly weepy-eyed and pushes her hands against his so softly, gently, that he must take them now in his own hands, a warm wonderful electricity filling them as he surprises himself, answers, "Yes, I do remember . . . it was a long time ago, when I was about eleven or twelve years old and I had run away from home for I think the third time.

"It was early spring and I was standing in the rain trying to hitchhike and I was wet and cold and lonely and this car, a big station wagon, suddenly pulls up and inside is this family, a mother and father and a daughter about my age, and there might have been a little baby . . . but they were all clean and dry and happy and they wanted me to come in out of the rain. They were laughing and seemed to treat my running away as a big joke! My first instinct of course was to tell them to leave me alone, but they kept coaxing me inside and I was so wet and miserable that I climbed in. It was warm, and I guess you could say, very happy, inside. They laughed and joked about everything and kept poking such fun at me that I laughed in spite of myself. They took me to a drive-in where I had the best hot ham sandwich with mustard and pickle relish I have ever had. To this day. I remember that sandwich to this very day."

"So . . . then what happened?"

Dunne sighs. "They took me back home. They said they were moving, I think, to Minnesota or Oregon or somewhere and I remember hinting about maybe going along, which of course they took as a huge joke, but I don't think I was ever more serious in my life. I have often reflected on that day and wondered what my life would have been like if I had been able to run away with the happy family. That's what I've always called them: 'The happy family.' I never saw them again. I never even got their name. I wish I had now. I could track them down and look them up, or at least deposit some money in their bank account."

"Clarence, now how would you do something like that?"

"Just an interbank electronic transfer. Simple and untraceable if—" he stops, realizes Lumpy Rutherford never would know any of this.

"Huh?"

"Oh, never mind. I was just kidding. So, uh, what is your happiest moment?"

"You know, I can't . . . remember. I just can't . . . my mind is so bad now, and the voices make it so hard to think. I was trying to remember and all I can come up with are some weird and exciting but thoroughly disgraceful memories of me as a very sexy model of some sort, and somehow as a college student, too. I just can't figure it out. That's why I asked if you could remember anything. I just can't anymore . . ."

Dunne sits silently, stunned and appalled by their evil handiwork, this poor, poor girl sitting before him. Although he understood logically, clinically, what was being done to her, seeing her now as an innocent flesh and blood being who has been so thoroughly compromised through the application of this sophisticated technology, he feels disgust and revulsion—and also tremendous sadness, realizing that all of *this* is what it takes to get this once-vibrant creature to accept him.

Suddenly the lighting in the room dims and hundreds of tiny white dots race against darkened window screens in perfect mimicry of the ballroom: the mirrored ball with the spotlight focused upon it—Clarence and Mary Ellen on the town!

"Oh!" Christin jumps up excitedly, "The dance is starting!"

And sure enough, the soulful strains of Mel Carter's "Hold Me, Thrill Me, Kiss Me," come through speakers hidden somewhere—those crazy guys are really going all out here—Dunne being pressed ever farther into social regions he never before dared enter. . . .

"Oh, please Clarence, dance with me! I love this song!" She pulls him into the center of the room and he clumsily follows. She guides his arms around her and, she leading all the way, they manage to glide around the room to Mel's soulful crooning:

> *Hold me, hold me*
> *Never let me go until you've*
> *Told me, told me, what I want to know*
> *And then just hold me, hold me . . .*
> *Make me tell you I'm in love with you . . .*

Dunne finds himself in a wholly unfamiliar universe, the music welling, the lights whirling, this beautiful warm young woman, intoxicatingly perfumed, dwelling lightly, softly, in his arms. He even dares to pull her slightly closer and thinks that he can't believe how truly wonderful, *wonderful*, all of this is . . . and then, as though there can be no unearned joy, regretful images flood his mind, of himself as the always-unloved, the always-rejected, the sorehead genius . . . and then descending even further, seeing himself as the evil one, the dark avenger, the murderer *in absentia* of beautiful hopeful young women such as these—even, almost, of she, Christin! How could he allow these atrocities to occur? How could he just stand by . . . and let them die? He feels truly awful now, so wonderfully, terribly, close to this very real, very human, onetime prey. He begins to weep on her soft fragrant shoulder.

"Oh . . . Clarence."

"No, don't stop . . . don't . . . I'll-I'll be okay."

"What's the matter?"

"It-it's just that . . . you're so . . . beautiful."

"Why, thank you."

The song ends and Dunne, staggered by a sudden overwhelming vision of reality, gently pushes himself away from her, ignores her entreaties to stay, stay and dance. . . .

He knows he must leave her now. He locks the door behind him, wanders down the fluorescent hallway, vowing that he will surely free her from all this insanity, and possibly . . . free himself, too.

Back behind his familiar monitor, Dunne grits his teeth and thinks, *My work for them is nearly done and soon I will be a dead man.*

He knew it was a sucker bet to come here and do their evil bidding and expect to get out alive, but—it was something he had to do: to finally commit to life, to come out of his desolate networked world and actually, meet her, touch her . . . and to think he almost—lost her.

The awful truth, he had realized as he walked out of her tiny patch of Elm Street, USA, is that he has caused her to die anyway, through a somewhat speeded-up version of the same fate that awaits most of us nonetheless, a slow subtle techno-death, courtesy of AlphaBanc and friends.

This I can certainly do, Dunne thinks, and begins seriously probing the housekeeping program O'Brian and Rascher have set up to run her hermetic life here: regulating the daylight, scheduling the cycles of the animated moon, the subliminal recordings, the release of drugs into her bloodstream. As he sits now before one of the hydra-heads of the AlphaBanc reticula and watches with overwhelming sadness his compromised beauty lounging alone in her quarters, he thinks, *I can stop this. I can turn this off . . .*

Dunne clicks away, secretly ending the flow of drugs and the constant subliminal babbling. He almost completely disables the software which communicates with her implant, but thinks better of it. At least for the time being he—and unfortunately, they—will be able to find her. Wherever she is. Which at some point in the crazy uncertain future, might just be needed.

Chapter Seventy-One

IT HAS FINALLY arrived, "Electronic Election Day," as all the media are calling it, America to select the next president of the United States, one third of the senate, and all congressmen, for the most part, electronically. Virtually all of the networked balloting data is being funneled through the Internet into the McCarthy complex's huge computers. All of AlphaBanc is naturally electrified, especially the crew underground at the complex itself. O'Brian hasn't gone home for the last four nights, has been bunking with the computer freaks down in geek-level (not really all that bad, he finds, so very close to the humming heart of everything). The Epenguin is working on the dark side with Norman Dunne and Maury Rhodden, up from AlphaBanc Chicago, adding final touches to their evil crack of the ElecTal vote tallying program and thus the ultimate subversion of the democratic process in America—what else is new?

Security is very tight. Blair and Clayborne, along with Haedler and the entire ISD team, have been putting in very long hours, working with federal marshals and a contingent from the FBI to ensure that the ElecTal system is secure. It is tedious and demanding work. Clayborne's current assignment is dealing with the press, specifically helping coordinate dozens of news crews' access to McCarthy's most photogenic features: the mammoth underground repository of stored data, the two-and-a-half story data screen arrays in the command center, and the cavernous computer room housing the great collection of networked servers known now officially to the press as "the Source."

Clayborne has had none other than Mario Pfalser assigned to him as a sort of assistant and guide around the underground complex, and through conversation during breaks Clayborne learns that, for a simple internal mail delivery person, Pfalser sure seems to know a great deal about computer systems in general, and the infrastructure at McCarthy in particular. Also, his job gives him security clearance to virtually all areas of the complex.

It is past lunchtime when they are finally able to turn over their duties to other ISD drones and grab some sandwiches from the underground commissary. The cafeteria is packed with employees and media people so Pfalser leads Clayborne down a couple of hallways to a locked corner office, room 101, according to a small metal plate on the door, which his security card is programmed to open. Pfalser closes the door behind them, sits behind a monitor on the desktop and fires up an old workstation.

Clayborne looks around, sees that the office is apparently used now for storage, with old chairs and books and boxes and papers stacked in shelves up to the ceiling.

"You know what the geeks are calling the supercomputer here of late, don't you?" Pfalser asks, staring at the screen.

"Uh, I've heard—the Beast."

Pfalser nods. "It used to be the Magic Mountain, then, the Source. Now it's the Beast. And I can see why. It's absolutely amazing—and reprehensible—what they've got in here. Your PERSPROF, for example."

Clayborne stifles a gasp, but again realizes that the underground keepers of the great machine would certainly have access to all of its vital parts. "Oh, really?"

"Really. You know how many PERSPROFs are currently in the system?"

"I give up."

"Let's see, about . . ." Pfalser squints as he types on the keyboard. "About thirty-eight million."

"No way!" Clayborne does gasp now. "Th–there's only around three hundred thousand AlphaBanc employees worldwide, even counting past employees—"

"They've found the PERSPROF format very useful in their efforts to keep track of people. It looks like they're adding about two to three hundred thousand records a month now. With their satellite and fiber optic networks nearly completed, they've really got the process automated—all part of the Grand Unification model. Now nearly all of an individual's transactions are recorded immediately: credit cards, debit cards, phone calls—whatever

comes across the Net. And of course that's all added to whatever's found by the huge batch jobs that run constantly now,
pulling data from health records, banking transactions, insurance
records, you name it—plus, now they've got IRS records,
criminal records, Interpol, Echelon, Carnivore, and any other of
the government databases the Beast has access to."

Clayborne is numb, doesn't want to believe any of it but
knows that it is of course all too true . . . and totally depressing.
"God, it's just, just—"

"Appalling? Well, there's another interesting PERSPROF that
I happen to peruse from time to time, a Christin J. Darrow. It
looks like she's a prime specimen in quite a few collections,
including AlphaBanc's. The best collection ever, of course. Man,
this is one hot babe. She thinks her postings on NEXSX are
anonymous and secure there, but of course we know better."

"Hey, damnit, Mario, c'mon now . . ."

"Know what the J. stands for?" asks Pfalser, clicking maddeningly away at the keyboard.

"No, but, let's just give it a rest here—"

"Julia. Christin Julia Darrow. Whoo, she is *too* hot."

"Mario! Goddamnit!" Clayborne finds it immensely disturbing
that Pfalser is able to delve so easily into Christin's file, which is
to say, into her life, an inordinately large portion of which is
undoubtedly encapsulated in this evil PERSPROF. He circles
around behind the workstation, knows that Pfalser is trying to
get a rise out of him, isn't really sure how to respond . . . and
then finds himself looking directly into the particulars of Christin
Julia Darrow's omniscient PERSPROF. And there she is in a
video clip obviously recorded by her webcam, purposefully
prancing around her apartment to party music by the GoGo's,
wearing a skimpy lavender thong, sheer bra, and purple suicide
heels—wow, she *is* hot. But he's vaguely jealous; it's a particular
erotic statement that he's never seen before. And, again he's
disgusted by just how much *They* really know. How *dare* they?

Clayborne looks over at Pfalser, speechless.

"Appalling, I think was the word of choice."

"Jesus, yes. . . ."

"Body and soul, man, body and soul. Well, we've seen the
body, some of the, er, collection, anyway, but, for the soul . . . it

seems that Christin has been visiting a Dr. Turing over the Net, a supposed online shrink."

"Yeah, she told me that she was doing some online therapy."

"Well, of course AlphaBanc knows, too. Let's see . . . the files are all nicely summarized by AlphaBanc's crack privacy invasion staff, some debauched branch of human resources, I gather, and there's something about her being expelled from college during her freshman year. Appears to be a sordid little tale. You know about that?"

"Uh, not really. But, again man, that's private, personal stuff, I'm sure . . ."

Pfalser rolls his eyes. "Nothing's private to anyone who's got access to this stuff, Jack. But the funny thing here is . . . Alpha-Banc ran a little check on this Dr. Turing. Turns out he—or *it*, actually—is for the most part a sophisticated AI computer program created by a fifteen-year-old kid, name of . . . Singer, from New York City. Very brilliant kid, apparently . . . we've got his middle school files here, somewhere. His father's a practicing psychiatrist, must be where he got the idea to set up a computer to do therapy, also the chutzpah to start up the bogus site."

Clayborne's heart sags. Christin had mentioned the therapy site to him when they were together, had been so hopeful when she told him how much Dr. Turing had been helping her. Now he isn't even real. God, what *is* real, personal, private, anymore? In a sense, even Christin isn't real anymore. At least to Clayborne. That's right—and the thought instantly angers him—They've got her. They, the goddamn Morlocks, have taken her away some-where and . . . maybe that location is in her PERSPROF. Clay-borne thinks he's got to gamble here to find her, roll the dice with Pfalser. It's the only chance he's got.

Chapter Seventy-Two

COULD HE POSSIBLY know where she is? Clayborne thinks, staring blankly at the glowing workstation. Strange as his request might seem to Pfalser, he's got to make it. "Hey, Mario, could you find out where . . . ?" Clayborne blurts, then checks himself.

"Yes?" Pfalser looks at him coolly, as though he knows what he's going to say.

"Er, can Christin's PERSPROF, or, er, anything else, tell us exactly where she is right now? You know they've got her, well, uh—" Clayborne trails off, isn't sure what to say next.

"Locked away somewhere?" Pfalser types at the keyboard, looks mockingly-blank up at him.

"Well, uh, actually . . ."

"How about right here?"

"Here? In McCarthy?"

"Alphaville, man. See for yourself." Pfalser pulls up on the screen an intricate grid that appears to be part of an elaborate 3-D floor plan of the McCarthy complex. "This is her. Right here." Pfalser points to a blinking red dot in one of the rectangular areas.

"Huh? What do you mean? What is this?"

Pfalser briefly describes AlphaBanc's Remote Personal Location program, a module linked to the Derived Dwelling Definitions system, and how it is able to precisely track people, that is, those people who have received an implant.

"Oh Jesus, the implant, oh no . . . so you mean that that crazy *dot* is Christin? Right here?"

"It's her location here at McCarthy. Obviously AlphaBanc's satellite network won't work underground here, so they've got several receivers mounted throughout the complex."

"I-I just can't believe this. . . ."

Pfalser clicks some keys and suddenly a dozen or so more red blinking dots appear scattered throughout the grid. As he moves the cursor over each of the dots, a small description tag appears. Over one of them it reads: Darrow, Christin, J., along with a trailing string of coded information.

"My God, so that's what the implant was really for."

"Among other things—"

"She thought it was to cure her-her Ménière's syndrome."

"Nope. She never had it. No one ever had Ménière's. It's something they artificially induced in all their, uh, guinea pigs. Even Bergstrom's daughter."

Clayborne's stomach is really knotted now; he's sure he's getting an ulcer. "Bergstrom's daughter? She's got one, too? How many are there of the goddamned things?"

"Fifty-one. At least that's the last one added to the database. Christin is glass house fifty-one."

"Glass house fifty-one . . ." Clayborne considers. "She's a . . . glass house?"

"They call them glass houses because they no longer contain any secrets; they're AlphaBanc's perfect specimens, utterly transparent. Hideously transparent, to my way of thinking, but I guess I'm old-fashioned."

"My God, in terms of this, aren't we all?"

"Some of us more than others, Rich. Some of us think maybe we're better off going back to the Stone Age, or least its information-age equivalent."

Clayborne instantly understands where Pfalser, speaking calmly to him from behind the omnipotent terminal, is going with this. Pfalser is a mole. "You're a Neanderthal, aren't you?"

Pfalser stares straight at the tube, nods very slowly. "You got a problem with that?"

"Actually . . . no. Not now. Not anymore. Maybe I never did." Clayborne feels the near-constant clenching in his stomach ease somewhat. He's told the truth.

"So, you know what I am. I can't tell you any more than that. Right now."

"Fine. I don't care."

"Okay, but care about this . . ." Pfalser reaches into a deep pocket in his cargo pants and pulls out a dark red anodized metal case, slides open a latch, and carefully lifts out one of a dozen or so miniature flash drives secured within. "I happen to think I can trust you. I've studied your PERSPROF; it describes you as a person who might have some integrity. At any rate, it's too late in the game to be choosy."

"Huh?"

"Never mind. The deal is . . . in case something should happen to me, I want someone to know about these."

"What have you got?"

"They're files that I've copied from the vast storehouses here. These, by the way, are the only copies I've got at the moment. I don't dare keep dual copies around here. Some are data files, some are captures of the endless videos they keep on things here, like Geli Bergstrom and Christin; some are recordings of conversations that I've found between O'Brian and Bergstrom and Gates and Blair and you—"

"And me?"

"Even you. Apart from the vast inputs of external information, many, many things are recorded within AlphaBanc itself. They've digitized everything . . . and miniaturized the cameras, the microphones, and placed them so cleverly that even people who ordered them installed don't remember where they are. People change jobs, buildings, offices . . . but the equipment keeps right on recording. It's only the drones, the trogs, the Morlocks who work down here, underground—where all the information ends up—who remember them."

"But—me? You said I was in your files."

"You play only a peripheral part in the Gnome affair. You come off pretty much as a patsy, a sap, actually."

"Oh, great . . . I love it."

"You should. It will undoubtedly spare you from prosecution. But not the others. They will ultimately do serious hard time."

"Good. My God, they should. What they're doing here right now . . . throwing the elections, virtually *choosing* the president. They've got to be stopped! I'm sick of it, I'm a mess, I can't sleep at night, my stomach is in knots . . . these guys have got to be stopped! God knows how far they've gone with their schemes. It, it makes me sick to think that I've played any part in it, even if it was, uh, as a stooge."

Pfalser seems to consider for a moment, then inserts the drive he holds into a port on the workstation and searches the file

listing. "In case you have any doubts whatsoever about your decision, or about just how much you were used—like anyone else
that AlphaBanc gets in their clutches—I want you to watch this
video clip. I have to warn you, it will be quite painful."

Clayborne feels an additional wrench in his gut—what more
could he learn? "Okay, roll it."

Pfalser clicks the mouse button and the screen goes entirely
black. Then, in the ragged slow-frame movements of a security
video, it fitfully lightens as though a door behind the camera, a
large door, is being opened . . . revealing a small airplane, beginning to gleam vaguely silver in the growing light. Clayborne
gasps, recognizes it immediately as the trainer that had crashed
with Natalie. Then a small man in blue mechanic's coveralls and
billed cap appears, opens a cover on the engine compartment,
pulls a small object from his pocket and places it inside the dark
cavity.

"This obviously isn't an AlphaBanc taping," says Pfalser, "but
somehow it found its way into the archives. Now watch this . . ."

Clayborne, thoroughly numb, watches as the man pulls down
the cover, and notices that the person's movements, even in the
jerky video, seem somehow awkward with the metal panel, as
though—it isn't really a man at all! And then the figure bumps
the bill of its cap on something in backing away, the cap falls off,
and a long lock of hair falls out—it is a woman! who retrieves the
cap, pushes her hair back under it and quickly walks out, this
time fully facing the camera. Pfalser freezes the frame on a fairly
good image of her face.

"Recognize her, Rich?" Pfalser says softly.

"Oh . . . God. It's Zara."

"Yep. Zara LaCoste. Apparently this was dirty work too sensitive to even trust to the drones. Or maybe no one else was available. Or maybe—"

"Or-or, maybe she had a motive of her own: me," Clayborne
chokes, feels genuinely dizzy, feels he has to sit down immediately and sinks to the floor.

"You okay, man? Sorry to show you that . . . but you had to
know. Their scheming knows no limits. They wanted Dunne like
nothing else. You had to be free, unattached, to help them. So
they detached you. Nothing is sacred."

"They just—*killed* her. Just like that. Just like that. . . ." Clayborne leans forward on the floor, his eyes fill with tears, throat constricts along with his heart, his gut, his soul. . . . He gasps for air, he needs air, some kind of fresh air right now that doesn't exist down here . . . rests his forehead against the side of the desk, feels like screaming, like strangling someone, like dying himself.

"Hey, hey! You gonna be okay, man? I had to show you. Take it easy now, you're in shock. They killed one of my friends, too. He was . . . like a father to me. I've never been able to find any proof, but while I've been poking around here I found a hell of a lot of other stuff . . . like your thing. Sorry about that."

Clayborne slowly pulls himself up, tries to catch his breath, "I think I'm gonna be sick," he says, feels he has to walk around, breathe some fresh air, real air, he just can't seem to get enough air down here. . . .

Chapter Seventy-Three

BLAIR HAS ALSO been trying to take a break from the crazy confusion of reporters, photographers, and equipment-laden camera crews stampeding through McCarthy's subterranean sanctity, but his accursed cell phone seems to never stop ringing with urgent dispatches from ISD central. Finally he turns it off, pretends to toss it into a wastebasket in O'Brian's office. Even though he doesn't much enjoy being in the intense IT director's presence—or actually with anyone anymore from the AFS inner circle—at least he's someone intelligent he can talk with, and he seems to have no problem with Blair's smoking; he puts up with it, anyway. Maybe he benefits from Blair's company as well.

From an inside pocket of his sport coat next to his shoulder-holstered Smith & Wesson, Blair pulls out a pack of Pall Mall's, secretly fingers a small gray flash drive which happens to contain a conversation he managed to record: of O'Brian when they discussed Christin's circumstances, his squealer's capital—also his death sentence if anyone here would discover it. He keeps it on himself at all times; the only way they could ever get it is if they get him. What the hell. It's a dangerous game.

"Hey Toby, there's something I've been meaning to ask you. From what I hear, the big conglomeration of computers you got down here, the Beast, the Source, the whatever, is going a little flaky on you guys. Rumor is that it's beginning to think on its own!" Blair laughs, lights up his cigarette.

"Well, that's ridiculous, of course," snorts O'Brian. "We think that the, ah, random messages are the result of the programmers' horseplay. Possibly even Norman Dunne himself hacking in. But that's all. Certainly nothing generated by the machine itself! You simply don't understand computers, George. Huge and powerful as the Beast, er, the Source, is, it is in the end simply a big dumb machine that cannot do anything, certainly cannot *think*, without our precise instructions."

"Like the poor bastards with your goddamned implants."

O'Brian smiles thinly. "Now, George, our test subjects are certainly still capable of independent thought—for the most part."

"Well, Toby, I've gotta tell you that I've gotten a couple of those 'random' text messages myself. On my phone. I told the Epenguin about it and he said he thinks some of the stuff is coming straight from the Beast itself."

"Then he's pulling your leg, George. He knows better. I tell you that it's got to be Dunne, or perhaps one of the programmers. They're absolutely brilliant, and at times, I admit, a trifle frightening. The alternative . . ." and here O'Brian seems to stop and ponder, shaking his head slowly back and forth, "is far too disturbing to contemplate."

Blair leans back in his chair, remembers something he's wanted to needle this brilliant, though not entirely puncture-proof techno-nerd with. "You're kind of a strange guy yourself, Toby. Didn't you say that you yourself started out as a programmer? Tobor—the Great?"

O'Brian winces, "Well, yes, many years ago, but I can assure you that I was never as—unusual, as some of these fellows."

"Sometimes I just can't fathom you, though. Like right now for instance. Doesn't it bother you that we've got . . . all this stuff going on here: the Darrow girl, Bergstrom's daughter, for chrissakes, the-the Gnome in his cave over there gonna subvert the entire American elections process, democracy itself going all to hell in this godforsaken underground rat hole . . . and now we've got all these reporters crawling over everything, every television network in the country and the world, and they're all just over on the other side of the wall . . . literally. Doesn't that bother you?"

O'Brian smiles, folds his pale hands together. "I understand what you're saying, George. I've given no less than seven interviews before lunch, I'm scheduled for at least a dozen more, and yet you see me here enjoying my break, checking my email, carving out my own little space, my own peace of mind. I've mastered the process, George. Compartmentalize, that's the ticket. A place for everything and everything in its—"

"Okay, okay, I don't need a lecture, Toby. Maybe I just haven't mastered managing my—space. But, Jesus, it sure gets to me. Maybe I'm just getting too old for this, I don't know . . ."

"George, let me ask you," O'Brian's smile gleams preternaturally from behind his glowing monitors. "Do you play chess?"

"Chess? Long time ago, I guess."

"Well, I love the game, and I've learned that it is, quite simply, a grand metaphor for the game of life. You see, in chess one can place a piece on a square right next to an enemy piece that could threaten it, capture it, annihilate it . . . but because that piece is protected by another, absolutely no harm can come to it. You see, it's a great deal like life—we protect, hide, if you will, our precious pieces, our treasures, through our own cunning and, of course, the help of ISD . . ."

"Well, ISD is here to tell you we got us a heap big problem!" O'Brian and Blair turn toward the door as Haedler storms in.

Blair instinctively reaches inside his coat, touches through the fabric the damning memory card. "What do you mean?"

"We-el," Haedler blusters behind O'Brian's monitors, "just flip over to camera R-G-Lev-D-9-1-3-1-0-1, will ya."

Blair steps around behind the monitors and watches with Haedler as O'Brian accesses that camera. "Look up there," says O'Brian as he sends the feed to the wall monitor . . . and up comes an image of Richard Clayborne and Mario Pfalser peering intently into a monitor, also quite visible, on a desktop.

"Ain't that your boy, Clayborne?" Haedler says to Blair.

"Looks like him. What are they doing?"

"Just watch. Toby, turn up that sound for us."

O'Brian clicks on the audio and a voice, apparently Pfalser's, comes through fairly clearly: "Take a look at this, Rich, if you want to see how sick it gets down here." He has pulled up a video of a dark Gothic-looking room with high-backed chairs, thick drapes, candles, and what looks like an altar. Seated at a massive table is a young attractive woman in a nun's habit. She is engrossed in reading a thick book, apparently a Bible.

"Looks like a nun in a convent," Clayborne's voice murmurs.

"Oh lord, no, they've got a feed of Geli Bergstrom!" gasps O'Brian. "One of our video action sensors picked up on this," grunts Haedler. "It's not good. You know who in hell this little Mario freak is, anyway?"

"He-he's just a clerk and internal mailman here, I think. A-a nobody."

"Well, we pulled up his PERSPROF and your little nobody happens to have access all over this place—"

"He's the delivery boy," says O'Brian, "he's got to be able to get around—"

"Don't gimme any of that shit, Toby!" growls Haedler. "You know what that little pissant is—he's a goddamned Neanderthal, an anarchist! Right here under our noses! We ran him through our files again and we're pretty sure he might be Leonard Huxley. Neanderthal number one! What thee hell!"

"Oh God, no! No! On this day of all days!" O'Brian wails.

"Compartmentalize, Toby . . ."

"Well, any day it's goddamn bad news," says Haedler. "But we're lucky we found out now."

O'Brian recovers somewhat, sniffs, "Well, Franz, apparently ISD didn't do its job when it screened him for the job."

Haedler's stare could freeze blood. "Mebbe not, but it looks like that little freak, Pfalser or Huxley or whoever! has been awfully busy here, copying God-knows-what sensitive stuff from our databases. Got it all on thumb drives. And it looks like your man, Clayborne, is in cahoots!" Haedler glares at Blair.

Despite himself, Blair feels his heart swell with pride. But he manages to pull his face into a scowl equal to Haedler's "Goddamnit! Are you sure?"

"Damn right I'm sure. One of our boys on the monitors got an alert—that room's supposed to be empty, and luckily, turns out it's one where we just installed a new itty-bitty camera . . . which that li'l smart-ass Pfalser don't know nothin' about. Well, don't matter now anyway, we got 'em. Georgie, take a couple boys down there and, uh, sequester 'em, eh?" Giving Blair what he knows to be the wink, if necessary, of death.

Chapter Seventy-Four

BACK IN RGLEVD913-101, Clayborne and Pfalser continue their compromised conversation: "It's a totally sick scene, man. Just shows what lengths they'll go to control people's minds. Now they've got AlphaBanc's own little convent. Right here in McCarthy. You won't believe it but that's Geli, Bergstrom's daughter. She's glass house thirty-nine."

"My God. So that's Geli Bergstrom."

"From what I gather, she spurned her daddy's blue blood choice for a perfect husband and chose to live with her boy-friend, a poor artist. Next thing you know, both of them disappeared, the story being that they had run off to travel the world together. I don't know what happened to the artist, God help him, but Geli ended up down here."

"So, what's with the nun getup and the convent setting?"

"It's the, I guess you could call it corrective action, that Berg-strom has imposed on her. One day she started having symptoms of Ménière's—or maybe worse—and then daddy provided a cure through AlphaBanc. Which happened to be an implant and a regi-men of Deludamil plus Nepenthine and—whatever. It's all in her PERSPROF. I can tell that you're puzzled, Rich. Let me explain what's going on here . . ."

And Pfalser tells Clayborne the ugly details of glass houses, the drugs, the subliminal stimulation, and apparently in extreme cases, the confinement down here in the catacombs.

"It's worse than you—or anyone—could imagine," continues Pfalser. "They've been having some sick fun with poor Geli, or Rascher has been anyway. I doubt that Bergstrom knows this, but Rascher actually walked into her convent room dressed up in a robe and a hokey crown of thorns and told her he was Christ himself! Can you believe it? What a crazy idiot. He had her bowing and genuflecting before him and promising to be chaste until eternity and he promised her everlasting life and . . . it was really a sick, sick scene. It's all in the digital archives here and I've got the clips. I tell ya, Rich, these folks are totally out of control. Which, uh, brings me to Christin. Want to see her?"

"Oh God. Yes, of course, but . . . I-I'm almost afraid to."

"Well, I guess it could be worse, but right now I'd say she's pretty darn close to June Cleaver . . ." And a video wobbles in before them, of unmistakably Christin Darrow, formally attired in pearls and a yellow ankle-length dress, softly humming to herself as she dusts the furniture in her 1960s-furnished apartment, an old "Father Knows Best" program inexplicably running on an authentic early black and white console television. Pfalser shakes his head. "Check out that TV program, man, complete with commercials of the day. That crazy O'Brian, man, he's—"

"The hell with O'Brian! What have they done to Christin?"

"Hey, calm down, Rich. I told you, it's just like they did with Geli—a wicked combination of drugs and suggestions through the implant. Zara's personally been involved with this—"

"I knew it, I knew it . . ."

"Yeah, she's got a makeup artist, Tatyana, doing her up. But it's sick, it's like The Manchurian Candidate or something. She's completely brainwashed. The term that army intelligence had for it in the early 60s was psychic driving. Although I think—I hope—these guys are a little more sophisticated than giving someone LSD and then letting them get too close to open upper-story windows—"

"Okay, Mario! Enough of this! We've got to get Chris out of there! Where is she? Flip back to the locator thing! Now!"

"Okay, okay . . . don't freak out on me here." Pfalser clicks around with the mouse and zeroes in on the blinking red dot that is Darrow, Christin, J., then turns to Clayborne, "Okay, she's on E-level. That's down this hallway, and then—"

And suddenly the door bursts open as Blair and two ISD goons storm in, pistols drawn.

"G-George!" All that shocked Clayborne is able to say as Blair, face cop-blank pulls his hands behind him, snaps on handcuffs, while another goon does the same to Pfalser.

Blair picks up the red metal case and puts it in his pocket, jabs the muzzle of his gun into Clayborne's back. "Let's go."

Chapter Seventy-Five

DOOM-TIME FOR Clayborne. Being hustled, handcuffed, down catwalks and back corridors of the McCarthy complex, well away from the swarming media army, he can't stop the sickening feeling of falling into the abyss, his carefully-wrought career shattered in an instant, ignominiously escorted out at *gunpoint* by the one person he thought he could trust in the ugly morass that AlphaBanc has become for him.

But who's kidding who? It was way past over.

The last few weeks had been a steadily worsening nightmare, culminating now in Pfalser's revelations of Natalie's fatal crash—and Christin's imprisonment. Now it's truly over, and actually, a tremendous relief. He never was in the same league as these ruthless sociopaths, knows now he never could be. So it is perhaps not surprising that a fluttering spark of pure joy wells up inside of him as he is urged along the corridors by the insistent stab of Blair's revolver. Now captured, he is free.

It's a catharsis; he's free now to finally strike back against the sick proprietors of this netherworld, against those who actually *murdered* his wife because it seemed expedient! And the first thing he's going to do is rescue poor Christin from the crazy Little Manchuria—or Elm Street, USA—that they've cooked up for her here just as soon as . . . well, what's going to happen here? They certainly don't dare turn them over to the police. No, there's no way they could ever . . . and then it comes to him, an icy shiver right through his heart . . . they aren't going to turn them over to anyone. They're dead men.

Clayborne, now truly frightened, thinks immediately of survival, tenses his arms to test how secure the handcuffs really are, looks furtively around the anonymous corridors: where are they? where can he run to?

Blair senses the change from submissive disbelief to escape-mode desperation, painfully drills the gun into his back, snags his arm, whispers menacingly, "So, now you get the picture, kid?"

"George, I-I—"

"Just business, kid."

Doomed. Clayborne looks wildly over at Pfalser, who walks along resignedly, head down, a model prisoner. Doesn't he know what's going to happen? He feels he needs an accomplice here. "Uh, hey, Mario—"

"Shut up!" barks Blair and pushes them along. And then they all suddenly come to a halt while Blair pulls his phone from his pocket. He shakes his head, announces to the other two, "Just got buzzed. Haedler wants us to take them up to Garage Four. Far away from here."

Where we'll be killed. Clayborne's heart sinks again. They are truly doomed. "Hey, wh-what are you going to do to us?"

"Shut *up!*" Blair yells and pushes him so hard he nearly falls over.

"Goddamnit, George!" Clayborne mutters and follows along the service corridor to a stairwell which he thinks is at the far back end of the complex, opposite the great repository. Silently they pass through the door and plod up the steps. Clayborne wonders if he should try to yell—after all, the place is full of reporters—but he fears being slugged immediately by Blair, the guy obviously now in full hyper-cop mode.

They clunk up at least a dozen flights of industrial stairway, all of them—especially Blair—puffing mightily at the effort, and run into no one, not a soul, Clayborne terribly disappointed, hoping, praying, that they might run into a hyperkinetic news team on a chance "behind the scenes" tour of the complex they might have wangled, but no such luck.

Garage Four is way in the back, dark and cluttered with maintenance equipment, tractors, a dump truck, snowplows and a beat-up old van, towards which, it appears they are headed. But then they all stop and Clayborne looks desperately around—there is no one else here of course. And then he gets a thought, looks up for AlphaBanc's ubiquitous surveillance cameras and there is one high up in one of the garage's dark corners, but it has a sheet of cardboard taped in front of the lens with the crude haiku: "Fuck You / McCarthy Maint."

Damn. Now there'll be no record at all of his miserable demise. Blair shouts, "Get on your knees! Now!" and pushes Clayborne and Pfalser onto the concrete floor of the garage.

Oh God . . . no. Clayborne is dazed, flashes to the many scenes of execution-style killings he's heard about and he knows it's over, he's a goner, there'll be no witnesses, that's why Blair was ordered to take them way out here, he's a dead man now, and suddenly he remembers running over corn-stubble rows in the dark Illinois night away from that quarry, away from the blast, from Billy and his craziness and he wants that sweet pure cool night air freedom again, away from all this insanity and intrigue— and he hears Blair spin the cylinder of his revolver and he tries to think quickly, thinks that he just can't die here, he's got an even greater purpose now, yes—he's got to avenge Natalie's death, he's got to rescue Christin . . . and he boldly looks back around, is horrified to see Blair screwing a black tubelike thing to his gun barrel, a silencer, the ex-cop amazingly casual, even chuckling a bit as he also notices the peevish placard before the camera above them, points up with the elongated barrel, addresses his fellow ISD assassins, "Looks like someone don't like old Darby O'Banknote checkin' up on 'em."

Both of them smile as they turn and look up at the camera and—suddenly—it's little more than a blur to Clayborne—Blair has jumped behind the two goons and cracked each of them— one-two—on the back of the head with his pistol.

They seem to hang in the air momentarily before crumbling. Blair quickly drops down behind Pfalser, reaches in his pocket for the key to unlock his cuffs while Clayborne watches in disbelief.

Thank God! He's still on our side! But then he notices one of the goons on the floor begin pulling himself up and at the same time reach beneath his sport coat for the gun in his shoulder holster. Blair has put his gun aside while dealing with Pfalser's handcuffs and Clayborne is now the only thing between them and the awakening thug—it's showtime!

Amazing himself, Clayborne springs to his feet and shouts, "George! Look out!" and, hands still cuffed behind his back, he runs straight for the goon who is presently standing upright and aiming his revolver at Blair but now quickly swings it around to point at Clayborne. *Oh God no!* But he can't stop, all he can see is the rapidly closing darkness of the gun leveled at his chest as he lunges forward, throws a body slam against the man . . . and then all sounds abruptly vanish as he seems to collide in slow motion, feels a vague thump on his chest as they fall silently together onto the concrete and Clayborne waits . . . doesn't hear the roar of the pistol . . . would he hear it? Is he dead? Or . . . what?

And then the world very quickly begins to swirl around him again, Blair scrambling over and Pfalser running up behind, bringing a large metallic object, looks like a wrench, swiftly down against the head of the goon who is trying to push Clayborne off of him . . . and the man lies silent once again.

"You okay, kid?" asks Blair leaning behind him, unlocking his handcuffs.

"I-I don't know," he says, shakily feeling his chest for blood, for a .38 caliber crater as he gets to his feet. He finds only a sore spot where the barrel of the pistol apparently hit him, almost collapses again with relief.

Blair picks up the man's revolver, looks at it, snorts, "Jammed. You are one lucky son-of-a-bitch, kid."

"No kidding? I-I thought it was all over."

"It almost was. In forty years I've never seen one as clean as this jam before."

"God almighty," Clayborne feels the blood drain from his face, fights to steady himself.

"Take it easy, kid. And thanks, you saved my life."

"Huh. Well, what else could I do?"

"Actually, I didn't think you had it in you."

"I-I didn't think I did either."

"But enough of that," says Blair, looking uneasily at the two men lying on the concrete. "We've got to get out of here. Let's get over to that van."

"But they've got Christin. We can't just leave her here."

"No kid, in a couple of minutes they're gonna be coming after us. We've gotta get outta here and regroup. If they catch us we won't be able to save anybody."

"But—"

"Mario, put down that thing and open the door!" Blair barks while running over to the van.

Pfalser drops the big crescent wrench he is still holding and runs over to push the button to raise the garage door, and Clayborne, still shaking, reluctantly heads for the van.

Chapter Seventy-Six

A MINUTE LATER the old service van roars out of the garage, Blair driving fast, sweating, smoking, swearing, Clayborne and Pfalser hunkered tensely in back. The entrance road to the complex is packed with traffic going both ways: cars, trucks, dozens of TV vans . . . and Blair drives steadily on the shoulder of the exit lane alongside the queue, skillfully cutting in front of a big commissary truck as they come up to the guardhouse. The truck honks at him, Blair casually flips him off and smiles over at one of the harried guards dealing with the stream of traffic.

"Hey, dago. How you holding up?"

"Hey, George. Like nothing I've ever seen before. Done for the day already?"

"Gotta run out for a little while. Good thing we aren't using the tunnel today, hey?" A very good thing. Normally all large vehicles going in or out of the complex have to pass through the "tunnel," a long low structure that x-rays the entire vehicle, with the occupants having to exit and walk through a similar, albeit smaller, room, so that no unauthorized material can be smuggled in or out of the complex. Very tight security, but Blair can see that all the traffic is being waved around it.

"Yeah, Haedler's orders. They stepped up security inside so's we don't have to check everyone. We never find anything anyway. Besides it's nuts here today."

The truck behind them lays on the horn again.

"You gotta move, Georgie." The guard waves them on and lifts the gate.

"Damn!" grunts Blair as they drive down the driveway to the main road.

"Wh-what's the matter?" a recovered Clayborne crawls up into the passenger seat, "somebody after us?"

"Naw, not yet anyway," Blair looks into the van's side mirror. "I just remembered, I left my Mercedes there. Damn it all."

"It's just bourgeoisie excess, anyway," Pfalser smirks, crawling up behind them.

"That's a fine way to talk after I save your ass back there."

"Your car will probably be okay," says Clayborne.

"I damn well hope so. We'll be coming back with a lot of law enforcement and I just hope it doesn't get trashed, or impounded, in the scuffle."

"I think I'm still in shock," says Clayborne. "I can hardly believe that all this unbelievable arrogance, and, and—scheming, has been going on for so long."

"Well, one of these days they were gonna get burned. Maybe, if we can get away, this is the day."

Traffic going east toward the interstate is backed up so Blair turns west towards the town of Red Rock, reaches in his pocket, pulls out Pfalser's red metal case, hands it over to Clayborne. "And here's how they're gonna get burned—real bad. Here, add this to it," pulling the small flash drive from his inside pocket. "This is our friend Mr. O'Brian admitting to some pretty mean stuff. Too bad. But I've gotta watch my ass, too." Blair reflexively looks in his mirror, grunts, "Speaking of which, here they come."

Both Clayborne and Pfalser quickly turn around to see a white AlphaBanc security Jeep, red lights flashing, siren wailing, barreling up behind them. "Jesus, George, step on it!"

"I am, I am . . . this old thing's a real dog," Blair flooring it, the van shaking badly as they try to speed away, the Jeep steadily gaining.

"C'mon, George, c'mon!"

"Goddamn it, I am, I am . . . we're screwed."

Up ahead, coming straight for them is another white Alpha-Banc Jeep, its lights flashing, too. There are corn fields on either side of the road right here, nowhere to go except . . . just ahead on the right is the road to the Blackwell Inn.

Blair nearly pushes the van into a four-wheel drift to make the turn and they rattle furiously down the lane to the rustic tavern, the two security Jeeps following behind in a cloud of dust. No one seems to notice a sign by the turnoff: Blackwell Inn - Closed.

Blair tears up the road, blasts right through the locked gate and roars into the central area by the well when suddenly Sally Thomas bustles out from one of the buildings and Blair shouts and spins the wheel and really does now slide sideways on all fours in an attempt to not run into her.

"Hoo-boy, we almost lost it there," gasps Clayborne as they shake to a stop.

"So what? We're dead men anyway," says Pfalser.

And at that moment the AlphaBanc Jeeps screech to a stop alongside of them.

"Maybe we can run for it . . ." Clayborne suggests weakly, gazing out toward the oaks as he opens the door.

Pfalser slides open the van's door and calmly steps out, but Blair remains in the driver's seat, lights up a cigarette.

O'Brian himself bounds out of one of the Jeeps, along with Haedler and, surprisingly, Zara. Clayborne freezes at the sight of her. Apparently she is also up here for the big doings. The two AlphaBanc security thugs from the other Jeep have their semi-automatics drawn along with Haedler and command the most respect, but O'Brian and Zara are also both armed, O'Brian with a black nine-millimeter, and Zara pointing a little silvered .22 caliber purse-piece at them. O'Brian visibly winces at her as they herd the fugitives together before the cobblestone well.

"Well, well, well . . ." O'Brian struts before the gang of three with a menacing twinkle in his eye, "what have we here?"

Blair groans, rolls his eyes while one of the goons frisks him, pulls the revolver-cum-silencer from his waistband. "Toby, if you're going to pop us, do it now and save us the idiot speech, okay?"

"Now, George, you remember what I told you about life being a game of chess? Well, I now think you play that game better than all of us thought—"

"Hey, hey, what is going on here now?" Up comes Sally toting an ancient shotgun that looks like it might have belonged to Daniel Boone. Forgotten by everyone zooming up in billows of dust, she apparently ran back into her house and retrieved the firearm.

"Ah, *Sally* . . ." coos benevolent O'Brian, "it's just a simple misunderstanding is all. These three gentlemen here have stolen something of ours and we simply want it back."

"Liberated the truth, if anything," says Pfalser.

"Well, so what's that supposed to mean?" asks Sally, eyeing Pfalser suspiciously. Then her eyes widen as she realizes who this is: the young man who had come into her tavern weeks ago for a Tarot reading. She gasps, understanding perhaps that whatever is going on here can now certainly come to no good end.

"Now, ma'am," answers Haedler, "we don't mean no harm at all. It's just a leetle misunderstandin' we need to clear up—"

"It's this he's after," Clayborne says, pulling the red metal case from inside his shirt, feeling Blair's and Pfalser's gaze upon him. "This has all the evidence anyone needs to prove that AlphaBanc has engaged in just about every conceivable crime to accomplish their goals—including the murder of my wife!" He nearly chokes as he says this, looks directly at Zara. "And probably others, you-you miserable sons of bitches! Not to mention unauthorized medical experiments on humans, and-and stealing the presidential elections, for God sakes! This very day!"

Sally—everyone—looks aghast. "Th-that *so*?" she says, squinting over her shotgun.

"As well as recordings of not a few AlphaBanc employees who may or may not be ready to turn state's evidence to save their respective asses . . ." murmurs Pfalser.

Blair immediately looks vaguely hangdog, and so, Clayborne notices, does Zara.

"Now, *Sally*," O'Brian's magnanimous voice gaining a distinct edge, "this really doesn't concern you. Why don't you just let us handle this ourselves—"

"Concerns me if it's on my land, mister. Place is closed today. Or maybe you missed the sign. You're trespassin' right now. Maybe I oughta go inside and call the sheriff, get us some *real* law enforcement around here." And keeping the gun leveled on them, she begins to back up towards the house.

There is a nearly imperceptible look Haedler flickers to his ISD security guards, which cowgirl Zara readily intercepts, opts to fire off a silver bullet from the little gun. There is a sharp pop, everybody jumps, and Sally falls back, drops her shotgun. Blair immediately runs over to her, shouting, "Goddamnit! Goddamnit, Zara! You stupid moron!"

But it turns out that Sally is okay, everyone more shocked at the loony accuracy of the shot, which miraculously struck the old blunderbuss at an angle, knocking it from her hands, the ricochet grazing her on the cheek. One of the guards runs up and takes the shotgun, two others pulling Blair and a slightly-bleeding Sally over to join the others at the well.

"Okay now, we've had our fun," says Haedler. "Now let's get down to business. First thing is that you hand over that l'il case to us, okay? And then no one will get hurt."

"Who are you kidding?" says Pfalser. "You're going to kill us all, anyway."

"Now, now . . . ain't nobody gonna get hurt, understand? Just as long as you comply, see. Now Clayborne, hand thet case over here so's the little lady don't get hurt any more, hey?"

"D-don't you give it to them. If what you say is in there!" yells plucky Sally, sneering, holding a hankie to her cheek. "I want to see these bastards *fry!*"

"Okay, well, nobody's going to get this then. It's just not worth killing anyone over." And Clayborne stretches out his arm, holds the burnished red case over the well, glances back toward them.

"No, sonny!" yells Sally. "Don't you throw away any of that evidence there. Don't let 'em get away with all that—whatever! That well's fifty foot deep with a strong flow at the bottom. Once it's down there it's gone for good."

"Toss it, kid. Don't make it easy for them. Either way, we lose it," grumbles Blair.

Clayborne understands, sadly, that Blair's right. He's got to do it. He extends his arm fully over the well and amid a chorus of cries from Sally and O'Brian and Haedler, he drops it. He watches it fall into the darkness, thinks he hears a soft splash and it's done.

"Well that's it," snorts Haedler. He raises his nine millimeter, aims it at Clayborne's head. "You pointy-headed little college punks are always so goddamn righteous."

"Franz, wait!" yells O'Brian. "Someone's coming." He points up toward the main road where a big white television van bristling with antennae is lumbering down the drive to the inn.

They watch in silence for a few seconds, then Haedler lowers his pistol, grumbles, "Don't they know this place is closed? Some people got no respect."

"Into the van, into the van," orders O'Brian. "We can't let the press find us in this—situation."

"Damn, that's just too bad. I was gonna fill this li'l punk here full of hot lead and let him sink in that stinkin' black well hisself," Haedler grumbles as he helps handcuff the tiny outlaw band.

"Well, kid," Blair says as they huddle in the darkness in the back of the van, "either way we were gonna lose it."

"Mario, you sure you don't have another copy of that stuff somewhere?" Clayborne whispers.

"No man, that was *it*. I told you. That's the end, finis."

Chapter Seventy-Seven

THEY ARE TAKEN back to the McCarthy complex, apparently to be kept on ice until a way is found to properly dispose of them. Also, with the elections in full swing, O'Brian, Haedler, and crew are required immediately back on the premises. They are brought in through the back garage again, and then down all the flights of stairs to sublevel D and its creepy corridor of forbidding doors with locking slide-panels over the little windows.

Haedler and the goons lock Sally in one of the rooms then Pfalser in another, but Clayborne and Blair are left, and Haedler purposefully walks them down the corridor to an empty corner room which looks very familiar to Clayborne, with books and papers piled nearly to the ceiling. It is in fact RGLevD913-101. Haedler pushes them in, gloats, "Well now, right back to the scene of the crime. Kinda fittin', ain't it? You boys gonna bunk together here, for the time being."

"You son of a bitch."

"Oh, this I *gotta* take care of . . . ." Haedler's fat fist pulls from his belt Blair's revolver.

Clayborne gasps, "No!" as Haedler points the silencer directly into Blair's face, then grins, swings around to the computer monitor on the desktop—it's an old CRT-type—and pulls the trigger. There is a loud WHOMP! and a small shattering of glass and acrylic from the black hole that erupts on the surface of the screen. Then he fires another shot into the PC tower only inches away from Clayborne.

"Jesus!"

"Allus wanted to do that, hey. Felt damn good."

They all fall strangely silent for a moment, everyone perhaps united in the satisfaction of seeing one of the heads of the hydra bite the dust.

"Gotta keep you boys incommunicado, so to speak." Haedler walks over, rips the phone out of the wall socket, carries it with him as he walks out the door.

"Hey, hey, at least unlock us!" yells Blair.

"Here Einsteins, you figure it out." He pulls a couple of keys from his pocket, tosses them on the floor. "They ain't gonna get you outta here though, ha-ha."

The door slams behind him and the electronic lock buzzes with finality. Clayborne sighs. It does seem somehow appropriate that they have come full circle, back to the office where Pfalser had shown him the secret evil that exists in the McCarthy catacombs, forever immortalized in the incriminating files he had copied, the ones, of course, that had just found their way to the bottom of the well. Clayborne shakes his head, scrunches down to pick up the keys, and after some contorting he and Blair manage to free themselves.

Blair tries the door, but it's unmovable and the back wall is solid granite, so it looks like there's no easy way out. Blair walks over to the monitor on the desk and sights a line up towards the ceiling. He points at a tiny darkish something up in the corner where the bookcase meets the granite wall. "That's the camera. Why Haedler threw us in this room, I bet. That's how O'Brian and I saw you and Huxley. Here, you can get up there easier than me."

"Who? Who's Huxley? You mean Pfalser."

Blair shakes his head, lights up a Pall Mall. "No, he's a Neanderthal, a mole, whose real name is Leonard Huxley. At least that's what Haedler thinks."

"Yeah . . . of course he would have to go by another name," says Clayborne. "And Haedler's right, he is a Neanderthal. He told me. But okay, first let's take care of this." Clayborne pulls over a chair, piles up some books and climbs on top, tears down the little device, snaps off a tiny antenna. "Huh. No bigger than a button. Incredible. They're making these things smaller and smaller."

"You can run, but you can't hide," Blair yawns, knocks some books off a couch along the wall and stretches out. "Might as well conserve our energy, kid. We're gonna need it when they come to get us. And come they will."

"That's a comforting thought." Clayborne turns on a desk lamp and begins to pull out drawers. "Maybe we can find something here to, uh, defend ourselves with."

"Yeah, well you let me know if you find a Smith & Wesson in there, okay?"

"Okay . . . well, how about some C4 explosive?"

"C—what? What are you talking about?"

"Well, this sure looks like a packing slip for C4, with 'Danger: High Explosive' warnings all over it."

"Lemme see that." Blair comes over and looks at the document, also at a mailing label Clayborne has found. It appears that 15 kilograms of C4 have been surreptitiously sent to a Dr. Rascher. "Jesus, what would he want this stuff for?"

"And-and why would the papers for it be stuffed way back in one of these desk drawers?" asks Clayborne excitedly. "You know, this is where Pfalser, or Huxley, I guess, did his dirty work. He told me that he got all sorts of strange packages for Dr. Rascher. Being the mail boy here it probably wasn't too hard to get something like this delivered to Rascher and then intercept it. He could have had one of his Neanderthals get it and mail it in. Or even do it himself. But he couldn't have carried it in himself—he never could have gotten past the scanners and the guards."

"Well, I guess that makes some sense, kid."

"Sure. Hey, you remember what he muttered in the van when we were brought back here, something profound like: 'The universe is so vast that the life of one man can only be measured by his sacrifice,' or something like that?"

"Hmm, and he's a what—a Neanderthal, right? Maybe he's planning on blowing something up right? Like maybe the computers down here. Bomb us back into the Stone Age."

"Yeah . . . that's it! That's it! And I wouldn't be surprised if it were sometime tonight! During the elections."

Blair lies back down on the couch. "Perfect timing if you're an anarchist—or a Neanderthal."

"Yeah, I guess you're right." Clayborne's heart swells with admiration and excitement. "Mario, or Leonard, he's gonna shut this place down. Big time! That's fantastic! That's great!"

"Yeah, but don't forget he's locked up just like us."

"Well, maybe he's got a timer set or something. Or maybe he's already broken out. He's a smart guy."

"Who knows? Thing is, if he can pull it off somehow, it's gonna shake things up. In the confusion we might be able to make a break for it."

"That's right. We've got to get Christin out of here, too. And the rest of them, of course."

"We'll do what we can. If we get a chance."

"I suppose we'll be able to hear the blast."

"That's a hell of a lot of C4. You didn't find any of the real stuff stashed in that desk, did you?"

"No."

"Well, I had demolitions training in the army, then more along the way, and I know you only need about three kilograms to blow through a concrete wall. He's got five times that. Dumb kid probably doesn't know what he's doing. Find any blasting caps?"

"Well, now that you ask . . . crammed way back in here happens to be some paperwork for blasting caps. Let's see here . . . number eight detonators, one hundred count, PETN five hundred-fifty grams, Lead Azide two hundred-fifty milligrams."

"Hoo-boy, that's the right stuff. A number six is too small for C4 . . . number eight is just right. Maybe he does know what he's doing."

"Well, I told you, he's certainly not stupid. Plus, as a Neanderthal, I'm sure he has access to all sorts of anarchistic bomb-type info."

"It's that goddamned Internet. Gives access to everything."

"That it does."

"Look, I'm bushed. Old man like me needs to get a nap in . . . before our favorite Neanderthal blows up all the goddamned computers. *Hasta la vista.*"

"Okay. But as long as were stuck in here, I'm gonna look through these old papers. Really interesting . . . all kinds of old engineering reports on the excavation of this place. Way back when."

"Well, maybe you can find a way to excavate us out of here, kid."

"Yeah . . . well, I'll let you know. . . ."

Chapter Seventy-Eight

ALONGSIDE COOL GRAY windows filled with numbing pages of computer code, program statistics, and constantly-updated test data, there is a small window on Norman Dunne's monitor that always remains on top. It is of she, beautiful and alive and for the most part, his responsibility, an odd situation, certainly the first time he has ever had such a fair and delicate creature under, more or less, his care. And now, ever since he has cracked their program and stopped all the evil drugs, the unrelenting subliminals, he watches her with a strange fatherly joy, as he might peer over the edge of a box by the stove at a small animal that he is nursing back to health.

But They obviously have other plans for her. He's seen that in the last few days Rascher and company have altered the mix, edging the Nepenthine ratio up over the Deludamil slightly, which as far as Dunne can figure, would tend to make her even more subject to suggestion, but less calm and controllable, more excitable, perhaps. And they also have changed the audio stimuli, to the "Mata Hari" femme fatale sequence which the online log shows was last used with a Deaver, Marcia M., when she was remote, in Lake Forest, Illinois.

But of course they only *think* they're changing dosages and audio and whatever as the Gnome has cleverly disabled the actual transmission to Christin's implant.

One thing he can't affect, though, is their control of the externals. This afternoon they had Tatyana come in and give her a complete makeover, from sober-sixties flowing skirt and prim white blouse to a hot-hot shiny black latex maid's outfit, complete with lace trim and a little white apron over the short skirt that molds so perfectly to her figure that Dunne's mouth waters in spite of himself.

Provocative as it is, this turn of attire troubles him; he knows that it is Bergstrom's particular fetish from not a few excursions into the CEO's own PERSPROF, the one Bergstrom thought he had ordered deleted long ago, but somehow only got moved to an obscure region of AlphaBanc's vast network.

So Christin must be going along with it, Dunne reckons; she has to be. She's been off the drugs long enough now to know what's going on, and with her keen intelligence she's got to just be playing along with this, biding her time. In this, he has gained a great deal of admiration for her; a lesser person in a similar situation might have gone completely off the deep end. He speculates also that if she really is being prepared for Bergstrom, there are going to be several more external adjustments to come, and when he sees them he's going to make his move . . . if she can only hold out until then.

But today is, of course, election day, and he watches his screen with satisfaction as his brilliantly-crafted crack of the government's vote tallying programs steadily nudge the returns ineluctably toward the AlphaBanc slate, certain to make the imbecile, Partridge, the winner—skewed along with many other AlphaBanc-targeted contests.

Dunne smiles grimly, suffers only the mildest disgust at subverting the democratic process, rationalizing that it is already contorted in so many other ways that at the least he considers it an exercise in z-hacking brilliance—a feat that only he could accomplish in such a minimal amount of time—and at the most, perhaps an exercise in good old Yankee ingenuity and efficiency. After all, huge amounts of capital are required to elect and then influence the decisions of the president and congress—and also, of course, to fund the tremendously expensive lobbying and legislative maneuvering that keeps the process more or less legal. What he has done is to simply streamline the entire mechanism, to enable the abuse to function so much more efficiently: one-stop-shopping at AlphaBanc. Pay your money and make your choice. Buy your bureaucrat directly from the source, the vote count itself. And AlphaBanc now controls the count.

Other windows that the industrious elf brings to his screens with increasing regularity are those of O'Brian's office and the ISD command center that Haedler inhabits whenever he visits the complex, both of which contain newly installed wireless micro-cameras that they, at least for now, know nothing about.

And presently some activity registers in Haedler's office. Dunne quickly enlarges the window to see Haedler and O'Brian and Gates and Rascher, and, yes, Bergstrom himself, here in McCarthy, apparently for the elections, heatedly discussing Christin, their fair captive. The Gnome turns up the audio.

". . . we don't have to do anything quite so drastic," O'Brian is saying. "That is, if it's even true that the drugs and the, er, therapy, aren't affecting her as much anymore. After all, the regimen has changed, don't forget, and really, a problem could present itself anywhere in the environment. It might even be a bug in the software. I can have Dunne look at it—now that he's finished with the election program."

Dunne smiles and increases the volume, adjusts the picture.

"Thet freak is a dead man," growls Haedler. "Now thet his work is done. Serves him right, too, fer makin' us turn thet girl into a common apple-pie bakin' mama."

Dunne sighs; this is exactly what he expected. He knew he was paying a steep price for such beauty, but when would he ever have had a chance like this? He will never forget his wonderful, wonderful moments with her. No matter what may become of him now, it has all been worth it.

"That's for sure," Gates agrees. "He's too crazy and dangerous to be let loose again. Besides, we'd be doing the world a favor. Make the streets a lot safer, anyway."

"Well, gentleman," O'Brian says, clearing his throat, "I was hoping we might be able to keep him, actually. Since we've gone to so much trouble to get him here. He's just such a wonderful resource. Maybe we could even make him a glass house."

"Ha!" snorts Rascher, "Fat chance. That would be like trying to bell the cat."

Dunne, in the midst of adjusting the contrast on his monitor, laughs out loud.

"Now, gentlemen," says Bergstrom, "we can deal with Dunne later. I'm sorry to have to even bother with this at all on such an exceptionally crazy day here, but Franz has very proactively informed me that we might be headed for a problem with the girl." He raises his eyebrows to O'Brian.

"Well, Karl, we're not sure there really is a problem—"

"There is to me," snorts Haedler. "I watch her pretty closely, ya know, and she just don't seem all that much under the influence."

"Again, Franz, I'm not sure," says O'Brian. "Although I have to admit I've been very busy, what with the elections . . . and all the problems with Blair and Clayborne."

"And Pfalser, Huxley, whomever he is," adds Rascher.

"Well, it's damn clear to me, real clear, that that filly is soon enough gonna be bustin' out of her e-lectronic corral," grumbles Haedler.

"I think I agree with Franz," continues Bergstrom. "It appears from the video he showed me that the girl's behavior is much different from before—and certainly a thousand percent different from when she first arrived . . . when she was docile, and sweet, and . . . much more attractively attired, also."

"Er, the retro-dress is really what Dunne wanted, Karl," says O'Brian.

"Okay, whatever," mutters Bergstrom. "But what really disturbs me, and Franz, here, is the fact that Dunne himself has actually visited her in her, er, quarters."

"That's right," snorts Haedler. "Talked for quite a while. Then, they even had themselves a leetle dance. After that, there were other times he came to visit. They would talk and talk."

"Er, yes," says O'Brian. "I did hear about that, er, dance. It seems some of the other programmers put on somewhat of a show for Dunne. They really love to impress him with their—"

"Yes, yes, we understand that," says Rascher. "But—what was Dunne discussing with Darrow? Do we have the video?"

"Sure, we got the video all right," drawls Haedler. "But we ain't got no audio. Funny how it just seemed to go out before he comes in to see her, and then goes on again after he leaves."

"Yes, well, he's the Gnome," O'Brian sighs. "You know, I wouldn't be surprised if these supposed glitches were attributable to—"

"Okay! All right . . ." says Bergstrom with obvious forced patience. "We've got to get these—parasites, out of our house here. I've got another interview in a few minutes, and I know that you all have better things to do. So I think we need to resolve the situation with the girl. She's no longer essential, and from what I have heard of her, uh, pre-confinement nature, she might be very difficult to control. In the future."

"Yes, yes, I would have to agree with that," says Rascher. "She seems to have deviated from the original profile we had on her. Although steering her into the NEXSX environment ended up working out very well for us, it also seems to have, ah, inspired her to discover within herself a quite strong and positive self-image that we didn't—"

"Okay, then we're in agreement," snaps Bergstrom. "God, what a nightmare today has become . . . Franz."

"Yes sir?"

"I will personally deal with the girl. O'Brian and I will handle her. Understood?"

"Yes sir."

"And then the final solution for Norman Dunne. And also Blair, Clayborne, and Huxley—whomever. The Gnome's the only one I hate to lose, but I think I have to agree with Roland, even if we kept him around, I doubt that we'll ever be able to motivate him again."

"Yes sir."

"Okay, everyone back to work. Oh, and let me say thank you, gentlemen, for all your hard work. Thanks to your efforts we will be living, at least for the next four years, in a world that will increasingly be safer and prosperous for those who, well, think the way we do."

They all leave, but Bergstrom asks O'Brian to wait. "Will the girl . . . be ready?"

"Er, just about, Karl. We've changed the whole regimen, as I said, and, by later this evening she should be completely, ah, compliable. If you're sure you still want to—"

"Oh, yes, yes, Toby. You know that we have spent a great deal of time and effort on this . . . whole process. And now that Dunne has served his purpose, and by default, the girl hers, I aim to get some reward for this, myself. Right after the elections close tonight and our mission has been accomplished. Do you understand?"

"Oh, yes, of course, Karl. You deserve it. You're entitled—"

"No cameras, no monitoring?"

"Oh, no, of course not. None whatsoever. Everything off."

"Not her though?"

"Oh, no. She'll be on, of course, ha-ha. You can, er, do with her as you wish."

"Excellent. I'll see you later tonight then. After our perfect dolt Partridge is elected."

"Everything will be ready, Karl."

Between keeping an eye on his (thus far) perfectly functioning election routine and the network television coverage, the correspondents trying not to sound too amazed at Partridge's slow but steady gain in the returns, Norman Dunne keeps a close eye on Christin's quarters and watches the ominous transformation: her quarters subtly darkened, sultry jazz coming over the speakers, she now pouring herself a glass of champagne—brought to her via AlphaBanc room service, some salivating moron whom Rascher no doubt owed a favor—while staring thoughtfully at the window animations, very impressive tonight, a starry summer night with an impossibly huge yellow moon rising over distant digital hills.

What can she be thinking? he wonders, watching her with fear and dread as the moment now suddenly comes in the form of a couple of AlphaBanc goons along with Zara in business suit, and Tatyana, fittingly attired in black leather, buckles, boots, chromium chains and carrying AlphaBanc-ubiquitous handcuffs, which Zara snatches, clumsily tries to force upon a balky—but to Dunne's wary eye, surprisingly compliant—drug-free Christin while the goons pinion her arms behind her, and fails miserably. Tatyana, "Oh for God's sake . . ." takes over as one obviously more skilled in the use of manacles.

"There, now she's ready for—da' man!" Tatyana jokes after snapping on the cuffs, wiping imaginary sweat from her brow.

"Hmm . . . good job," Zara begrudges and looks at her watch. "Let's get going. There's a certain little nun we've got to tidy up, too, before daddy checks in on her."

"Time to boogie . . ." Dunne whispers to himself as he summons up the software application called "The Housekeeper."

He pauses briefly to admire again not only O'Brian's droll wit in naming these mean little things, but also the very slick GUI interface the programmers have come up with. He enters it through the back door he's constructed and proceeds immediately to the dosimeter function, but then on a lark, jumps over to the "outside" windows animation feature and from a dropdown list selects the ambience that he feels is most appropriate, the "Crystal Ballroom" again, which gives him goosebumps and maybe a tear or two as he remembers that precious time with her so close to him, so soft and warm . . . the "Crystal Ballroom" it is. He clicks OK and watches his monitor. The lights in her apartment dim further and suddenly the whirling white lights again dazzle the darkened windows. Good.

Now he adjusts the dosage for rapid unconsciousness, and locates the drug release icon on the GUI screen, a clever little cartoon face with + +'s for the eyes, which, when clicked instantly releases multiple nano-buckets of a heavy sedative into her bloodstream. He clicks the face and watches his monitor. In just a few seconds her eyes suddenly roll backwards, she staggers, struggles briefly against the cuffs, and manages, thankfully, to make it over to the couch before she collapses.

Dunne picks up the phone, orders a forklift and a driver he knows well to her quarters, tells them he's got to move a big carton to storage, to a special place in the repository. And hurry!

Chapter Seventy-Nine

BLAIR IS STRANGELY with LuAnne again on a sunny Chicago afternoon in that apartment she had off of Armitage in the 1970s. He thinks it's a Saturday or Sunday and he's off duty, but he's still nervous as nutty LuAnne passes him a smoking reefer that spells instant dismissal from the force, although of course he knows for a fact that Jackie and Teddy and Terry smoke it too, and they're in Narcotics, for chrissakes, so what the hell . . . and anyway she's so hard to resist here in blue jean cutoffs and a too-short T-shirt, giggling and tossing her long blonde hippie hair in the sunlight . . . so beautiful and so happy to be with him, and he happy too as the hard edges of reality begin to soften . . . except she has to play with his service revolver again, fascinated with guns, why? Just to make him nervous? Yet he indulges her, captivated and excited himself, the gun must be loaded, lethal, she stoned and somehow getting more turned on with the mean thing in her small pink hands, softly caressing its trigger, giggling as she holds it delicately and pulls back the hammer with her sweet thumbs, an even better game now as she rubs the barrel against her fragile body, crazy dangerous, pointing it now at her heart, her throat, her temple, when the heavy piece slips, she tries to catch it—

"Hey, George, wake up! Wake up! I've found something! Pfalser had to have seen it, too!"

"Huh? Huh? What?"

"Hey, George. You okay?"

"What? Wh-where am I?"

"Underground at McCarthy. Locked in a room. Remember?"

"Oh . . . oh yeah."

"You okay?"

"Yeah, must've been dreaming. Nightmare, actually," Blair wipes sweat from his forehead, slaps his cheeks.

"What—what was it?"

"Nothing. Just . . . something from long ago." He coughs, clears his throat. "So . . . did they blow us up?"

"No, no, I've just found out the reason why they decided not to use this place as the site for NORAD, and chose Colorado Springs instead. Didn't you ever wonder why that was?"

"Well, to tell the truth kid, I never lost a lot of sleep over it. Like right now."

"Listen. The reason they gave up on this site is because they found themselves drilling and blasting right toward an underground river! It's right here in the engineering reports! The drill holes came within ten feet of a flow of . . . estimated to be thirty-eight thousand gallons per minute! That's a lot of water, hey."

"Oh . . . so you think—"

"Pfalser's not going to blow up the computers at all! He's going to blow the granite between the underground river and here! That's got to be his plan! It would destroy everything, all the data in the repository as well as the computers. Someone has circled that area on the blueprint! It's got to be him. It was right on top of the stack of binders."

"Where is this—underground river?"

Clayborne walks back to desk, scrutinizes one of the diagrams. "It looks like the far end of the repository. That's opposite to where we are."

"Jesus. We're gonna drown like rats. Are you sure that he's gonna blow it tonight?"

"Well, remember what else he muttered in the van? Something like 'no one's ever going to know who won this election, anyway.' So whether he's going to blow the computers or all of McCarthy, it's probably going to be tonight."

"What time is it? The bastards took my watch—along with my phone, my key card, my gun. You still got your watch?"

"Yeah, it's . . . nine twenty-five."

"Hmm, most of the returns are already in—"

"And a winner projected. I hate when they do that . . . with one percent of the vote in. And they're always right."

"Maybe not this time, ha!" Blair snorts.

Suddenly there is a ka-chink behind them. They turn around to see the door swing open . . . and it's the Epenguin, in black tux coat and homburg. "Greetings, gentlemen. Heard you needed some help."

"Pengy! Am I glad to see you!"

"I can guess. How did you get locked in here, anyway?"

"It's a long story. How'd you find us?"

"Norman told me to come down here. He's got an alert set for any activity coming from this node. Apparently Pfalser had been using this room for hacking around and Dunne likes to keep an eye on what's happening on his turf. He said it looked like you were in some trouble—"

"That's an understatement. But, hey, who's winning?"

"Ah, interesting, interesting. First Partridge was behind— down but not out. But actually enough for them to declare our distinguished opponent the winner, with like ten percent of the returns in. And then, would you believe it, our boy slowly starts gaining, the rural precincts and western states coming in later, always last to be tallied, of course," the Epenguin blinks his big eyes. "And now they're neck and neck, much to the surprise of all the pundits and pollsters. Wouldn't be surprised if Partridge pulls ahead at the end, with just enough of a margin to avoid a recount."

"You think so, eh?"

"I know so. I had the privilege—the honor, actually—of working with Norman on his programs. They're flawless. We've captured the presidential election. And a lot of local ones, too. Partridge is going to have a lot of support in Congress. Anywhere there's a close race, Partridge and his kind are gonna take it."

Clayborne shakes his head. "Even though I knew this was going down, now that it's really happening, I think I'm gonna be sick."

"Easy, kid," says Blair, "we've got to get moving. We've got to get to Pfalser right away. He's in one of these rooms down here."

"Sorry, not anymore."

"What?"

"I just let him out. I think he's crazy. He grabbed me by the lapels and said, 'E.P., you've got to get out of here by ten tonight!' And then he ran off. Really spooked me."

"Ten tonight . . ." Clayborne and Blair both echo.

"So, is something, er, else, going on, boys?" the Epenguin half-laughs.

"Listen, we think Pfalser—Huxley, is going to try to blow this place up. Tonight at ten, apparently."

"W-what? Who's Huxley?"

"Pfalser is. We'll explain later," Clayborne says, running into the hallway. "C'mon, Sally's in one of these rooms, too. . . ."

They open all the doors the Epenguin's card will access, find only Sally, and soon the four of them are racing the corridors of McCarthy, yelling to each other as they run.

Blair explains the basic situation to Sally while the Epenguin tries to keep up with Clayborne, who explains what he can to the bewildered birdman. " . . . So we've got to get to the back of the repository and see if we can find that bomb. Unless we can find Pfalser, or Huxley, first."

"So Pfalser's just an alias? Man, I can't believe this," puffs the Epenguin. "And you really think he's got a bomb planted? With all these people here? On election night?"

"Perfect timing for a Neanderthal."

"What?" The Epenguin nearly stops. "He-he's a Neanderthal? An anarchist?"

"That's right. He told me. C'mon, Pengy, we gotta keep going!"

"Oh, man, no! Huxley . . . now I remember that name! He's General Ned Ludd, chief Neanderthal! So then he's gonna do something to the system, too. You watch. Oh no, no, I just thought—omigod, I'll bet you he's brought that Plague virus in here somehow! Of course! We've got to—"

"Screw the virus, Pengy!" Clayborne yells as they come off a catwalk and stop on a sort of high mezzanine with a row of unused offices that run above the repository business counter directly below. It's dark and littered with trash, obviously not in use for some time, but it affords a good view out across the huge room. "He's got a real bomb, man, fifteen kilograms of C4 planted somewhere in the back . . . way out there!" Clayborne points over the railing, and his and perhaps everyone's heart sinks as they look out over the crowded expanse they will have to traverse to get to where the bomb might or might not be hidden.

"Glory be! Well, would you look at all that down there . . ." says Sally, awestruck.

Many people are swarming below, AlphaBanc staff and security, along with scores of reporters armed with cameras, microphones, and sound and lighting equipment.

"Man, I've never seen that many people on the floor!" exclaims the Epenguin.

"My God, what are we going to do?" Clayborne desperately asks Blair.

"What time is it now?"

Clayborne checks his watch. "Nine forty-five."

"It's hopeless, then," Blair replies. "What are we even gonna do when we get there? We're just not gonna have enough time to defuse it—if we can even find it."

"Well then we've got to find Christin! She's locked up in here somewhere. Pfalser showed me. If there really is a bomb, she's going to . . . a lot of people could die!"

"Including us, kid." Blair pulls out a cigarette, shakes his head, "We've gotta warn 'em somehow. If it's true what was in that old report you found, a lot of water's gonna come in here."

"You know, that's a subterranean river that runs under Blackwell, the geologists tell me," Sally interjects, "and if it's the same one, then you ain't a-kidding, buster. It's a goodly flow."

"Oh God! Then we've got to warn everyone!" Clayborne runs to the front of the mezzanine, cups his hands around his mouth, shouts, "Attention everyone! Attention! May I have your attention please! There is, uh, an emergency, and we all must leave the complex immediately!"

Several heads turn and look up. He must be hard to see from below, but one of the heads is O'Brian's in the process of being interviewed, glancing up, and then recognizing Clayborne, scowling directly at him, the word "Fuck!" clearly visible on his lips.

"Please, listen to me!" Clayborne shouts again. "We have to evacuate the complex immediately! We believe that an explosive device is about to—"

But he is suddenly drowned out by the absurdly loud BLATT-BLATT-BLATT-BLATT-BLATT-BLATT of the fire alarm system, and then the calm, obviously recorded voice of Mario Pfalser speaking through the complex's loudspeakers: *"Attention everyone! There is an emergency situation and the complex must be evacuated immediately! Attention everyone! There is an emergency situation and the complex must be evacuated immediately! Proceed to the marked emergency exits in an orderly manner and . . ."*

"Well, at least he's a humane mad-bomber revolutionary anarchist," observes Blair.

Down below it is instant pandemonium as reporters, camera crews, and myriad AlphaBanc personnel scramble for the exits, O'Brian's face now clearly contorted with rage as he glowers up at the mezzanine and the escaped Blackwell Inn crew.

Meanwhile the Epenguin has wandered into one of the darkened rooms on the mezzanine, has found a computer and fired it up, his pale face beatific in the old monitor's cathode glow. Clayborne bursts in, "Pengy! We've got to find Chris! Can you find out where they've got her?"

"Hoo-boy, this is an old box, but it's networked. Let me try a search through those rooms around the marketing labs."

"Okay, just . . . hurry, hurry." The fire alarm blares maddeningly overhead, interspersed with Pfalser's message, and Clayborne watches tensely as the Epenguin finds a directory named Darrow_CJ, and clicks through camera views of a well-appointed set of rooms—all very empty.

"Not there, man. That was where they had her, and they must've moved her somewhere or—"

"Oh, no, no, no . . ." moans Clayborne, looks at the Epenguin. They both instantly understand the horror of the situation. With the elections nearly over, and the Gnome's mission complete, she is utterly expendable—as are they all right now.

Blair appears in the doorway, face grim in the dim glow, "Guys, we've gotta move. We gotta good chance to get out of here if we run for it now."

"Okay, okay. You go out with them. I've got to stay and find Chris."

"Kid, you don't even know if she's—"

"Omigod," gasps the Epenguin, who has been clicking around through the network, "we've got a virus! Must be the Plague!"

"Something's wrong with the system?"

"The Neanderthal's virus! The rumors were true . . ." says the Epenguin breathlessly as he jumps from file to file. "We've sure got it all right. A lot of our stuff is already garbage! He must have just unleashed it!"

"Hey, forget the stupid files—"

"Okay, it's a huge pain, but-but everything's archived, and we can always restore as long as nothing happens to the backup—"

And then there is a tremendous vibration, the desktop shaking mightily, the Epenguin throwing his arms around the monitor as the sound follows immediately, an unbelievably loud KRAAKK-BOOOOOOOOOOOOOOOOOOOOOMMMMMMMMM! that reverberates through the underground chamber.

Chapter Eighty

THE EXPLOSION SHAKES the mezzanine so violently that Clayborne is afraid it might collapse. He is thrown forward over the desktop next to the Epenguin, the birdman desperately hugging the illuminated monitor.

Blair and Sally are knocked instantly to the floor and all of them hold their breath for several long moments until it seems there will be no aftershocks.

"Jesus, I guess Huxley wasn't kidding," says Blair, slowly standing up and stretching, checking for broken bones. He helps Sally up, Clayborne and the Epenguin come out of the office, and they all cautiously step up to the railing to witness the apocalyptic: the main aisle at the far end of the repository where there had been rows of storage racks and a huge red and white banner proclaiming: *AlphaBanc – Guardian of the World's Data*, is now only bare red granite with a huge gaping hole spewing an ugly frothing torrent of dark water.

Blue and white sparks crackle on the floor where the water plows into the reporters' abandoned lights and camera equipment. A couple of intrepid news crews who have tried to continue reporting throughout this incredible breaking news story are forced to flee, splashing through the already ankle-deep flood.

"Omigod!" yells Clayborne, breaking everyone's spell. "We've got to find Chris! She's locked up somewhere. You guys get out! I-I've got to look for her—"

"Not so fast, kid," Blair grabs him by his shirt sleeve before he runs off. "I think I know how we can find her." He turns to the Epenguin. "Can you run that crazy program on the computer over there? The one that can pinpoint a person's whereabouts?"

"Oh, Jesus, yes, good thinking George," says Clayborne. "I forgot all about it, her implant."

378   **G L A S S   H O U S E   51**

You got it, kid. I saw that program locate Marcia Deaver in Georgia. But I don't know if it will work down here—"

"Yes, actually, it will. I saw it work with Pfalser—"

"Yeah, I can access that," says the Epenguin. "If it hasn't been hit by the virus. Only works on glass houses, you know—"

"She *is* a glass house, goddamnit!" Blair barks, dragging the beleaguered birdman back into the room with the computer. "And you damn well know it!"

Clayborne blinks. "You-you, knew? All along?"

"Well, uh . . . Rich."

"Yeah. Of course . . . you would have known."

"Sorry, man. It's totally top secret. I knew she was basically okay, but there was really nothing I could do under the circumstances . . ."

"Okay," says Clayborne. "I get it, just . . . hurry!"

"I'll try. I just have to enter her number—"

"Fifty-one."

"Right . . . and hopefully she's still local." The Epenguin clicks away and Clayborne and Blair watch as he drills down through several grids, finally zeroing in on a spot in the complex that perplexes him. "Jeeze, that's weird."

"What, where is she?"

"She seems to be, uh, actually out in the repository. This can't be right. It looks like . . . aisle 284, bay 57, top level. There must be a problem with the program, unless, unless—"

Suddenly the screen corrupts to a scrambled mass of numbers, letters, and characters.

"Damn, we're cooked now. The virus got it."

"Whoa, lord!" Sally runs in. "We'd better get a move on. That water's just a-comin' on in, fillin' up like a big swimmin' pool. I hope you boys can swim, 'cause I can't!"

"Unless what, E.P.? Unless *what*?" asks frantic Clayborne.

"Unless she's up in a nest."

"A nest?"

"Yeah, this repository is so big that sometimes the workers will push some boxes together somewhere at the top level of the storage racks where there's not a lot of activity and bunch up some old printouts and sleep for a while, hide from the boss. They call it a nest. In fact . . . you know the reason I know this is because Norman once showed me his nest. That's where he'd go when people couldn't find him for hours at a time."

"Is that Dunne's nest then? The top of aisle 284, bay 57?"

"I don't really remember . . . it was out there somewhere."

"Okay, I'm going to find it," declares Clayborne.

"Then you're gonna have to swim!" yells Sally as they run back to the railing. Clayborne is appalled. The water is rising shockingly fast, a dark swirling soup of floating boxes and papers that has covered the lower levels of storage racking—already at least eight feet deep.

"Okay, we gotta get out of here *now*!" orders Blair. "E.P., can you lead the way?"

"Sure. We're gonna have to run on the catwalks. I just hope the main gallery down here isn't flooded. Rich, come on. I'll show you where you can get into the repository if you want to see if she's actually there."

They run off the mezzanine, down several flights of stairs and through a door which the Epenguin unlocks, opening onto the main underground gallery. It is a scene of minor pandemonium: ragtag bunches of reporters, AlphaBanc staff, and security personnel dash past them, headed for the stairwells. The lights blink fitfully, then go out completely and they are suddenly plunged into darkness pierced with random shouts and screams until, five seconds later, the lights flicker back on, although much dimmer.

"Looks like it hit the main power station; now the emergency backups are on," says the Epenguin. "They aren't going to last for very long."

They run by the massive steel vault doors which have thankfully been closed. Several AlphaBanc workers have perversely paused here to be fascinated by small sprays of water issuing from the seams in the doors which might be bulging slightly outward. The harried crew also find themselves inexplicably slowing in the dimmed light, there some strange fascination with omnipotent black liquid death so huge and near, so close they could almost reach out and touch it . . . and then the lights blink several times again and they all seem to come to their senses and run for the stairwells, splashing through several inches of water that has leaked onto the dark granite floor, passing the useless elevators when Sally yells, "Wait! Wait, there's somebody in there!"

"What?" Blair, Clayborne, and the Epenguin stop.

"I thought I heard some pounding from the elevator!"

They run up to the doors and listen. Sure enough, there's the faint sound of yelling and pounding. Someone is stuck inside. They frantically look around the gallery and find nothing that could conceivably help them pry open the doors, which appear to be severely out of alignment, twisted no doubt during the explosion. Then the lights flash again, the elevator makes a sickly thudding sound inside and the doors actually open slightly, less than an inch. The end of a metal rod protrudes through the opening.

"Hey, you okay in there?" yells Blair.

"Oh, *thank God*, someone's out there!" comes a desperate woman's voice. "We're stuck in here! Three of us from WTFF news. I *told* them we shouldn't take the elevators, but we had a lot of equipment and—"

"Okay!" shouts Blair as he futilely tries to pull the doors open with his fingers. "We've got to move fast. Do you have anything we can use to pry these doors?"

"We've been using a pole from our light stands. I think that's how we got the doors to open at all."

"You got another we can use?"

There is some hurried muffled talk inside the elevator car. "He wants the other pole . . . get the goddamned pole off the other light!"

A few stragglers running frantically for the stairway splash past them, but no one offers to help.

"Hey, George," Clayborne says, "I've got to get moving—"

"Jesus, kid. Can you just leave these people here to drown?"

"I-I've got to get to Chris . . ." Clayborne offers, but is immediately ashamed: *Is that really it? Am I just trying to save myself?*

"If she's even there, if she's even alive. Kid, look . . . you've gotta face the facts. I can't do this alone." They both look over at the Epenguin, soft white little bird, forever digital, methodically, maniacally pushing the elevator buttons on the wall.

"Okay. Let's do it."

A steel pole is passed through the crack. Clayborne and Blair quickly grab it, jam the end nearly vertically between the doors to get some leverage, but the doors won't budge. Behind them there is a frightful creak and groan from the vault doors, water now spraying constantly through its seams.

"Sally! E.P.!" Blair barks. "Get up the stairs! It's gonna blow!"

"No!" shouts Sally. "I'm staying with you. These people might need some assistance!"

"Goddamned optimistic . . ." Blair grumbles, glances over with the faintest of smiles, then he and Clayborne kneel down in several inches of water and lean ferociously into the pole.

Meanwhile the Epenguin stands stoically, patiently tapping the elevator buttons with his white fingers.

"Jesus, Pengy!" shouts Clayborne. "Go! Run! Get out of here! You're driving me nuts!"

"I can't," replies the cool little bird. "This is really the only way. Don't you remember how the doors opened before when the power surged? All we need to do is to stay on these buttons when it comes back again—"

And suddenly, as if there might be some strange affinity between the Epenguin's dauntless hope and McCarthy's dying electrical grid, the lights flicker on and off again, the Epenguin hollers, "Lean into it!" while clicking madly on the elevator buttons, the motor inside whines horribly, and the doors creak open, wide enough for a person to pass through. A miracle indeed.

The elevator floor is about three feet off the landing and Clayborne, Blair, and Sally help the terrified reporters to the ground.

It is just in time. Behind them, several new plumes of spray have burst from the vault doors and the water on the floor has risen nearly to their knees.

Blair takes one look at the bulging doors, shouts, "LET'S GET THE HELL OUT OF HERE!"

They all run for the stairwell just as a tremendous wrenching EEEEEEEEEEEEEEEEHHHNNNNNNNNNNNNNNNNHHH! reverberates throughout the chamber, the doors fly off their hinges and tons of dark swirling water flood onto the gallery floor.

Chapter Eighty-One

"RUN, RUN, RUN!" a multiple mantra echoes through the underground lobby as they scramble up the stairs, Blair bringing up the rear, only a step ahead of the dark surging tide.

About four frantic levels up, they seem to have escaped the flood—for now—and the Epenguin, puffing, turns to Clayborne, "If you want to see if you can find Chris, this is where you can get over to the mezzanine we just left. The water's probably dropped a little after busting through the doors, but that river's sure going to fill it up again. If you could jump in there, you might be able to swim over to the racking. I don't know any other way."

"I-I've got to do it."

"Okay, go through this door and follow the catwalks we were on before all the way back to the mezzanine. But hurry, man, this place is going to be nothing more than a big underwater cave real soon!"

Clayborne takes off, clanging along deserted dark catwalks until he gets back to the mezzanine, which is now vista to a fearsome sight under the feeble auxiliary lighting: a dark placid sea that is shockingly close to the railing. The Epenguin's right, this place is going to be underwater for some time. It's an eerie scene, almost tranquil, and Clayborne suddenly realizes that what's missing, or at least muffled, is the hum, the constant drone of the machines that he has heard, accepted, allowed to become a part of him ever since he descended to the lower levels of the complex. It's nearly gone. The Beast is dying.

But where is she? In long soldierly rows the tops of the racks protrude above water level, dim backup lights on girders crisscrossing the ceiling reflected eerily in the black velvety surface of the water below. Clayborne looks out over the dark sea like a sailor at night and wonders if Christin can really be out there somewhere. Aisle 284, bay 57 is way, way out, and, well, maybe

Blair is right, maybe they have simply taken her away. He shouts: "CHRIS! CHRISTIN! CHRIS! CAN YOU HEAR ME?! CHRIS? CAN YOU HEAR ME?! CHRIS? CHRIS? CHRIS?"

He strains to hear, but there is no reply, only the echo of his voice and vague creaking noises all around him. He can still see the aisle markers out there; they're at the top of the racks, will be covered soon by the rising tide. He takes a deep breath, knows he has to do this. If she is out there, maybe tied up, maybe already the latest slasher victim of the Gnome, he's got to know. He left Billy and has regretted it forever; now fate has granted him one more chance. He kicks off shoes, pants, and shirt, sees he happens to be wearing his lucky green boxers with the gold $ print, a good sign, holds his nose and jumps in.

It's a cold plunge and he sucks deep breaths to ease the shock. Somewhere he has read that it is always a constant fifty-something degrees in a cave, water the same temperature, awfully damn cold—so he's got to start moving right away, begins swimming fitfully through the darkened pool, a sort of modified breast stroke toward one of the racks up ahead to read the aisle number: twenty-one. He's got a long way to go.

He pushes ahead past floating debris: printouts, boxes, and many bobbing plastic data containers . . . aisle after aisle, the racks going by like miniature oil rigs silhouetted in the ghostly half-light, the topmost storage platforms nearly submerged, the water continuing to rise, the ceiling girders hard above.

He swims faster, thinking: *Maybe this is crazy, maybe E.P. and his stupid computer is wrong, wrong, wrong.* . . . He makes the mistake of looking back, can't see the balcony at all now, either it's too dark and too far now, or maybe—most likely—has flooded over. Oh God, now he is truly frightened, there's no turning back, nowhere else to go but onward. His legs begin to cramp and he crawls up, shivering, on a rack to rest, at aisle 203. This top platform is a full inch underwater, and he knows this is undoubtedly lunacy but he can't give up now, plunges back into the black sea, thinks, *all my life I've given up, taken the easy way out . . . but not now, no more, no more, no more . . .* a chant merging with his breathing as he slowly pushes ahead, finally reaching aisle 284, and then it's a turn into the dark channel between boxes and stacked reels of old magnetic tapes, antediluvian data soon to be purified in the earth's cleansing waters . . . and by God, up ahead between some boxes he thinks he sees some movement! He swims faster, finds himself at what must be bay 57, and by God, yes, she's here.

She's here! It is Christin! lying prone on soggy cardboard in a couple inches of water, wearing what looks to be some kind of strange rubberoid maid's outfit, but, but—alive! Apparently just rousing from a state of profound unconsciousness. Clayborne climbs up on the platform, kicks away some of the surrounding boxes, and begins to shake her, reaches over and scoops up water, splashes it on her face. "Chris! Chris! Wake up! It's me, Richard! Wake up! Wake up!"

"Ummm . . . Richard?"

"Oh Chris, Chris . . ." he pulls himself alongside her, holds her close, trying to warm her, presses his lips to her clammy face, ghostly pallid in the feeble light. He's so happy to find her, to hold her again, he can't speak, can't think, never wants to let her go . . . but realizes that something's wrong here.

He lifts her to a sitting position, shockingly finds that her wrists are handcuffed behind her. *Damn!*

"Ohh . . . Richard, Richard . . . I feel . . . so tired . . . where, where am I?"

"Uh, up on top of a storage rack. In the repository. In the McCarthy complex."

"Ohh, my God," she slowly shakes her head. "I feel like I've been hit by a truck. And why . . . where, where are my arms . . . ? Am I—handcuffed?"

"Yes, yes, you are. I don't know why. Dunne did it, I guess—"

"Why is it so dark? What . . . what is all this water?"

"It-it's a long story, but now . . . now we've got to get out of here. There's been a flood. The water's rising, see. We're on the top rack. There's at least twenty feet of water below us, to the floor."

"I-I don't get it."

"Okay, listen. We're in this big warehouse room underground in the McCarthy Complex. There's been an explosion and a-a subterranean river is flowing into it, filling it up. In less than an hour, I bet, it'll be filled to the top, completely flooded. If we don't get out of here now, we'll drown!"

"Oh, oh my God! How did I get here?"

"I-I think Norman Dunne brought you in here. To hide you. I think he actually might have saved your life—in a weird way."

"Oh, yes, Norman. He said he would come to rescue me. I guess he really did."

"He came and talked to you? When you were—confined?"

"Yes, after I started to get better, my mind . . . got better, he came once at night, secretly I guess, and told me what was going on. He told me I was in danger, and to be patient, that he would come and save me. Although, I guess this isn't much better."

"What did he tell you?"

"He said that they—Haedler and O'Brian and Blair—would be coming to get me! They were trying to keep me drugged and stupid—and were doing a pretty good job of it too, I'd say. But Norman told me that he had shut down the-the microchip that—" her voice breaks and she sobs quietly "—that they implanted in my head! Oh they're evil, Richie, they're evil, they're just pure evil. . . ."

He holds her tighter, "I know, I know now . . . they are."

"So," she sniffs, "Norman said to just keep pretending, even though he had stopped the drugs, the goddamned Deludamil and whatever else they had been pumping me with . . . and I had been getting better . . . God, I must have been out of my mind . . . I-I thought I was in an old, old TV show. It was crazy . . . I-I still can't see colors. It's like my color vision is totally gone!"

"Really?"

"Uh-huh. You . . . you're all . . . just gray. I don't know if I'll ever be right again. . . ." She begins sobbing again.

"Sure, sure you will," whispers Clayborne hollowly. "The light's just bad in here . . ."

"And, and so I was getting better and thinking about planning a way to get out of there, and then Zara and Tatyana came in, they were the ones that handcuffed me . . . and I still played along, and then everything went dark and the stars came out and swirled around me . . . and that was the last thing I remember."

"God. Well, you're safe now, sort of . . . well, not really."

Clayborne tries to assess their situation, realizes that the water has continued to rise as they've talked, easily another inch or so, gently lapping against their cold clammy flesh. He is exhausted after his swim but pulls himself around to get a better look at her manacled wrists. It's instantly depressing. Her arms are pulled behind her, locked with as solid-looking a set of cuffs as he's seen recently, and that not so long ago. He tries feebly tugging on them, but they are secure. His heart sinks. *Why oh why did they have to cuff her?*

An evil thought insinuates itself, whispers the truth: tired as he is, he could leave her, could swim back, be free—even if it took every last bit of strength he had, he could escape. Otherwise, he will somehow have to make it back with her, two hundred and eighty-four aisles back to the mezzanine—if it's not completely flooded by now. The urge to flee, to save himself, is enormous. But he knows that he can't do that. Not again. Even if he must die here with her. *I will not leave her*, he vows to himself. *This time I will not leave; I will not. . . .*

"H-Hey Chris," he asks, beginning now to shiver continuously, no doubt the onset of hypothermia, "c-can you swim, er, f-float?"

"Uh-uh. I'm sorry, I sink like a stone."

"Damn!"

"I'm going to die here, aren't I?" she whispers.

"No!"

"I am. You go, save yourself."

"No! Don't t-talk like that! Don't you worry! We'll f-figure out something here . . ." Richard trails off, not believing a word that he is saying.

Chapter Eighty-Two

THE WATER CONTINUES to rise and Clayborne looks out over the dark sea, tries not to speculate on the short amount of time left for them in this world, one that, only a couple of months ago had seemed so bright, open, and huge, for him and for her, too . . . considers how strange it is that life can suddenly turn around on them like this . . . and now he thinks, must be the cold and the fatigue getting to him, he's beginning to hallucinate in the dimness . . . thinks he's just seen a brief flash of light over the misting waters.

It's only trick of the eye, he tells himself, but strains to see down the nearly submerged dark long aisles . . . and then he thinks he hears a splash of water, and another, and then he does see the light, yes! way down at the end of aisle 284 a tiny round beam ghosting through the mist.

"Oh! Oh my God!" he gasps. "Someone's coming!"

"What? Who's coming?"

"I-I think it's . . . it's a boat!"

"A-a boat?"

And as he and Christin strain to see down the aisle, the light comes closer, filtering between the rack uprights, enlarging until it breaks into full view.

"It-it's Norman Dunne!" Clayborne announces, more amazed to see the legendary man he has pursued for so long than the fact that it is him here, now.

"Oh, I knew he'd come back. . . ."

Dunne cautiously paddles up to them in a small rubber lifeboat, a flashlight affixed to its bow with duct tape.

The disappointment in Dunne's eyes is unmistakable as he gazes at Clayborne kneeling on the rack beside Christin, but Clayborne, grateful and oblivious, greets the fabulous ferryman heartily, "Hey! Hi there! G-glad to see you there, uh, Norman! R-really, really glad to s-see you!"

"Oh, Norman, I knew you'd come back for me," says Christin.

Dunne steadies his craft a good twenty feet away, sits looking silently at them.

Clayborne, shivering steadily, tries to calculate what it would take to jump in, quickly swim over and seize the little vessel . . . but at that moment Dunne pulls a small pistol from his pocket, holds it gently in his lap.

"Norman," Christin asks, "would you happen to have the keys to these uncomfortable handcuffs?"

Dunne remains silent, staring as the boat rocks gently in the water. There is the sound of distant muffled booms and structural groans coming from somewhere deep below them, immediately followed by a particularly disturbing series of short sharp boom-boom-booms that seem to agitate the underground lake. At the same time, the lights overhead blink several times, going completely out, and then blink on again, even weaker than before.

"Norman," pleads Christin, "talk to me please. My arms are aching terribly and I'm cold. We're both very cold, Norman."

"Hear that?" asks Dunne softly. "That's the Source . . . or the Beast. The flood finally got to it, found its way around the locked doors and shielding and now . . . it's killing my friend."

Both Clayborne and Christin silently consider Dunne's pronouncement. In the dim light he looks very sad.

"That's the third power backup we're on, too," he says. "Once it goes, darkness will descend upon these waters . . ."

"Oh, Norman, I'm so very sorry about your big friend," says Christin, turning as best she can to face him. "I know that you loved it, and . . . and I'm sure that it loved you, too."

Dunne's eyes light up. "Yes, I think it did. I truly think it was capable of love—and therefore, also of jealousy. It communicated such things to me, you know, sent me messages . . ."

"Oh, I'm sure it did, Norman."

"H-hey, I believe you Norman. I even got a message from it a few times, I think," adds Clayborne. "Never could figure—"

"It knew so very much," Dunne says, eyes distant above the flashlight glow. "Strange things, improbable things . . . things well beyond our feeble reasoning."

"Uhm, Norman, could you please, puh-le-e-ase, just throw over the key to these things?" pleads Christin.

"I do, of course, have a master key," says Dunne. Cautiously, he paddles closer, points the gun directly at Clayborne. "Didn't expect to find you here, though. Don't try anything."

He reaches inside his pocket and pulls out a small key, tosses it, a silver sparkle in the flashlight beam, to Clayborne, who reaches out his clammy hands, bobbles it dangerously over the water, but manages to hold on. He immediately spins around to Christin, gets behind her and unlocks her cuffs.

"Oh, *thank you* Norman, thank you so much," says a very grateful Christin, rubbing her wrists, then quickly whispering to Clayborne as she stands and stretches, "He's completely crazy. Keep him talking. Talk about the Beast."

R-right. Richard stands, turns toward Dunne. "S-so, uh, Norman . . . how do you think the B-Beast, er, your friend, knew—all these things?"

"I have often wondered that," Dunne answers. "It is—or was—the largest massively parallel processor in the world, you know, handling amazingly huge quantities of data, many, many terabytes day and night, down here surrounded by all this massive granite. I somehow think that the tremendous concentration of all those electrons working together at nearly the speed of light, computing together, thinking together, somehow might have created a sort of critical mass . . . a soul . . . a true ghost in the machine."

Clayborne shrugs, shivers, "I-I guess anything is possible."

"It was my only real, true friend, in the world." Dunne chokes, wipes tears from his eyes. Then he stiffens, sucks in a deep breath. "But then I think, for mankind's sake, maybe it is for the best."

"For, for the best, Norman?" asks Clayborne. "That your friend dies?"

"Yes, I have come to think that what we called the Beast, or something like it, will become the dominant force on this humble planet. It seems the process has already begun. We humans are so willing to acquiesce to its immense power in order to receive gain, people like Bergstrom and O'Brian, obsessed to reduce people to digits, numerics, metrics, that could first be predicted, and then induced, to buy, act, think—as directed. In the course of this, their souls are reduced to silicon, to dust, to nothing. And people's souls in this post-industrial world are for the most part dead, anyway, inextricably bound to the machines from birth to death.

"Of course, there might be a few rebels: artists, philosophers, poets, perhaps, who try to free themselves from the oppression, but all the machinery, all of the gigantic monolithic system, is stacked against them. All the great Beast knows, all it sees with numeric eyes, are great multitudes of fat, dumb, consumption machines, purchasing whatever it commands, despoiling whatever is necessary in the process, and ultimately bringing a baby Beast back into the home with them."

Dunne sighs heavily. "In a sense, I'm the worst of all. I'm the one who knows the great system best, I helped create it and tonight . . . tonight I watched it being destroyed by the terrible virus and I-I did nothing to stop it . . . because it had to die."

"It-it had to die?" asks Clayborne, trying to fathom just how far removed from reality at this moment the man might be.

"Yes, you see, being a machine, it had none of the moral sanctions that humans might have, none whatsoever, and yet had developed what I can only describe as a sense of jealousy to explain the ugly things it did—"

"Er, what do you mean?" Cold and tired as he is, Clayborne's interest is piqued. "W-what ugly things did it, the Beast, do?"

"Well, it killed them, you know, or, actually, arranged for their deaths—"

"Whose deaths, Norman?" asks Christin.

"Why those girls, the ones I conversed with via NEXSX, including yourself. At first I couldn't believe it myself, but I checked the system logs and—"

"You mean, it wasn't *you* who had those girls killed? It was *the Beast*?" Clayborne asks, amazed.

"Oh yes, yes indeed. It was the great machine, all right. It was connected directly to the Net, to messaging, to voice-simulation software. It acted entirely of its own volition. But I am just as guilty because I allowed it to happen. It-it was my friend, of course, and it amazed me to see that it was capable of the murder of human beings, all to satisfy me, to provide for my dark side. It knew me, you see. It knew me very well. And I simply allowed it to happen. In the end, the blood is certainly on my hands."

"Oh, Norman, I-I don't know what to say," says Christin.

"But now you see that's why I had to let my great friend die. It had become more dangerous than I had ever imagined. So I simply let the Plague take it, staying a step or two ahead of the virus as it leapt from server to server, saving what few things I could."

Christin, standing now waist-deep in the water with her arms crossed, is shivering and sniffling, "Oh, Norman, I'm so sorry. You did a wonderful, noble thing, to let it die like that."

"Yes, in the end it was because I couldn't bear to see the Beast destroy you, your precious beauty, that I let it die. This mess, this flood, will be cleaned up eventually, but the Plague wiped out a tremendous intelligence. I doubt that we'll ever get it back."

"H-h-hey Norman, old p-pal," Clayborne shivers, "d-do you think you could f-ferry Christin over to—whatever d-dock you pushed off from? She's been in this w-water quite a while now . . . and-and it's n-not getting any w-warmer. Or lower."

"Yes, ferry you out . . . it's time for that, all right. Well, I'm going to let you two take this little boat. . . ." Dunne paddles over to their submerging island, grunts, and jumps out, sinks up to his chest. "There's certainly not enough room for three in it."

"Gee, thanks!" Clayborne doesn't quibble, urges a wide-eyed Christin up on some soggy cartons to climb into the shaky craft, then quickly follows her and climbs in himself.

"Here are some discs I want you to take," Dunne reaches into a pocket and retrieves several plastic-encased discs, hands them over to Clayborne.

"And these are . . . ?"

"Some key programs I helped create, FINIRG, SEXIRG, and several kernel programs, the very heart of the Beast itself. Just in case I wouldn't . . . survive this. It won't be easy after . . . all this, but it'll give AlphaBanc a slight chance to rebuild their systems. Maybe give civilization a chance to get going again, if the Plague has spread as far as I fear it has."

"Don't talk like that, Norman," says Christin. "You'll be right there to help build it all up again. We'll be coming right back . . ."

Dunne doesn't seem to hear. "Now you paddle down to the end of this aisle, turn left and go all the way. Keep hugging the wall and you'll come to a steel ladder that's hanging down from a catwalk. Better go now. The water's going to rise up against the ceiling girders before long and you won't be able to float underneath them. Plus, the emergency lights will soon short out and then, that'll be the end."

"Oh thank you, thank you, Norman," Christin calls out as Clayborne digs into the water with his paddle, backs the boat into the channel. "We'll come back for you right away, Norman."

The Gnome waves perfunctorily, looks pointedly at Clayborne, says, "Will you really come back for me? Will you? Or will you run away and save yourself and leave me to die here? Leave me to blow myself away? Is that who you really are?"

Clayborne stops paddling, looks hard, unbelievingly, at the diminutive balding figure standing chest-deep in the water, accusatory ripples rolling toward him in the dim light, thinking: *So he knows! It was him all along!*

A distant muffled boom and a faint hissing sound from somewhere far below catches his ears and he fancies it to be the last dying gasp of the great machine, deep, deep underground.

"Richard! We've got to keep going!" the voice of beauty herself breaks his reverie. He turns to look at Christin, who leans anxiously forward in the little boat, looking tired, but extremely determined, and, well, beautiful, in the strange little outfit, gleaming wet in the shadowy lighting, distracting him long enough to miss Dunne's revolver rising from an inside pocket, pressed lightly against his right temple, followed by the sudden sharp explosion echoing over the waters.

"No!" Clayborne yells, drops the paddle, sees the body slump into the water, pushing rings of blood, intelligence, and strange unrequited love out and across the black lagoon. "No! No! No!" Clayborne wails at the floating body. "I was going to come back! I would have come back! I would have, I swear I would have . . ." he breaks down. "I swear . . ."

Christin is sobbing too; perhaps she had gained some affection for the misunderstood little man who undoubtedly had saved her life, her soul. "Poor Norman, poor, poor, Norman. . . ."

There is only the soft sound of weeping over the dark waters for several minutes, then, "Chris . . ." Clayborne leans over to her in the unsteady craft, tries to comfort her as best he can, but there's nothing anyone can do, so much has died this troubled night.

Christin straightens up, wipes her eyes. "He had such a sad, sad life . . ."

"He did," agrees Clayborne, picking up his paddle. "But we've got to get out of here."

"Yes, yes, we've got to get moving."

"But this first." Clayborne reaches down, grabs the discs that Dunne has given him, holds them up for her to see: silvery seed-containers of magnetic instructions, the soul of a new machine. "Norman Dunne's legacy," he says.

"Do it."

He tosses them over the side; they briefly watch the ripples fan out over the watery grave of lost information, and then they paddle away.

Chapter Eighty-Three

IT IS THE next day, late afternoon, when Clayborne opens his eyes to subdued pastel periphery, white tiled ceiling, a shadowy hospital room. He kicks off a sweaty sheet and tries to scratch a vague itch on his side, finds that he can't seem to make his left hand function, looks over a little panicky, discovers his wrist handcuffed to the railing of the hospital bed. *Oh great.* And he's really got to pee. He fumbles with his free hand to find the thing with the button to signal a nurse and there's nothing there, calls out, "Hey, hey! Anyone out there? Is there a nurse or . . . ?" and the door opens and a male nurse comes in, big guy, accompanied by an even bigger Wisconsin state trooper—guy's name has got to be Bruno.

"Can I help you?"

"Uh, I gotta go . . ."

Bruno unlocks him and the nurse, keeping his distance, points him to the bathroom while Bruno takes a position between him and the door, guarding his exit.

Clayborne tries to engage them in conversation after he comes out, but Bruno replies with, "Sir, I have nothing to say to you," and although the nurse is a little more talkative, introducing himself as Victor, he clearly doesn't want to get too close to him, seems relieved after criminal Clayborne is locked to the bed again before he and Bruno walk out.

Clayborne lies back, tries to recall the events of the night before, remembers he and Christin making it to the catwalk, covered by then with easily a couple feet of water, then finding their way to a stairwell only moments before the lights went out for the last time, plunging them into total terrifying darkness.

Using the Gnome's rapidly dimming little flashlight, they made their way up step by wet step to a wholly dry level where they ran into the beams of many flashlights and a rescue unit of the state police just arrived with oxygen and scuba equipment, obviously amazed that anyone could still emerge from the deluge below.

Clayborne, exhausted and shivering, still clad only in his boxer shorts, ignored their long looks at the disheveled Morlockian maid, told them that there were sure no more people down there that *they* knew of, and soon they were draped in scratchy green dry wonderful wool blankets and escorted up through ever greater numbers of people and brighter lights and then much jostling and cameras and microphones and ignored questions and disturbing surreal glimpses of Haedler and O'Brian . . . and then the saving ambulance ride to the hospital, this hospital, in the lakeside town of Oshkosh.

Victor returns an hour later to check on him, seems somewhat friendlier now, tells him what he can about the outside world, the biggest news, certainly, that what was supposed to be the first all-electronic election in the United States was thwarted by a mysterious explosion at AlphaBanc's McCarthy complex. Also that an incredibly annihilative computer virus called the Plague has been unleashed, hitting lots and lots of businesses, banks, law enforcement agencies, and other institutions—countrywide, and apparently worldwide. Not to mention all of the radio and television stations, because everything's silent, dead, at least around here.

"So, the virus was as bad as the Epenguin thought it would be . . ." muses Clayborne.

"What was that?" asks Victor. "Did you say something about a penguin?"

"Er, no, just muttering, I guess. So, how do you know about all of this . . . if there's no news—?"

"My brother's an amateur radio operator, lives practically next door. He's been on it all night. It's really spooky. There's reports of shutdowns of services in a lot of cities and of looting in Detroit, Miami, Chicago, New York, and Los Angeles . . . but that's all I know, man."

"Can you try the TV again, please?" Clayborne asks. "Maybe it's come back on."

"We've got it on out there and there's nothing, but see for yourself, buddy . . ." and Victor, smiling smugly, quickly clicks the remote through a couple dozen channels for him: nothing but static on every one.

"Also, there's no cell service right now, and the Internet's down too, man," calls Victor cheerily as he walks out.

Clayborne lies back and smiles at the ceiling. Absolutely no radio and TV! And no phones and no Internet! Maybe everywhere! *Wow*. It's incredible, and somehow tremendously heartening. He feels an odd sense of relief, of crazy freedom . . . that all of the world's computers may simply no longer be there, for him, for anyone.

Victor comes back at dinner time, drops off a depressing gray plastic meal kit, removes the lid to reveal rubbery fried chicken, canned green beans, a spongy white bread roll, and a yellow and green cube of Jell-O . . . ugh. Clayborne takes one look, pushes the tray aside, closes his eyes, wonders how anyone gets well in hospitals anymore, how anyone ever gets out . . . and seriously wonders now how *he's* going to get out of all this crazy trouble, thinks that it might have been better if he had never listened to Huxley, had never accepted the Neanderthal's grand plans in his heart of hearts . . . wonders where Christin and Blair and Sally and the Epenguin all are . . . probably locked up somewhere, too.

This is a depressing thought. Clayborne realizes that right now he is probably a key suspect. That will all get sorted out soon enough, he hopes, but he becomes more morose, thinks that it's going to be really tough going in the days and weeks ahead, undoubtedly a legal nightmare going up against the tremendous team of attorneys that A-Banc will pull together to defend itself, wonders, even though he's got the truth on his side, if it will count for anything in this crazy AlphaBanc-owned world, anything at all. . . .

Chapter Eighty-Four

CLAYBORNE IS DREAMING again . . . this time strangely finds himself in a little boat floundering in a dark sea, along with Christin and Norman Dunne. They are all terrified by the rising storm, the boat tossed in the churning, foaming black water and at some point Christin falls overboard, and Clayborne, fighting his fear, determines that he must jump in to save her. Dunne yells for him to stay, save himself, but he doesn't hesitate before plunging in, the oneiric water delicious, cool and wonderful, as though washing away his fears, his cowardice, forever. Finally, he has made the right decision, is truly proud of himself. He retains this good glowing feeling even as the dream fades away and he finds himself awake, sweating . . . and still chained to the bed rail.

"Goddamnit!" He rolls back, grits his teeth, closes his eyes.

"Welcome to the club, kid."

"Huh?" A familiar gravelly voice. Clayborne turns, looks over. "George?"

"Howdy, kid." Blair smiles, raises his left hand, extending his handcuff above the bed rail. "Guess they've got us again."

"They, they, They! When are we ever going to be free?"

"You got me, kid."

"When did you get here?"

"Rolled me in this morning."

"Oh. But what are you doing in here? I thought you made it out okay."

"Broke my stupid ankle." Blair smiles sheepishly. "Slipped on my ass on those wet stairs, trying to run up and light a cigarette at the same time. So now I took the pledge. Quit cold turkey. Sally wouldn't help me up unless I agreed."

"Uh . . . and Chris?"

"Down the hall is what they tell me. You obviously found her all right. In that crazy hell hole."

"Yes, yes . . . thank God . . . but she's probably locked up now, too."

"Probably. It's our word against theirs."

"Damn! Well . . . how's Sally? She made it out okay, then?"

"Don't know, actually. I haven't seen her since they took me off in an ambulance, and frankly I'm kind of worried. She's dog meat just like us."

"Oh, God . . . we're all doomed," groans Clayborne, lays back to stare at the ceiling. "I should have never thrown Pfalser's—or Huxley's—files into the well. Everything that could save us was there."

"Well, they would have gotten 'em anyway. Don't be so hard on yourself, kid. Better gone than in their hands."

"You're darn tootin, mister!" booms an enthusiastic voice. "They had the drop on us. There's nothin' we could of done any different, that's for sure!"

Clayborne turns to see Sally Thomas walk in with a bandage on her cheek, followed by four dark-suited exceedingly sober men. "Sally!"

"Hey there, Sal! You bring me some smokes?" Blair calls cheerfully.

"You've had the last smoke you're ever going to have, buster." Sally wags her finger at Blair. Then she turns to Clayborne, "Yep, but don't you worry, boy—there's a little old video that I got of a bunch of AlphaBanc bigwigs shootin' up your gal Sal that has convinced these fellows that maybe they aren't as pure as the driven snow."

"What do you mean . . . video?"

"Well, there's a little old video camera I had installed about a year back on one of the buildings. Keeps watch on the place, you know. And I went back and got the thing and gave it to these gentlemen from the F-B-I."

Clayborne's heart leaps. "Oh! Great! Good thinking, Sally."

"Modern technology, boy."

"Yeah. Fantastic. Hey, do you know how Chris is?"

"She's doing just fine. A case of hypothermia like you. I was just over to see her with these fellows. You know they're mighty interested in having her go for an x-ray to look at what might be beneath the little scar behind her ear." Sally raises her eyebrows significantly.

"She told you then . . . about the implant?"

Sally nods. "That poor, poor girl. . . ."

"Ha! Well, we got them, then," grunts Blair with satisfaction. "Let them try to explain that little bit of . . . biotechnology."

"I'm agent Heywood," says one of the suited men who walks up, flashes his badge. "And I can say, Mr. Blair, that we are very interested, not to say—shocked—by all that Ms. Darrow has told us. But we wonder if there might be some other evidence against the executives at AlphaBanc that you might have in your possession, or access to, at least? Ms. Darrow suggested that you might have something, some data files?"

Clayborne groans, "No. Not other than our own testimony. We had . . . a great deal of evidence, but . . . it was lost."

"You might try this fellow, Pfalser," says Blair. "But . . . that was his alias. Richie, what was—"

"Huxley, Leonard Huxley. He was a Neanderthal, a member of the anarchist group. He worked at AlphaBanc as a kind of mole, I guess . . ." Clayborne trails off, sees that the agents have been exchanging glances since the mention of Pfalser's name.

"A Mr. Pfalser, or perhaps, Huxley, as you say, was found in a back garage of AlphaBanc's McCarthy complex. A bullet to the head from a nine millimeter, we think it was, took his life. At first sight it appeared self-inflicted," the agent looks over at his cohorts, "but now . . . we're not so sure."

"Oh, God . . . Mario. . . ."

"Apparently someone may have been very upset at Pfalser's alleged actions. And I think we can certainly see why."

"Yeah, yeah . . ." says Clayborne. "He set the bomb, let in the flood. I think there's no doubt about that. And then, I guess this Plague virus of the Neanderthals turned out to be a pretty bad thing, hey?"

Again, the agents look at him somewhat sideways.

"Er, did I say something funny?"

"The understatement of the millennium, kid. Here, give him this." Blair holds up a Milwaukee *Journal Sentinel* toward agent Heywood, but Sally is closer, takes it and hands it over to Clayborne, its headline blaring: "CYBER-DISASTER!"

"Oh boy," says Clayborne as he scans the subheads: "Elections Compromised, 'Worthless' Says Official," and "Plague Computer Virus Cripples Globe," and "U.S. Defense Systems on Full Alert."

"One of the few major newspapers actually able to get out an edition," says agent Heywood. "Now you see, Mr. Clayborne, why we're all here. I'm with the computer crimes special unit of the FBI, out of Milwaukee. I have a degree in computer science, so I have a pretty good understanding of what's occurred here and I've got to tell you that we are in the midst of near-total disaster. We've been watching the Neanderthals for some time, but I have to admit that this character Huxley had eluded us. We knew who he was, but not where he was, unfortunately—most unfortunately—and never suspected he would have been a mole within AlphaBanc itself, and certainly not the secure McCarthy complex. Just goes to show how nothing is ever really safe . . . another lesson for our brave new e-world, eh?"

"Like you say . . . another gigantic understatement," says Clayborne.

"Anyway, that's why you're locked up, gentlemen. I apologize, but it's a necessity until we get statements from you and ultimately get to the bottom of this whole thing. The virus that hit the world yesterday has been devastating—the only way to describe it. It appears that anywhere from fifty to sixty percent of the world's computer systems have been compromised—if not completely disabled. It's like a neutron bomb exploded, leaving the hardware standing, but destroying all the data inside. And of course, most of the available backups are now at the bottom of an underwater cave, from what I've been told."

"You've got that right," says Clayborne. "That whole repository is underwater now. We—Christin and I—were the last ones out and we barely made it. It's a total mess. . . ."

"Yes, it'll take some time, months certainly, possibly years, to restore the systems to their, er, pre-Plague, state."

"Well, that might well be," says Sally, "but I can see that the electricity is on and the water's running—"

"Yes, although we only have preliminary reports, it seems that the Neanderthals, and their supporters—very many supporters—it turns out, were surprisingly humane in their unleashing of the virus. Hospitals such as this one, schools, libraries, airports, fire stations, power plants—including nuclear power plants, which surprises me—were all spared. We don't have one confirmation of any of those facilities being infected. But so many other—'establishment,' institutions were hit." Heywood pulls a notebook from the inside pocket of his suit coat. "It got many, many major commercial institutions; all the world's financial markets, stock exchanges, etcetera, are closed—probably for their own good, they'd sink like stones if they were open—almost all governmental agencies, including the FBI, and—if you ever say I said this, I'll deny it—a couple of large national security agencies—"

"The CIA and NSA," offers Blair helpfully. "And I'll bet everything in the Pentagon is toast."

"No comment," says agent Heywood. "But the fact that our nation is currently standing at DEFCON 3 ought to indicate something."

"So, who else has been, er, trashed?" asks Clayborne.

"It's widespread, and worldwide. This is no simple little virus. Businesses were certainly the hardest hit. We don't have any good numbers yet, but it is certainly many thousands, with more instances reported every hour. And since so much business is now ecommerce, we estimate the losses to be in the billions—worldwide—daily. A real catastrophe. All major transportation is down, all major airlines, rails, Amtrak, even bus lines—everything's computerized now, of course, from ticketing to operations. There are no commercial aircraft in the air as we speak, only military jets and transport. It's exactly like it was after 9/11. Only now there are no trains or buses running, either."

He looks down at his notebook. "There's no end to it . . . the telcos were hard hit, too. Land line and mobile. There might be some isolated local traffic, but no long distance, no cellular. Another casualty—surprising, really—is the Internet. There are small pockets up here and there, some ISPs with very good antivirus protection mostly, but nothing is moving out there, no real traffic at all."

"I guess I am surprised at that," says Clayborne. "I thought that was the original purpose of the Internet, communications that would stay up even during nuclear attack."

"Well, that's the theory," says Heywood. "You know that, from its inception, the Internet was supposed to be a decentralized network championed by the Department of Defense to provide communications during times of national emergency, on the order of nuclear war. The fact that it isn't dependent on any central source, like national broadcasting networks—all of which were hard hit by the virus, by the way—is supposed to enable communications to proceed from independent server to independent server. Well, it turns out that that's a myth. We've learned that there are quite a number of bottlenecks in the great network—one of the biggest in Red Rock, obviously. Just seems to be economies of scale, pushing all of the traffic through singular high-speed hubs with the result that, if they fail, so fails a great big piece of the world's communications. . . ."

Agent Heywood continues talking about disaster near and far, but Clayborne finds himself daydreaming, nurturing a surprising bubble of joy in his heart. Finally, without a doubt, a huge chunk of the electronic infrastructure that dominated so much of our lives has been destroyed and will take no small amount of time to rebuild. And it's not just him, he realizes; everyone in the room seems in surprisingly good spirits, almost euphoric as they glance at each other, look dreamily out the windows at the sunny world beyond, contemplating, each in their own way, the prospect of a simpler life, a world that, for at least the time being, is free from the ubiquitous glowing hydra-heads of the AlphaBanc Beast.

Chapter Eighty-Five

THAT CRAZY OZONE hole at the north pole must be sucking all the cold air into outer space, Clayborne thinks as he rolls toward Red Rock sitting next to Blair in the back of agent Heywood's Buick, the windows open, the strange warm November weather continuing throughout the Midwest, record highs in the 70s, sunny and breezy. Or is it at the south pole? Or both? Well, everyone knows these temperatures are quite abnormal, preternatural even, but no one complains—who wants cold and gray? Which happens to be the approximate atmosphere in Clayborne's heart right now.

He and Blair have been spilling their guts before FBI video cameras for the past two days, telling everything they know about the insanity at AlphaBanc—in Blair's case, almost everything. The good news is that federal election fraud is still apparently a very serious thing and most of the AlphaBanc execs have been or are in the process of being rounded up for questioning: Bergstrom, Sturgis, Van Arp, Lefebre, O'Brian, Gates, Haedler, and Zara LaCoste, herself.

To keep them talking, agent Heywood made promises: to Clayborne, that he would be able to see Christin just as soon as she came out of surgery to remove the implant—whatever it was—from her neck; to Blair, that they would take him back to the McCarthy complex to try to retrieve his precious Mercedes.

The next day, however, Clayborne learned that Christin had been taken away in the night to another hospital in Milwaukee for the operation. The FBI wanted to make a professional video recording of the procedure and they didn't have the equipment or personnel at Oshkosh Memorial.

"Sorry, chief," Heywood consoled Clayborne, "it's only for a day or so. We'll bring her back up here right away. That is, if she wants to. She's not under arrest, you know, and I really wouldn't be surprised if she just wanted to head back to her home in Chicago. . . ."

Great. Just great. Why would she want to come all the way back up here anyway? To see him? She hardly even knows him when you really think about it. . . .

So it is a gloomy Clayborne who sits next to Blair, coming along supposedly as designated driver of the soon-to-be-liberated classic car—Blair's cast ankle in no shape to manage the pedals—but it's more just a chance for all of them to get out and see what's happening at McCarthy.

"Aw, cheer up, kid," smiles Blair, coughing and absently reaching in the breast pocket of his shirt for the pack of cigarettes that are no longer there. "Looks to me like everything's come full circle. How long did those guys think they were gonna get away with . . . everything?"

"Yeah, I guess," says Clayborne, rolling up the sleeves of his shirt, one retrieved from his Red Rock motel room by the FBI.

"Would've been the perfect crime."

"Yeah, it would have been," Clayborne sighs, looking blankly out the window at the farmland rushing by the dark shoulders of agent Heywood and his partner, agent Schuman, "if it hadn't been for Huxley. The world owes him a lot. . . ."

"Yeah, that's right," Heywood, overhearing their musings, yells back. "The world would really like to thank him for that stinking Plague virus. That's gonna keep our agents—and a lot of other people—busy for years to come!"

"Well, at least they've got work," says Blair. "Nobody else does now."

They come to the turnoff for the McCarthy complex and pass long lines of cars, trucks, and various service vehicles that seem to have some role to play in the aftermath of the great disaster. At the entrance they are confronted by a lot of law enforcement: state and local police, what seems to be several platoons of FBI and other dull-suited federal-types, even a contingent of National Guard troops. But Heywood and Schuman, credentialed liegemen of the new world order, get them inside the grounds which, after they slowly thread their way between the trucks and vans lining the drive, reveals a fantastic scene, of hundreds of people milling around numerous heaps of salvage: colorful carapaces of de-

ceased thinking machinery and piles and piles of plastic containers, magnetic tapes and disks, and miniature sodden mountains of
cartons and bales of printouts dredged from the underwater cave.

"They're diving around the clock, I hear," says Heywood.

"That's right, twenty-four hours, with divers called in from all
over the Midwest," adds Schuman.

"Jesus," grunts Blair. "It's going to take them twenty years to
sort out all that stuff."

"If even then," smiles Clayborne.

Although their ostensible mission is to get Blair's car back, all
of them feel a need to get out and wander around the amazing
tableau taking place on the long green lawn before the McCarthy
complex's main building, vaguely reminiscent of the "Last Judgment" by Hieronymus Bosch: milling cops and national guard
troops, AlphaBanc employees, and many neoprene-suited divers
wandering around like golliwogs carrying wire baskets or pushing
carts full of drenched data.

It's a busy, busy place: tents are being erected over the growing mounds of debris, catering trucks are pulling up, portable
toilets are being delivered, along with more lights, electric gen-
erators, hoses, pumps, and other postdiluvian supplies.

Clayborne can't keep himself from grinning hugely as he
strolls along. Up ahead there seems to be a large crowd of
AlphaBanc employees gathered together, some of whom
Clayborne seems to recognize from the catacombs. As they get
closer Clayborne gasps, for in the center of the group is O'Brian,
wearing an orange prison jumpsuit, his wrists manacled with long
chains, but obviously directing the efforts, waving a clipboard
and barking orders to a circle of cops, federal marshals, FBI
agents, AlphaBanc drones, divers, and anyone else who is able to
help him retrieve fragments of his precious data from the big
dark drink.

"Hey buddy!" a squawk from behind. Clayborne whirls around
and faces the Epenguin, although this time surprisingly bare-
headed in an orange jumpsuit with chained wrists and ankles,
accompanied by two suits who smile and nod at Heywood and
Schuman.

"Pengy—"

"It's a bad scene, man . . . what can I say?"

"Yeah, yeah . . . amazing what a little C4 will do."

"I'll say. Not to mention the Plague, man. It's screwed the world."

"From what I hear."

"Well, they're letting me and O'Brian and all the programmers who made it out, survived the flood, that is, help with the recovery. We hope maybe it'll impress the courts, you know?"

"Yeah. You worried?"

"Not too. I've been telling them everything—or most everything—I know. I guess from what you guys told them and then what they got from Christin with her crazy implant . . . that's a lot of evidence. I heard they're bringing in Marcia Deaver from Atlanta, too. But the thing is, Bergstrom, Lefebre, and Sturgis are already out on bail, you know. They got some heavy lawyers up from Chicago, and pulled not a few strings."

"I guess I'm not surprised. But what about Zara? She out on bail, too?"

"Oh, you didn't hear. They found her dead, man. Overdosed on 'ludamil and booze and whatever. . . .'"

"Oh no. Zara . . . dead." Clayborne lowers his head, rubs his temples. Zara. Gone. Forever. He doesn't know what to think, except . . . if she hadn't done that, he might have come after her himself. She, as part of They, murdered Natalie, coldly, calculatedly, as if the evil deed was just a line item on a project plan. . . . In the end, Zara was just another piece of the evil that flowed around here, who never loved or cared for anything that wasn't herself.

"She always was bad news, man. Maybe she finally realized what she was, what she did."

"Yeah maybe, just maybe. . . . You know about Dunne, Pengy?"

"Yeah, I heard . . ." the Epenguin sighs deeply. "We're not gonna see another like him come along again soon."

"Maybe that's for the best."

"Yeah . . . but I still feel honored to have been able to work with such a genius—even if it was for something despicable."

Clayborne nods. "So, who else didn't make it?"

"Well . . . Jacob for one. Nobody's seen him and you know, he's the kind of guy who would program underwater until somebody told him to swim—"

"Poor bastard . . ."

"Also, Bergstrom's daughter, who he had down there thinking she was a nun, or the Virgin Mary or something."

"Aw, no . . ."

"Yeah, it's sickening. No one, except O'Brian and maybe Haedler, knew who really was locked up in those rooms."

"Jesus, it could've been us. But you got us out, Pengy."

"Dunne's idea. But don't forget to tell the judge."

"Don't worry."

"Hey! Check it out!" the Epenguin squawks excitedly, looking past Clayborne at one of the haystack-size heaps of recovered boxes of cassettes and old magnetic tape reels. "Is that what I think it is?" Chains clinking, the Epenguin shuffles over to the pile and retrieves a damp black something that he proceeds to shake and shape until a battered, though recognizable homburg appears. "I can't believe it. One of my old hats . . . rescued! Hooray!"

The Epenguin looks around to the agents, asks, "Uh, I know this doesn't exactly go with orange. Any conflict with the dress code here?"

They look at each other and nod, and the Epenguin pops the dented lid on his head, happy to be nearly himself once again.

"Hey, hey! There they are!" someone yells in their direction. Clayborne turns quickly, thinks he recognizes that voice. Could it be . . . ?

Chapter Eighty-Six

CLAYBORNE STRAINS TO see through the close milling throng, the voices nearer now, one of them calling him by name: "Richard! Richie!!!"

Omigod! Can it be? He begins walking forward and the crowd opens up and suddenly he sees them, Sally and-and Christin! Chris! She's come back! They come running up the slope around and through people and equipment with Christin in the lead. Clayborne dashes toward her . . . and they're soon together, she grabbing him tightly around the neck, kissing him over and over again . . . and he too, holding her once again tightly, forever, this time he's never going to let her go. . . .

"Oh, Richie, they wouldn't let me see you until I had this operation they had to film . . . in Milwaukee. For evidence." She pulls away, tilts her head, shows Clayborne a gauze pad secured below her ear by adhesive tape.

"Oh . . . Chris." His heart melts as he pulls her head against his chest; he can't think of anything to say, only wants to hold her, protect her, finds tears welling up, grateful that the evil appliance has been removed. "I-I'm so glad you got that damned thing out."

"Oh, God, yes. It was a horrible, evil thing. I can't believe I ever let them . . . I feel so stupid, now. . . ." She casts her head down, sadly shakes her soft brown hair, stands beautiful before him in blue denim bib overalls and a Green Bay Packers T-shirt.

Christin notices him looking, smiles, "They got these for us—at Kmart, I think."

"That's all the clothes we had time to pick up for her, sonny," says Sally with a chuckle, standing behind her.

Clayborne blinks. He hadn't noticed her, or anyone else, actually, around them.

"Hi, there, Sal-gal," croons Blair, hobbling over with his cane, doffing an imaginary hat.

"Well, hello yourself, Mr. Non-smoker."

"How'd you get in here?"

"Well, when Christin got back to the hospital and found she had missed Richie here, she and yours truly sweet-talked Erin and Shirley, the agents in charge of us, to bring us over here."

"I'm so glad you did," smiles Clayborne. "But what a crazy scene, huh? We can walk around some more, but not over there," he motions behind Christin with his chin. "I don't feel like going over where O'Brian is. I might try to strangle him."

Blair snorts. "I hear you, kid. Something I've been repressing myself for some time now."

Christin whirls around. "Is that-that O'Brian himself? In the orange thing?"

"None other than . . ." says Blair.

"Well, I want to strangle him, too," says Christin, frowning, clenching her fists. "And . . . goddamnit, I will!" And she suddenly dashes away from them through the crowd, pushes through the marshals and agents surrounding O'Brian, screams, "YOU SELF-RIGHTEOUS SON-OF-A-BITCH!" and lands a roundhouse on his nose. It happens so quickly everyone freezes, enough time for her to sink another couple of blows into his soft white face before he collapses and the agents come to life, pull her away, she screaming, "How dare you lock me up like an-an animal! How dare you put an-an implant in me?! How dare you treat me like nothing more than a, a—"

"Sweetie, you're under arrest," says Blair, who has limped up behind Christin, efficiently pulling her hands behind her back, snapping on a pair of handcuffs that seem to have materialized from nowhere.

As everyone leans over the fallen O'Brian, Blair, and Clayborne, who has also run over, lead a squirming, snorting Christin away, back to Heywood and Schuman, who both seem quite amused.

"We gonna book her?" jokes Heywood.

"Nah," grins Blair, "not this time. Let's get her out of here."

"Damnit! Let me go!" grunts Christin. "I wanna stick something in his stinking neck!"

"That's what we're afraid of . . ." mutters Blair as they all move quickly away from the crowd, up toward the main building. Blair speaks softly to her, "Sorry to lock you up again, kid, but there's more cops here than at a doughnut convention. Better me than one of them."

This seems to calm Christin down somewhat, along with getting her away from O'Brian

"God! Just the sight of him! I-I wanted to *kill* him! I-I could kill all of them. . . ." She begins sobbing.

Clayborne pulls her closer, holds her as they continue moving away from the commotion. Finally they seem to have distanced themselves enough and Blair gestures, raises his eyebrows to Schuman, who chuckles, tosses over a small black key.

Blair unlocks the handcuffs, hands them back to Schuman. "Thanks for the loaners, pal."

Schuman laughs. "Next time, George, please ask first. These are federal property."

"Sorry, had to move fast. Take it out of my taxes."

"Ooh!" Christin rubs her knuckles. "My hand is killing me."

"I'm not surprised," says Blair. "You really smacked him."

"Good. Good! I wanted to kill him—"

"Now, now, honey," says Sally. "He'll get his. Bergstrom too. They all will, just you wait."

"Well, I hope so," says Clayborne quietly. "The Epenguin just told me that Bergstrom and some others are already out on bail."

"No!" wails Christin. "You've got to be kidding."

"Wish I were . . ."

"Well, what goes around, comes around, is what I always say," says Sally. "And I've been around enough to see that it sure happens . . . eventually. But for right now, you've just gotta believe in the powers of the natural world. It's still here for us. Trouble is, you young folks don't get out enough, out in nature, that is. If you're closer to the earth, where you can really feel it, not just think or dream about it . . . good things happen naturally. Believe me, kids."

Clayborne and Christin walk on in silence through the growing piles of conglomerated techno-salvage. On the other side of the building, they come in sight of Blair's white Mercedes.

Blair sighs, "Yes!" and hobbles as quickly as he can over to the car, the agents trailing along.

Clayborne begins to follow them, but suddenly a flash of color glinting in the sunlight catches his eye. He spies something that looks vaguely familiar in the very last pile of dredged-up debris. There, sitting atop a freshly dumped agglomeration of disks and tapes is a red metallic case. Just like the one that Leonard Huxley had given him and he had tossed into the well. Could it be? Water is still beaded up on the glistening red anodized sheen . . . could it possibly be?

Clayborne feverishly looks around, no one's looking—not even Christin and Sally, walking slightly ahead now—so he snatches it up, strolls further away with the women. Blair and the agents are out in the parking lot and the busy salvage operations are now fairly far behind them, so, hands trembling, he finds the catch and flips open the lid. And—yes! It *is*! It is *the* case, containing the same black plastic flash drives that Huxley had made, and the gray drive that Blair had added, still on top. *Yes!* A crazy miracle!

"Um, Richie, what have you got?" asks Christin, turning to see why he hadn't kept up with them.

"I-I think I've got all of our AlphaBanc evidence back again!" he gasps, smiling incredulously. "But I don't know how—"

"Is that—is that the little doodad you threw in my well that day?" asks Sally, smiling hugely. "I'll be . . . it's come back to us."

"But how could it . . . ?"

Sally slowly nods. "It's the good earth, comin' through, just like I told you folks. Why, nothin' more than the big ol' underground river that flows under Blackwell Inn. A dowser gal from Wasson's Bay up on the peninsula came by once and told me that it runs down from north central Wisconsin and then straight over toward the McCarthy complex. So your case just must just have been carried along by the current of the river and—"

"Sucked right through the hole blasted by Huxley's bomb!"

"Omigod, so that's the collection of evidence against these guys you were telling me about," says Christin excitedly. "The stuff you thought you lost. Oh, this is fantastic! This is wonderful! We'll be able to nail these bastards!"

Clayborne nods and smiles. "It truly is some kind of miracle for it to have made it all the way from that well to here . . . absolutely amazing. . . ."

"It is a miracle, son," grins Sally. "A real miracle, indeed."

"You're right, but . . . now we've got to get these into the right hands. And you know, as much as I trust George, he's getting to be so buddy-buddy with these agents that I'm afraid he might just turn it right over to Heywood if we show it to him, and I *think* I trust him and Schuman, but—"

"Yes, you're absolutely right, Richie," says Christin. "You lost it once and you don't want to lose it again. The first thing you've got to do is make a copy."

"That's what I was thinking. A bunch of copies. This is all we've got."

"I understand completely," says Sally. "I think old Georgie can be trusted all right. But who knows about the FBI?"

"That's right, at some point, even in the FBI, AlphaBanc's probably got a connection that could make this stuff disappear—"

"Forever," concludes Christin. "There's no telling where their influence ends."

"Well, I'll hide it in my shirt then."

"Or I could put it in the pocket of my overalls," says Christin. "No one would notice it there, I don't think."

"We-ell, I don't know, one of the cops scoping you out just might just notice. . . uh, they're actually kind of tight for overalls, you know."

"I think they got me a size too small. Do you disapprove?"

"No, no, are you kidding? Not at all. . . ."

"Er, well, you kids figure out what you want to do," says Sally. "I'm going to go over by Georgie for now."

Sally walks away; they decide that the case is safest in Clayborne's shirt, and it is hidden away.

"Now that we're free to go, more or less, all we need to do is get to someplace with a computer where we can—"

"Like maybe my place, down in Chicago?"

"Um, that would be perfect. Just perfect."

"I think so, too."

"Well, we really are getting out at the right time," says Clayborne, taking up Christin's sore hand and gently massaging it.

"They don't have any real security set up yet, but they will soon. Probably by tomorrow."

"Ooh!" Christin grimaces. "Easy on the hand there, Richie. That hurts."

"Sorry. You know, I thought you were going to pulverize him. Wish you had, actually. You really went, kind of wild . . ."

A small proud smile. "Yeah, I did, didn't I?"

"Uh-huh. Heh, seems you're always ending up in cuffs—for one reason or another."

Bigger smile, an arched eyebrow. "Hmm, you're right."

"Ahem . . . well, uh, maybe we ought to get going here, see if we can get old George to get a move on."

She puts her arm around him, pulls him close. "Maybe you can ask him if we can borrow those handcuffs . . ." she whispers.

"Hoo-boy, yeah . . . I might at that."

Chapter Eighty-Seven

ONE DAY IN early May, Clayborne stands high on a balcony in the Lambert Towers complex, looks out across the Chicago skyline and thinks that the worst is over.

It has to be. It's a bright spring morning with warm westerly breezes, the smell of Christin's homemade croissants fills the apartment, every residual nanogram of evil Deludamil is gone from his system, and just yesterday her attorney called to say that AlphaBanc has made a substantial offer to head off her pending juggernaut of a lawsuit against them—very substantial. It is welcome news to grace this marvelous morning, as they, and the rest of the world, have been on quite a ride since those dark days of November.

Though the Neanderthals' success in obliterating the databases of the civilized world didn't achieve the near-totality Huxley had dreamed of (latest estimates place it at less than thirty-five percent), it was enough to send the planet into serious recession— what the press, taking a cue from the Neanderthals' perversely proclaimed mission, settled on calling the Great Chaos. Millions of people were thrown out of work, the stock market crashed, banks failed worldwide, street corner messiahs appeared everywhere, and everyone blamed AlphaBanc. Huxley had accomplished his mission. They noticed. And maybe They understood. Time will tell.

Clayborne and Christin had retreated to her apartment in Chicago to weather the troubled times, living primarily off their assets like so many other young out-of-work professionals, as those who worked primarily with digitized information were the hardest hit. In a strange reversal of techno-fortune, non-computer skills suddenly became much in demand and armies of clerks working once again with pencil and paper, calculators, and isolated personal computers missed by the virus displaced the banks of glowing monitors and sophisticated programs that had for so long defined the modern workplace.

Nearly all of the government computers in Washington, D.C. were trashed, almost the only place in the country where the electric grid was also compromised due to an unbelievably complex and internecine networking of systems—but that's Washington. Sensing emergency, congress stopped its latest round of political probes and investigative hearings and actually tried to *do* something, and, well, immediately called for investigative hearings on the AlphaBanc scandal and the Plague virus nightmare, but also began the process of trying to authorize billions of dollars in aid to stricken families and banks and businesses (debate still continues), and, almost as an afterthought, set new (non-networked) elections for June. Despite the political perversities, society as a whole endured surprisingly well; no one starved, no one went homeless (except, of course, the homeless), and no one suffered terribly—due in part to the Neanderthals' consideration in leaving the nation's computerized services infrastructure for the most part intact, and also to the mildest North American winter in recorded history, with chrysanthemums still in bloom on New Year's Day in Duluth, icebergs the size of Connecticut floating toward Tierra del Fuego, and the appearance of the equivalent of alpine meadows in Antarctica. God bless global warming—at least this winter.

The economy, as economies will, began to sort itself out after months of confusion, and by March a recovery was underway, the markets climbing, people returning to work, with nearly all of the crashed computer systems up and running once again, although not a small amount of the data in them was still suspect. . . .

The Internet came back too, in fits and starts after the corrupted servers were cleansed and new high-speed routes built around the forever-defunct link at the McCarthy complex. Clayborne, in spite of himself, was glad to be able to get online again, having first rejoiced that the nervous system of the great Beast was dead, but discovered that he missed the electronically-linked world more than he ever would have guessed. Christin had never wanted to look at a computer screen again—although, at Clayborne's urging and after a few glasses of wine she still deigns to cavort upon her big monitor, for consumption only in the privacy of their apartment, nevermore to be globally broadcast across the Net. Well, maybe never. . . .

Their big project over the winter, of course, was the creation and dissemination of numerous copies of Huxley's secret files, which they found to contain mostly the abominations of Grand Unification, Huxley's selected samplings of the huge amounts of data collected on innocent citizens. A particularly disturbing discovery was the linkage of each specimen to a set of potential informants: family members, relatives, friends, enemies, and co-workers—AlphaBanc's groundwork for a virtual police state. It was more intrusive, more comprehensive and integrated than Clayborne had ever suspected. There were also numerous incriminating video and audio clips of Bergstrom, O'Brian, Haedler, Gates, and the whole sick crew scheming together—solid irrefutable evidence—including a couple that pertained to Blair and peripherally, even Clayborne. Those particular items never made it to the copied files, with smashed-up shards of the originals somehow finding their way to the bottom of the Chicago River on a particularly dark winter evening.

Aside from the short ugly imagery of Zara—unmistakably Zara in repeated viewings—tampering with a silvery airplane, the most disturbing video sequences were those from AlphaBanc's sinister laboratories in the catacombs of the McCarthy complex, of the compromised Christin, McClelland, and other poor enslaved subjects of as yet indecipherable proceedings, and then the very dark and sad sequences of Bergstrom's own doomed daughter, sentenced to a virtual nunnery. They found those quite difficult to watch.

One of the greatest casualties of the Great Chaos was the postal service—a lot of Neanderthalian grudges apparently floating around there—which began delivering mail again only after two full months in letter-sorting limbo. Clayborne and Christin each received notices for further depositions in Milwaukee and Chicago, at which they reluctantly, but dutifully appeared, bringing with them the bombshell files, having first sent copies to various icons of the press: the Chicago *Tribune*, The New York *Times*, the Los Angeles *Times,* et al., with the headlines quickly following: "AlphaBanc Execs Plotted, Stole Elections," "Americans Nothing More Than Numbers, Bought and Sold," the poignant: "Death of Freedom, Privacy, America Itself," and the New York *Daily News* screaming: "ALPHABANC SECRET LABS KEPT HUMANS FOR EXPERIMENTS."

With nothing really to do other than wait to be called as witnesses in the coming trials, Clayborne and Christin hunkered down in the safety of Lambert Towers and worked through various degrees of yuppie guilt over taking it easy during these trying times: leisurely shopping during the day for the evening meal, sharing a bottle of wine on the balcony before a candlelit dinner, prelude perhaps to an evening of lovemaking—such a complete change from the plotting and pressures and overall insanity of AlphaBanc that the guilt is sometimes really hard to come by.

Clayborne surfs the reviving Net and dabbles in the recovering stock market, and one day notices an item in the online edition of the Chicago *Tribune*: the Club Ventosus mysteriously caught fire the night before and was gutted. Clayborne thinks immediately back to his evening there and the old man, Uncle Nick, pompously open-mouthed: *What do you think about that?* Imagines him there still, sunk deep in leather chair, smoking, smug, dead.

One night out clubbing with Christin, Richard notices something oddly *glowing* on the back of her neck when she passes under a random black light in a tavern. Hands trembling, he pulls back her hair and the number 51 appears, of course, along with a barcode beneath, just like that nurse in the catacombs of McCarthy! It's freaky and depressing, to think that Christin carries still the mark of AlphaBanc's apocalyptic depravity. The dermatologists they visit tell her that the ink, visible only when excited by a UV light source, appears to be benign, but none of the modern laser tattoo removal processes, designed for vaporizing pigmented inks, can eradicate this abomination. There are other, more invasive surgical removal methods, they learn, but for now she decides to live with the evil icon as a sort of invisible badge of courage that she and the other victims of AlphaBanc's excesses will bear. She even thinks she may contact the other fifty glass houses and begin a sort of support group, to build public awareness of the evils of a transparent glass house society.

Meanwhile Christin's color vision has returned completely, and, feeling as though the shackles of too many years of repression have been removed, she begins painting again, starting with the long-neglected oil on her easel in the corner. She sees it literally in a new light, the colors of the grass, the sky, the sunlight, so vibrant now, the children in the park seeming to be *her* children, joyous childish spirits that have been locked up inside of her for too long now. Sitting at the painting once again on her bright balcony, holding a fauvist palette of alizarin crimson, cadmium yellow, mauve, and viridian, she begins weeping. She can't remember the last time she was this happy.

Out of the blue (cerulean) comes an email from Stevie Denton, for Clayborne. Stevie has been avidly following AlphaBanc's travails, catching his old boss running a gauntlet of reporters on national TV news, and, thinking that he might be ready for a break from the big-city bedlam, invites him to visit his little farm in Washington State. He is welcome to bring a friend along if he likes—maybe that gorgeous girl who seemed to be dodging the press with him.

They are seriously considering this when another invitation arrives, this one by snail mail, from Red Rock, Wisconsin. It is from Blair and Sally, inviting them to, surprisingly, their wedding, to be held at the Blackwell Inn, where else? Joyous news. Apparently the old gumshoe felt it was time to settle down and enjoy life with Sally, take care of the beer garden, the ancient well and the landscaped grounds, and dwell peacefully under the beauty of the spreading oaks forevermore.

This is a combination of offers they cannot refuse. Christin absolutely has to visit her parents in Seattle, she growing weary of fending off their repeated requests to come and rescue her from the AlphaBanc-plagued Midwest. So why not combine a trip up to Stevie's and a visit to her parents—they're certainly in the same northwestern neighborhood—right after stopping in Red Rock for the wedding? They can rent a car and drive it up to the namesake rubicund granite town, and from there to Minneapolis, where they can catch a plane west. Even with gasoline jacked up to six dollars a gallon for no discernible reason, this sounds like a pretty good plan.

Epilogue

RED ROCK IS beautiful in the late spring, the woods awash in trilliums, may apple, jack-in-the-pulpit, showy pink wild geranium, the oaks wearing their first full leaves of the season. It's a great day for a wedding, sunny and warm. Sally has lavishly decorated the Blackwell Inn grounds with flowers everywhere, lots of outdoor tables, an organist, a string quartet, and an altar set up under a rose-entwined arbor.

One thing is sure, Blair is marrying into a lot of family. It seems the whole town is here, Clayborne and Christin being introduced by a bubbling Sally, glowing in white satin and tulle, to more Wisconsin uncles and aunts and cousins and second cousins than they could ever hope to remember the names of. The ceremony is less than an hour away and Clayborne can't seem to find Blair anywhere, but thinks to sneak away and take a look inside the tavern where, sure enough, he finds the groom-to-be, dapper in a white coat and a white rose boutonniere sitting alone at a table in the empty room, nursing a scotch.

"George?"

"Richie! Kid, I'm glad you could make it," Blair waves, points to the bar. "Pour yourself a drink."

Clayborne sees a bottle of Glenmorangie on the bar and a tumbler, as though waiting just for him. He splashes some in the glass, carries it over by Blair, clinks glasses with him. "Congratulations."

"Thanks, kid. Never thought I'd do it, huh?"

"Well . . ."

"You and the girl are next, kid."

"Huh. Well . . . maybe."

"I'm not much for the circus out there," Blair points to the windows at the throng of people milling around the grounds. "I don't really know anyone here and I hate to mingle."

Clayborne looks around. The tavern is gaily decorated for the reception afterwards, with crepe paper and flowers, a vase of carnations and roses on each table. "It's kind of nice in here too, I guess . . ."

"Yeah. Anywhere there's some booze. But, unfortunately no more cigarettes," he sighs.

"You're better for it."

"So they tell me."

"Well, They got their's, huh," says Clayborne. There's no need to explain who They are.

"Ha-ha. Just like we had thought. I got to tell you kid, I feel like I dodged a bullet here. I have to thank you for that. I've been in communication with Heywood and it turns out there's nothing incriminating about me on those files you sent out there. I would guess there might have been a little bit of editing somewhere along the way."

"Maybe just a little. I'm amazed we were able to get those files again at all. It really was a miracle."

"That's an understatement. Without them, I might be behind bars, maybe you too. And those sons of bitches would be free. Maybe forever."

"Yeah, it was a miracle," Clayborne says, takes a sip of scotch.

"You know, kid, we all make mistakes. Sometimes we get so caught up in the job we're doing, we don't see how far we step over the line, into the dark side. You see where I'm coming from?"

"Yeah, I guess . . ." Clayborne thinks right away of Darby O'Banknote and the Christin conspiracy for himself; he isn't exactly sure what Blair is referring to, but he can imagine.

"So if it was a really big mistake, and you understand that, and feel completely rotten about it, maybe it kind of makes up for it in the end somehow."

"Yeah, I would think so . . ."

"Good. That's the way I feel, too. But, listen kid, I really am glad you're here today. I gotta ask you a favor. I happen to be light a best man here and I wonder if you could fill in. It'd be kind of embarrassing not to have one. I asked some guys, old buddies I had on the force, but no one seemed to be available. Maybe we weren't as close as I thought."

"Well, sure, George, I-I'd be honored." Clayborne gets a lump in his throat. "So it's just . . . you, here, then?"

"And now you. As I say, it's kind of embarrassing. She must have fifteen bridesmaids. We've even got a flower girl and ring bearer. My side of the equation is a little light."

"Ahh-hah!" a sudden squawk.

They both turn toward the door and in walks the Epenguin, resplendent in a very sharp brand new black suit, hatless, and—nothing ancient, borrowed, blue.

"Pengy!" Clayborne gasps.

"Greetings, gentlemen. It's my new look. Time for a change. Anyway, I thought I'd know where to find you. A super-duper day for the nuptials, hey?"

"Pengy . . . w-what are you even doing here?" asks Clayborne.

"I invited him," Blair grins. "He's out on bail, with a little help from agent Heywood."

"Absolutely. Although I was looking at doing some time for my help with the elections scam and a few other trifles, I have been granted immunity and have been doing a lot of, ahem, squawking."

"Pour yourself a drink, E.P.," says Blair.

"No thanks, it's still a little early for me. I'm high on fresh air and sunshine, only. I've kicked the Deludamil."

"Nice going pal!" exclaims Clayborne. "Welcome to the living. And the somewhat sane . . ."

"Yes, true, very true. When I think back I can't believe some of the things I did for AlphaBanc . . . I suppose while under the influence. Some of it, like working with Norman to throw the elections, was pretty bad, but we were all kind of caught up in the AlphaBanc madness."

"Pengy, you know something strange . . . before Dunne, uh, left us, he said that it wasn't him who had killed—or had someone kill—those girls on NEXSX. He said it was the Beast itself."

"Yes," sighs the Epenguin, "he's partially right; it wasn't him."

"The ones that McClelland murdered? It wasn't Dunne behind it?" asks Blair.

The Epenguin shakes his head. "That . . . that was the worst, probably the greatest evil of all perpetrated during this, this . . . incredible mess," the Epenguin says softly. "But it wasn't him."

"Well then—who?" asks Clayborne.

"It was . . . O'Brian. He was the real Beast."

"O'Brian!" snorts Blair. "Why am I not surprised?"

"Wow, so it really wasn't the Gnome . . ." breathes Clayborne.

"Nope, it wasn't Norman. Exactly what I told the FBI. It was O'Brian all the way with that bad scene. He set up each one of them, faked the logs, the message origins, to make Dunne think that the big machine itself was ordering the killings, supposedly because it was jealous of Dunne. Apparently it worked, too, 'cause Dunne bought it, and he's definitely not an easy geek to fool. But then he is, or was, a hopeless romantic."

"It didn't fool those dead women," growls Blair.

"No," the Epenguin sighs again, "it was a real tragedy. But that was the high-stakes game they were playing—at least the one that O'Brian was playing. No one but him knew that it wasn't the Gnome doing the killing; that is, no one but me. But I only found that out the week of the elections, after doing some pretty extensive digging into the system. Before that I was clueless. O'Brian was obviously obsessed with getting Dunne back, and each murder upped the ante for him with Bergstrom and the boys. O'Brian played all of them, just like he played Dunne. And I think it really helped bring Dunne in, too. I think it totally intrigued him that the Beast seemed to be ordering the executions of his carefully selected specimens."

"Well, then O'Brian's plan seems to have worked."

"That it did. It was the perfect crime. Almost."

"Hmph . . . just like he said it would be," mutters Blair.

"Huh?'

"Oh, just something O'Brian told me once. That he was going to pull off the perfect crime." Blair leans back and stretches. "And he almost did it; it almost was the perfect crime."

"Yep, almost. O'Brian had everything worked out to the smallest detail. In fact, I didn't know it at the time, but it was him who had run the original data to find McClelland. Did a perfect job, even using one of Dunne's old ID's to hack into the system. If Norman was the best-ever hacker, then O'Brian was a close second."

"That explains a lot," says Clayborne. "But I always wondered about the strange messages I was getting . . ."

"From what I saw, they were all, or almost all, from Norman himself. Like that tiger's eye message that led us to his spy setup on Christin? It was him that sent it to you. I traced it myself."

"So why would he do that?"

"O'Brian and I wondered about that, too; we think it just made it a better game for him. We think he really just wanted us to admire all the work he had done, with the telescope and stuff, show us how brilliant he was. He didn't have much of a life, you know."

Clayborne slowly shakes his head. "So Dunne truly is an innocent."

"In the murders, definitely yes. The only thing he really is guilty of is maybe spying on NEXSX babes and helping us rig the elections, and, uh, maybe falling in love with Christin. If that's a crime. I don't think he expected that to happen."

"The poor bastard," says Blair, downing the last of his scotch.

"But, you know," says the Epenguin, shaking his head, "there are still some things, weird messages and system quirks that came out of the big Beast that we never could explain. I think it really messed with O'Brian's mind. Mine, too."

"Well, maybe, just maybe, it *was* able to think for itself—"

"Hey there, Mr. Blair!" Sally pokes her head through the door. "The future Ms. Blair would like your presence at her wedding, unless, of course, you've changed your mind."

"No, way!" Blair laughs. "You think I'd want to face all that family out there?"

"Well, then, get a move on!"

"So it starts . . ." Blair says softly to his companions, raising his eyebrows and smiling as he stands up.

The wedding ceremony is dignified and joyous, the energy in the grove high, all of Sally's relations obviously overjoyed for her. The minister performs the rites with warmth and wit, everyone cheering and applauding when Blair finally kisses the bride.

Afterwards Clayborne and Christin sit at a table in the grove with Blair and Sally and the Epenguin, sipping champagne. They are immensely enjoying this excursion into nature, far away from the big city. They will stay at a motel in Red Rock tonight, and then head to Minneapolis in their rented convertible.

"Well," says Sally, "I always thought that them AlphaBanc-sters down the road were up to no good, but who'd have thought how no-good it really was!"

"We were all shocked," says Clayborne.

"Yeah, even me," says the Epenguin. "And I was in on a lot. At least starting with our scheme with Dunne." He looks sheep-ishly over at Christin, "Really sorry about all that other stuff . . ."

Christin sighs, "Well, you were only doing your job . . . as you saw it at the time."

"Hopefully, some good will come out of all this," says Blair. "I see that there are not a few bills up in Congress now to actu-ally safeguard our privacy. Once I looked into it, it was shocking to see how much of what A-Banc did—with the information, anyway—was pretty much legal."

"Sure, it's all new to us," says the Epenguin. "Legislation just hasn't kept up with the new technologies, Internet spyware, the tracking of people through RF chips, the huge amount of our personal data that is out there in digital form. It was all ripe for the picking. AlphaBanc just got there first. If it hadn't been them, it would have been someone else."

"Yes, you're probably right," says Christin, "but would anyone else have sunk to the depths of depravity that they did?" She un-consciously rubs the scar behind her ear.

"I think it's a matter of degree, of increments," Blair says, gesturing with his champagne glass. "Once they found they could get away with something, they moved on to the next thing, from keeping people's personal history, to keeping people themselves. Bergstrom and O'Brian never knew when to quit."

"Yeah, I can vouch for that," says the Epenguin. "You can pretty quickly lose sight of what's right and what's wrong. It's really bad when it happens to someone powerful like Bergstrom, an intelligent, driven, sociopath. That's the most frightening thing in the world today, I think."

"Well, what I think is remarkable is way that the world, the Internet, the economy, has recovered from the Plague virus," Clayborne says. "And the United States from corrupted elections.

People just seem to accept the insanity and deal with it. Nothing seems to shocks us anymore. We move on."

"I agree," says Christin. "The pace is just so much faster. Communications are instantaneous and ubiquitous. Nothing is spared. Nothing is sacred. We hear of incredible doings: disasters and horrible crimes, as well as scientific breakthroughs and discoveries, not even every week or every day, but every hour, every minute. As a society we're all numb, we're immune . . . and I think we're simply forced to adapt. To maintain our collective sanity."

Everyone pauses and thinks. It's true, the world is spinning much, much faster.

"Well, maybe then it isn't really the Beast down in the depths of AlphaBanc that we have to fear," says Clayborne, raising an eyebrow, "but the beast that lies deep within us all."

"Oh c'mon now, such talk . . ." says Sally, raising her glass. "Let's have a toast and celebrate. The Beast is dead!"

They all smile, raise their glasses and clink them together.

Clayborne and Christin exchange a glance, raise their glasses again, "Long live the Beast."

About the Author

John Hampel, the acclaimed author of the strange and wonderful novel of the great Midwest, *Wherever You Go, There You Are*, has worked in information technology for over 20 years. He currently lives and works in Wisconsin.

CPSIA information can be obtained at www.ICGtesting.com
Printed in the USA
BVOW07s1851230913

331918BV00002B/120/P

9 780962 799228